Moon Island

'Rosie Thomas's new novel features the sort of emotions and cast list favoured by writers such as Anne Tyler . . . May Duhane is fourteen, overweight and sensitive. She and her sister have been brought to the beach house opposite Moon Island by their father, hoping to achieve normality after the death of his wife four years before . . . Thomas excels at sinister atmosphere. The mood shifts like the unpredictable summer weather' *Sunday Times*

'[Thomas is] intense, closely focused and a perfectionist. The portrait of the motherless, rudderless May is affecting, pulling up from a deeper well than anything else' Libby Purves, *The Times*

'Swathed in morning mists and drenched in mystery, Moon Island looms over the faded beach town of Pittharbor on the Maine coastline, eerily controlling the lives that intermingle there. May Duhane comes to spend the summer in a clapboard house facing the sea, and discovers the diary of a young girl who died in an accident the year before. As she pieces together the real cause of the girl's death, she confronts other truths – about her family, herself and the nature of love. A powerful portrait of the pain of growing up' *Good Housekeeping*

'An amalgam of love story, ghost story and historical novel, told mostly through troubled teenager May Duhane. Thomas is a marvellous storyteller, *Moon Island* a compulsive read . . . there's an understanding of the complexities of adolescence and the intricacies and treacheries of adult love' *Hampstead and Highgate Express*

'*Moon Island* is an extraordinary novel. It has the haunting quality of a dream and the tenderness of a love story. Intelligent, readable and atmospheric, with the background of beachcombing and tidal movements that are so much part of our own memories of summer seaside holidays. Every woman will identify with this moving and mysterious tale' *Woman's Realm*

'Love and sex, loss and disappointment burn their way relentlessly through this intense and involving novel. The shores of Maine during a long hot summer provided a setting soaked with history and atmosphere. Thomas gives a superb portrait of the emotional pains of adolescence, of a bereaved and lonely girl poised on the brink of womanhood' *Ideal Home*

'The characters are privileged but laden with emotional baggage. None more so than May Duhane, a motherless teenager. She finds the diary of a young girl who tragically drowned on the island, stirring secret ghosts and her own strength. Colourful and compassionate' *She*

'A feast of a book, achingly true in parts and totally bewitching in others' *New Woman*

'May Duhane is a plump teenager, ill at ease with herself and her father and overhsadowed by her confident older sister. When she discovers the idary of a fourteen-year-old who drowned the previous summer, she begins to identify with her . . . May feels hemmed in by other people's sexuality: her father's developing relationship with a married neighbour; her sister's casual romps with a local boy . . . As the tension mounts, Rosie Thomas knits together the various strands of this complex and satisfying novel, bringing it to a dramatic and fulfilling conclusion' *Woman and Home*

Rosie Thomas is the author of a number of celebrated novels, including *Bad Girls, Good Women; Other People's Marriages; A Simple Life* and the Top Ten bestseller *Every Woman Knows a Secret*. She lives in north London with her family, and when not writing fiction spends her time travelling and mountaineering.

ROSIE THOMAS

Moon Island

ARROW

Published in the United Kingdom in 1999 by Arrow Books

3 5 7 9 10 8 6 4

Copyright © Rosie Thomas 1998

The right of Rosie Thomas to be identified as the author of this work has
been asserted by her in accordance with the Copyright, Designs and
Patents Act, 1988

First published in the United Kingdom in 1998 by William Heinemann

Arrow Books Limited
Random House UK Ltd
20 Vauxhall Bridge Road, London, SW1V 2SA

Random House Australia (Pty) Limited
20 Alfred Street, Milsons Point, Sydney, New South Wales 2061, Australia

Random House New Zealand Limited
18 Poland Road, Glenfield
Auckland 10, New Zealand

Random House South Africa (Pty) Limited
Endulini, 5a Jubilee Road, Parktown, 2193, South Africa

Random House UK Limited Reg. No. 954009

A CIP catalogue record for this book is avilable from the British Library

Papers used by Random House UK Limited are natural, recyclable
products made from wood grown in sustainable forests. The
manufacturing processes conform to the environmental regulations of the
country of origin

Type by SX Composing DTP, Rayleigh, Essex
Printed and bound in Germany by Elsnerdruck, Berlin

ISBN 0 7493 2342 6

For everyone who went to Gokyo & back

The boat turned a fresh furrow of ripples in the flat water. Doug Hanscom opened up the outboard motor and set a course from his dockside moorings towards the mouth of the harbour. There was a midday haze today, not a fog but a thickness of heat and moisture in the air that almost blotted out the islands lying off at the edge of the bay. Their crests of spruce trees stood black and two-dimensional against the pearly sky.

Another boat was nosing towards him. It was Alton Purrit in the *Jenny Any*, with a half-dozen visitors he'd taken out to see the seals basking on the ledges at the tip of Duck Island. Alton raised his arm, as they passed and called out, 'Hope they're crawlin' right today, Doug.'

Doug nodded an acknowledgement. He was not noted for loquaciousness.

He turned towards the rocky teeth that guarded the south headland of the bay. The current ran viciously here and slapped collars of white foam against the rocks, but he negotiated the tideway without a thought. He had been a lobster man out of Pittsharbor, Maine for twenty years and he made the same run to haul his traps every morning. Today he had stopped first for hot coffee and a cherry muffin at the store on Sunday Street, and he could still taste the pleasant sweetness on his tongue. He was thinking that he could well have eaten another of Edie Clark's muffins and at the same time began rummaging in the side pocket of his oil-stained pants. He took out his pipe and chewed on the stem, even though his daughter had long ago nagged him out of smoking it.

Beyond the headland the water was flat again. The first of his marked buoys floated here and he swung the tiller over and cut the engine to bring the boat alongside. There were gulls and cormorants standing sentinel on the rocks, and a dozen more made a slow circle over the buoys. Doug tilted his head to look at them and shrugged as he bent to work. The first trap he hauled was a good one. Two nice two-pounders, along with the dross of snails and hermit crabs.

The lobsters went into a tub of water in the stern and the rubbish was tipped back into the sea. The gulls widened their circle to glide overhead.

Doug manoeuvred his boat between the buoys, the stem of his pipe gripped between his teeth. The second trap was empty, but the sun was warm on his back, and he was dry and comfortable. He whistled as he worked, a sibilant 'sss-sss' that bubbled in the pipe.

He was leaning over the boat's side to the third buoy when he noticed the woman's body. It was the hair he saw first. It fanned out like fine weed, rippling gently in the current. She was hanging face down in the water, perhaps five feet below the surface.

x

Doug bumped down on to his knees, his hands fastening on the boat's side as it rocked with his sudden movement. Looking again through the skin of the water he could see her quite clearly, it was no submerged log or trick of the light. Her pale shirt or vest, or whatever it was, ballooned lazily around her curved back.

The shock of seeing her had made his throat tighten and his heart bang in his chest, but now he began to breathe again. It was not the first drowning he had seen, nor did he imagine it would be the last.

With cold fingers he replaced the pipe in his pocket and groped beneath the thwarts for his boathook. Gently he fed the pole down into the water and tried to twist the hook in the loose cloth of her shirt. But his hands were not yet steady and the hook snagged, then jerked free. The body sank a foot deeper and Doug grunted with despair. If she went down any more he would lose her.

He waited a moment, gripping the hook in his right hand and bracing himself to hold steady against the boat's rocking. Prickly sweat had broken out on his forehead and under his flannel shirt. Once again he lowered the boathook and drew wheezy breaths clogged with concentration as he tried to take a secure purchase on the clothing. He twisted the hook sharply and hoisted the pole. This time the body rose sluggishly but obediently. Doug eased it slowly closer, bending as far as he dared to meet it. When it hung a foot below the surface he knelt down again and reached with his left hand to grasp her arm. He let go of the boathook and the woman rolled over as he pulled her wrist towards him. Her head, then her face, broke the surface. The gulls circled closer over the boat.

Water streamed off her, plastering dark tendrils of hair across her features. She was not much more than a child. Perhaps fourteen or fifteen years old. Her eyes were closed and her lashes made delicate black crescents against her white skin. He could see no fish or crab damage yet, so she couldn't have been in the water very long. But there was no question that she was dead.

Doug looked away. His granddaughter was pretty much the same age as this one. The difference was that he saw to it Stacy never went near the water without her lifejacket, and still he sometimes had bad dreams.

He raked among the gear stowed under the seat and found a good length of strong line. The waterlogged body was heavy and he didn't think he could haul her in over the gunwale single-handed. To make her secure and tow her into the harbour was the best he could hope to do. He tied her wrist first to a cleat. Then the body bumped awkwardly against the hull as he struggled to pass more line under her arms and at one point the boat rocked so fiercely that he was afraid they would capsize. He waited until it steadied again. Sweat ran down his face as he rolled her over and tightened his methodical knots around her chest.

A huge gull settled on the transom, its hooked beak pointing at him. He cursed briefly and waved his arm at it and the bird took off again. It drifted in an arc around the stern.

Doug saw the sailboat then. It was one of those lightweight fibreglass affairs the visitors liked to sail about the bay in, a Mirror dinghy or Heron, or some such thing. It had drifted into a narrow cleft in the rocks and now it was wedged there, banging its hull as the waves slapped against it. The mainsail flapped as the boom swung dismally from side to side.

It was more than possible that the girl hadn't been out alone.

She was tied fast now. He checked the knots and let out a length of the line so that she would ride free of the rudder and outboard. Then he made the rope fast to the cleats inside the boat.

He pushed her away from the side, fired up the motor again and cast off from the mooring buoy. At low throttle he nosed towards the inlet. The weight behind him sagged in the water, as if greedy to pull him in beside it.

Doug Hascom searched thoroughly among the rocks and weed. But there was no sign of anyone else, in the dinghy or in the water.

When he was convinced that the girl had been sailing alone he turned his boat again and made slow progress with the unaccustomed weight sloughing at his stern, back around the headland and into the mouth of the harbour.

One

The rain fell in a steamy curtain. It hissed into the sea and blurred the windows, and pounded out a drumbeat on the roofs and decks of the five houses. Unseen in the darkness, rivulets coursed down the beach steps and washed the day's sand prints into miniature river deltas and estuaries.

The car windscreen washers swept plumes of water aside as John Duhane followed the unfamiliar road out towards the beach. The route from Pittsharbor to the bluff was narrow, twisting back on itself two or three times, and as he drove he hunched forward to try to see ahead through the downpour. A flicker of lightning hollowed the sky and an instant later a thunderclap shook the car. The echoes rolled overhead for long seconds and the rain beat harder.

'Great,' Ivy sighed. 'Just great.'

She sat slumped in the seat beside her father, twisting her body away from him even though the seatbelt bit into her bare neck.

'It's only a summer storm.'

In the back seat May said nothing at all. She hadn't

spoken for more than an hour, since they had passed Bangor and turned towards the coast.

They had driven all the way up from New York, stopping for a night to stay with John's sister. May was tired of the journey and of Ivy's sulking, but even so she was not looking forward to their arrival at the beach house. Everything would be the same as it always was, except that it would go on being the same in a different place. How could a family vacation be anything of the kind if there wasn't a family to live it; if there were only a father and two daughters who didn't get on?

May leant her head against the window of the station-wagon and closed one eye, squinting so the smears of rain blurred and shimmered into rainbow fragments against the lights of the last houses on the road out of Pittsharbor.

Elizabeth Freshett Newton stood in the window of her house up on the bluff. This was the evening room, that was what her mother had called it. It faced north and west, away from the beach and the ocean, and over-looked part of the sheltered pocket of garden, which had once required the full-time efforts of a man and a boy to maintain in the English style favoured by her mother. Elizabeth's parents had liked to entertain in the evening room, where blinds filtered the setting sun and brightened squares of pattern in the old rugs. She remembered bridge evenings, and impromptu piano recitals on the baby grand that still stood between the two tall windows. The memories of those parties of

2

fifty years ago made the house seem the more empty and silent now.

The lamp at her shoulder shone on the window glass and made broken reflections in the wash of rain. Aware that her silhouette against the light would be visible to anyone outside, she reached up and clicked off the switch. There was no one out there to see her, of course, but she felt easier in the dark. Until the sudden crack of thunder came the only sounds were the measured ticking of the long-case clock and the rain. Her hand held the cord of the curtains, ready to draw them and close out the storm. Then she leant forward, peering into the dark. The headlights of a car were veering slowly along the road.

Elizabeth stood still. The beam of the lights came closer and swept across her windows, before turning towards the gateway of the Captain's House. She heard the engine stop and through the drumming of the rain a car door slammed.

Another sheet of lightning ripped the sky. In its split-second eerie brilliance she saw a girl, running, with her shoulders hunched and one arm crooked over her bent head in an attempt to shield herself from the storm. The flash froze her into immobility and left the image burning behind Elizabeth's eyes.

The thunder crashed again. Elizabeth's hand had flown up to her mouth, but as the darkness resettled she let it drop. She waited for her heart to stop pounding with shock.

It wasn't the same girl.

It was someone else, just another girl of a similar age

and build. The Bennisons had rented the old house out for the season and these were the summer tenants, that was all.

Two or three years ago Sam Bennison had laid out fancy garden lighting along the path to the Captain's House and now these little flares suddenly shone out, lighting up sopping-wet billows of overgrown foliage. The back door of the house stood open and two girls were trailing mournfully back to the car, their hair already draggled and soaking. The lights picked out their T-shirts and denimed legs and big white sneakers. A man gave each of them an armful of luggage from the open back of the station wagon and they trooped back to the house.

The younger girl was indeed in her early teens, just like Doone. She was stocky, too, with the same shoulder-length hair. Otherwise, Elizabeth now saw, there was no real resemblance.

She turned away from the window, leaving the curtains open.

May dumped her bag on the bed in the bedroom Ivy had not chosen. Then she sat down beside it and looked around her.

The bedhead was made of curly wrought iron, kind of French-looking, May thought, although she had no idea what a French bed might really look like. There was a pine bureau with a framed mirror screwed to the wall above it, an armchair with a worn slipcover and a set of bare shelves. Beside the bed lay a blue and grey rag rug hiding, as she saw when she pushed it aside

4

with her foot, a burn mark in the haircord carpeting. The walls were wood panelled and painted a greyish white that reminded her of a bird's egg. There were sticky-tape marks on the panelling showing where someone else's pictures had once been fixed.

Except for the faintly exotic bed, the room looked what it was – a bare shell in a beach house, stripped ready for a summer's rental. A smell of dust and salt was trapped inside the closed windows.

But there was also a forlornness about it, which went beyond mere emptiness. It made May shiver. Or maybe she was cold because her hair and T-shirt were wet from the rainstorm. She hugged herself and tried with numb fingers to rub some warmth into her arms.

Ivy pushed open May's door with the toe of her sneaker. She came in without waiting to be asked and leant against the door frame. 'You going to sit there all night?'

May shrugged.

Her sister sighed and her pretty top lip lifted. Once, at school, May had heard an older girl describing Ivy. 'She's drop-dead gorgeous, of course,' the girl had whispered in what had seemed a knowing, adult way. Ivy was just eighteen and May fourteen. She supposed that Ivy was gorgeous, if you went for that sort of thing. She also knew that she herself was anything but.

Ivy said in her condescending way, 'Look. We're here, aren't we? Can't you try and be half-way happy about it?'

'Yeah, all right. I notice you've been Miss Sunshine since we left home.' And without waiting for Ivy to answer she got up and went to the window. After a small struggle she pushed up the sash and leant her elbows on the sill. Needle points of rain drove into her face, but the storm was already passing. Patches of faintly paler sky showed in places through the ragged masses of cloud.

'Dad's sending out for pizza,' Ivy said to her sister's back.

'I don't want any.'

'Why not? Are you on another of your diets?'

'Is that any of your business?'

'Jesus. Suit yourself,' Ivy snapped. She went away, slamming the door.

Left alone again, May moved slowly around the room. Lightly, with the tips of her fingers, she touched the exuberant metal curves of the bedhead, and the empty bookshelf, and the faintly splintery grooves of the panelling next to the bed, then circled with her forefinger and thumb the worn knob of one of the bureau drawers. There was a distant, fluctuating, deep-throated sound, which she only now identified as waves breaking on the beach.

The sad room seemed to enclose her, embedding her within itself in a way that was almost comforting. She sank down again on the bed. Sitting motionless, with her arms hanging between her parted knees, she let her mind wander.

'May? Can you *hear* me?'

She became aware that her father had been calling from downstairs for some time. She stood up reluctantly and went to the door. Yeah?'

6

'What's the matter with you? Will you get *down* here?'

'Yeah. Right, I'm just coming.'

Ivy dropped a fistful of cutlery on to the table. In the low, L-shaped downstairs room were chairs and two battered chesterfields, and a television set at one end of the long arm, and the heavy old oak table with a collection of unmatched dining chairs at the other. Even with all the lights on, the corners of the room remained obstinately shadowed. There was a yawning hearth with a stacked log basket beside it and the stone chimneypiece was blackened with smoke. The room still smelt of the driftwood smoke, as if the walls and beams were ingrained with it. In the wall facing the sea was a set of new-looking french doors, flanked by the original small-paned windows.

The unmodernised kitchen was in the short section of the L. John opened and banged shut cupboard doors as he searched for plates and glasses. Two pizza boxes stood unopened on one of the worktops. 'There must be some goddamn glasses somewhere.'

The steep stairs rose straight up from the back of the room. Surprisingly the banister rails were carved with leaves and flowers.

May drifted down and hesitated beside the table. 'How old is this place?' she asked, looking around.

'Pretty old,' John answered, pleased by her question. 'The original house was built sometime in the eighteen-fifties, by the captain of a whaling ship. Which is why it's called the Captain's House. Probably it was just this room and the bedroom above. The rest was added later.'

Under her breath Ivy made a small, dismissive sound, 'Tchuh', to show she couldn't care less about the house or its history, or about being here at all.

John found the glasses in the last cupboard. 'Let's eat, shall we?' he said patiently.

They sat at the oak table, wide spaces between them. Ivy opened her pizza box and began to eat the doughy triangles straight out of it, ignoring the plate she had laid. A thread of cheese looped out of her mouth and she caught it with a silver-varnished little fingernail and pushed it between her pursed-up lips. Ivy could make even such an inelegant manoeuvre look cute and sexy.

May felt hungry enough to have wolfed down Ivy's entire pizza and her father's as well. But the waistband of her jeans bit into the solid slab of her belly and the stiff fabric dug into the creases of her thighs. She ate fruit and some plain crackers from the box of supplies they had brought up from the city. She cut the pieces up small and ate very slowly, as the plump mother of one of her friends had once told her they were advised to do at WeightWatchers.

Ivy left two-thirds of her dinner. The mozzarella solidified into a greasy waxen mass around the chunks of mushroom and pepperoni. Even so, May still eyed it covetously.

'We'll do the marketing tomorrow,' John said. 'It'll help us to find our way around.'

'Great,' Ivy said without inflexion. She tipped her left-over food into the garbage pail, meticulously removing the traces of her own dinner and touching nothing else. 'Mind if I go upstairs now?'

The taut thread of John's patience finally snapped. 'For Christ's sake, Ivy, couldn't you sit here with us for five more minutes? You know, family together time? Talking. Sharing things, the three of us?'

Ivy only stared at him. 'Fantasy,' she murmured. 'I told you all along.'

John stumbled to his feet as if he might hit her.

'Don't you,' Ivy breathed. 'Don't you ever.'

There was a silence. He had come close to it sometimes, after Ali had gone, but he never had hit either of them.

Ivy went briskly up the stairs. After a minute they heard music thudding out of her room. May sat still at the table, her bottom lip stuck out in a mixture of embarrassment and depression. John went back into the kitchen with the plates. He stacked them in the dishwasher and rubbed down the counter-top with a folded cloth. Then he poured himself a Jack Daniels. There was no ice yet.

Looking at him, May noticed dejection in the slope of his shoulders. Her father was a big man, broad-backed and still dark with only a few feathers of grey showing in his hair, but in her eyes he suddenly appeared smaller and weaker, the way he might turn out to be when he was really an old man. Although what she actually wanted was to hold back and keep herself safe inside the confines of her own skin, she made herself put her arms around his waist and rest her head on his chest.

'It will be all right. Ivy'll get over being mad because you wouldn't let her stay in the city all summer. We'll have a good time up here, I know we will.'

The warmth of her gesture was contradicted by a much stronger impulse, which kept her body stiff, micromillimetres removed from him, all the way from her forehead to her knees.

'I guess so.'

He patted her shoulder and she stepped back in relief. 'I think it's stopped raining,' she offered.

John tilted his whiskey glass in the direction of the doors.

'Want to come out on the beach? Take a walk before bed?' Slowly, May shook her head. Knowing that she should have accepted and returned his peace gesture, she wanted more urgently to be on her own in the melancholy stillness of the new bedroom, to lie on the European bed and lose herself in a book.

'I'm pretty tired tonight. I'll come tomorrow, okay?'

'Okay.' He smiled at her.

He refilled his whiskey glass and opened the door to the beach. As he slid the screen aside and stepped out on to the deck a blast of salt-laden wind hit him full in the face. He shivered and lifted his head. There was a covered porch and sandy wooden steps led down from it to an expanse of soaking grass. John walked carefully, waiting for his eyes to grow accustomed to the dark. Rainwater drenched his ankles. Glancing up, he saw a wan moon momentarily revealed by flying clouds.

At the far end of the rough patch of garden was

another deck, and a heavy wooden post and rail fence on the seaward side. When he reached it John saw that the fence ran along the top of a low wall of rock. On the other side was a short drop down to the beach. The tide was out and he caught the windborne reek of low water. Only a few years ago he couldn't have stopped the girls from racing out here to explore, even in the wet darkness. Now the deadness of their indifference weighed them all down.

A gate in the fence gave on to a short flight of rough wooden steps. He took a long pull of whiskey and descended to the beach. Crescents of coarse sand lay between patches of shingle. The stones grated beneath his deck-shoes as he crossed to the water's edge. Ahead, across the mouth of the little bay, he could see the black hump of an island. John knew from the realtor's description that this was Moon Island. And so the sheltered beach that faced it was known as Moon Island Beach. On the map it was just one of the dozens of bays and inlets that fretted this part of the Maine coastline.

He stared out towards the island until his eyes smarted in the wind. Then he swung south and began to walk the curve where the waves ran out in murky lacings of foam. Up on the bluff the Captain's House lay directly behind him. There were four other houses overlooking the sheltered bay, strung in a line to his left. From down here their roofs and gables looked gothic and sinister against the storm clouds, but the lighted windows made cosy little squares of glowing amber.

The tide had turned. A seventh wave ran over his feet and soaked his shoes. He swore and directed his path further up the beach.

Back in the spring John had suggested to his daughters that they should share a last, proper summer vacation before Ivy went to college in California. He had in mind that he would teach the two of them to sail, and they would picnic and barbecue and take cycle rides together along the coastal paths. He and his sister Barbara had enjoyed just such a holiday with their parents thirty years ago.

The girls had protested. But in the end, in their different but equally reluctant ways, they had agreed that they would come.

John had written at once to the local realtors and almost by return, from Pittsharbor, they had received the details of the Captain's House. It sounded perfect. The house was old and picturesque. The beach was partly sandy, unusually for this section of the coast, and private except for a short length at the southern end. One of the bluff houses was occupied year-round by local people, the others had been owned or rented by the same families for years. Pittsharbor was a pretty fishing town with a thriving artists' colony. It was busy in the summer season but not yet spoilt.

The woman realtor had been quite direct. 'It's an unusual opportunity,' she told John on the telephone. 'We almost never get one of these houses becoming available for a summer let. The Bennisons have owned the Captain's House for – oh, let me think – it must be

12

ten years now. They're doctors, from Chicago. I'm sorry to say that last summer their daughter, their only child, was tragically killed in an accident up here. The family haven't yet decided whether or not to sell the house. We have been instructed to find a suitable tenant for the place for this season only.'

'I see. That's very sad,' John said. 'But I think we'll take the house. It sounds just what we want.'

The whiskey glass held in the crook of his arm was empty now and he had reached the southernmost end of the beach. There were sailing dinghies and little rowboats beached here, tethered at the extremity of anchor chains that ran from concrete blocks half-buried in the sand. The running tide was just lapping at the bow of one of the dinghies, a fourteen-footer with a white tarpaulin cover that shone in the dark.

A flight of stone steps cut in the sloping headland led from the public part of the beach in the direction of the Pittsharbor village road. John retraced his path up the beach towards the Captain's House.

The wind had dropped and the house was silent. He turned off the downstairs lights and went slowly up the steep stairs. The girls' rooms were in darkness, their doors firmly closed. His ears sharpened in the stillness and he heard the old timbers overhead shift and creak, as the house settled itself after the storm.

In the sunshine next morning Leonie Beam stood at the top of the steps and surveyed the beach.

Marian, her mother-in-law, was wading into the sea.

Her faded cotton skirt was tucked up out of the water, tight across her generous backside. She was wearing a rakish straw hat and a crumpled white smock, and there was a fat, naked baby hoisted astride one hip.

The sky was pearly, washed by the night's rain. On a patch of sand scraped by the receding tide Marian and Leonie's husband Tom had already laid out the day's paraphernalia. There were canvas chairs and a pair of parasols with their white cotton fringes teased by the breeze off the water, sand toys and beach bags and rubber rings, and a rug spread for the babies.

Tom was doing his run. He was at the far end of the beach now, his feet sending up little sparkly silver plumes of spray as he plunged along at the water's edge. Next he would thud up the stone steps and disappear down the coast road to the village. In Pittsharbor he would buy bagels and newspapers, and come home with snippets of gossip about whom he had seen and what messages they wanted relayed to Marian.

Leonie stood expressionlessly watching him until he reached the end of the beach. Then she went on down the steps and laid her book on one of the canvas chairs.

'Leonie!' Marian called to her from knee-deep water. 'Angel, there you are. What have you been doing? Ashton needs his little sun-hat. Will you find it in the bag there . . . no, no, the *red* bag, darling. And bring it to me.'

Leonie obediently paddled out with the hat. Marian swung round and the baby on her hip waved his fists and laughed with delighted pleasure.

'There's the boy. Hat on for Grammer, *there* we are.' She smoothed the white cotton with a sun-tanned, capable, heavily ringed hand.

Marian Beam was a widow. In her middle sixties she remained handsome, her broad face creased with the lines of a lifetime's emphatic emotion and marked with the irregular sepia freckles of sun damage. Marian liked to be noticed. She emphasised her large, dark eyes with smudgy charcoal pencil and kept her silvery streaked hair long and flowing. For convenience she pinned it off her face with a series of combs.

Marian loved children. She had had five of her own. Kids were her *thing*, she often said. And as for grandchildren, well, they were the greatest gift God could bestow. It was her sadness that poor Dickson couldn't be here to share the joy of seeing them grow up. Dickson was Marian's late husband. He had died fifteen years before, most probably, Leonie thought, of sheer exhaustion from living alongside Marian for nearly thirty years.

'You could have married again,' Leonie remembered saying to Marian years ago, not long after she had married Tom. 'You were only fifty when Dickson died.'

Marian smiled luminously. 'My dear, Dickson was my husband. I couldn't have thought of anyone else. And I had my boys, and Karyn. I felt rich enough.'

That was how she always talked about them. There were the four boys, of whom Tom was the second, all strapping replicas of their father, and then there was the late, longed-for girl. Karyn was thirty now. She had given her mother plenty of problems but lately she seemed to have settled down. Ashton was her second baby by her live-in partner Elliot. Elliot was black and the two children were exquisite, plump *café au lait* armfuls.

With the addition of Sidonie and Ashton, Marian now had eleven grandchildren. None of them was from Tom and Leonie.

The two women stood side by side in the water, looking back at the bluff and the houses. The old clapboards and pointed gables were softened by the benign light. Even the tarry dark-stained shingles of the Captain's House shimmered as if washed with a milky glaze.

The Beams' was the largest of the five summer cottages overlooking the beach. It stood majestically in the centre, the complicated pitches of its steep roof pierced by dormer windows and surmounted by a widow's walk. From the flagpole in centre front a faded and frayed American flag twitched in the fitful breeze. Marian always hoisted the flag as soon as she arrived at the beach. Dickson's flag, she called it.

The house was entirely surrounded at ground level by a wide porch, the home of sagging hammocks and swing seats and surfboards awaiting rehabilitation and windsurfer sails and ancient bicycles, tangled up with driftwood trophies and shells and all the other relics of past holidays. It was just this endless continuity about the place, the silted layers of historical minutiae, which oppressed Leonie.

'We've always done this,' Tom explained to her at the beginning. 'Moon Island Beach is embedded inside us all. I can't imagine spending a summer anywhere else.'

'Not Europe?' Leonie had protested. 'Venice? Tuscany? The French Riviera?'

He had dutifully taken her to Italy for their honeymoon. But the next year, and every year after that, they had returned to the beach. And at the beach house Marian was the matriarch. She presided over daughters-in-law and children and grandchildren like some fertility goddess.

Leonie stirred one leg in the water. She could feel warmer and cooler layers swirling around her calves, cooler on the surface. The storm had stirred everything up. 'Where is everyone this morning?' she asked. There was only Sidonie asleep on a towel in the shade of one of the parasols.

'The kids are playing tennis.'

There were four of them, Lucas and Gail and Joel and Kevin, the children of Marian's eldest son, Michael. All four of them came out every summer to stay at the beach, just as their parents had done all through their own childhoods. This year, unusually, their mother and father had gone to Europe. 'And Karyn and Elliot are out in the boat.'

Leonie looked and saw the white mainsail and jib of the Beams' Flying 15 running out beside the island. She nodded, wondering with a part of her mind exactly how she would occupy herself for this morning, and the afternoon that would follow it, and

17

the nights and days after that. The beach and Marian and the family affected her like this.

A man Leonie didn't recognise was standing up in front of the Captain's House and a young woman in a double sliver of bikini was spikily descending the steps. 'Who are they?' she asked Marian.

'They're the Bennisons' tenants, I guess. I hope they're going to be an addition.'

Marian meant an addition to the local texture and colour, to the ever evolving art-form of the family summer holiday.

At the same moment there was a loud whoop from the garden of the Beams' house, signalling that the tennis was over.

Marian said, 'Take the babe for me, Leonie' and handed over the peachy weight of him without waiting for Leonie's agreement. She waded out of the water, ready to welcome the older grandchildren, her tucked up skirt revealing navy-blue thickened veins behind her heavy knees.

They came streaming down the beach, headed by a sun-tanned young man of twenty in tennis shorts and a faded vest. He wore his long hair pulled back in a stringy pony-tail.

'Lucas,' Marian called to him, but her eldest grand-child's attention was elsewhere. He had seen the bikini girl, who was wandering across the shingle and occasionally turning over shells with one languidly pointed toe.

May walked from the window of her bedroom to the

18

door and pressed her knuckles against it, making sure that it was firmly closed. She was repeating a manoeuvre she had made only five minutes earlier but she could not have explained the need to make sure she was alone. She knew the house was empty; she had seen Ivy disappear down the beach steps and John was sitting reading a book on the bench above the sea wall.

With the door closed she felt safe. A fly buzzed against the window-pane. The forlorn room held her enmeshed in its drowsy heat. There were thirteen steps from the door to the window; she had already counted them. Her belongings were unpacked, sparsely laid out on the shelves. There was nothing else to do up here and the sea and the island were bathed with clean blue light. The water of the bay was dotted with cheerful coloured sails. She should put on a swimming costume and go out, like Ivy, into the sunshine.

May had bought a new one-piece from Macy's. It was red-and-white plaid and she had thought she looked okay in it. A bikini was out of the question and now when she put it on she saw that even this suit showed the cellulite at the top of her legs. She stood for a long moment looking at her torso in the mirror over the dresser, then blindly turned away. If she didn't go out now she was afraid she never would. She might climb back under the bedcovers and stay there with her knees pulled up to hide her stomach.

The fly had fallen to the window-sill. The buzzing was louder and desperate. May retraced her steps to the door. But when she grasped the handle and pulled it wouldn't open. It only shifted slightly, resisting her efforts. It was as if someone else were leaning a shoulder against it. To keep her there, within the stuffy confines of the room.

With her breath catching in her throat May pulled harder. The door suddenly sprang open and she gave a muffled croak of surprise. Without looking back she fled down the stairs and through the screen doors on to the deck. There was an old woman in the garden of the next-door house. She had been bending over a clump of tall blue flowers, but she saw May and stood up, straight-backed, watching her with uncomfortable intentness. Even at this distance May didn't like it. She ducked her head and ran down the sandy path, rough grass whipping at her ankles.

John looked up from his book. 'Sun cream,' he called after her as she raced by.

'Ivy'll have some.'

She wanted to get to Ivy. Without thinking, May ran down to the beach. She could see her sister in her bikini, standing gracefully, her weight all balanced on one long leg and angled hip. She was raking back her hair with her fingers and talking to some boys.

When May panted up to her she half-turned, startled, and smiled. 'This is my sister, May.'

The three boys were standing in a dazzled semicircle. Of course Ivy drew them like moths with no thought but to incinerate themselves in her flame.

'This is Lucas, May. And . . . um . . .' She didn't try to conceal the fact that she hadn't remembered the names of the others.

'Joel. And Kevin.'

The middle one fell over himself to supply the information. Ivy gave him a small, considered smile and he blushed. Joel was about sixteen and Kevin a year or so younger. They looked just like the two hundred boys May knew in school in New York, who all wanted to date the same twenty skinny girls. Lucas was different. He was older, perhaps even as old as twenty. He had beige-blond hair pulled back in a pony-tail, a slippery golden tan and a lovers' knot tattooed on his left bicep. May realised that she was openly staring at him and felt dull colour rising in her face as she dragged her eyes away.

'Your sister?' Lucas said in amusement.

May stood with her arms folded across her chest, numbly exposed in her stupid red-and-white swimsuit, feeling the sun hot on the top of her head. 'Have you got the sun cream?' she demanded of Ivy. She had forgotten the eeriness of the house. It was time to retreat from all these pairs of eyes. There were two women sitting on rugs only a few yards away and John was strolling across the sand with his hands in the pockets of his khaki shorts.

'Sure.' Ivy produced a tube from her straw bag. 'Want me to rub some on your shoulders?'

'No thanks,' May snapped. She took the cream and marched away.

'And this is my Dad,' she heard Ivy saying.

'Hi. I'm John Duhane.'

Marian was already on her feet, on her way to greet the newcomer.

'I'm so pleased someone has taken the Bennisons' place. I couldn't bear to think of it sitting empty, with all that sadness trapped inside it. Are the young women your daughters? They'll make the house laugh again, I know they will.'

John hadn't yet told Ivy and May about the death of the Bennison girl. It had seemed the last of too many negatives about the whole trip, but now he knew that he should have done so.

For the moment Ivy's attention was fully occupied by the blond boy. The two of them had already begun to wander away, the younger brothers in attendance.

Marian Beam introduced Leonie, whose arms were full of baby. 'This is Ashton and that's Sidonie asleep on the rug.'

'They're beautiful,' John said dutifully. But it was the babies' mother who held his interest. She had a narrow, brown-skinned face and dark eyes, which met his briefly and slid away. She was pretty in a boyish way, but what struck him about her was the way her face looked tucked in, as if she was used to concealing things.

Marian was saying, 'There's plenty of company here for your girls. I've got eleven grandchildren altogether, from Lucas down to Ashton, and they all come to spend the summers with me. Is your wife here with you?'

'I'm a widower.'

And he saw the mother look at him over the baby's sun-hat. 'You're here on your own with them?' Marian protested. 'I call that plain heroic.'

22

'Or plain foolish,' John anwered and was rewarded by another veiled glance from the daughter-in-law.

'You must come over and join us whenever you feel like it. How about tonight? My daughter Karyn is here with her partner and Leonie's husband is here too . . .'

Ah, John thought. Of course.

'Unfortunately the other two boys and their families won't be getting here until later, and you must meet them then.'

'Perhaps not this evening,' John said. 'We should settle in up there first. We only arrived in the middle of the storm last night.'

He looked beyond the frayed brim of Marian's hat to the Captain's House. It stood at a slightly different angle from the others, seeming to turn aside from them and away from the full assault of the sea and wind. He could imagine that a seafarer had built it, a man who had had enough of the weather and the elements, but still couldn't quite leave them behind. May had been standing on the lower deck looking down at them, but now she had disappeared.

Marian was insistent. 'Tomorrow, what about that? Come over and have a meal with us tomorrow evening.'

'Thank you, we'd like to.'

'That's settled then.'

Evidently Marian Beam was a woman who knew what she wanted and insisted on getting it.

The garden between the sea wall and the deck was not really a garden at all, more a strip of grass and sand, which had been decorated in places with big rounded beach stones and low bushes. May prowled aimlessly around the limits of the area, turning back when she came to the fence painted in faded blue that separated the garden from the one next door. Orange, scarlet and ginger flowers growing on the other side spilled over the fence, making a little oasis of brilliance.

May followed a stony path down the side of the house. There was an outside shower behind a screen, a big evergreen tree with a dilapidated hammock slung from the branches, a coiled-up hosepipe, which stopped her short for a second with its resemblance to a snake. When she recovered her breath and stepped forward again she immediately knew that someone was watching her. She peered behind her and up into the branches of the tree, to the little screened windows in the side of the house. There was no one to see. A cold breath fanned the nape of her neck, even though the day had turned hot.

She turned her head slowly.

The old woman she had seen before was standing on the other side of the fence, half hidden by the green leaves of her garden. 'I didn't mean to startle you,' she said.

'You didn't.' May was relieved. 'I saw you before.'

The woman held up a big pair of shears to show May. 'I'm doing some pruning. Turner's supposed to come and see to it but he doesn't always have time to do everything. Turner's my gardener. My mother loved this garden and I try to look after it for her sake. I suppose it's a kind of memorial.'

The woman really was quite old, so her mother must have died long ago. May liked the idea of her daughter keeping up the garden in her memory. She wished that she had something like it to do. Sometimes she and Ivy talked about their mother, but not very often nowadays. And John hardly ever even mentioned her. He just expected them to accept Suzanne or some other girlfriend instead.

'I like your garden. It's pretty.'

'Thank you. I saw you looking at the Japanese garden the Bennisons did out the front. What did you think of that?'

'Japanese? I thought it looked like someone had dumped a whole lot of stones and left the rest to itself. Gardens ought to have flowers and stuff. Lots of colours.'

The woman laughed. 'I think you're right. And my mother would have approved of your ideas too. Should we introduce ourselves? My name's Elizabeth Newton.'

'Hi. I'm May Duhane.'

'I'm happy to meet you, May. I saw you arriving last night.'

'Yeah? All that rain.'

'You reminded me a little of Doone. You still do remind me of her, as a matter of fact. Perhaps only because you're the same age.'

'Doone? Who's she?'

In the quiet that followed voices carried up to them from the beach. One of them was Ivy's and a burst of laughter came after it.

Elizabeth said, 'Would you like to come round to my side and have a closer look at the garden?'

'Okay,' May said. 'I can get over the fence here, look.'

After the tour of the garden they sat in deep wicker chairs on Elizabeth's porch. At first sight of her May had thought that Mrs Newton must be dressed up ready to go out somewhere, maybe to a coffee party or a town meeting, or whatever it was that old ladies did in Pittsharbor. She had on a dress, silky and pleated, with a brooch pinned to the collar. She was wearing tights, too, fine pale ones that showed the brown marks on the skin of her legs, and proper leather shoes. Then, when she didn't mention having to hurry off anywhere, May came to the conclusion that this must be how she always chose to look. It made her seem even older than she really was, as if she belonged to history instead of to May's grandparents' generation.

Elizabeth had proper lemonade, which she served in a tall glass jug with intricate diamond patterns cut into it. She also offered May a plate of very good chocolate fudge brownies. May took two, telling herself it would not be polite to insist that she was on a diet.

'Who's Doone?' May finally asked again.

Elizabeth was looking out to sea. The island was a solid shape in the middle distance, its beach fringed with a rim of silver. 'Perhaps I shouldn't have mentioned it. Her parents own your house.'

'The Bennisons.'

'Yes. Doone was their daughter. She died in a boating accident last summer. She drowned.'

May looked at her glass. There was a sweat of condensation on the smooth rim and a greasy mark where she had put it to her mouth.

'I *reminded* you of her?'

'Just because of your age. And your size and build are similar. Actually you are nothing like her at all.'

May thought again. 'Which was her bedroom?'

'The one on this side of the house, looking over the sea.'

'It's mine too,' May said. And in case her new friend should be concerned, or think that she might be unnerved by this idea, she added firmly, 'I like it. It's a good room. And I'm sorry about Doone, I just didn't know.'

Her words seemed to echo in her own ears, as if she were listening to someone else uttering them.

Two

May sprawled on the bed in Ivy's room where her sister was getting ready for dinner at the Beams' house. Ivy had already changed her clothes twice and May was still in the baggy shorts she had worn all day. 'Ive, did you know about the kid?'

Ivy snapped the cap off a lipstick and coloured her mouth. She lifted one eyebrow at May in the mirror. 'What kid? What're you talking about?'

'The daughter of the people who own this house.'

A shrug. 'Nope.'

'She drowned. Last year. Elizabeth told me. She was out sailing by herself and she fell in. She was the same age as me.'

Ivy lowered the lipstick for a second. 'No. I didn't know. That's really sad.'

The shadow falling on Ivy's face made her beautiful by dimming her china prettiness. May noticed it and for all the jealousy that clogged her veins and weighted her feet, she knew that she loved her sister. She gnawed viciously at the corner of her chapped mouth, not knowing how to deal with the realisation._She complained, 'Why do you think Dad hasn't told us about her? I'm only sleeping in her bedroom. He never says anything, does he?'

'Perhaps he thought it would spook you.'

'I'm not spooked,' May insisted. 'I'm not a baby.'

Ivy shrugged, losing interest. 'Well, ask him, if you want to know. How do I look?'

'Nice.'

Ivy had finally settled for a halter top and a tiny skirt. They left uncovered a slice of smooth flat belly. Her legs and shoulders were already turning a pale gold. 'Nice? Don't go crazy, will you?'

'What d'you want me to say? How about hot? You look like you put out big-time, as it happens.'

'Little bitch,' Ivy retorted, not without amusement. She was in a good mood. 'Are you going in those clothes?'

'Does it *matter*?' May jumped off the bed, needing to hide the fact that it mattered too much. 'Anyway, what about Steve?' Steve was Ivy's steady boyfriend back in the city.

'What do *you* care about Steve?'

'I don't. I thought you did, that's all.'

Ivy had spent weeks protesting that it was because of Steve that she didn't want to be dragged away from Brooklyn Heights and made to spend half the precious summer in some God-forsaken seaside town like a kid being sent to camp. 'I'm here and he's there. Besides, Lucas is okay.' Ivy combed out her glossy hair. 'I saw *you* checking him out.'

'I didn't. I wouldn't.'

29

Ivy only grinned. 'No? One of the kid brothers would do for you. Whatshisname, Kevin. He's cute.'

'Shut the fuck *up*, will you?'

May stared in fury. That's how it was between them. They veered from being almost friends to raw-skinned irritation, and back again, without any episodes of moderation. Sometimes May wondered if their mother had been around whether she might have been the mediator, smoothing over the spikes of anger and making their attempts to like each other seem less clumsy. John didn't do anything of the kind. He and Ivy seemed to occupy a different territory, adulthood maybe, which left May stranded somewhere apart. It intensified her loneliness and made her angrier still with both of them. Yet sometimes only Ivy would do: only Ivy understood anything.

She slammed back into her own bedroom. She had spent the whole day in here while Ivy lay sunbathing. The cracks in the paper and the vertical shadows that ran like thin ribs in the grooves of the panelling had already become familiar. May imagined Doone Bennison sitting reading in this same armchair, or lying on her back making figures out of the spidery lines that traced the ceiling. Perhaps she had swung her legs off the bed like *this* and ducked down the stairs, and then gone out to sail the boat across the bay for the last time.

What was it like to drown?

May pressed the back of her hand to her mouth, experimentally stopping the air. Her heart fluttered against her ribs and she found herself gasping for breath.

Ivy banged on the door as she passed. 'You coming?'

It was too late now for May to do anything about the way she looked. She could have fixed her hair, at least, or chosen a looser top to hide her fat.

She vented some of the pressure of dissatisfaction with herself by kicking the skirting beside the base of the bookshelf. A neat section of it immediately fell forward and lay on the worn carpet with the unpainted splintery back exposed. There was a rectangular black space behind it.

May knelt down and peered into the hole. Something was hidden in there.

Carefully she reached in and drew it out. It was a hardback notebook with dusty black covers and a scarlet cloth spine. She opened it at the first page and saw girl's handwriting not much different from her own. The first word on the top line was *May*.

May licked her dry lips. The faint murmur of the sea swelled in her ears until the room seemed like a giant shell that amplified the greedy waves.

The book was Doone's, it had to be. This was her bedroom, and May had kicked against her secret hiding-place. Now Doone was writing from somewhere directly to May, and the roar of the sea rose up in her ears and almost deafened her.

She read on with reluctant fascination, her fingers shaking as she turned a page.

It wasn't her name, she realised. It was a date: 15 May, last year. This was a diary. The dead girl's diary, tucked into its hiding-place and forgotten.

31

John and Ivy were calling her.

May closed the book and blew the dust off the covers. She slid it back into the hole in the wall and pressed the loose section of skirting back into place. It fitted closely, with only two vertical cracks to betray its existence. No one would bother to investigate unless they accidentally dislodged the section as she had done. She scrambled to her feet.

John was standing downstairs next to the smoke-blackened chimney stones. He had put on a clean blue shirt.

May rocked on the bottom step, glaring her latest accusation at him. 'Why didn't you tell us about what happened to the Bennisons' daughter?' It was typical of May not to offer an introduction, just to launch straight into her offensive.

John temporised. 'All right, May, I should have done. Okay? But I didn't want it to be a reason right off for you not to like the place.'

She recognised the expression on his face. It was a taut mixture of conciliation, impatience and anxiety, and she often saw it when her father looked at her. Thinking about the hidden diary she felt defiance harden within her. Somebody's drowning shouldn't be wrapped up and hidden, just in case it might spoil someone else's holiday. A person took shape in her mind, a girl, with her skin mottled by sea water and her clothes streaming with it. The momentary vision was real enough for May to see her pale features.

Holding her discovery to herself, May felt the secret settle in place like an invisible shield.

The diary was lying in the darkness, waiting for her to read it. Finding it in its secret hiding-place drew her into a conspiracy with Doone: Doone must have something to tell her that shouldn't be shared with anyone else. 'The place is okay,' she said tonelessly. 'Why wouldn't I like it?'

John's face relaxed. This was better than he had hoped. 'Good. We're going to have a good time. These people seem friendly.'

'Are we going, then?' Ivy sighed.

The Duhanes walked down their own driveway, passed Elizabeth Newton's mailbox and doubled back between the overgrown trees and bushes that lined the way to the Beams' house. They skirted the tennis court and various cars drawn up on a gravel sweep, and climbed the porch steps to knock on the back door. There was plenty of time before anyone answered it for them to survey the sagging chairs, heaps of shells and discarded shoes that lined the unswept boards. John and Ivy exchanged questioning glances.

At length the screen door was tugged open by a man none of them had seen before. But it did seem that they were expected.

'Hi, I'm Tom. Come on in, we're all out the front.'

The glimpse of the house confirmed their first impressions.

It was huge and chaotic. Open doors revealed chairs piled with children's toys and floors patterned with sandy footprints. At the beach, Marian favoured freedom and space for self-expression over domestic order.

33

The houses had been built so that they turned their backs on the land and the lane leading away to Pittsharbor. The wide porches and front windows faced the curve of beach, the island and the open sea beyond, and they were separated from the edge of the bluff by their gardens. Elizabeth Newton's and the Bennisons' gardens were cultivated, but the other three were not much more than sandy spaces stitched with seagrass. Tonight, the porch and the decks at Marian Beam's house appeared to be crowded with people. Lucas and his two younger brothers and two of their friends from Pittsharbor were playing frisbee between the deck and the bluff, with Gail looking on.

Ivy stepped forward, smiling, knowing that she would be welcomed. May hung back, disabled by shyness.

Marian surged forward to greet the Duhanes. Once they had been processed by her, John and Ivy were drawn straight into the party. May edged around the group and positioned herself where she could watch Lucas covertly and survey everyone else. After a minute's quiet observation she saw that, apart from the four Beam siblings and their friends, the crowd was only made up of five Beam adults, Elizabeth Newton and an elderly couple May had not seen before.

Marian was introducing the old people to John. 'This is Aaron and Hannah Fennymore. Your neighbours from the opposite end of the beach, John.'

The woman was about the same age as Elizabeth Newton, but she looked completely different. She had none of Elizabeth's stately bearing or gracious manner. Hannah Fennymore was small and bent-backed, dressed in layers of nondescript brown and grey clothes as if the evening were cold instead of soft and mild. She was sharp-eyed and inquisitive-looking, rather like a small busy bird.

The man, her husband, must once have been tall and imposing. He was bent now, too, and a stick lay on the floor beside his chair. He had white hair, long and a little unkempt, which stood out around his hollow, beaky face like a lion's mane. Everyone, even the boys, stepped carefully when they came near Aaron.

The Fennymores were Mainers, not weekenders or summer visitors. They lived all the year round up on the bluff.

At last, feeling more confident, May slipped into a seat near Elizabeth.

'I remember parties at this house in the nineteen-thirties and forties,' Elizabeth murmured to her, as if they were resuming a conversation they had broken off only minutes before, not a full day and a half ago. May liked the implied intimacy of this. 'Long before Dickson Beam bought the place. Marian makes believe the Beams have been here for ever, but they're just newcomers, really.'

'What were they like, the parties?'

'They were grand affairs, for a summer cottage. Everyone in evening clothes, a uniformed maid. Of course, the house looked *quite* different then. Marguerite Swayne wouldn't recognise it if she saw it now. Mr Swayne was a friend of my grandfather's.

35

They were an old family. Their money was in fruit shipping: bananas, up from Jamaica.'

May scratched at an inflamed bite on her ankle, half-closing her eyes and trying to conjure up the scene. Movie images of marcel-waved ladies fox-trotting with gentlemen in white gloves danced in front of Joel and Kevin Beam. The pictures clashed with May's own much darker impression of the beach and its houses. Another face swam by, drowned features framed by tendrils of wet hair. Water blotted out the dancing couples.

Elizabeth was saying, 'This house was built ninety years ago by the Swaynes, at about the same time as my paternal grandfather bought our parcel of land. He was Senator Maynard Freshett. *His* family business was timber, lumber mills. There's a rather forbidding portrait of him in my dining-room, but he was the kindest man. My mother brought me up here every summer to visit her parents-in-law, from the time I was two years old. Her family were from Portland, originally, but *her* mother died when she was just a girl.'

May nodded politely. 'Who else lived here in those days?'

'When I was a child?' Elizabeth laughed briefly, showing the soft crow's-foot skin beneath her jaw. 'Aaron, Mr Fennymore did, for one. Not in the house along there, that came later. His people lived back in Pittsharbor.'

'What was their family business?'

Elizabeth gave her a quick glance. Then she

36

touched her throat with the tips of her fingers, as if needing the powdered wrinkles as a reminder that the skin was an old woman's. 'Fishing. His father and grandfather were fishermen.'

May wondered if she had inadvertently strayed on to some sort of forbidden ground. She didn't like the look of Aaron Fennymore very much. He was stern, yet alarmingly frail – ill-looking. As if he might die or something.

Marian clapped her hands and walked between the groups. She was wearing a tiered hippie skirt and the toe-nails of her faintly grubby feet were painted ripe purple. 'Everything's ready, plates are right here. You have to help yourselves, now, no ceremony. We're just family, John.'

Aaron Fennymore's white head jerked and his wife patted his hand. 'I'll fix you a plate,' she soothed him.

'Go on,' Elizabeth said to May. 'You'll be hungry.'

'Not really,' May said coldly, while her stomach clamoured for hamburger.

The food was barbecued with some aplomb by Tom Beam, aided by Lucas, and served up by Lucas's laid-back friends from Pittsharbor. Leonie always let Tom do the cooking. He ran two successful restaurants in Boston, and he had precise ideas about the right way to do anything connected with food. She sat back in one of the canvas loungers, wondering vaguely when the salt-rotted fabric would finally tear apart and deposit her on the deck. The size of the gathering allowed her to feel that for once she needn't make a particular effort to be cheerful and talkative. No one would notice if she withdrew and let her thoughts wander.

Everyone had eaten and Tom made regular circuits of the adults with the bottles of Californian Merlot. Lucas and his friends, and his sister Gail and Ivy, drank beer. Marian looked pleased with her success in having been the one to draw the new people into the little society of the bluff. They would be her protégés now and she liked that.

Marian had stopped to listen courteously to something Elizabeth Newton was saying. Leonie knew that privately Marian considered Elizabeth to be an old Boston snob and an anachronism, but she was always polite to her in public. Maybe they were talking about the land behind the beach and the development. Elizabeth's son Spencer and his partner wanted to buy a piece to build condominiums, but Aaron owned it and flatly refused to sell. Elizabeth tried to promote Spencer's cause whenever she could and she was well aware that Marian's relationship with the Fennymores was more cordial than her own.

Leonie drew up her knees and rested her chin on them. She was happy watching without having to respond to anyone. She saw her husband lean down to say something to Karyn and their physical likeness struck her all over again. All Marian's children resembled her and one another. Their wide, handsome faces with broad foreheads and big noses might have come from the same mould. Karyn was dark like her mother, whereas Tom had inherited his father's sandy fairness and prominent chin, but they were unmistakably brother and sister. They laughed now, the same noisy burst of amusement that was the signature sound of Beam family gatherings. Leonie's gaze travelled on at once.

The sky over the sea had turned pistachio green and now the light was fading into navy-blue darkness. The teenagers had begun to talk about taking a boat out to the island and lighting a fire, so they could carry on their own party there.

'Aw, c'mon, we've done it plenty before,' Joel was protesting to Tom and Marian.

Leonie did not try to intervene. The older of the two sisters from the Bennisons' place was as graceful as a gazelle, but she was wearing too much make-up for a summer's evening and her eyes were bold to the point of hardness. The younger one with the round, sweet face hovered watchfully at one side. She kept tugging at the hem of her shorts as if she wanted to cover herself up. Leonie wondered how long ago their mother had died.

Their father moved around the circle, making a polite point of talking to everyone. He had sat for a long time with the Fennymores and now he was nodding in the midst of a brief conversation with Elliot. Watching them, Leonie reached down and groped unseeingly for the glass of wine beside her chair. She finished what was left of it, her third of the evening. She didn't often drink more than one. Abstemiousness over food and drink was part of her carefulness, her exercising of control in all the areas of her life that remained susceptible to control.

The children began a shift down the beach steps. Marian and Tom moved in their wake, issuing warnings and instructions. The sea was calm and the tide was right, so they had been given permission to row across to the island. Leonie saw how the younger Duhane girl waited until her sister motioned her on with a hitch of her chin. Then she followed on after Kevin and Joel, who took no notice of her. They clattered down the steps and out of sight and the adults came back into the circle, simultaneously smiling and shaking their heads.

'They'll be okay. You can't stop them doing everything because of what happened,' Tom proclaimed to no one in particular.

'May I sit here?' someone asked.

Leonie turned her head and saw it was John Duhane. She was convinced that he had taken care to talk to everyone else except her because he had been saving her until last. 'Please do.'

At first, he didn't say anything at all. They sat in companionable silence watching the glow of candles around the deck and as the quiet stretched between them Leonie let her head fall back once more against the salty chair canvas. A thin wire loosened between her shoulder-blades and her breathing steadied. The murmur of the sea grew louder.

When he did speak it was in a low voice that she had to turn her head to hear. He was telling her his daughters had been reluctant to make this trip and how pleased he was that there were other young people for them to be with. 'Vacations have been the hardest part to deal with since their mother died.' He spoke softly but without hesitation.

'How long ago?'

'Four years now.'

'I'm sorry. They must miss her. And you must too,' she added hastily, disconcerted to discover that she sounded clumsy.

John was sitting on the edge of the decking. He reached down to the coarse grass arching beside his ankle and pinched a blade between his thumb and forefinger.

'One of the babes is crying,' Marian called. There was a nursery alarm plugged in close to the porch door. Karyn swayed past and the hem of her skirt brushed over John's arm. A moment later she came out again with Ashton in her arms. His dark pin-curled head lolled and his thumb was wedged in his mouth. Over her shoulder his wet saucer eyes blinked at the world with tearful reproach.

John moved a little to one side, but Leonie sat motionless with her hands locked behind her head. 'They're beautiful children,' he said. 'You don't believe they will ever grow up, do you? But they do. They grow up and they stop thinking you're the best person in the world. Overnight you become the enemy.'

Leonie followed his surprised gaze as Karyn went to Elliot. Elliot took the bundle of damp baby and unconcernedly rocked it and went on talking. She made a small sound that might have been laughter, or something altogether different. 'Oh, I see. You thought they were mine? From the beach, yesterday morning? No, they're Karyn's kids. Elliot's her partner, obviously. My husband is Tom.'

'I'm sorry.'

'Don't be. It's a natural assumption to make, a woman with a baby in her arms.'

'So which of all those children *are* yours?'

'None of them. Tom and I don't have any.'

'Ah.'

Leonie stood up. A spoon that had been hidden in the folds of her skirt clattered to the decking but no one looked round. She retrieved it and replaced it with the others. 'Will you come for a walk on the beach? Just ten minutes?' she asked abruptly, without having pre-planned the invitation in her mind.

'Of course.'

They crossed the deck and descended the steps without anyone seeming to notice their withdrawal.

Once they were there, Leonie kicked off her sandals and hooked her forefinger through the straps. The sand was pleasantly cool and coarse underfoot. They began to walk, side by side, their heads bent.

'I wanted children,' she heard herself saying. 'I wanted a family.' Even the word itself had become taboo, so that it lay unwieldy on her tongue. 'But I couldn't. I had all the tests. The problem was me, not Tom. We tried the . . . the alternative methods. Quite a lot were undignified, most of them painful, all of them were expensive. None worked. I sound sorry for myself, don't I?'

John listened, but said nothing.

'We were told to consider adoption, but Tom didn't want to do that. He felt it wasn't right for him. So. No children.'

'I'm sorry, I made a clumsy mistake.'

'Don't be. I said, it was natural enough. I'm spilling all this out probably because . . . because of the wine.'

Laughter and the splash of oars travelled across the water to them. Two boats were making their way out to the island.

'Why don't you and Tom take your vacations somewhere else?'

She was taken aback for a moment. The question leapfrogged further than she had been prepared for. 'Oh, it's a movie, isn't it? The beach, the island . . . that house, Maine itself. It's woven into all of them, a picture, that was what Marian wanted. It's her *oeuvre*. Family, grandchildren, the tradition of all the summers. Tom wouldn't consider cutting us out of the celluloid.'

'Not even for your sake?'

Leonie considered in all seriousness, wishing to do her husband justice. At length she said, 'No.' It was the truth; it was so important to Tom that the two of them should remain part of this extended family. The connection compensated him for the lack of his own children, even as comparisons deepened the sense of loss and failure for her. 'It isn't so much to ask, you know. It's just a summer vacation. Some tennis, a couple of barbecues. Aunt Leonie and Uncle Tom. In the winter we go on a ski trip, usually with friends. Last year we went to the Caribbean . . .'

43

She knew that she protested too much. It was part of a contract she had agreed with herself, to be as positive as she could manage. There seemed no way, any more, to give expression to the desperation and craving and sense of futility that were all her body did manage to breed. At the beginning, in the first years, she had talked – ranted, sobbed – to Tom about her longing to conceive. But now, driven into blankness, they hardly ever even mentioned it. Except maybe as the bitterest, the most oblique of jokes at their joint expense.

Athough she had told John Duhane the bare facts, Leonie couldn't have conveyed to him or anyone else how it felt to hold Ashton or Sidonie in her arms. The simultaneous longings to smother them, to inhale the scent of their skin and hair to the point of narcolepsy, to hurl them aside, to rake and pummel her own disobliging flesh . . . *I'm crazy,* Leonie thought. *Raving. There's no hope for me.* . . . She grinned in the darkness. There was relief in acknowledging her madness.

An onshore breeze had sprung up, and it blew a hank of hair across her face and flattened her skirt against her thighs. Being at the beach made her crazier, being inundated with babies and pounded by teenagers and chewed up by the clan of Beams, up here where everything was so god-damn clean and healthy and salt-scoured and plain . . . at least back in the city there was dirt and confusion, and work, and even a couple of women friends who had elected not to have babies. . . .

She laughed now, a low noise that made John look sideways at her tucked-in face. 'Something funny?'

He touched her wrist, guided her around a mooring chain snaked over the shingle. She resisted an impulse to take his hand.

'In a way. Tell me about your girls.' She wanted to ask about his wife.

'They're growing up.'

'They would do, in the end.'

They reached the far point of the beach, where the steps led up towards the Pittsharbor road. Leonie had the sense that John was also thinking of Doone Bennison, who had not grown up in the end.

Which was worse, she wondered, for the thousandth time, to have had a child and lost her, or never to have had one at all? She didn't know, any more than she had known on the afternoon a year ago when the fisherman brought Doone's body ashore. She had been there, with a brown bag of shopping and a quart of ice-cream from the Ice Parlour. There had been a flurry down at the dock and one of the men had run forward with a tarpaulin and another had dashed along the harbour wall to the wooden hut where there was a telephone. At the same time there had been a hideous silence, and all the running and hoisting and sluicing of water had seemed to take place in slow motion. They had lifted the body, laid her on the dock and covered her over. Leonie remembered the white hands and feet.

The breeze off the water was cold now. Leonie and John turned and began to retrace their slow steps along the tide line.

'I miss their smaller selves,' John said. 'Even after Ali died, I was certain I could look after them. Now I don't believe I know anything. They think I'm the enemy.'

'You said that before. I'm sure it isn't true.'

She had seen the girls, she wasn't sure of anything of the sort. But you reassured parents about their children, didn't you? That she was uncertain even of that much made Leonie aware how useless she had become around the whole business. Parents, procreation. Cut off from the chain of heredity, except via aunthood. What was there to do? she wondered. What, exactly?

Out on the island beach two tongues of fire made wavering figures that were answered by fainter reflections in the water. They stopped walking, stood still to watch. The fire torches dipped and a third flame sprang up between them. The young were lighting a bonfire.

'Looks kind of fun. Do you think they'll be okay out there?' John asked.

'The kids row or windsurf or sail across all the time. The beach on this side is safe enough and there's not much to go over the top of the island for. A lot of thick scrub, rough ground. Once there was a whalers' retreat out there and a native American settlement before that. Plenty of legends about it.'

'Tell me one.'

'Ask Hannah Fennymore. She's the local historian.'

John took this to mean that Leonie didn't care

enough for the place to absorb its history herself. They resumed their walk.

At the foot of the Beams' steps Leonie said, 'Come and have a cup of coffee. Or another drink.' The thought of going in on her own was not inviting. She felt a connection to this man and wanted to hold on to it.

'Perhaps another evening,' John said politely. He was half turned towards the island, listening to the murmur of breaking waves.

'Do you play tennis?'

'Yes. Not quite championship standard.'

'Good. Come and play. I need a partner, Tom's too competitive. Marian likes to see a family tournament.'

'I'm sure she does.'

They allowed themselves a moment's sly amusement *Oh, God, an ally*, Leonie thought. *I need an ally so badly*.

'Goodnight. Will you thank Marian for me?'

'Of course.' She went up the steps and left John to cross the remaining expanse of shingle to the Captain's House.

The Fennymores were preparing to leave. Aaron leaned heavily on his stick with Hannah guiding him. When Marian kissed them both, Aaron submitted to her.

'You'll come again? You won't let the whole summer go by this year?'

'Time doesn't mean as much as it once did, Marian.' Aaron's voice was deep and hoarse, as if it cost him an effort to propel the air from his chest.

47

'All the more reason,' she answered, patting his hand as it rested on the knob of his stick.

They passed Elizabeth, who was also making ready to go. Hannah and Elizabeth mimed a kiss, Aaron looked at her once and nodded his big head.

'Let me help clear up,' Elizabeth politely said to Marian.

'Let the boys do it. Tom will walk you home, Elizabeth.'

'Aaron has aged ten years since last summer,' Karyn said, after they had all gone. 'It's quite a tribute to your new friend, Mom, that they came to meet him. I wonder if he realised it?'

'Why should he?' Leonie demanded, too sharply. When they looked at her in surprise she added, 'I mean, understand all the social and historical nuances that rule this place? It takes years to figure exactly where the Fennymores stand in relation to the Newtons, who said or did what to whom twenty years ago. John Duhane's only just got here.'

Marian smiled at her. 'You are very good at it yourself, Leonie. You humour us.'

Leonie lifted a bunch of dirty wineglasses on to a tray. 'When do the Stiegels get here?' she asked.

Elliot took it from her. 'I bumped into Marty and Judith at a gallery opening in SoHo,' he said. 'They'll be arriving in a week.'

'Great,' Leonie said. Athough they had rented the fifth house for several years the Stiegels were outsiders too. Like John Duhane. And herself.

The younger boys brought driftwood from the ends of the stony beach, and Lucas and one of his friends knelt by the fire and fed it. The flames fanned upwards, washing their faces with lurid light. Ivy and Gail reclined on the rocks. Their long legs folded on either side of the other friend, flirtatiously penning him in. The three of them watched the fire, smoked and murmured and joked together. Lucas had brought beer in his boat, and from time to time one of them lazily tipped a can and gulped from it.

May sat apart. When Kevin and Joel were tired of collecting wood they squatted head to head and produced cigarette papers and a packet of weed wrapped in tinfoil. They offered her a draw from the resulting roll-up but she shook her head, wishing at the same time she had accepted and could melt into the group as easily as Ivy had done. It was cold at this distance from the fire, so she edged a few inches closer, feeling the meaty weight of her buttocks as she slithered a trough across the sand.

Lucas was kneeling, staring into the fire. A pale slice of hair had worked itself loose from the rubber band that held it and fell forward, bisecting his face.

May gazed at him.

To one side of her Joel coughed as he inhaled, then snorted with laughter. In her flat, slightly nasal voice Gail called for another beer.

'What's happening, then?'

Lucas shrugged in answer to Joel. From his place between Gail and Ivy the other boy said, 'I've got a couple of ideas. How about this for a start?' He rolled

49

over and flopped on top of Gail, pushing his knee between hers.

Lucas briefly glanced over his shoulder at Ivy. To May he said, 'You okay there?' She nodded, unable to speak. The metal braces on her teeth felt like a gag. 'How old are you anyway?'

'Fourteen,' she managed. She kept her lips folded down over her teeth.

'Yeah. Well, Kevin's fifteen and Joel's sixteen. Not that much difference.'

From their snuffles of laughter it was plain that his brothers thought otherwise.

'What's with these names?' Lucas's friend asked. 'I mean, Ivy and May?'

It was Ivy he was looking at but May said loudly, 'Our mother was English, she chose them. She said they were Victorian housemaid's names.' She remembered the day when they talked about it.

They had been in the kitchen, the three of them, the one in the old apartment, so she must have been still small, perhaps five or six. They were baking. Ivy was running the bendy plastic blade around the mixing bowl, scraping up a pale creamy ruff of coconut cake mix, ready for licking.

Alison bent over to peer inside the oven, at the first batch of cakes. She straightened up and her face looked shiny from the heat. 'They are English names,' she said in her definite way that made you know whatever she said was right. 'Old-fashioned names, not modern trendy ones like Zoe or Cassie.' Victorian housemaids. 'They'll come back in style one day, you'll

50

see.' May had felt proud of her name and distinguished by it.

She saw that everyone was laughing at her. Kevin and Joel had collapsed sideways in a heap and Gail and the two other boys were grinning, showing their big teeth. Ivy was glaring in fury.

Lucas stretched out a foot and stirred the logs with the toe of his boot. 'Ivy and May,' he mused. 'I think they're cute names, your mom was quite right.'

May looked at him again. The wedge of hair had fallen loose and now he pushed it back with a flat hand. The firelight neatly divided the planes of his face, light and shadow, rose and umber. Gratitude hammered in her chest, and as he turned his head their eyes briefly met and held.

In that single second May fell in love.

Adoration and devotion seeded themselves and flowered, and overwhelmed her with their cloudy scent. She felt dizzy and elated even as she watched his attention leave her and return to the fire. She didn't care any longer what the others thought. Lucas had defended her. The island and Pittsharbor and the world itself were bearable, even beautiful, because they held Lucas. The music of amazement and awe hummed in her ears.

Lucas scrambled up and sauntered over to sit down next to Ivy. She made room for him, curving her leg so that her hip tightened in the little skirt. Lucas put his big hand there.

Humbly May ducked her head. The moment was already forgotten, it had meant nothing to any of the

51

others. With the tip of one finger-nail she scratched minutely in the sand. *Lucas,* she wrote, the letters engraved on top of each other so no one could see.

Later, Lucas and Ivy strolled away from the fire. With her chin resting on her knees May watched them. As they crunched to the end of the little beach Ivy curved her pliant body inwards so that her thigh and hip and shoulder touched his. Lucas's arm rested lightly around her waist.

Kevin and Joel tried to talk to May but she couldn't listen. She kept saying *what?* or nodding her head and in the end they gave up.

After what seemed like a long time May stood up. Ivy and Lucas had climbed beyond the beach and vanished into the scrubby trees. She dragged a log to the fire and dumped it on, raising a cloud of powdery sparks. Then she slipped off from the others. She wanted to get away from Kevin and Joel and their monotonous stoned giggling, and from the two other boys tussling over Gail. Perhaps she would stumble across Ivy and Lucas. If she interrupted what they were doing, Ivy wouldn't be able to have him all to herself.

The darkness in the shelter of the spruce trees was intense. May stood still, widening her eyes in an effort to see ahead. A path revealed itself as a just discernible glimmer of paler ground and she ducked forwards, her breath growing loud in her ears. The ground rose steeply and a claw of undergrowth ripped her calf as she climbed. When she stopped to take her bearings the silence was absolute: solid, it lay like a suffocating coat over her skin, pressing down against her lips and eyelids. She rubbed her bare forearms and felt the fine hairs prickle under her fingertips. She was breathing in little irregular gasps.

May sat down suddenly on a broken tree stump that was furred with moss. The silence swelled, rushing away from her at a speed that made her dizzy, then became a vast shell containing tiny noises – the rustle of an insect in the vegetation at her feet, the whisper of the sea, the furling of leaves and the slow surge of her own blood.

Terror suddenly expanded in the narrow space of her chest. May felt each hair at the nape of her neck rise. She stared wildly around her, fearing what might be concealed behind the trees. Every impulse told her to run but she was frozen, pinned to her log like a dead moth in a case.

Then she looked up through a gap in the trees. The stars were cold but she saw the reassuring blink of a jet making its way down the coast. Carefully, brushing her fingers against the mossy dead wood, she stood up. She could move, she could return to the beach; she would be all right if she made no sound.

May crept down the path. Her only thought was to get back from this eerie place into the firelight and warmth; she had forgotten about Lucas and Ivy. But now she came to the lip of a little hollow. She must have missed the original path because she didn't remember it from the way up.

They were lying in the shelter of a clump of bushes. May saw the pale blur of Ivy's discarded halter top, then Lucas's pale profile burned itself against her eyes. He was leaning over her sister, his hands busy, and even in the thick darkness May could read his delighted absorption. Then he dipped his head and their faces greedily blurred into one. Ivy's thin arm reached up, lazy and proprietorial, and wound around his neck like a noose.

A small sound escaped from May's mouth. She tasted something sour and burning in her throat, forgot the need for silence and began to run.

The sudden crashing and flailing in the undergrowth flung Ivy and Lucas apart.

'Shit,' Ivy gasped. 'What's that?'

Lucas rolled on to his back and relaxed. He was laughing, his white teeth split the pale oval of his face. 'These woods are haunted, baby.'

Tom and Leonie went to bed in the room that had been Tom's since he was a boy. The windows overlooking the beach stood open and moist, salt-laden air washed in. Lying on her back, Leonie imagined that she could see mist wraiths sadly hanging in the corners.

'Are you cold?' Tom asked. He sat on the edge of the bed with his back to her, the mattress dipping under his weight.

'Not really.'

'Did you enjoy tonight?'

'Yes,' Leonie said truthfully.

Tom eased himself under the covers with a sigh of satisfaction and clicked off the bedside lamp. He settled down for sleep. Experimentally, Leonie rubbed her cheek against his shoulder.

'You reckon I should just confront him then?' Tom asked. He had been having a battle with a temperamental chef and as they undressed they had been talking about ways of dealing with the situation.

'I guess so,' she answered. She moved her head so that her cheek was no longer touching him. They did not often make love nowadays. When she been trying to conceive it had become one of the hurdles to be scaled on the way to a baby. Now that they had given up, Tom seemed to prefer to roll on his side and fall asleep immediately. Leonie would have welcomed the warmth and affection of familiar sex, but she no longer commanded the language in which to ask for it.

Elizabeth wound the clock in the evening room and replaced the key on the ledge where it always rested. On the way to make herself a cup of herbal tea she passed through the dining-room and stopped in front of the portrait of Maynard Freshett. He did look severe, but she remembered how patiently he had taught her to play canasta, sitting at this very table.

Grandfather Freshett had always been very sure of everything. Of his own worth and that of his family. Of his place in the world. Of what he expected of himself and everyone around him. It was this sense of order and expectation that Elizabeth had wanted to convey to May Duhane. Instead, she had come out like an old-fashioned snob. What was *their* family business, the child had asked. She was a sharp little creature. Smart, that was the word. Her sadness didn't obscure how smart she was. Fishermen. The Fennymores had been fishing out of Pittsharbor for generations.

The look of Aaron had shocked her. It was her first sight of him since last fall and he had turned other-worldly, as dry and leaf-brittle as if only the most fragile stalk held him connected to life. He and Hannah had barely spoken to Elizabeth beyond expressions of politeness. Even now, it was difficult.

On the mahogany sideboard under the senator's portrait was a silver-framed photograph. It was Spencer, Elizabeth's only child, on the day he graduated *summa cum laude* from Harvard. Bob would have been proud of his boy, but he had died the year before the photograph. Elizabeth picked it up and stared into Spencer's eyes. She could almost hear the dust, gathering and layering itself in invisible soft motes all through her empty house.

Tonight she was oppressed by the relentless passing of time, by the accumulated, stifling deposits of wasted and missed opportunity.

Three

The morning sun shone into the room again, driving a bright wedge through the salt-veiled window.

May checked that the bedroom door was properly closed, then tried it again to make sure. In the absence of a lock or bolt, she came up with the idea of wedging the back of the armchair under the handle. But when she trundled it across she discovered that the chair back was too low.

Nobody would come in, logically she knew that. John was playing tennis with the Beams and Ivy was on the beach with Lucas. When she leaned on the window-sill to look for them she saw her sister wearing Lucas's wetsuit, perched on his sailboard in the shallow water. Waves no bigger than ripples fanned around the board and ran out into the glittering shingle. Lucas himself stood alongside to encourage her, but as Ivy braced her arms and pulled on the bar, she wobbled and toppled backwards into the water.

May's mouth curled with pleasure, but Lucas waded forward and hoisted Ivy in his arms. As he set her upright she turned her face up to his and they kissed.

It was only the lightest brush of a kiss, but it filled May's teeming imagination with images of other less public embraces. Her smile turned stiff and bitter. It felt like a Hallowe'en mask on her burning face.

Lucas.

As far as Lucas was concerned she was invisible. Since the night on the island he had hardly glanced at her. She didn't really expect otherwise, but the glaring hopelessness of her attachment intensified the pain of it. May felt diminished and squat, trapped at the wrong end of some monstrous telescope. Sometimes it was hard to breathe when she covertly stared at him, her arms and legs seemed to waver and soften, and threaten to buckle underneath her. She didn't know how to position herself, even how to sit or stand when he was around. The only solution seemed to be to hide in the room she shared with Doone and her secrets.

Nobody *would* come in.

Only there was nothing logical about her fears that someone might. May left the chair pushed hard up against the door and knelt down in front of the loose section of skirting.

She had resisted the impulse of curiosity for two days. Part of her recoiled from the very idea of reading the diary. The act of invading the other girl's thoughts, making this intimate connection with somebody *dead*, was as much fearful as fascinating. But now the desire to read what Doone had written overcame her misgivings. Without giving herself more time to think she pushed the board so it fell forward and revealed the space behind. She slid the diary out of its hiding place and sat down with it in the armchair. Holding the book in her lap she began to read one of the earliest entries.

Six more weeks until 4 July. Six weeks, forty-two days. I can *see* the days lined up in front of me, like brown empty envelopes. Mom says we can go up to the beach house right at the beginning. Then at least I'll be there, seeing the same places, the old places, even if I have to wait . . . but I'm used to waiting and watching. I know how to be patient. I can keep it all wrapped up inside me, my secret. Mine.

Then a whole summer, a long chain of days, shiny beads in a necklace . . .

Do I feel happy or scared?

I don't know, I don't know.

Sometimes I wish I could tell someone, just talk, but who? Imagine telling Amy, or Mel. Ha ha. That is so weird it is almost funny.

May frowned. The next line was just numbers.

66 7 10 146 12 2 67 10 9.

And then the writing resumed.

Went to Amy's last night. We just hung out and painted our nails and watched TV. She talked about Scott T. all night. That is just so dumb.

Forty-one more days.

What did the numbers mean? They weren't dates, nor did they suggest anything else May could think of. She flipped forward through the blue-lined pages and saw there were more groups of numbers, of two and three, sometimes whole paragraphs of them. Interspersed between the numbers were ordinary jottings, about school and sleep-overs and parties and friends, reassuring to May because they sounded so familiar. If the names were changed they could have applied to her own life as readily as to Doone's.

Then, among the numbers and the scribbles about everyday events, there were the other paragraphs. These were passages of introspection, which caught May's attention and held it hooked as if the barbs bit into her mind.

Argument with Mom.

I know everyone has rows with their mothers. You're supposed to, even. Only I know there's a difference with ours.

I'm like two people. There's the one they all want me to be and I pretend that I am, the A-student and the choir leader and the student councillor; and the one I really *am*, that's so dark and strong and deep that sometimes I can't stop it bursting out of me.

Like tonight when we were arguing, about nothing at all, just what time I should come in on Saturday nights, and I couldn't keep up the control: I felt the real me speaking.

Not shouting or any of that stuff. Just cold and quiet and sure. I said I didn't care, their rules didn't touch me, nothing really touches me except things they would never know about.

I could see Mom staring at me like I'm an alien. And fear in her face that she kept trying to rub out.

She said did I want to talk, I could trust her, I could tell her anything I wanted.

And I had to keep my mouth still to stop it making this crazy smile. Because I know what I am and what I have, and I know what I hold on to, and it's nothing I could tell. Never.

Sometimes just the knowledge, the memory of it does make me feel so strong. Like I could hike up the highest mountain or live alone on a deserted island – oh, an *island* – just with this for food and drink and warmth and company.

And if I'm truthful there are other times when I doubt it all. All the wishing and waiting. Miss Straight-A says in my head, *who are you kidding?*

But it's easy to quieten her. And the easiness makes me sure that I'm real and what I have experienced is real.

And then I feel happy.

After that there was a long sequence of numbers, scribbled and jumbled close together so that the hasty digits were barely legible. They looked as if they had been written in high passion.

Because May read too quickly she sometimes missed the sense, so she went back and made herself study each line. After a while she yawned, and the yawn caught in the back of her throat and swelled into a greasy surge of nausea.

She realised that the diary frightened her.

It was the combination that was unnerving. The way the accounts of normal everyday experiences were linked by the fierce jumbles of numbers to the passages of declaration. And Doone's declarations of strength made her uneasy. If she was so strong and happy, why did she keep writing it down and why did what she wrote make her sound so lonely? What secret was hidden in the numbers?

May looked at them again. They were usually groups of three, sometimes only two. Once or twice the same number or similar ones occurred several times close together, but otherwise there was no apparent link or pattern. If it was a code, she had no idea how to break it. The thought of what the numbers might spell out increased the sick pressure so that May wondered if she might actually vomit. Holding her legs tensed against the chair's worn slipcover she closed the book and waited.

Slowly the nausea subsided, but she couldn't get Doone's words out of her head. *I could never tell. I could live on a desert island with nothing but this for food and warmth and company.* It made her sound so isolated. And yet, May thought, *I know* her. This bed was where she had slept. From the window she had looked at the view of the island and had gone out and drowned in the blue water.

Somehow, with her diary and her introspection and her coded secrets – and her loneliness – Doone Bennison was slipping under her skin. Now that the knowledge of her was there, hooked in beneath the surface, May did not know how she might rid herself of it. She remembered how finding the diary had made her feel that she hugged the secret to herself like a shield.

Perhaps I'm like her, she thought. As if she were looking down from some vantage point up under the cracked ceiling, she saw herself sitting splay-legged in the old chair, with the closed diary in her lap and the chair wedged up close against the door to keep out intruders. Or, maybe, was it Doone she was seeing and not herself at all?

'I would tell my mother,' May said. The words sounded startlingly loud in the enclosed room. 'I wish I could tell her.'

One grey, sleet-filled afternoon in the weeks after Alison's death, driven by an impulse she didn't understand, May had gone to the boxes where John had stored her clothes. She had taken out the dresses and jackets one by one and cut them, making long tattered ribbons, with the kitchen shears. 'See?' she had angrily demanded as she did it. 'Do you see what I'm doing?'

She hadn't expected her mother to hear the question, or to be hurt by the destruction of her clothes. Nor had the frenzy been a relief, only another shame to add to the ones May was suffering already.

The therapist John took her to see after this episode had advised May to search for something in nature that reminded her of her mother, and to look at it and think about her when she felt overwhelmed by grief or anger. Reluctantly May had chosen a tree, one particular tall, graceful tree, which grew in a little park near to their house, and in a way the strategy had worked. She thought of it secretly as Mom's tree and tried in a stilted way to address her mother through it. Now she felt a sudden urge to run out and put her arms around the rough trunk.

There didn't seem to be much variety in the trees around here. They were mostly hostile pointed firs.

May jumped to her feet and the diary fell to the floor. She shoved it back into the hole and clumsily wedged the skirting back in place, then pulled the chair away from the door. She didn't have to trap herself in this room. Ivy was with Lucas but she could try her father. There were enough reasons why she didn't usually turn to him, but she dismissed those for this moment.

May ran down the steep stairs. As her head came below the upper floor level she saw that he had come in from tennis; he was in the kitchen with Leonie Beam. The corners of the room were thrown into deeper shadow by the slices of light that angled from the windows. Dust specks floated in the sunlight, making the old beams and the blackened hearthstones seem the darker and heavier.

John was making coffee in the old-fashioned per-colator. Leonie was leaning against one of the counters. She was wearing white tennis shorts and shoes, and her long legs were crossed at the ankles. Both of them looked up at May in momentary surprise and smiled at her.

'Hi,' John said. 'I wondered where you were. We had a good game, Leonie and I won both sets.'

Her smooth dark hair was damp, sticking to her forehead, and his shirt was darkened in a great patch across his chest. The two of them were smiling in exactly the same way – the neutral way that covered up other things. May had interrupted something.

'Do you play tennis, May?' asked Leonie.

'No. I can't think of anything more boring.'

'*May . . .*' John began, but she didn't wait to hear him out. She marched across to the porch screen and slammed it open, leaving it gaping behind her.

After a second's awkward silence Leonie gently closed the screen again. She took the mug of coffee that John handed to her.

'Sorry,' John said shortly.

'No need.'

The child had materialised like some avenging angel. Her eyes had skewered them both, as if she could have uttered something much worse than mild rudeness. But her reaction at the sight of them had been so quick that Leonie knew jealousy was a familiar feeling for her. John must have plenty of girlfriends. Not surprising, she thought with resignation.

'May didn't like Suzanne, the woman I was involved with until recently. Neither did Ivy, really, although it mattered less to her.'

'I see,' Leonie said. She sat down at the over-large oak table and looked through the window at the pillars of the porch and the sky, waiting for what he would say next.

*

Out on the deck May hesitated, blinking in the brightness, remembering the people down on the beach and her sister's golden limbs twined around Lucas's. There was no going back into the house either, so she slipped down the dank space that separated the Captain's House from Elizabeth Newton's garden. She moved quickly, because Elizabeth might be working with her pruning shears again amid the thick greenery. She didn't want to talk to Elizabeth now, or even to be seen by her.

There was no way to go but round to the road side of the house. There was a path and dogwood bushes, and the open patch of grass and stones where John left the car. The Pittsharbor lane petered out here at the Captain's House, the last building on the bluff.

May wandered slowly along the road. She hesitated at the sound of a car and saw a black Lexus coming round the bend. She thought it must be more members of the endless Beam family arriving, but the car slowed before their driveway and turned towards the house that stood between theirs and the Fennymores'.

The name on the mailbox was Stiegel. The occupants of the car were a couple, quite young. May waited in the shelter of the hedge. The car drew up at the door and the man got out. He had dark curly hair and wore smart New York clothes; a pink Ralph Lauren button-down shirt and polished shoes. There was a thick gold band on his wedding finger; she saw the light catch it as he opened the rear door of the car and unbuckled a baby seat. He swung the seat into the air, using two hands, as if it were a prize he had just been awarded. There was a fat, impassive-looking baby strapped into it. '*Here* we are,' the man cooed into the baby's face, '*here* we are at last. Was it a long way for her? A long way in the nasty car?'

The woman had got out too. She was big, May saw, and swathed in those no-colour linen clothes that some people try to hide their size inside. 'Come on, open up the house, Marty,' she said. 'You know she needs her feed.'

Marty handed the baby over to her and ran up the steps to the door, tugging a bunch of keys out of a slim leather bag. He fumbled, then unlocked the door. He pushed it open and held it for the woman, who walked by with the baby lifted aloft in its seat. They all disappeared inside, but a minute later the man re-emerged and began taking heavy bags from the trunk of the Lexus. May slipped out of her hiding-place and walked on aimlessly.

The Fennymores' house was smaller than the other four. It was a plain box but the steep pitched roof and low windows made it look hunched, even forbidding. There was no suggestion of a garden, only a piece of open ground where their old tan station-wagon stood next to a dilapidated shed. Shading the car and the shed was a big tree. It had pale, almost silvery bark and branches like the fingers of an elegant woman's hand. A sweep of leaves looked like the layers of a skirt.

May hardly knew one tree from the next, but she thought this one might be a kind of birch or maybe beech. It wasn't exactly the same as the one in the park she called Mom's tree, but it was quite similar. On an impulse she left the road and went to it. She rested the flat of her hand against the smooth, sun-warmed bark, then tipped her head forward so that her forehead touched it.

Alison had been tall and elegant like the tree. The rustling skirt of leaves was like one she had brought with her when she moved from England to New York in 1970. Alison had been a student of American history and part of her degree course had been a year at Columbia. She had met John Duhane sitting on a bench at the Frick and had stayed to marry him.

The skirt was made of watery tie-dyed cheesecloth, sea-green and jade, with a handkerchief-point hem sewn with tiny emerald beads. The beads had rolled and scattered as the scissor blades sliced the cheese-cloth into tatters. Once, long before that, May had implored Alison to let her dress up in the skirt. She had worn it to a fancy dress party as a sea nymph and Alison had plaited green ribbons for seaweed in her hair.

May pressed her face against the bark of the new tree, but she couldn't conjure up any words, for her mother or for anyone else. Instead, her shoulders heaved and her face contorted. She rolled and scraped her forehead against the tree as the tears came.

Aaron Fennymore had been in the shed, chiselling a new dowel to replace a split one from one of the old chairs. Hannah had been asking him for weeks to do it, and today he had felt enough of a lick of energy to attempt a job that once would have taken a matter of minutes. It was slow work now; the wood slipped in the vice and the mallet had grown almost too heavy to lift.

He saw the girl as soon as she walked in from the lane. He frowned at the sight of her, then stood with the mallet in one hand and the chisel in the other as she stretched out her arms to embrace a tree trunk. He let his spectacles slide down his nose. Old age had made him long-sighted and he could see the child's face squeezed with suffering. Gently, he put down the tools.

She didn't hear the creak of the shed door or his slow footsteps. When he asked, 'Can I help?' she leapt backwards, hand to her mouth to stifle a scream. 'It's all right,' Aaron said.

May rubbed her eyes and nose with the back of her hand. They stood looking at each other, not sure what to say next.

'Are you in trouble?'

She shook her head, sniffing. 'Sorry. I'm in your garden.'

'Yes. I was going to chase you away with my big stick.' He held up his knobbled walking stick. 'But I can't hardly do that if you're crying, can I?'

May had been afraid of this old man when she had seen him at the Beams'. Now, closer up, he was a little less formidable. There were silvery fans of lines around his deep-set eyes and the hand resting on the knob of his stick shook uncontrollably. Even so, he did not look particularly benign.

'Come inside.'

69

She would have made an excuse if it had been more of an invitation and less of an order. Instead she followed him into the frowning house.

The door opened into a little wood-panelled lobby hung with thick old curtains that smelt of dust. May imagined that the Fennymores would need all the draught insulation possible during the winters they spent alone up here on the bluff. Aaron held open a door for her, and she passed through into the middle of the house.

There was just one big room. Around three of the walls were floor-to-ceiling shelves made of thick, rough timber and the shelves were filled with dim-looking books. On the small spaces of wall that weren't covered with books there were framed maps, and old brown-toned photographs behind glass, and little nests of smaller shelves made to display bits of what looked like carved bone. Against one wall there was a big wood-burning stove, with a chimney alcove stacked with cut logs. The seaward windows looked out at the bay and the island, but the curtains that framed them cut out a lot of the sparkling light. The room smelt of woodsmoke like the Captain's House, and musty book bindings and old people.

May wanted to wander around and stare at the thick deposits of things, but felt too wary of Aaron Fennymore. Instead she glanced sidelong at a small table near at hand, where a vaguely spoon-shaped piece of the bone material was laid out like an ornament. It was an ugly yellowy-cream colour and she noticed now that it was minutely carved. Without

70

thinking she picked it up. The carvings were patterns of tiny leaves and flowers.

'What do you think of that?' Aaron demanded, making her jump.

'What is it?'

'Don't you know?'

'No, I don't.'

'It's scrimshaw.' Seeing that meant nothing to her either he snapped, 'Where have you spent your life?'

'New York City.'

'Well, then your ignorance is hardly surprising.'

He hobbled over to a chair beside the stove and sat down, pointing to another seat opposite it. May obediently took her place, wondering how she was going to escape. The room and its crammed contents were overpowering rather than fascinating. Aaron took another of the yellowy carvings in his hand and gently turned it in his fingers. His fingernails were almost the same colour, thickened and horny. May looked away.

'Imagine you are a hand on one of the old whaling ships. Away from home for years at a time, at sea for months on end. You live in the forecastle with the other hands, a space not much wider than this.' Aaron pointed the fragment of scrimshaw, indicating an area of a few square feet. 'And your berth and sea chest are the only space you can call your own. It's the middle of a windless day somewhere near the Equator, and the sun's so hot and so high overhead you think your little ship's the centre of its burning eye. What do you do with yourself, eh? What's your name?'

'May,' she said quietly. The picture he conjured up for her was so vivid that it interested her, even though she didn't want it to. 'I suppose I might read a book, or write a letter to my family.'

'And suppose you'd never learned to read or write properly? You might just scratch your name to a contract of hire, no more than that.'

'They're sailors' carvings, aren't they?'

He gave a sharp nod of satisfaction. 'They are. They took the materials they had plenty of, pieces of whale bone or tooth, and they carved them like this. They took their carvings home as presents for their wives or sweethearts, or they sold them for a few cents on shore. What do you think of them now?'

She looked again at the tiny whorls and fluted cavities, which with their unwholesome colour now made her think of inner-ear parts, or fragments of joint that would have been better left covered by merciful flesh. 'I think they're kind of sad.' So much time taken, so much skill lavished.

Aaron's face tightened into vertical grooves as he regarded her. To her relief he only said, 'Yes. Maybe that's why I like them.'

'Can I look at the pictures?' May indicated the old brown photographs. There was a noise out on the deck and Hannah Fennymore opened the porch door.

'If it's history you're interested in, you should ask my wife to tell you some stories. Hannah the historian, she knows all about Pittsharbor and Maine. I've been talking to our neighbour about scrimshaw, Hannah. I

72

found her out the back of the house making friends with the tree.'

Hannah put down a bucket which left a sandy ring on the floorboards. It was half-filled with clams; the Fennymores had clam beds on the portion of beach fronting their house. For fifty years Aaron had rowed out to his lobster traps, too, but now he was too infirm to handle the boat. May remembered that Elizabeth Newton had talked about all this in one of their conversations about Moon Island Beach. She had only half listened then but her interest stirred properly now.

In her clamming boots and thick brown jacket Hannah looked more than ever like some unshowy little bird. Both the Fennymores wore several layers of clothes even though the day was warm, and May wondered again how and why they lived out here all the winter through.

'Historian? Hardly. No letters after my name. Aaron, haven't you offered your friend a drink or something to eat?'

May stood up quickly. 'I have to go anyway.'

'Come again,' Hannah said, pleasantly enough. 'Aaron likes to talk about his collections. Doone Bennison, poor Doone, used to come and listen sometimes.'

'Did she?' There was an edgy note of curiosity in May's voice.

'Once in a while.'

'What was she like?'

The two old faces turned to her. They were of an

73

age to have grown to look alike, even though Aaron's features were much sharper and stronger than his wife's.

'She was a lonely little thing,' Hannah said at length. 'But I used to think it was by choice. She didn't spend much time with the other children, the Beams and the local kids. It was as if she didn't have time for them. I lent her a couple of books to read, I thought she might enjoy them if she spent so much time on her own. Sam and Jennifer Bennison sent them back afterwards, after she died.'

'Can I look at them?' May asked.

Hannah paused, as if considering the propriety of the request, then went to one of the bookshelves. She took down two nondescript books in dingy cloth bindings and handed them to May. One of them was titled *In the Country of the Pointed Firs* and the other *Voyages of the Dolphin*. 'You're welcome to borrow them', Hannah said, forestalling May's question.

'Thank you. I'll take care of them. Why did she choose these, out of so many books?'

'She just seemed interested in the place as it used to be and the local whaling legends. As interested as Doone ever was in anything, that is. There are some old stories, you know. I don't know if she ever read the books in the end.'

May nodded. 'Thanks. Look, I'd better go. My dad'll be wondering where I am.' Perhaps, she thought. Or perhaps not.

Aaron levered himself painfully to his feet to accompany her to the door, although she wished he would not. Outside again beneath the shade of the tree he said, 'I'm too old to remember why young women cry. I remember enough tears, but I've forgotten most of what stirred them up. You forget nearly all of it, however bad it seems at the time. You learn to live. That may not seem much of a comfort to you right now.'

May shifted her weight. She did not want to talk to Aaron Fennymore about any of this, although it was true he was only trying to be comforting. 'It's nothing. It's just me.'

'I told Doone the same thing. She didn't believe me either.'

'Was she unhappy?'

It was not the kind of question, she understood, which Aaron was interested in answering. 'You know what happened.'

'But wasn't it an *accident* that she drowned?'

At length Aaron replied, 'Yes. That was the verdict.'

Curiosity and a chill, queasy premonition crawled together up May's spine. She wanted to know and feared the discovery, whatever it might be. She persisted, 'Do you mean that the truth is different from the official story?'

To her surprise Aaron walked a little way away from her and stood staring past the house to a thin segment of the sea. When he turned his head again he spoke quietly, so that she had to inch forward to catch the words. 'It's more that there are always layers of truth. Some aspects of the truth you can measure and explain, and others defy you to do anything but accept them for what they are. I haven't known so many other places that I can compare, but I believe the Beach is particularly resistant to rational explanation.'

May thought, *I know that. I knew it as soon as we came here. Before I even knew about Doone.*

She didn't want to ask any more. There was enough to absorb already. 'Thank you for lending me the books.' They were tucked under her arm.

'They belong to my wife. As for the girl, you're not like her,' Aaron said, as if that settled their conversation. He waved his stick in dismissal and hobbled back towards the house. May wandered slowly along the lane to the dark full stop of the Captain's House.

Traffic in the main street of Pittsharbor was almost at a standstill with jeeps and RVs and station-wagons tailing back from the lights. Cyclists threaded between the cars and a steady stream of pedestrians flowed between the shops and the open-air vegetable and fish market. At the stall that Leonie knew always had the best fish John debated with the young stallholder, then bought a sweet, silvery chunk of tuna. She watched him, with her own shopping piled in her arms, as he took the neat paper package and stowed it in his bag.

Tom always did the food marketing swiftly and as if it was a test of his professionalism, prodding and irritably rejecting any merchandise that didn't please him, and adopting a triumphant air when he brought his kill back home to the lair. By contrast, John seemed to take a mild and uncompetitive pleasure in wandering between the baskets of muddy lettuces and pyramids of melons, settling on his purchases apparently by whim instead of iron rules of quality and value. Leonie found this refreshing.

When they had finished they hesitated beside the road, watching the tailback of traffic.

'Thanks for the ride,' Leonie said. 'Looks like I've brought you into town at just the wrong moment.'

After May's exit Leonie had told John she must do some shopping. It was true: Tom had gone back to Boston to undertake the battle with his chef, otherwise the job would not have been delegated to her, but Marian had handed her a list that morning. Everyone else was busy with children or watersports.

John had said at once, 'I'll drive you. I've got some stuff to get, too.'

Now he turned his back on the glittering lines of cars and looked down at her. 'I think we should have lunch.'

Leonie thought for a moment. She had the impression that there were unspoken negotiations taking place within this bland exchange. The realisation made heat prickle beneath her hairline and the picturesque and fully restored old façades of Main Street took on a more highly coloured focus. 'What about all this shopping?' she asked. Of course, Tom would never have left fresh fish broiling in the afternoon sun in the back of a car.

By way of answer John went back to the fish stall and returned with a bag full of ice. They bedded their purchases beneath it in the trunk of the station wagon. Then he led the way to Sandy's Bar, the best place to eat in Pittsharbor but no longer patronised by the Beams because Tom had had a disagreement with the proprietor the summer before. It gave Leonie an agreeable feeling of disloyalty to settle herself with John in a corner booth draped with fishing nets and studded with shells.

It was cool in Sandy's; she pushed her damp hair off her face and eased the armholes of her cotton vest where they cut into her armpits. She was conscious of John watching these small movements; it felt like a long time since a man had watched her in just this way, but she accepted his gaze, letting it lie on her skin like warm honey.

With Tom there would have been critical deliberations over the menu, but now she chose food and drink at random. They were talking about their lives, filling in details that needed establishing before they moved on. She learned that John ran his own business mail delivery service. It was a successful company, but he found the demands of it difficult to balance against the need to take care of Ivy and May. In her turn Leonie described her work as an editor for an art and art-history publisher in Boston. She told him about the economics of high-quality colour printing and her plans to commission a series of monographs on women artists of the twentieth century. A plate of griddled shrimp with a hot Thai sauce was put in front of her and she blinked in surprise, having forgotten what she had ordered.

The talk threaded between them like a line of stitches. After the first connecting seam was made they

78

felt free to change direction. Leonie said suddenly, 'I'm not comfortable in that beach house, but just the same, Tom always wants us to spend the summer vacation up here. Marian makes me feel that I deliberately don't conform. That I must be denying her more grandchildren on a whim.'

'Hasn't she got enough already? What about the population crisis?' Their eyes met, testing the strength of the seam. 'Doesn't she know you can't conceive?'

'Of course she does. But perhaps if I just *tried* harder. Babies were so easy for her, and for Anne and Shelly and Gina. They're the other daughters-in-law. Even Karyn, who didn't manage to get much else right before that, cruised it.'

Looking down at her food Leonie thought of the hospitals; the tubes and the needles and the drugs and the waiting, and the increasingly desperate connections with Tom that had led them there. Tom had become angry with her, that was what had happened. She didn't blame him for his anger, just for the form it had taken. He had retreated from her, and left her marooned on her island of sterility.

'Is it difficult to talk about it?'

'Only in the sense that there isn't anything to say any longer.'

The waiter removed their plates. Outside, the sky turned the solid, passive blue of mid-afternoon. Back at the house, Karyn or Marian would have put the babies to bed for their afternoon rest and the adults and older children would move softly, allowing them their sleep.

'Will Ivy and May wonder where you are?'

'Ivy won't. I don't know about May. You saw her, this morning.'

Skewering them with her eyes. Jealous and dismissive at the same time. 'Yes.' The talk veered again. They were zigzagging close to intimacy.

'They were both so hostile to Suzanne. I was amazed by the intensity of it. She was the first potentially serious involvement I'd had after Alison died, and it was almost three years later. At the beginning, when I first introduced her, they were welcoming enough, even friendly. And Suzanne did everything she could.'

I'm sure she did, Leonie thought.

'She used to come round for dinner at first, and the girls and I would get together and plan a meal we could cook for her. Then she went shopping with them once or twice. May wanted a special outfit or something and Suzanne was a store buyer. Then the four of us went on a couple of weekend trips, which worked out fine. I thought we were going to make something of it, in the end maybe turn into a family.'

Leonie could see how John would want a mother for his girls, as well as a woman for himself. That was natural. But she guessed there were cross-currents of jealousy and mistrust in children, which ran invisible and powerful against the tide of what seemed natural. 'What happened?'

'Suzanne began to stay over at the apartment. Not all the time, not even often. But as soon as she did they turned against her.' He rotated the stem of his glass in his fingers, watching the splintered lozenges of light it

80

threw on the table-cloth. 'Not difficult to understand why. But it finished everything off in the end.'

Leonie could imagine it. Suzanne's retreat, John's resentment, the girls' pleasureless triumph in their achievement. She began to understand what a landscape the unspoken negotiations between John Duhane and herself might have to cover. A sudden jagged breath caught in her windpipe and even as she pressed her thighs together against the loosening between them, she was forbidding herself anything more. She was married and none of these silent phrases had been in her vocabulary for a long time.

Then something happened. She was gazing at some paired cherries on John's plate. And as clearly as she saw their waxy sheen and wishbone stalks in front of her she knew that she no longer loved Tom any more than he loved her in return.

The cherries looked so ordinary, and the detritus of the meal spread over the cloth, and yet her bearings had shifted so suddenly and radically that she half-expected them to mutate into different objects. A knife-blade reflected a little asterisk of light at her as she stared at it. For more than ten years she had made her judgements and interpreted her place as Tom's partner. Now she understood that each of those daily measurements was wrongly calibrated and therefore worthless, because they had no love left for each other. All the pressure of needing a child, and the bitterness and anger and violence that blossomed between them, were rooted in this one truth. A child would just have been a diversion. A bandage for a mortal wound.

For a moment she felt cold and calm, like the oily sea under a flat Maine mist. Then a wave of panic shrugged itself up and washed over her. The plump cherries blurred in front of her eyes, turning to dull blotches of crimson.

'Are you all right?' There was a crease between John's eyebrows and one corner of his mouth was bitten in.

'Yes. But I'm . . . thinking. We should take that shopping home.'

The crease stayed, but he was already signalling to the waiter for the check.

Outside he took her arm and steered her between the cars. The line of traffic at the lights was shorter now, and an afternoon daze of heat and lassitude had settled on Pittsharbor. They crossed the car-park to John's station-wagon and he leant forward to open the passenger door for her. Leonie heard the words in her head. *What the hell?* she was saying. *What does it matter now anyway?* She tipped back her head and tilted it sideways a little, so that her mouth connected with his. The kiss shivered through her.

He would have put his hands on her shoulders, gently drawn her against him, but Leonie opened her eyes and over the hot metal curve of the car's roof she saw Spencer Newton. His dark-green Jaguar was parked in the next slot, there was a brown bag of groceries under his arm and Alexander Gull was following behind him.

'Hello, Leonie,' Spencer said, with his feline smile.

'Spencer, I didn't know you were up here. Hi, Alexander.'

'We've just arrived. I'm taking some supplies home to mother.' The corners of his smile curled higher.

Without looking to see his expression Leonie introduced John to them, explaining that he had rented the Captain's House.

'I see,' Spencer murmured.

The men shook hands and accepted one another's assurances that they would meet again on the beach.

John drove with his eyes fixed on the road, but Leonie saw a twist of concern around his mouth. She said as lightly as she could, 'Spencer is Elizabeth's son. So he's an old Pittsharbor man, like Tom. Alexander is Spencer's partner, they have a rather wonderful gallery in Boston. Alexander paints. Hopperish. Not bad, in fact.'

'I thought they were sweet,' John said, and Leonie laughed and broke the tension between them.

'Oh, Spencer and Alexander are anything but sweet. Spencer is trying to bully his mother and Aaron Fennymore into selling him the land behind the beach. He and Alexander want to build rental condos.'

'I see. That would change the old place, wouldn't it?'

'It won't happen. Aaron will never let go.'

'And what about what Spencer just saw?'

'Can't I kiss a friend who just bought me lunch?'

'Of course. If that was what it was.'

Neither of them spoke again. When they reached the Beams' entrance John took Leonie's shopping out of the trunk and piled it into her arms.

She said defensively, 'Marian'll be waiting for me.

83

There are no cookies for the kids until I get back.'

He touched her arm. 'Did something happen back there?'

Their eyes met. Leonie wanted to acknowledge to him what her words and manner denied. We're both wary, she thought. And defensive. 'Yes,' she said simply.

He nodded, and turned back to the car.

She called after him, 'Thank you for lunch'and he lifted his hand in acknowledgement. Leonie's breath was jagged in her chest again as she carried the bags of groceries up to the house.

May idly let her paddle rest across her knees and the canoe drifted, the prow turning parallel with the island's beach. The sea was flat, like oiled glass, and the afternoon sun plastered thick layers of light across the water and over the lip of beach. The rocky crescent reminded her of a mirthless smile and the trees and scrub that fringed it became a throat, opening, ready to swallow. She hoisted herself abruptly, causing the canoe to rock violently, and stepped into the shallow water. Even at only calf-depth the shock of cold made her yelp. The water was always cold here.

She grasped the prow and dragged the canoe up on to the stones. There was no one else on the island this afternoon, no other boat or beached sailboard and no sign of swimmers or picnickers. Once her canoe was safe above the tideline she hoisted her pack on to her shoulder and began to pick her way across the sand. In the wrack along the water's edge she found the prehistoric-looking shell of a helmet crab. She examined it and trailed on, holding the thing by the tip of the jointed tail so that it banged dully against her thigh. There were other different shells caught in the washed-up debris. She squatted down to examine their shape and quality before pocketing them or hurling them out into the water.

Neither Ivy nor John had come back to the house at lunch-time.

May was used to making meals for herself, but today she had sullenly rejected the option and eaten a pack of Oreos instead. Her stomach was distended and she could still taste the sugar thick in the back of her throat. There was no wind, not even the smallest stirring to ruffle the water or cool her face. Beads of sweat pricked her top lip. She felt sick and solitary, and disgusted with herself.

It was the day's motionless hour when time seemed to hang for ever between early and late. Even the shade within the woodland looked bruised and resentful. May dragged a few steps away from the water and sat down in the sand. In her backpack were some more cookies, but she stopped herself from reaching for them. Instead she took out the book she had brought with her, one of the two that she had borrowed from Aaron and Hannah Fennymore. The books that Doone might, or might not, have read. Listlessly she flipped open the warped board cover and began to skim the pages.

The ship's log records that the *Dolphin* sailed from Nantucket on 1 May 1841, under the command of Captain Charles S. Gunnell. She was bound for the Cape Verde Islands and the west coast of Africa with a full crew of experienced officers and good men. Captain Gunnell was recognised as a fair master and a lucky whaleman.

Among the crew that left the sanctuary of Nantucket harbour on that spring morning was a green hand who had signed up for the voyage only two days before. He was eighteen years old and slightly built, but he assured Mr Gunnell most vehemently that he was a strong worker and ready to learn the whaler's craft, and that he wanted nothing more than to take his share of risk and reward aboard the *Dolphin*.

The boy gave his name as William Corder. The crew-list indicated that he was a 'down-easter', a native of Maine.

The early part of the *Dolphin*'s voyage was without incident. The new hand did indeed prove to be willing and quick to learn the duties of the ship. He possessed courage enough for a man twice his size, showing no fear when sent aloft to furl a sail. And he could keep his head and secure footing when the ship's head fell from the wind and the sail filled with enough force to tear a man from the yard and pitch him into oblivion.

But William Corder was sadly afflicted by seasickness. For all of his first month at sea he struggled with severe attacks, sometimes to such a degree that the first mate sent him to his bunk to groan out the worst of his trouble in peace. This perceived weakness caused some of the more experienced hands to joke about him, and to suggest that his smallness and gentlemanly demeanour would fit him better for a lady's parlour or a draper's shop than for the forecastle of a whaling vessel.

Then, after the first weeks of misery, William overcame his affliction overnight. He awoke one morning in his bunk and told his companions that he would never be ill again. His prediction proved correct. However rough the seas and however viciously the stubby vessel pitched and rolled, William steadily continued in his work from that day forward. He was not a high-spirited young man, never indulging in horseplay or coarse behaviour with the other hands with whom his life in the forecastle was necessarily shared, but he was always good-humoured and willing to apply himself to whatever the officers required of him.

For his quiet and modest demeanour he slowly gained the respect of his fellows, but their liking was bestowed on him in time for a different reason.

By the very nature of their arduous life, the whalemen's clothes were frequently bathed in perspiration, coated with whale oil and grease and dirt of every description, and saturated with sea water. Any cleansing of their few articles of clothing had to be performed with cold salt water and the roughest soap, so this necessary labour was among the least popular of all the deckhands' duties.

But William Corder, it was soon noted, went about the business of laundering his clothes in the deftest manner. He would stand up to the wooden tub containing water set aside for the purpose, and rub the soap into his loose sailor's shirts and breeches in a shipshape fashion that betokened long familiarity with the washtub.

One of the hands chanced to make a passing joke about this unlikely talent, and William blushed and let his shirt fall back with a splash into the water. But he quickly explained that he was the youngest of several brothers whose mother had died of the fever when he was still an infant. While his father and brothers attended to the heavier domestic chores, as William grew up it became his responsibility to launder all the family's clothing. 'I have had a good deal of practice,' he said, smiling a little. 'I could not begin to count up the number of shirts I have washed in my life.'

'Do you miss the privilege, then?' one of the older hands asked mischievously. 'Because if you do, you may certainly scrub mine for me.'

'I'll do it gladly,' William replied.

So it happened that William Corder cheerfully undertook laundry duties for his crew-mates, continuing to perfom the disagreeable work with a neatness and economy that did indeed speak of years of practice. William accepted whatever small payments of coin the deckhands were able to offer him in return for his services, but he had no interest whatsoever in the more common currencies of tobacco and rum.

The *Dolphin* continued her voyage towards the fertile whaling grounds of the Central Atlantic with William as an accepted member of the crew. It was noted that whenever the vessel drew alongside another whaling ship for an exchange of news or the barter of other sought-after shipboard commodities, William was the first of the sailors to run to the rail and scan the faces of the opposing crew.

'Are you looking for someone, young Will?' the mate enquired one day.

William's face coloured up again. He was young and beardless, and his fair skin showed his blushes for everyone to see. 'My brother. My brother Robert signed to a ship a year ago and I would be more pleased to see him than any other person in the world.'

'What ship is he aboard, under what master?' the mate asked curiously. Something about this story stirred his interest, although he could not have explained exactly why.

'I don't know the name of either,' William said quickly, and turned away from the rail when the strange faces across the neck of water did not include the one he searched for.

Bored by the old-fashioned language and impatient with the close-set type, May looked up. A woman was standing under the trees, motionless, watching her.

At first May thought it was Ivy or Gail. But it wasn't either of them, nor any of the other women from the houses on the bluff. She was wearing loose, wide trousers that hid her feet and a colourless shirt with some kind of deep collar. Her hair was pulled severely back from her pale face.

Stillness lay across the rocks and flattened the sea

and pressed on May, so that she found she could not move. A chain of tiny cold droplets trickled down her spine. She stretched her fingers and they touched the discarded crab shell. She picked it up again and slowly, against the heavy weight of the air, she lifted her hand and arm upwards and backwards. Then, with an effort she flung the shell away from her. It flew in a great spinning arc and dropped into the sea, her eyes following it. She waited until the memory of it in her mind's eye was swallowed up by the ripples.

When she looked again the woman had gone.

Four

On some windless mornings, even in July, a fog closed in on the bay. The waves rolled in from the invisible distance, oily and soundless, to break in melancholy ripples on the beach shingle. Out beyond the island a foghorn sounded, spacing the seconds for shipping passing down the coast. The air held layers of salt and tar and fish smells trapped with the earthier inland scents of wet leaves and woodsmoke. The Beams and their friends took advantage of the cooler weather by stepping up the intensity of their tennis matches. Their cries of triumph or challenge drifted over the bluff.

Elizabeth heard them without listening as she followed Turner around her garden. She was convinced even though he had worked for her for ten years, that if she didn't watch the gardener he might inadvertently cut off the mopheads of the hydrangeas, or uproot the tender unfurling shoots of her Japanese anemones. She paused in her circuit at the head of the beach steps, where Alexander Gull was sitting with a drawingboard resting on his knees. He was trying to capture in water-colours the view of Marian Beam's house lapped in pearly light. 'Pretty,' Elizabeth said, looking over his shoulder.

'Ever heard of damning with faint praise? But you're quite right.' Alexander dropped his brush with a shrug of exasperation. 'Pretty is what it is.'

Elizabeth and Alexander had grown fond of one another in the years that he and Spencer had lived together. For Elizabeth it was like having a real daughter-in-law of whom she had disapproved at first, but who had shown herself to be loyal and adept at making a happy partnership, and who was therefore to be valued. The only material difference now, Elizabeth thought, was that of course there would be no grandchildren. That was a sadness. There were plenty of Newtons, from her husband's brother, but she and Spencer represented the last of the Freshetts. She was glad that at least the old Senator couldn't witness the ending of his line with a lonely and regretful old widow and her homosexual son.

Unless his shadow somehow inhabited this beach house that he had built for his bride, observing his granddaughter's solitary rituals and the occasional visits of her son and his partner. What would he have made of that, of the room and the old scroll-headed bed, and the life that the two men shared?

But Elizabeth did not think that her grandfather's ghost haunted these rooms. She didn't feel his presence, although he had dearly loved the house and the bay, and Pittsharbor. It was because he was so conclusively gone and because he had loved the place so much that Elizabeth wanted to strengthen the family connection with it. But Spencer didn't much care for the beach as a place to spend his time. She was afraid that after she was gone, unless he could find some better way of using the house and making money out of it, he would sell up.

Of course, if Aaron could be persuaded to sell his land, if Spencer could build the rental condos he envisaged, that would be different. New building would change the beach and the bay, but that was progress. Old Maynard Freshett had always believed in progress.

The foghorn gave its disembodied, bleating moan out in the sea mist.

'I hate that noise,' Alexander said.

'Why?'

'For being so relentless. And so depressing. Why not a cheerful bell, or a whistle, or a happy tune?'

'Because it's a foghorn.' Elizabeth smiled inwardly. There was progress and there was the pleasing counterpoint of what was fixed and enduring because it worked, because there was no need to change it. 'You'd be glad of it if you'd lost your bearings out there in a small boat.'

Spencer had been sitting reading on the swing seat on the porch. Now his mobile rang beside him and he snapped up the antenna and began a discussion with his assistant at the gallery. One polished loafer swung from his bare foot as he talked.

Alexander sighed and closed his paintbox. 'I'm going to make lunch, Elizabeth. Fish soup, I think.'

'Good,' Elizabeth said. Alexander was an excellent cook.

The fog had thinned enough for a game of tennis to be just feasible. Beyond the netting of the court the rear of the Beams' house was still no more than a dark, formless mass, but the players were visible to each other as they paced on the back line for the knock-up.

When the game began John Duhane was partnering Marty Stiegel against Tom and Joel Beam. John was an adequate player but he was out of his class in this company. Marty was slightly built and several inches shorter than John, but his toned muscles and stamina suggested enough time spent in the gym. He was friendly and laughed easily, but there was an edge of competitiveness in him that showed whenever John dropped a point. It was clear that he and the Beams had a long and complicated history of games won and lost on this court, and that Marty was at least as eager for a victory as his opponents.

John lost his first service game and Marty turned to him with a shrug. 'Hey, tough luck,' he judged. 'You get a good topspin on your first serve,'

They were changing ends. Marty towelled the grip of his racquet and spun it aggressively.

This display of vigour made John want to slow down even further. 'So, you're a photographer, I hear,' he began.

'Mostly advertising,' Marty grinned. 'I leave art to Judith.'

'Ready?' Joel called from the other end. Without

waiting for an answer he unleashed a powerful serve, which shot past John.

The morning had been too foggy for the beach, so Judith Stiegel and Marian were sitting in lawn chairs drinking coffee and watching the game through the veils of mist. Marian held Ashton on her lap and Judith was nursing the baby Justine.

The Stiegels were in their early thirties, several years younger than Leonie and Tom, but a little older than Karyn and Elliot. They fitted comfortably into the beach society; Marty was high-spirited and always ready to play any game, or to help out with a beach barbecue. Judith was more restrained, but Marian forgave her that because she was an artist. Judith was a sculptor and Marty had already told everyone that she was about to have a big show in the city. Spencer Newton had taken four of her pieces to Boston and had sold them all. She worked mostly in bronze and even when she was still single and only pleasantly plump, Judith's best work had tended to big, swelling shapes seamed with a vague cleft or dimple. With her first pregnancy it was as if she grew into her own art. Now she was like a monumental composition of curves and cushions of flesh waiting to be cast in sumptuous metal.

The baby, Justine, was ten months old. Judith finished feeding her and leaned forward to compress the blue-veined billow of breast into her nursing bra. Marty looked round from the net to check on her and Joel took advantage of his momentary distraction to send an overarm smash past his ear.

'Tough luck,' John took the opportunity to murmur and Marty shrugged unsmilingly. They were about to lose the set.

Karyn had been playing with Sidonie in her sandbox near the porch steps. The little girl wore pink jellies and a vest, and her hair spiralled in damp corkscrews around her face. Now she trailed her bucket across to Judith and asked if the baby was ready to play yet.

'She's still a bit too tiny for that. And I need to change her.'

Tom and Joel were high-fiving each other. The first set was theirs.

Marty came over to Judith's side. 'We're taking five minutes. Let me do that for you.'

He lifted the baby and massaged her rounded little back. He was the most eager of new fathers. Judith watched him with shining affection as he spread the baby's rug on the tufty grass and began the business of wipes and plastic Pampers tags. Justine gave him her smile starred with new teeth and her fists balled into soft knobs. Marty blindly pressed his face against her tiny belly and blew until she wriggled with pleasure at the game.

'I want that,' Sidonie demanded. 'Do it to me.'

Leonie came out on to the porch. There were the babies and mothers and Tom in the background, swishing his racket at the willowherb bordering the path. She stood with one foot on the step, hesitating, feeling that if she obeyed her inner compulsion to turn round and leave she might well march through the

96

house and out the other side, across the rocks and over the headland and never come back again.

The fog was shimmering and turning opalescent as the sun grew hotter.

John was at the other side of the group with Joel. To see him felt to Leonie as if someone had thrown her a rope across treacherous water. Every impulse told her to snatch at it. She nodded at him, a curt, awkward movement, and descended the second step to Marian's side.

Lucas and Ivy drifted round the side of the house from the direction of the beach. They were wearing faded shorts and windbreakers, so they looked like male and female versions cast from the same perfect androgynous mould.

'Young love,' Judith sighed. 'Just look at it.'

Marty's head jerked as he handed Justine over to her.

'They're welcome to young love,' he said, so sharply that his wife stared at him in momentary surprise.

No one caught sight of May who had followed Lucas and Ivy from the beach. She found a temporary refuge in the thinning fog.

The Fennymores' house was out of earshot of the Beams'. Aaron was in his chair with a rug wrapped around his thin legs because even the occasional faint chill of July penetrated his bones and threatened him with the winter to come. Hannah sat opposite, wearing her old-fashioned reading glasses and with the week's *Pittsharbor Record* folded in her hand. She read the more interesting titbits aloud to him, although she was not sure that he was listening. More and more often Hannah performed small services for Aaron because she had always done so, not because she was convinced that he still required them. He had withdrawn where she couldn't follow him, into memories and the recesses of the past.

Yet sometimes he startled her with the relevance of his train of thought. 'What was the girl's name?'

'Which girl?' She wasn't sure whether he meant Doone Bennison.

'I found her outside.'

'Ah, that girl.' Hannah had been thinking about her too. 'May Duhane.'

'She needs something.'

'Mothering, perhaps.' Marian Beam, of course, had told them what she knew about the death of Alison Duhane.

For so many years Hannah had watched her husband's uncompromising features – at first in anxiety, then in bitter resignation, and now, at last, in affectionate acceptance. She knew all the nuances of light and shade in him, and the expression he wore as he looked at her at this moment was the best because of the warmth in it. 'You would think so.' He smiled.

'I know so,' Hannah answered composedly.

She had been a successful mother, that was one of her compensations. The demands of her children had seemed easy to meet and the easiness had passed itself on to them. All three of them were unremarkably grown up now, moved away and settled with partners and children of their own in Cleveland and Dallas and Burlington, Vermont. She missed them less than she had imagined she would while she was still waiting for them to fly away. Now, as he had been at the beginning, Aaron was her central concern. Her books and papers and investigations of local history and legends were a distraction, a way of not letting him know how important he was.

But he knew in any case. His wordless acceptance of her devotion was a measure of his arrogance. He had been arrogant as a young man, too, with an unshakeable pride in his roots and his place in Pittsharbor, which bound him to his home. He had never been tempted to wander elsewhere and his self-assurance had been overturned only once.

He had allowed Hannah to rescue him then, and she had been glad to do it, but the history of the damage and his debt to her had been buried silently between them.

Aaron nodded, his hands folded on the knob of his stick, apparently satisfied with this brief reference to May Duhane and her possible needs. Hannah refolded the paper and began to read a contributor's letter about the success of the Pittsharbor Fourth of July parade.

May wasn't afraid that Ivy and Lucas might have been able to see her spying on them. She knew they wouldn't look at anything except each other and the thought made a jealous knot twist in her chest, so that she had to suck hard to draw air into her lungs. She

99

stood at the side of the road away from the houses with her arms weightily hanging at her sides, panting with the effort of drawing breath.

May felt that whichever way she tried to direct herself there was a precipice yawning at her feet. If she focused on Lucas – and there was no conscious effort in that, the thought of him filled her head, and she saw the fall of beige-blond hair and the tattooed lovers' knot in her contorted dreams – there was always the accompanying swell of jealousy and self-dislike, and the hopelessness of wishing that she could be like Ivy.

Her father was even less of a resort because of Leonie Beam, who seemed always to be around him, friendly and smiling like a shark in lipstick. To see them, even to think of them together, reminded her of how it had been with Suzanne.

Disliking Suzanne, steadily hating her, had made a guilty cloud that still hung around May. But feeling regret for driving her away didn't make any difference to her mistrust and resentment of Leonie – who was *married,* who shouldn't look at her father in just that way, which only May seemed to notice.

Ivy shrugged it off, if she was aware of it at all. 'Don't use your imagination so much,' she told her sharply when May tried to share her anxiety.

And if she concentrated on this place, on the vacation itself, she only became miserably aware of her inability to fit in. The tennis and the barbecuing and beach volleyball jollity generated by the Beams made her shrivel up. She was too fat, too awkward and too used to being unhappy. But May didn't recognise her

100

unhappiness for what it was, merely having a sense that there was something the matter with her – for which she could only blame herself.

There were the old people, she grudgingly acknowledged, Elizabeth and the Fennymores, who had tried to be kind to her. But May didn't welcome kindness because of the accompanying suspicion that people felt sorry for her. If only she *could* be like Ivy, who was slick and thoughtless, and dismissed what she didn't care for with a shrug and a single sarcastic lift of her plucked eyebrows.

May sat down heavily on the grass bank, shuffling her back up against a convenient wooden post. She drew up her knees and rested her forehead on them, staring down at the blades of grass between her feet. The enormity of everything, all the countless profusion of grass stalks, and beads of moisture and minute insects, was suddenly terrifying. May rocked her head on her bent knees and screwed up her eyes to ease the burning behind them.

More and more often she found herself thinking about Doone. The sense of collusion, the feeling that she was following Doone's footprints clearly printed in the sand or the grass, grew steadily stronger in her mind.

The first time she had read the diary she had gone straight through it, devouring every page, unable to disentangle herself from the fascination it exerted. Even though she now knew some of the passages almost by heart she still found it hard to extricate herself from Doone's wild scribblings. The night before, she had gone through every entry yet again – those she could decipher, at least – sitting up late on the French bed and staring at the now-familiar handwriting. The scrambled numbers still danced in front of her eyes, maddening her with what she could not interpret. If Doone had left these messages for her, why was it that she couldn't read them?

There was also the woman on the island. The image of her returned to May as often as the thought of Doone, so that the two of them became connected and inseparable in her mind. The picture came back now, superimposing itself on the canvas of grass and moss. A pale woman in loose, colourless clothes. Standing still, watching and waiting.

Sometimes May convinced herself that she had been just a picnicker, someone who had landed a boat on the seaward side and walked over the hump of wooded land to the bay beach. Perhaps she had been resting in the shade of the trees before making the scramble back to her friends or her husband, her children even, waiting by their sailing dinghy for her to come back from her explorations.

At other times, when she lay awake in Doone's bed following with her eyes the cracks in the ceiling, she knew that the woman was different, nothing to do with the bright and wholesome holiday place that was dominated by the Beams. The white oval of the woman's face and her very stillness had been too alien. She was part of the water and the fog, and the low, brooding hump of the island itself. In some way she belonged with Doone, or Doone belonged to her.

102

Aaron Fennymore had said that Moon Island was resistant to rational explanation. The words stuck in May's head, scratching her with an insistent point of fear.

Someone was coming across the road. May looked up and saw Elizabeth.

'Good-morning, May. Are you busy or would you like some company?'

She was wearing a straw hat, although the sun still hadn't burnt away the last layers of mist, and a waisted dress printed with little flowers. May liked the way she looked and her old-fashioned politeness that managed to be quaint without being weird. 'It's okay. I don't look busy, do I?' She scrambled up and scrubbed at the wet seat of her shorts.

'Perhaps we should take a walk together.'

May gave a nod and a shrug, and fell into step beside Elizabeth. They turned along the road in the direction of Pittsharbor. May found it a relief not to be looking towards the crazy peaks of the Beams' roof and the dark timbers of the Captain's House, which seemed to suck in the light. Further on in this direction there were cottages in the woods, with towels drying on rails and couples putting cool-boxes in their cars, and ordinary families with little kids and babies in strollers. It was nice, with a friendly feeling. She felt suddenly that she shouldn't walk on beside Elizabeth without saying something appropriately companionable. She racked her brains, then asked, 'Do you like having your son up here to stay with you?'

'Yes, I do.' Elizabeth adjusted her hat and May saw

103

the inside of her arm, the loose white skin seamed with thin spreading veins. 'But he has to go back to Boston unexpectedly this afternoon. Some business he must see to at his picture gallery.'

The way she glanced away and settled her face again, levelling her chin with determination, made it clear to May even in the depths of her own self-absorption that Elizabeth was lonely. 'That's a shame.'

May wondered what she was doing on her own up here if it made her lonely and the speculation led her to reflect that the adults she knew mostly didn't seem to suffer from loneliness. They had partners and friends, and complicated lives filled with choices, as her father and Ivy did. Being lonely had seemed an immature problem, most specifically her own. 'Do you stay here all summer?'

'I do, nowadays. I like to look after the garden, because my mother loved it so much. I told you that, didn't I? When my husband was still alive we came only seldom, because he liked to go to Europe and to visit his sister in Virginia, and there was only so much time. He was a lawyer, you know. A busy man. Then, very soon after he retired, he was taken ill. He died six months after that.'

'I'm sorry,' May mumbled. She was thinking how horrible it must be to be old, a widow like Elizabeth or Marian Beam, or frail like the Fennymores. Once you had grown out of the horribleness of being a child, which must surely happen some day, how long did you have before it closed in again as old age? The seeming pointlessness of it all weighed down on her, so that her

104

feet dragged beside Elizabeth's brisk steps. Doone had written something like this in the diary, she remembered. It was one of the crazy despairing bits, when her exhilaration had evidently deserted her. She would read it again when she was back in her room.

They walked on to a point where they could see the whole of the bay. The sun was stronger now and the island shimmered in nothing more than a faint haze. It would be a warm afternoon, perhaps even hot. Looking back over her shoulder from the top of the steps May could see a rowboat beached on the island sand. Perhaps Lucas and Ivy had gone out to their hollow together. Imagining them, May felt a contraction in her stomach and a shiver of nausea.

'Let's go on this way, shall we?' Elizabeth pointed down the road and May could only nod, silenced by misery. As they walked, she listened to Elizabeth talking about what it had been like to spend summers here when she was a girl.

Half a mile further on, set back under the shade of some crooked spruce trees, stood a little saltbox shack that had been turned into a restaurant named the Flying Fish. There was a blackboard at the roadside with the day's dishes chalked on it, and a couple of tables crammed on the narrow front porch.

'I used to play with the kids who lived here,' Elizabeth said. 'They've all moved away now. It's been the Flying Fish for about ten years. Shall we stop for a drink?'

'Okay. Please let me buy you one.' For once, May had some dollar bills folded in her pocket. Enough, she calculated.

'Why, thank you,' Elizabeth said.

They sat at one of the porch tables. Bright sunlight suddenly made the shadows inky dark. Until this minute neither of them had noticed that the moan of the foghorn had stopped.

'Iced tea for me, please. They have good jelly doughnuts,' Elizabeth advised.

'Just a Coke. *Diet* coke.'

'You'll fade away.'

'I don't think so.'

When the waitress had put their drinks in front of them Elizabeth asked gently, 'Is something wrong?'

May was exhausted. Even if she had wanted to, how could she specify one thing when it was everything? 'No, Nothing.'

'Are you sure?'

The concern in the old woman's face affected her, all the pursed lines around her ladylike mouth and the wattly flesh of her throat pulling with the effort to be kind but not intrusive. May was afraid she might, embarrassingly, cry again. It was unthinkable to mention even John or Ivy and Lucas, let alone the feeling she was always trying to hide and duck away from, that the insides of herself were wrong and guilty, and less adequate than everyone else's.

'May?'

For the sake of saying something, deflecting this concern at all costs, she blurted out desperately, 'I saw a woman on the island.'

Elizabeth leaned forward and took a slow sip of her iced tea. At this range May could see that tiny filaments

106

of her lipstick had bled into the furrows around her lips. Then she lifted her head again and their eyes met. 'What kind of a woman?'

'I don't know. Just . . . just a woman. Pale, with her hair all scraped back. Funny clothes, I guess. She was just standing looking at me.'

To her surprise Elizabeth nodded, as if she knew already.

A noisy family group came up the steps all together and banged in through the screen door to the interior of the restaurant. When they had gone, Elizabeth looked away towards the road and Pittsharbor. An RV passed with three bicycles bracketed on the back. 'Have you ever been in love?' Elizabeth asked softly.

May blew angrily through the straw in her Coke. *Being in love* was what Ivy went in for, and the thin girls in her class who whispered endlessly about boys and dating. 'No.'

What she felt about Lucas was beyond love, at least the way Ivy and the others defined it. It was fascinating and appalling, and he had barely directed five words to her. She wished she could free herself from it, but it had wound her in its tentacles and she could not.

Elizabeth was still staring away down the road, the fingers of one hand gripping her glass of tea. 'I fell in love for the first time when I was your age,' she said, so quietly that May had to lean forward to hear. 'Or perhaps I was a year or so older. Of course, we were less sophisticated then. We didn't know all the things that you young women seem to take for granted now.'

'I don't think I know much,' May said, and the tone

of her voice made Elizabeth smile at her. 'Tell me about it,' May asked.

'I will, if you think it would be interesting.'

May didn't think it would, particularly, but she was glad to settle for anything that spared her from having to talk and therefore risk the ignominy of tears.

Elizabeth repeated, 'I was so young. Perhaps nothing that happens to us afterwards in life ever quite matches the intensity of that first falling in love. Nothing, not marriage nor having children nor acquiring age and experience.'

Her gaze had turned inwards, May saw. She was looking at something that was no longer there.

It had been a day not very different from this one, misty at first, then shimmering with the afterthought of heat. Elizabeth clearly remembered the dress she was wearing. It was crisp linen, banana yellow, with a full skirt and cuffed short sleeves, which flattered the smooth, summer-golden skin of her forearms. Bought with her mother on a shopping trip to New York and put on for the first time for her grandparents' party.

It was a luncheon for Maine friends and families, most of whom Elizabeth had known from childhood. There had been white sailcloth canopies slung from ribboned poles to shade the garden, and English silver porringers filled with white and yellow roses to decorate the tables. The house had been scented with lavender and filled with music from the piano in the evening room, and the women's heels had clicked out an intermezzo on the old wooden floors.

Elizabeth had drunk her first glass of champagne as a birthday toast to her grandmother, the Senator's wife, and after the speeches, as she had dreamed all day of doing, she wandered away from the heart of the party to the kitchen where the cook and two maids were working. From there it was only a short step through the side door to the back of the house facing away from the hammered-metal sea. A line of cars was parked there, two or three of them attended by lounging chauffeurs. Elizabeth slipped past them into the lane and began to walk slowly in her ankle-strap high-heeled shoes, feeling the eye of the afternoon sun fixed on her head. She had turned in the opposite direction from Pittsharbor and now she passed the Captain's House. A low whistle stopped her in her tracks.

He was waiting for her in what had become their place. The house was empty and dilapidated, because the old woman who was the captain's daughter had died in the spring. Pittsharbor talk had it that the place had been bought for a summer cottage by rich people from off, but there was no sign of them as yet. In the meantime, Elizabeth and the boy had found a screen and an inner door that they could prise open, so the whole house was their domain.

He held the door ajar now, and she ran across the turf and up the sagging steps so that he caught her and snapped the door shut behind them. For a long second they stood looking at one another, the gloom of the house shifting and re-forming into welcoming shadows as their eyes grew accustomed to the dimness.

109

He kissed her then, tasting the champagne foreign in her mouth.

For weeks, ever since the beginning of the summer when Elizabeth had come up from Boston with her mother, they had been waiting and watching for opportunities to meet in the old house. Their meetings happened seldom enough, because Elizabeth had to explain every absence and the boy had his work to do, but today was perfect. Everyone at the house was busy with the party and the tide had brought the fishing boats back early.

'You look so pretty,' he told her, and ran the tips of his fingers over her shoulders and down to her breasts. The yellow dress had a row of tiny covered buttons, and he bit his lower lip between his teeth and stopped breathing as he undid them one by one. Elizabeth thought of the protests she should make, but even as the thought came she gasped and abandoned it, letting her head fall back against the peeling wall.

They had done this before; when the two of them had grown bruised and sticky with kissing he had touched and stroked her breasts with his salt-cracked fingers. He had been almost too gentle, and without properly understanding her hunger Elizabeth had snatched his hands in her own and greedily bitten and sucked at them. She had licked the cuts made by running lines and gutting knives, and the punctures from fish-hooks until he had muttered roughly, 'Don't, don't you do that.'

Today was different. They hadn't talked about why,

110

but they both silently accepted that the difference was momentous.

In the corner of the room he had spread a rug on the bare boards and a pillow with a split in the seam that exposed the feather innards. He took her hand now and led her towards it. The seaward windows were sealed with storm shutters but cracks had opened in the old wood and they let in long streaks of light to lie like fuzzy blades on the floor. When they knelt and faced each other a few puffs of goose-down escaped from the pillow and floated like minuscule clouds. Elizabeth's arms rested on his shoulders, and with careful movements he lifted the rustling folds of linen and slid his hands up her thighs.

She shifted a little, hesitant, then yielding. Their mouths met again, familiar after weeks of touching but wider now and wetter, until each of them felt they might slip down the other's throat and be swallowed up for ever.

A minute later, it seemed, the yellow dress had been dropped to one side and Elizabeth lay back naked with one hand crooked to pillow her head. She had imagined this moment, and feeling ashamed and exposed, but now she was wiser she understood that neither shame nor exposure was at issue. Nor were questions of right and wrong. This was right and it was what she wanted.

He knelt between her spread knees, as naked as she was, his hair as black as ship's tar and his beaky tanned face taut with longing and concentration. He was holding himself with one hand as if he was afraid he might spill too soon. 'Is it what you want?'

111

She hadn't felt herself to be the leader in any of their doings before this minute. He was two years older and belonged here with the rocks and currents of the shoreline, and he knew and was able to do much more than she ever would because she was a pampered city girl. But still by some alchemy she had become the navigator and the helmsman now. 'Yes,' she said. 'It is.'

Looking at his face and the muscled lines of his body she thought she would melt with love. She lifted her hips, her eyes slanting with a smile, offering herself to him. With a helpless groan he pushed himself into her.

It hurt. The pain of it took her completely by surprise. She turned her head aside, biting her tongue and the inside of her mouth, staring over his heaving shoulder at the walls marked with the ghostly outlines of pictures and furniture. For an instant the room seemed full of ghosts who crowded in to watch her crossing into womanhood. Suddenly fear unfolded terrible wings in her stomach. She gasped, 'Be careful. Please be careful.'

He was already shuddering. He shouted something she couldn't decipher and pulled away from her, and she lay motionless with her eyes wide open as he ejaculated. Afterwards she held his head in her arms, strands of his sweat-soaked hair caught in her mouth. The pain had gone as quickly as it had come and her fear had subsided with it. Nothing that happened now, whatever there was in the future, could take this moment from them.

Their first time had been together.

A tiny beat of triumph and relief and happiness began to tick in her throat. She peeled his hair away from her mouth and waited for him to come back to her.

When he opened his eyes he looked dazed, overcome in a way that she had never even glimpsed in him before. He locked her in his arms, pinning her against him. 'I love you. I want you to marry me.' The declaration was almost violent.

Elizabeth said, 'I don't know.'

'You're sixteen now. When you're eighteen we can do it. We can make them say yes.' He meant her parents and grandparents, and their old-money objections to a mere Pittsharbor fisherman. His family might be equally old, but they were also poor. It was a big obstacle, a huge barrier set across the future.

'I love you too,' she said humbly. It was the truth. 'Will you wait until I'm ready to tell them about us?'

He smiled then, believing that he would get what he wanted in the end. Elizabeth Freshett would marry him and they would live in a house overlooking the bay and Moon Island.

'I'll wait. I'll go on loving you until I'm an old man and I'll still love you after I'm dead.'

They lay in each other's arms in a drift of goosedown, awed by the magnitude of their commitment.

Later, when she walked back alone to her grandfather's house with the linen dress creased and dusty, Elizabeth was facing the end of the summer and separation from the boy she had just promised to marry in the sun-barred stillness of the Captain's

113

House. The party was ending and her mother had been looking for her. Amazed that the truth wasn't clearly written in her face, Elizabeth told her that the sun and heat had given her a headache, and she had been walking on the beach to try to rid herself of it.

'Look at your dress,' her mother exclaimed. Appearances were always crucial to her.

'I'll go and change,' Elizabeth answered, the meek daughter with rebellion and love twirling in her heart.

Some of this, only the bones of it without the precious details that were still as clear in her mind as yesterday, Elizabeth told May on the porch of the Flying Fish.

May heard her out politely. She finished her Coke and jabbed the straw into the mush of melting ice at the bottom. 'You used to sneak off and meet this guy in our house?'

'The house where you are staying now, yes.'

May didn't want these confidences. In any case it was inconceivable that this old lady had once been young, let alone had sex – that must be what she was saying in her genteel way – had *screwed* some nameless fisherman in an empty house they had broken into together. The idea of adult sex, *old* sex, all the teeming sequences and varieties of it, even and especially Ivy and Lucas, was revolting and threatening. It made May more conscious of the lump of misery lodged inside her but she could only admit obliquely, with her thoughts sidling up to the idea and skittering desperately away again, that the misery was something to do with John and Suzanne, and the threat of John with

114

Leonie Beam. She hunched her shoulders rigidly and glared down into her empty glass.

'Would you like another Coke, May? It's my turn.'

'Uh, no, thanks.'

She wasn't sure how to extricate herself from this uncomfortable conversation. In an attempt to sanitise the story's ending she mumbled, 'So he was your husband, right?'

'No. I married someone else.'

The bleakness, the note of pure despair in the old woman's voice made even May look up and beyond her own concerns. 'Yeah? Why was that?'

Elizabeth paused. 'I don't know that it will be in any way intelligible to you. I was a Freshett, my mother was an Archbold from Portland.'

May waited for further explanation.

'A year went by and I was as much in love as ever. At last, when I was eighteen, I told my mother who the boy was and why I wanted to marry him.'

'And?'

'They refused their permission. They were quite adamant, so the choice I had to make was between my family and the life I knew, and a boy whose life and background were entirely different from mine.'

'Well, that doesn't sound so hard, in a way. Doesn't everyone kind of have to make choices when they pick people?' May was interested now in spite of herself and impatient with the irrelevance of all these family names.

'Yes, they do. I didn't understand that really I was free to choose, or at least could try to be brave and set

115

myself free. That's what I meant when I said you know all kinds of things that I didn't at your age.'

Was that the case, May wondered? She didn't feel she had the luxury of any choices in the plodding discomfort of her daily existence. 'So what happened?' The end of the saga must surely be in sight.

'I was sent off to Europe. I spent eighteen wonderful months travelling, and living in London and Paris. When I came back I met and married my husband, to please my family. He was a good man, quite a lot older than me, and we lived comfortably together.'

Elizabeth's glass clinked in its saucer as she gently laid her spoon beside it. Her mouth made a thin riverline with its tiny tributaries of lipstick bleeding away from it. It hadn't been a happy ending. May guessed clumsily at the implications of regret and missed opportunities threading back through years and years of an old woman's uneventful life, then she bundled up the thought and pushed it away from her.

In as careless a voice as she could manage she demanded, 'So what happened to him? The other guy?'

'He married, not so long afterwards, and had children too.'

The waitress brought the check and laid it on the table beneath Elizabeth's saucer.

May snatched it up and glared angrily at the total. 'Why did you tell me this?' she demanded. She felt close to tears again, unable to deal with the way Elizabeth's loneliness and long-ago hurt nudged and pressed against her. She felt too fragile to withstand it.

116

'Because you told me about the woman on the island.'

May counted her dollar bills and laid them neatly with the check. She knew Elizabeth was waiting for her to make some knowing response. There was some connection between the two stories but whatever it was she didn't want to make it, or even to think about what it might be. She wished only to regain the safety of Doone's bedroom, where the diary was brooding in its secret place. She had meant to reread one of the bits, about the pointlessness of everything. She would look at it as soon as she was back there with the door safely closed. John and Ivy would both be busy somewhere, for sure.

'Well, yeah, okay. One for one.' She eased her chair back from the table, awkward in the small space, and made a show of looking at her watch. 'I've got to get back, you know?'

Elizabeth reached out and took her hand. May had to force herself either not to snatch it away and run and run, or to stand still and let her shoulders sag while the tears slopped down her face.

'Can I do anything to help you?' Elizabeth asked softly.

'What, how d'you mean help? No, I don't need anything. Really. Thanks, okay?'

'Go on, then. If you're in a hurry, that is. I walk much more slowly than you. Thank you for the tea.'

'You're welcome. I mean, I enjoyed it.' May turned and almost ran down the steps and away from the Flying Fish, back towards the house on the bluff. She was almost there when Spencer Newton and his friend passed in the opposite direction, in their spiffy green Jaguar with the top down. They looked the same, in their designer shades with the breeze blowing their pale hair straight back off their foreheads. Elizabeth would be on her own in the house again.

Down on the beach there was a small group of people gathered around a trailer hitched to the Beams' jeep. They were wrestling with the transfer of a boat from it to the sea. Tom and Karyn were there, and two other adults, and a fringe of children and teenagers milled around ignoring instructions and loudly contributing their own.

John had been wondering where his daughters were. Ivy and Lucas weren't in the group, but he caught sight of Leonie in her black swimsuit. He strolled across from where he had been sitting on the steps up to his house. 'Can I lend a hand here?'

'Sure, thanks. Grab a hold,' Tom called over his shoulder. From the driver's seat of the jeep Elliot shouted a warning and backed the trailer closer to the water. A wave ran up and slapped against the wheels, and the younger children danced around with pleasure at being soaked.

Karyn introduced John to the newcomers, Richard and Shelly Beam. Their three children were pointed out to him.

'Is this the complete family now?'

Richard grinned, showing a strong resemblance to his brother. 'Nope. There's Clayton and Gina and

118

their two still to come. Mike and Anne are in Europe, of course.'

Leonie was on the opposite side of the trailer. When she lifted her eyes to meet John's she saw that he had acquired the beginnings of a sun-tan and some of the lines of strain had faded from his face. Elliot was still easing the trailer deeper into the water. Leonie looked away, to where Marian had come up to watch the proceedings.

When the trailer had gone far enough Tom directed them to put their shoulders to the boat's fibreglass hull again. They gave a concerted heave and a shout of triumph as it slid off the trailer and the keel scraped the sand in shallow water.

'Push her out,' Tom commanded and they ran it forward into deeper water where it floated free. Children were already swarming under the tarpaulin cover and Elliot was easing the jeep forwards up the shelving sand. John and Leonie were left alone, separated by the space where the boat had been. Among all the cries and laughter and diamond-glittering splashes of water Leonie could hear nothing but a question vibrating between them with a tuning-fork's meticulous note.

It was absurd to go on meeting and deflecting each other.

In the time that had elapsed since their lunch together she had convinced herself that a question could have two answers. If she and Tom didn't love each other as they once had done, they were still friends and they were knitted together by history and shared experiences. It was possible to live a calm and ordered life surrounded by siblings and their children, and to take pleasure in work and companionship.

Even as she made these measured decisions a current of revolt ran through her, snapping her shoulders back and her head upright. The opposite answer reverberated deafeningly in her head. It wasn't *enough* of a life. Not enough, not enough. It was like a sour chorus to the song of the beach.

She didn't think Tom even noticed that she handed her allegiance over to him. She was just here at the beach as a part of a landscape, not even making the foreground of the picture.

With three precise and deliberate steps Leonie crossed the barrier of stones to John's side. She felt gleeful and reckless, as she had done with the kiss in the car-park, and at the same time as awkward as a teenager. Dressed only in a swimsuit she couldn't find anywhere to put her hands, so she crossed her arms in front of her stomach, cupping her elbows in a stance that reminded her of May Duhane. John was no less fenced around than she was herself – almost all she knew about him was to do with his daughters and his widowhood, and the cautious path he steered through the thickets of responsibility.

A greedy longing to know more, to excavate him and at the same time to be dug out of herself, suddenly blazed up in her like ravenous hunger after a long swim in the sea. She said coolly, 'Would you like to come for a walk this evening? There's a good one along the cliff to the next bay and over the causeway to another island. You can do it when the tide's right.'

Lucas and Ivy were rowing back to the beach. At least, Lucas was rowing; he bent over the oars and the muscles in his back and arms smoothly bunched and lengthened. Ivy lay back in the stern of the boat, one leg lazily hooked over the side. She looked creamy and sated, and at the same time triumphant. *Just-fucked* was the phrase that came to Leonie's mind.

John watched them until Lucas shipped the oars and let the boat drift in to the shallows. Ivy sketched a little wave at her father. Leonie knew that John was also weighing the significance of small signals and the major movements they flagged.

Marian had gathered a flock of children around her and was beckoning Leonie. Tom and the jeep had driven away.

'Yes, we could do that,' John said. His voice was light, giving nothing away.

Five

The stagnant air of Doone's bedroom breathed and
sighed in May's ears. Hannah Fennymore's two books
and Doone's diary lay in a row beside her on the bed
quilt. She let her chin fall on her chest as she stared at
them, trying to imagine Doone putting her writing
aside and picking up the whaling story. To mimic her
actions, as if it might help her understanding, she
opened the book herself.

The *Dolphin*'s was an uneventful voyage for the first six
weeks. No whales were sighted, but favouring winds
assisted the ship's progress across the Atlantic and
Captain Gunnell gave orders for the four whaleboats
to be lowered from their davits at regular intervals so
that the boat steerers and oarsmen might at least
practise their seaborne maneouvres as often as was
practicable.

William Corder learned his part in the boat as
readily as he had about the decks and masts of the
Dolphin. He was assigned the position of stroke

oarsman in the third mate's crew, from which place he bent to pull his oar at the mate's command, assisted with handling the small mast, and when the light-weight, sharp-ended craft took in water in rough seas it was his allotted task to bail her out with a canvas bucket stowed for that purpose among the copious whaling gear. The rest of the paraphernalia looked threatening enough to William – there were the tubs with their great coiled lengths of line, the razor-edged harpoon and long lances to be plunged deep into the creature's innards, and the cutting spades with which great incisions could be sliced in the blubber for holding the whale fast, while it was towed back to the ship's side.

The boat was headed by the mate, who directed their turns and twists with the steering oar while the boat steerer pulled from the forward thwart until they could draw close enough to their target for him to jump up in the bow and throw his harpoon. The four oarsmen rowed for their livelihood, but always with their backs blindly turned to the scene in front, for they were forbidden even to glance over their shoulders at what might lie ahead of them. Their only clues were the headsman's guttural commands and imprecations, and the light of terror or exultation in his eyes.

Even in practice it was deadly hard work, and William and the other green hands were in no doubt that the difficulties would multiply when there were whales in the offing. They listened with apprehension to the able seamen's tales of closing in on their quarry

– the great sperm whales. They heard how an ugly whale could stove in a boat with one thrash of his flukes and of the perils of a 'Nantucket sleigh ride' – when a running whale would drive across the surface of the water, dragging the boat and its occupants in a wild dash in its wake.

The third mate was named Matthias Plant, a Nantucket native and a great veteran for a whaleman, being almost forty years of age, swarthy from the sun and with a body like one of his own barrels of whale oil. Matthias had been married for twenty years and out of that span of time he had lived just weeks, in all totalling barely thirteen months, at home with his wife. The rest of the time he had been at sea. It was Matthias's pleasure to regale William with stories of the chase and the catch, embellished with the most vivid and gory of details. William heard him out with his invariable courtesy, and tried manfully to hide his fears behind an expression of calm unconcern.

In truth, the rowing and paddling and hauling on the mast and sail under Matthias's brutal direction was an exhausting trial for William. His narrow shoulders and slender arms were racked with the effort, and when the order came at last to row for the *Dolphin*, riding a mile or so distant like an ivory ship on a sapphire sea, he would have uttered a cheer if he had possessed sufficient voice for the task.

'We'll make a whaleman of you yet, my little parlour-maid,' Matthias would roar and clap the boy heartily on his aching back.

After these expeditions William returned almost

with pleasure to the shipboard routine of two-hour turns at the helm and as look-out at one of the three mastheads. He was keen-eyed, and it was one of the few joys available to him to stand at the high vantage-point and scan the glassy miles of water for a whale's spout. In his commanding position, with the ship beneath him riding along under easy sail, he felt like a giant striding across the waves. He could even lean forward, his eyes stinging with the lick of the salt wind, and believe he wished for the spout of a whale as much as for the sight of another ship that might contain his true quarry.

The *Dolphin* was just two days short of a full two months out of Nantucket when Captain Gunnell took the observation and worked up the latitude before announcing to the second mate that the ship would cross the Line, or the equator of the earth, at about sundown that evening.

The mate sagely nodded his head, then spoke to the helmsman who happened to be one of the green hands. 'Do you hear the Captain? I believe that Old Neptune himself will be coming aboard tonight. Every whaler who passes through his empire must pay homage to him and from every first-timer he extracts the proper dues.'

'What dues may these be?' the sailor asked, thinking anxiously of his supplies of tobacco and other small luxuries safe in his sea-chest in the forecastle.

'That's not for me to predict,' the mate answered. 'All I know is that the old man will be aboard this ship tonight.'

As soon as the wheel was relieved, the man scurried

below to spread the news to the other first-timers. William sat tight in the narrow space of his bunk, the curtain partly drawn, as was his habit, to afford the smallest protection from the squalid conditions of the forecastle. He heard the rumours and assertions of the other hands with misgiving. At sundown, as the last watch came down from the mastheads, the green hands heard the hatch over the heads slammed closed. They were shut tight in their living quarters until such time as Old Neptune came aboard.

'I see a ship,' the mate loudly cried out overhead. 'The Emperor himself!'

Up on the deck, the biggest and broadest of the able seamen had padded his chest with mats, wrapped himself round in a white sheet from the Captain's cabin and pulled on top of the whole a great dark coat blackened with smoke from the try-pot. He had a wild nest of hair made of frayed yarn decked with seaweed, whiskers of the same, and a cloth mask that covered all but his eyes and nose. In his hand he held a four-pronged harpoon. Against the dimming sky and the limitless horizon he made an alarming sight.

In the meantime the other hands dragged up from below decks the largest of the blubber tubs, a great vessel they filled to the brim with salt water. Over the lip of it, secured at the other end to the summit of the brick furnace where the whale-oil was boiled out of the blubber, a broad plank was fixed. The Captain's own chair was brought from his cabin and set next to the near end of the plank, and Old Neptune took his seat upon the throne.

In a great roar he demanded that the first of the youngsters be brought up without delay.

In the forecastle the young men had heard the tramping and thumping over their heads, and waited with great trepidation for what would happen next. At the command they hustled forward the boldest of their company and sent him up the steps to the deck, and whatever fate was awaiting him. There were a few long moments before there came some confused shouting and the sound of splashing, and the call for the next victim.

One by one, they put their reluctant heads out into the night air. When it came to William's turn he had no sooner appeared from the forecastle scuttle and tried to see around him in the blaze of lanterns than he was seized from behind and blindfolded. He caught no more than a second's glimpse of Old Neptune towering on his throne, but it was enough to send a thrill of fear through him. He was hustled up the ladder and set in front of the sea's Emperor. William's common sense told him that all this was no more than a sailors' prank, but still he could not stop his limbs from trembling.

'What is your name?' Neptune roared into his face, sending a great wave of tobacco and rum breaking over the boy, which would have knocked him backwards if he hadn't been pinned by both arms.

'William Corder, sir.'

'And why do you travel through my domain, William?'

The young man hesitated for a long moment, as if debating with himself the best answer to give.

Neptune roared at him, 'I have a dozen ships to visit tonight.'

'I . . . I am hoping to catch a whale, sir.'

Amid a great roar of laughter Neptune said, 'Aye, you and Captain Gunnell also. I have a piece of advice for you, William, before we make a sailor of you. If you want to see Nantucket again don't look backwards when you can look forwards and don't you look forwards in the whaleboat or Mr Plant will have your two ears for bait. Do you hear me? Open your mouth wide in answer.'

William opened his mouth as wide as it would go to say *Yes, sir,* but at once a filthy brush covered with tar and soap was crammed between his teeth. All over his face the vile paste was slapped on until he was gagging with it, then invisible hands pretended to shave his soft skin with a rusty knife.

'There's no beard on the boy, not a whisker,' cried a voice he recognised as the first mate's.

'Can you swim, William?' Neptune roared at him. 'It might be better for you if you can answer yes.'

William remembered the shouts and splashing he had heard from the victims who had preceded him, and knew that he was going to be thrown overboard. He could not swim a stroke, and the green water would close over his head and he would sink like a stone. 'No,' he screamed, his voice rising to a shriek of terror.

But a bucket of water was thrown full in his face, so that his scream became a gasp, and he was lifted off his feet by what seemed a dozen men and pitched backwards into the water. As his heels flew over his head he heard the crew sing out, 'Man overboard!'

William was kicking out for his life even before he hit the water in the blubber tub. He wrenched off the blindfold and looked up through the froth as he sank to see the grinning faces of his shipmates encircling the tub. He was choking and retching as he rose to the surface, and no more than two floundering strokes carried him to the side. Rough hands seized and hoisted him out, and a mocking attempt was made to strip him of his soaking shirt and trousers.

But the threat of having his tender naked flesh revealed was much greater to William than the fear of death by drowning. His fright was seemingly forgotten as he rounded on his tormentors and spat at them like a wildcat. 'You have done enough. Take your hands off me at once.'

One or two of them were jeeringly ready to take the matter further, but Captain Gunnell called out from his place at the front of the little crowd, 'Leave the lad alone now. He has shown spirit enough and there are more of them waiting below.'

At once, attention turned to the next youngster who was hustled up the forecastle ladder. William saw that those who had preceded him in the cruel ritual were awaiting the show as eagerly as any of the other hands, but he did not choose to take his place alongside them as Neptune began his roaring again. Instead he turned his back on the fun and leaned over the taffrail to gaze out over the wide black sea.

Not one of the men saw that his face was wet with tears as well as tub-water.

May frowned. She could hear the endless sea beyond her window and wished that she could shut out the sound. The whaling story seemed to bring it closer and to amplify the threat in its lazy whisper. She opened the diary yet again.

Doone always wrote the date in full at the beginning of each entry. The last one was for 15 August but it ran to only a handful of numbers, scrawled with such heat that an impression of the digits clearly showed on the blank page beneath. Almost all the later entries were in code, except for the dates and a tantalising handful of words and phrases – *mirror, photograph, dinghy* – out of which May could piece together nothing significant. She was tired of staring at the code as if the intensity of her concentration alone could dissolve the mystery.

The plain-written page that held her attention was dated 13 June, not long before the Bennisons left Chicago for their summer vacation. The curve of Doone's mounting excitement about the impending departure for Maine had been almost unbroken, but now it dipped into a chasm of despair.

Talked with Mom, back from the clinic early for once. Says she and Dad have been thinking about maybe going up to the coast a bit later, say a week, because Dad has some work to finish off and she 'could always use a bit more time'.

What did I think?

Think. As if it's anything to do with *thinking*, like whether to have relish or extra fries. It's like I've made a little tower of stones balanced on top of each other, dragging them to their place and building up hopes and dreams all the year, then my parents knock it down and scatter the stones with a flick of their feet and don't even see what they're doing.

I need so much to be *there* in the places where I remember him, even if he won't be there yet himself. I have got everything fixed on this, it's what I've kept going on all these months and it's so fragile that Mom can just change it, going hmmm? over the pasta as if nothing matters except her work and Dad's.

There's no defence and no control anywhere in my life.

I'm so scared.

I've got to *be* there, on the beach and the bay, closer to the memories and the promise of him arriving. A week longer to wait is longer than I can bear to imagine. There isn't anything else I care about.

And as soon as I write that I think, God, what kind of a person am I?

And I know the answer to it is that I'm dumb, and a kid, and an ugly, fat-bottomed one at that – and perhaps it's actually because nothing matters or means anything at all to me that I've fixed on this *thing* as a meaningful structure in my life. Probably that's what Dad would say about it, only with a whole lot more jargon.

How pathetic of me, and how pathetic to hope for anything more, that *he* might want *me* for any reason at all, even though I love him so much I'd be glad to die for him.

And yet, and yet. I remember what I remember.

I didn't say anything to Mom. I ran out of the kitchen and went to my room and lay under the covers, and in the end she came to look for me. She saw my face and I saw the dawn of *fright* in hers. And that made me feel really strong for a minute.

She asked me, 'Are you okay?'

It's a funny question, as meaningless as just about everything else. If your parents are a pediatrician and a shrink, what room is there for you not to be okay?

Then she said, 'Honey, we'll go up to the beach as planned if it means so much to you. Is there some reason why you so badly want to get away from here? Do you want to talk to me about something?'

I told her there was nothing. Nothing nothing nothing, like it's my signature.

Nothing except him.

Who is he? May asked herself for the hundredth time when she finished reading.

It must have been someone up here at the beach; someone who had been here the year before as well as last year. A regular summer visitor, not a year-rounder, because Doone wrote about waiting for him to arrive. Was he from one of the five houses, or Pittsharbor, or further afield? Doone had written about the beach and the bay as if that was where he belonged, so surely that indicated *here*, the beach itself?

It was clear to May that he could only be Lucas, even though Doone never wrote his name. There were no other possibilities except Joel and Kevin, and how could either of them inspire such intensity of feeling?

The year before last something had happened between Lucas and Doone – *I remember what I remember* – and it had been enough for Doone to make it the *structure* of her life. *Pathetic*, Doone had judged her attachment to be and the judgement had extended to herself as well, but she had still acknowledged it to be the centre of her life. She had believed her love to be strong enough to die for and it was true that it had brought her moments of ecstasy as well as despair.

And she did die.

Was that because of Lucas or had something else intervened?

The Beach is particularly resistant to rational explanation. Aaron Fennymore's dry words again, somehow more alarming for their very lack of colour.

May studied her bitten finger-nails and the ragged cushions of flesh surrounding them. They looked like a stranger's hands.

Was it possible, might she have to love Lucas just because Doone had done so before her? Was this helpless longing for a tattooed arm and dirty beige-blond hair inherited from a drowned girl? Is it me or her? Which of us is which? And the one on the island – who is she?

Suddenly May hurled the diary away from her. It

133

landed face down with the pages splayed. Her hands flew up to cover her ears and she rocked in the old armchair.

There *was* a difference, a big one – Doone had had her mother to confide in, even though she was angry with her for her absences. Doone's mother had come up to her room, hadn't she, and put her arms round her troubled daughter and tried to make her talk?

An angry sob cranked itself out of May's chest.

She knew how people could just die, like they could just go shopping or on vacation.

When she thought about her own mother in the earlier times the memories were dressed in colours: the clothes Alison wore, brilliant slabs of saffron or mint or cerise like exuberant abstracts out of one of her art books, and spiked with the scent that clung to her, and the sound of talk and laughter.

Then there came the reversal of all that, the dissolving of Alison into silence and darkness. She had gone so suddenly there had been no chance for anyone to make ready for the loss of her. There had been no packing, no goodbyes and all the tears had to be spent uselessly afterwards. She had left her clothes hanging in the closets, lurid ghosts of her, which still seemed ready to stir with her movements.

Alison's disappearance out of May's life seemed such a terrible and random assault that it had put every remaining corner of her world under threat. All the warmth and certainty drained away, leaving a place of yawning shadows and whispers she couldn't hear.

134

May remembered the uneasiness that seeped through the apartment, filling the rooms like poison gas. She wondered who was guilty and what it was they were guilty of so that Alison had had to die, then she pinched down on the thought to press it into oblivion. Questions simmered in her head, about the time before her mother's death and voices behind closed doors and murmured telephone conversations and Ivy's mute, accusing face, but they were never spoken aloud. When Alison was gone there was no one to answer anything.

Maybe her father had never been very good at looking after people or answering their needs and she had never really noticed the deficiency because Alison had always been there. He made the right movements and gestures, and after the first weeks he found a housekeeper to take care of them all, but he did everything mechanically and painfully, as if he was too disabled by his own grief to attend to May's. She tried to spare him by keeping still and quiet.

Ivy had been the strongest, but she turned her strength into icy withdrawal. She spent her time with her friends, and would hardly speak to her father and sister at all.

For months May had been afraid every day that Ivy and John would die too and leave her behind. One day she couldn't keep the fear of it locked inside herself any longer. John was just leaving the apartment, in his business suit with a file of papers under his arm, and May clung to him and howled that she was sure he would be run over or murdered on the way.

He was in a hurry. He needed to get to a meeting and to win a contract; the business wasn't doing well. 'Nothing will happen to me, baby, I promise. I'll be back at six o'clock, just like always.'

And he had handed her over to Carmen the house-keeper, murmuring that May seemed a little spooked and needed some extra attention. Carmen did her best, but May pushed her away. She lay on her bed, waiting and shrinking from the inevitability of the phone, the knock that would bring the news. What had once been safe was now precarious.

A few days later she cut up her mother's clothes.

Dr Metz had been through all this with her. It was normal, she had told her. It was fine and natural for May to feel what she felt.

'If it's fine,' May had snarled once, 'why does it feel so *bad*?'

Dr Metz had smiled at her. 'We can talk about it next time.'

If I had been Doone, I would have told my mother I loved Lucas. I'd tell Alison now, if she were here. May didn't know whether she had spoken out loud or not, and the realisation made her feel that she might not even have her solid self to rely on any longer.

Restlessly, searching for an escape from her thoughts, she turned back to the story of the whaler ship.

It was the afternoon of the third day after the crossing of the Line ceremony when the exultant cry came at last from the look-out at the masthead. 'There she blows!'

Captain Gunnell sprang to attention at once, and the rest of the watch on deck and William Corder with them.

'Where away?' the Captain howled.

'Four points on the lee bow, sir.'

'How far off?'

'Two miles.'

'Sperm whale?'

'Yes, sir. A large school. *There* she blows again.'

'Call all hands. Haul back the main yard and stand by to lower.'

The men from the watch below decks swarmed out of their places and joined the rest in the scurry to the boats. This urgency was like none of their practice games and even William felt the thrill of the chase in prospect, as the bow boat hit the water and he sprang over the rail and landed in his accustomed place. There was great rivalry between the boats to be the first under way and the fastest over the water, and William bent to his heavy oar with great alacrity as the mate sang out, 'Give way, my lads, give way. A long steady stroke and we'll have 'em.'

The four boats flew over the water, steadily closing the distance on the school of whales. They had travelled a mile and a half when the whales went down. The oarsmen stopped their work and lay on their oars until the headsmen directed them to paddle gently towards where the great beasts had last been seen. The sudden quiet and the tension prickled at the nape of

William's neck where the sweat- and spray-damped clothing stuck to his skin. He could hear Matthias Plant breathing hard and counting off the seconds into minutes. Then there was a sudden shout as a bull whale blew a great plume of water not a hundred yards away from them. He lay rolling comfortably in a trough of the waves.

William's boat was caught at right angles to him, dead on the eye as whalemen called it, because the sperm whale has the best field of vision at that angle. As Matthias howled at his men to row round to bring them head to head, the remaining boats scattered in pursuit of the other whales now blowing all around them.

Heggy Burris, the boat steerer, stood up with his first iron grasped in his hand, ready to send it into the whale's body once the head had slid past. At exactly the right instant he braced his foot against a cleat and set his thigh in a half-circle cut for the purpose in a gunwale plank, bent his body back in an arc and drove the iron through the air and into the whale's flank. It buried itself deep and an instant later the second iron followed it home.

Pain bent the creature almost double as he flung himself away from them. He thrashed his mighty flukes and sent a column of water high into the air before he sounded. The line ran out so fast as he dived that smoke rose from it and the headsman hollered at William to douse it with water from his canvas bucket. The line had half run out before the whale rose once again and in agony beat the water with his flukes and tail, so that it churned and rocked the little boat like an eggshell. William could not make himself look to see, but he heard the whale's jaws snapping like cannon fire seemingly inches from his own head.

'Oh, my boys, my lovely boys, we have him now,' Matthias was crooning. The lines held fast and blood welled up and clouded the water between boat and prey. The other craft closed in to assist the bow boat with the kill.

The poor whale proved no match for all of them. Soon his thrashing ceased altogether and he rolled belly up. Immediately they had the huge carcass secured Matthias set the signal to the ship. As luck would have it, it was riding to windward of them, so it beat down towards the boats while they rested next to their prize. A leeward wind or a flat calm would have meant a gruelling row back to the ship with the great dead weight of the whale dragging in the water behind them.

William was full of the exhilaration of chase and kill as they made the whale fast against the ship's side, but he soon found that his day's labours had hardly begun. Once the whale was properly tethered with hawsers and an iron chain passed around the narrow part of the tail before the spreading flukes, the work of cutting-in commenced. This was the stripping off of blubber, to be completed in the shortest possible time before sharks could begin to feed on the carcass and because the ship could make no further headway towards fresh whales with the unwieldy bulk of the dead cousin dragging alongside.

The Captain and mates began digging with their long-handled cutting spades. After an hour's work of hoisting oily and bloody strips of blubber over the ship's side, William knew that any notions of exhaustion he had entertained before this moment were no more than a sweet afternoon's dream compared with the reality of stink and pain and retching disgust he was experiencing now.

At last the whale's mangled body, headless and stripped bare of every other valuable shred, was cut adrift and left to the mercy of sharks and circling sea-birds. Matthias patted the crumpled boy on the shoulder as he came aboard from the cutting platform with the last of the animal's blubber. 'Well done, lad,' he said simply. 'Now you're one of us good and proper.'

'I think not,' William retorted and turned away, with a display of energy and feeling that surprised them both.

Already the fires were blazing in the brick furnaces of the try-works. The seamen had fed the hungry iron mouths of the furnaces with wood carried for the purpose and now began the business of feeding blubber into the two huge pots mounted above. It was boiled to release its barrels of oil and when each load had yielded its all the tried-out scraps themselves were used to feed the red heat.

William sank down, mesmerised with exhaustion, on to the hatch-cover that up until now had protected the try-works. The boat steerers were the ship's stokers, and they stirred up the roaring flames and

140

used long poles to pitch reeking piles of blubber into the boiling pots.

The smell was all of terrible singeing, a sick oiliness that filled every throat with a taste of decay and death. Dense clouds of black smoke billowed up from the pots to darken the sails overhead with broad brush-strokes of filth. The ship surged forward in the night, freed from the encumbrance of the whale, with the inferno of fire and smoke blazing on its deck.

It was a twelve-barrel whale, William had learned. A good enough start to the *Dolphin*'s voyage

As he huddled on the hatch he watched the hissing pots and the belching flames of the furnace, and the figures of his shipmates bending and gyrating in the lurid light. Their naked upper bodies gleamed with sweat, their faces were black masks of smoky grime and their exertions drew their lips back from their teeth in a stark grimace so that white teeth shone cruelly out of the tangles of black beard. They looked like the devil's own imps tending the subterranean fires.

'I am in hell,' William whispered aloud. 'Truly I have descended into hell and this is the payment for my sins.'

He locked his hands together and tried to pray, but no form of prayer would come to him.

May lifted her head. She could see the dead whale and the oily fires glimmering on the deck of the ship. A shiver crawled over her skin. The sea was greedy and

she felt how close it was to her, gnawing and worrying at the shore.

She thought that if only she listened a little harder she would be able to understand its language; maybe interpret the warning it was whispering to her. It was like breeding an extra sense that was not yet quite ready to use, a painful knob under her skin to which her fingers kept returning, pressing to test the growth.

The book was more than just a book, but she couldn't put a finger on why or what it might mean. Hannah Fennymore had lent it to her because she had asked for it, because she was curious about Doone. And beyond Doone's bedroom window there was nothing to be seen except the beach, and Kevin and the others fooling about on or in the water.

And Lucas, slant-eyed, who made her feel things she did not understand or welcome.

May didn't want to be shut up alone any longer. She left her chair and ran to the door and for a second it seemed again that there was a weight pressing against it, trapping her in the room. But it yielded and banged open, and May ran down the steep stairs.

John was sitting by the window overlooking the sea. There was a book on his lap but he was staring out at Moon Island, his chin resting on one hand, as if waiting for something. 'Hi,' he said. 'What's happening?'

May hovered in front of him. She was pricklingly conscious of her father's outstretched legs and the sinews on the backs of his hands. Her own legs felt thick and over-elongated, and her hips wide and heavy. Her arms hung clumsily at her side.

He made the little beckoning movement she was waiting for, putting his book aside. May could see that he was afraid she might reject his gesture. She bundled forward and piled herself on to his lap, an awkward mass of jutting elbows and knees.

John held her, resting his chin on the top of her bent head and stroking her hair. Her weight and size surprised him. It was a long time since she had come asking for a cuddle like a little girl. 'What's wrong?'

May picked dully at a three-cornered tear in the pocket of his chinos. *Where to begin? I wish I were like Ivy. I'm afraid I'm turning into someone else. There's a ghost on the island and now I'm scared of the sea. . . .* 'I don't like it here,' she said. It came out as a whine instead of an explanation.

John sighed. 'I know that. What do you want to do, May? Go home early?'

He had unintentionally wrong-footed her, turning her into the saboteur of other people's pleasure when she had only wanted reassurance. It seemed always to happen this way between them. When he offered his concern it made her feel awkward. She retreated in guilty embarrassment. And when she asked for it he couldn't interpret the question.

May shook her head violently, bumping his jaw. 'No. It's okay. I don't mind staying.'

'Is there something going on between you and Ivy?'

'Nuh-uh.'

She had blocked off the channels already and had

no idea how to clear them. They both sat still, locked by the failure of communication.

'Just feeling blue?'

'I guess.'

At least he was holding her. But as soon as the thought came she was uncomfortable with the weight of his arms, the thump of his heartbeat against her ear. Her flesh shivered. The physical solidity of him was an invasion.

There was a tap on the door-frame. Leonie was standing there wearing a plaid shirt and hiking boots. She said uncertainly, 'I was wondering about that walk. But we can easily do it another day.'

John lifted his hand an inch from May's head and as soon as he did so May leapt to her feet and backed away, hump-shouldered and frowning.

'May, how about coming with us?' John asked.

'No, thanks.'

They made an attempt to persuade her, then John went to put on his boots and Leonie tried to talk to May. May managed to answer every question with a monosyllable, but this victory gave her no satisfaction. At length John and Leonie went out together and May was left to drift out on to the porch, to watch their figures disappear northwards across the headland.

Ivy came up through the garden from the beach. 'Hi. What is there to eat?'

'How should I know?'

Ivy ignored her and busied herself with hauling food out of the refrigerator. 'I'm starved. D'you want something?'

144

May could see that Ivy was wearing her marijuana face. Her eyes were pink and heavy-lidded, and she had a stupid, muzzy smile. She had been smoking with Lucas; it made her obliging and affectionate instead of the way she usually was. And it made her hungry, too.

Why did John never notice what was so plain? May felt angrier still with his lack of perception. 'What have you been doing?' she asked her sister sharply.

Ivy's shapeless smile widened. 'None of your business, kid.'

'You've been smoking weed.'

Ivy turned her silky, sun-tanned back. 'Grow up,' she drawled.

The coastline above Pittsharbor and Moon Island Beach became a ragged fringe of wooded promontories and narrow green inlets lined with sloping ledges of granite. By staying close to the tideline it was possible to walk or scramble the two miles to a rocky causeway linking Berry Island to the mainland.

Leonie knew the route well and most of the owners of the summer cottages that stood back from the water in their secluded clearings. She liked walking and often came this way alone, but John turned out to be a good companion. He didn't press too close on her heels where the path was narrow and on the strips of shingle beach he moved unobtrusively alongside her. He seemed content not to talk very much. They found a rhythm of step and breath, and stuck to it.

The causeway itself was a narrow spine of rocks from which the tide dropped to expose shoulders of

145

sand and stone. It was low water when they crossed over, and they walked easily between lacings of driftwood and sea wrack and the occasional battered reminder of a lobster float. The soft, still afternoon had faded into an early evening the colour of smoke and the only sound apart from the chafing of the sea was the regular spoon-in-sugar crunch of their boots on the shingle.

Berry Island hung at the end of the rock chain like the dot of an exclamation point. There were no trees on it, only a scrub of blueberry and wild raspberry bushes, rocks and rough marsh grass, and the occasional painterly splash of a turks-cap lily. A path led over its mild convex hump to a tiny shelf of sand uncovered by the receding tide.

When they came to this ghost of a beach they sat down by unspoken agreement on the sand, from where they could look back at Moon Island and the needle spire of Pittsharbor Unitarian Church beyond. Leonie held out her hand and revealed a little heap of raspberries glimmering in their own juice. They took and ate one each, in turn, until they were all gone. The eastern horizon slowly turned the colour of pewter, ready to draw up the darkness.

'They're biting,' Leonie said, pinching a mosquito off her wrist. 'No-see-'ums, the Indians called them.' She took a bottle of insect repellant out of her pocket and anointed her face and hands with it before passing it to John. He tipped it and went through the same motions, his gestures exactly mirroring hers. When he handed back the little bottle their fingers touched.

146

Leonie held herself still. There was a tranquillity about the place and the evening that were at the opposite end of the scale from the way she had felt in the town car-park. She feared the betrayal of some inappropriate gesture or movement, from herself as much as from John.

He was sitting with his knees drawn up, one hand clasped on the other wrist, gazing across to the bay. *It's like I'm setting both of us a test*, she thought. *Dare to come to my good place and see if we don't spoil it.*

She had been disconcerted by John's casual suggestion to May that she might come along too. But now it came to her that it might have been a good idea. Dreamily, lulled by the repetition of the waves, she imagined how May might even have liked it. They might have talked quietly, about ordinary things. 'It can't be easy for you,' she said, speaking her thoughts without preamble. John did not seem surprised, as if they had all the time been thinking in parallel.

'No. It isn't easy,' he agreed. 'For Ivy and May, or for me.'

'What happened to your wife?'

'It was a cerebral haemorrhage. She was dead within minutes. She was at a friend's apartment, I wasn't there. She had had a headache, that was all.'

Leonie stared ahead of her at the gulls strutting on a rib of rock that jutted out of the sea. When the space grew too crowded one of them would lift away and slide through the air to another vantage point.

She was imagining the impact of this sudden death. The magnitude of it and the details that must have gone with it. Telephone calls, news to be broken, a funeral, children to be guarded. In an unregarded hollow within herself she felt sympathy expanding, the pressure of it tightening against her chest wall. 'I'm sorry,' she said, a sudden breathlessness making her inarticulate.

John ducked his head. 'She didn't deserve it.'

Leonie wondered why he should use those words.

He went on, looking out to Moon Island and the houses of Pittsharbor, 'Al was a vivid person. She lived at double the pace of everyone else, at twice the intensity. If she disapproved of something she fought it, if she loved something she would defend it to the end, right or wrong.'

A picture began to form in Leonie's head. A woman, not just a shadow of a dead wife and mother. Her fleshed-out presence lent different nuances to the way John sat here on the beach, how their arms didn't touch, and they both gazed ahead at the birds and the darkening horizon instead of looking at each other. 'How did Ivy and May deal with losing her?'

'Differently. Ivy grew up too quickly. May was sometimes angry, sometimes withdrawn. You've seen something of how she can be.'

'Yes,' Leonie said. Truthfully, she did not think John's daughters seemed much different from any of the other children she knew of their age. But she understood nothing about being a parent. It would be presumptuous, she thought, to offer an opinion.

'Sometimes I catch myself saying to her, *Alison, I'm sorry. I've screwed up with our children.* Then I'm surprised at having said her name way inside myself. I guess the truth is I don't miss her that much, not any more. I did, but she's so conclusively *gone*.'

'I think I understand that,' Leonie said. To be gone didn't necessarily mean death. There were other with-drawals and disconnections that were no less final.

'And other times I think that the two of them might still have grown into the angry, pained women they seem to be now, even if their mother had been around.'

'Perhaps. Or perhaps their anger and pain just seem more pronounced to you, because they allow you to see it. Even expect you to deal with it for them. Which means they have faith in you.'

'I don't know.' The words broke out of him. 'I don't know anything. I thought I did, when they were younger. Then, after Alison died everything seemed to break up and and get washed away. I shouldn't have brought them here this summer. Neither of them really wanted to come and I thought it would be good for us all.'

'You don't know for sure that it isn't. And it is only a vacation.'

Leonie heard rather than saw that he was suddenly smiling. 'You could be right. And if we hadn't come, you and I wouldn't have met.'

She considered this. The acknowledgement that their meeting was significant was important to her, but all the time she was aware of taking steps that she couldn't retrace. *Nor do I want to retrace any steps*, she thought. *I don't want to go backwards, to anywhere I already know.*

She nodded her head and let her chin rest on her knees. The day's heat was beginning to drain out of the air. They sat in silence for a while, listening to the sea fretting at the shingle, comfortable with the beach and the sky, and with one another's company. They had come to the good place and nothing had happened to discolour it.

In the end it was only the thought of the rocky causeway and the rising tide that made them turn back again. Leonie led the way across the top of the island, familiar with the twists of the path even in the fading light. When they reached the last headland and the secluded crescent of Moon Island Beach they stood for a moment to look at the five houses. Their roofs and gables were black and strong against the navy-blue sky.

Neither John nor Leonie said anything more before they reached the Captain's House and bade one another good-night, but she knew they had come an extra distance together. As she went up the steps to the Beams' house she felt happy and calm, as she had not done for a long time.

Six

Elizabeth laid a tray with a lace cloth and three bone china cups and saucers, and set a silver cream jug beside them with a beaded net over the rim. She was folding napkins, in case her guests chose to eat fragile lemon cookies, when she heard the knock at the door.

Marian and Hannah were standing together on the porch. They looked so incongruous side by side that Elizabeth had to tuck in the corners of her mouth to conceal a smile. Marian was eye-opening in a full-skirted scarlet sun-dress, which showed the top of her freckled cleavage, and her hanks of hair were tied up with a red bandanna. Silver hoops the size of handcuffs swung in her ears

Hannah wore brown and a long-sleeved woollen cardigan that denied the heat of the day. She inclined her little round head towards the pots of marigolds and cineraria splashing over the step. 'The garden looks fair, Elizabeth,' she murmured.

'Thank you. Turner Hanscom does well enough, if he's watched.'

Marian was exclaiming that she and Hannah had

151

met out in the road and they were both ready for business. Elizabeth led the way through the cool house to the evening room. When she brought in the coffee tray Marian was sitting back in one of the armchairs with her skirt making a creased pool of colour around her. She nodded at the cut flowers in the vases and an embroidery frame standing close to the hearth.

'Always makes me feel I ought to be on my best behaviour, your house, Elizabeth.'

Elizabeth glanced at the other woman's big bare feet. Marian had been wearing flipflops, but she had kicked them off. 'Is that so, Marian?'

She handed the coffee cups that had been her mother's and her grandmother's before that. They were gold-rimmed with a pattern of blue flowers, and the touch of them and their fragility always gave her satisfaction, even today.

It was time to finalise their arrangements for Pittsharbor Day. The twenty-first of August was only a short time away.

The date was said to be the birthday of Benjamin Pitt, who had arrived at the coast from southern Maine in 1770 with a group of settlers in search of grazing land. There were still Pitts living in the vicinity, but the commemoration of their ancestor had been a date in the local summer calendar for little more than twenty years. It was true that the festival was regarded as something to please the tourists rather than the townspeople themselves, but the summer visitors liked it and it raised some funds for the town, so every year there were fun runs and craft stalls, exhibitions of local

152

artwork in the library and Main Street galleries, and a Fish Fry on the town landing. Bunting was zigzagged across the street and a softball tournament was held on the green alongside the church.

Marian Beam was a great enthusiast for the day. It had become a tradition in the last few years for the houses on the bluff to run a wild blueberry bake stall. Marian had suggested the idea originally and the others had fallen in with her, because baking and selling was in the end easier than playing softball or taking a part in one of Amy Purrit's Pittsharbor Musical Revues. Marian contributed her energy, her army of family helpers and tubs of wild blueberries bought from one of the farmers on the town road. Elizabeth lent her name and her mother's recipes, and did some of the baking, but it was Hannah who did the bulk of the work. She was the best cook out of the three of them, although Jennifer Bennison had been a good assistant.

Marian took out a pen and began writing in a notebook. 'I don't suppose we can count on the Duhane girls for too much.'

Her pen stopped. The room went so quiet that the sea sounded like the steady pulse of blood in the chambers of their ears. Doone Bennison had drowned on 22 August last year. Elizabeth remembered the bunting flags hanging motionless from their strings as the police vehicle drove her body away from the town landing. Only an hour before, Jennifer Bennison had telephoned her to ask if she had happened to see her daughter sailing out of the bay. Jennifer said she must

153

have taken her boat out early, while everyone was still asleep.

'Don't worry,' Elizabeth had reassured her pointlessly. But still, she had been unable to settle to any of the tasks that were waiting for her. She had walked into town, telling herself she would collect the plates and dishes she had lent out for the bake stall. And she had been standing outside the town house as the news had run up Main Street like a freak wave.

When she heard that the child had drowned she had to grope for the nearby fence to hold herself upright. Her head turned towards Moon Island, although she couldn't see even the harbour water from where she was standing. What had Doone seen or done? She was an awkward child with an air of melancholy about her and Elizabeth had not known her well. But now she was possessed by certainty that there was a link between Doone and the old story; one which seemingly renewed itself, generation on generation. Elizabeth's stomach had churned with a mess of shock and guilt, as though she might have saved Doone if she had tried, as if the drowning was her fault.

Then Leonie Beam had come white-faced towards her. 'They've gone to the house to tell Jennifer and Sam.'

The two women had put their arms around one another, Elizabeth wordlessly grateful that Leonie was there.

'We should speak to Marty Stiegel again.' The silence was broken by Marian, of course. She scribbled another line and Elizabeth reached out to her coffee pot, lifted it with an effort and refilled Hannah's cup. This annual enforced contact was always difficult. Marian was a vulgarian and Hannah a provincial mouse, but a silently critical one, always appearing to judge and find wanting. Yet, Elizabeth reminded herself in her mother's voice, the job had to be done, whether she enjoyed it or not, because she had undertaken it.

The previous year, Marty had brought along a gas barbecue and had made wild blueberry pancakes for all comers. It had been the success of the stall.

'I'm sure he'll help out again,' Hannah judged.

'They do have the baby this year.'

'Marian, it's only a couple of hours we're asking for,' Elizabeth said.

They wouldn't show their dislike too plainly, any of the three of them. It was muffled about with coffee and china cups and decorous arrangements for the bake stall. Elizabeth looked at Hannah's pursed mouth and sharp eyes half veiled with pink lids, and thought of the years they had known each other, since they were both young women, all the years that had been pressed into shadowy negative images by no one admitting to their real feelings. Owning to nothing had kept Elizabeth away from Pittsharbor and the beloved bay, and the spellbound heart of the island itself, for the whole of her married life.

Impatience with lists of ingredients and estimations of plates and forks needed, and calculations of charges and change crawled down her spine. It was an imposition to be old and look back on an unfulfilled life. Her memories bore a patina like clouded pewter, without colours or depth. Elizabeth wished she were young again and tasting the luxury of choice, with a passion that made her fingers tremble around the shell of her bone-china cup. And as she gazed downwards she was reproached by the sight of her own hands, age-blotched as they were and roped with sinews.

'Do you agree, Elizabeth?'

It was Marian demanding and she hadn't heard the question.

Marian was a bully. Elizabeth felt sorry for her children and their partners, and the grandchildren, driven into acquiescence by an overbearing old woman. Or was it better to be dominating in just the way that Marian was, rather than an accumulation of shadows, a prim negative, like herself? 'I didn't hear what you said.' And she added with a certain satisfaction, 'I'm afraid I wasn't listening.'

Marian's tongue clicked. She repeated the question, which was to do with limiting the order of blueberry pancakes to one per customer because last year the line had wound all around the stall and caused a crowd, and in the thick of it some of the kids had pinched muffins off the dish at the front.

'I don't believe it matters a dab.' Elizabeth sighed at the end of it.

It was a phrase Aaron used. She couldn't have given a proper reason for why she had come out with it now. Hannah's expression was inscrutable. Her ankles were set together and her hands rested in her lap; she looked as if she was drawing herself in and away from the other two, and from the polished order of Elizabeth's drawing-room.

Marian pursed her lips and drew a line in her notebook.

Under her direction they agreed next on who would make pies and who muffins, where the cold-boxes would come from and how many quarts of cream to order, as they did every year. At last the agenda was covered. Marian said, 'I'll have Karyn and Leonie help out, and I'll ask Gail and those Duhane girls if they'll do some of the marketing and washing up. They'll like to be part of the day.'

If Hannah and I had ever liked each other, Elizabeth reflected, we could join forces now and set Marian Beam exactly where she belongs. But the years had gone by and even the pain of long ago had been blunted and tempered by time. All that was left was the dilute sparring that took place over coffee and town celebrations, and the triviality of it made a mockery of what had been powerful enough to divide them in the first place.

It was more than fifty years since Elizabeth had last seen the woman on the island. But the memory of her was still sharp in her mind.

Marian was talking unstoppably as the three of them came out on to the seaward side of Elizabeth's porch. Hannah had announced that since the tide was low she would walk back along the beach and Marian agreed that she would do the same.

Elizabeth escorted her guests through the garden to

the head of her beach steps, where they met Marty Stiegel climbing towards them. There was a little camera slung on a strap around his neck. He gave them his sociable smile and pushed his hair back with two hands, smoothing his temples. 'I heard there was a summit meeting. I've come to offer my services again.'

Elizabeth said, 'That's very good of you, Marty. I should have telephoned to tell you we were going to talk about the bake stall this morning.'

'Marty, you're a jewel. Are you certain Judith and Justine can spare you for the afternoon?'

'Sure thing, Marian. It's good that we summer complaints can give something back to the town.'

Hannah offered him a nod and made to move past at the top of the steps, but he blocked the way with a sun-tanned arm. 'Let me take a picture, ladies.' Without waiting for their answer he lifted the camera and snapped off a couple of shots.

Elizabeth could already see the photograph in her mind's eye. The three of them ranged in a line, Marian's floridness and Hannah's unwinking, suspicious gaze, with herself in the middle, caught, so insubstantial as to be almost permeable to light.

'That'll be ten bucks,' Marian laughed. She was waving to grandchildren on the beach. She kissed Marty flirtatiously on the cheek and swung her red skirts down the steps to the shingle.

After Marty had gone there was a moment when Hannah and Elizabeth stood on their own. Elizabeth could have counted almost on one hand the number of

158

times they had been alone in the past fifty years. 'How is Aaron?'

'Not as strong as he was,' Hannah said. 'But still himself.' She thanked Elizabeth formally for her hospitality and descended the steps, straight-backed, without putting her hand on the guard rail. Down on the beach she seemed to melt into the background of the bay, like one of the birds she resembled.

The island lay in its skeins of water and rock. If it were not for the boats and holidaymakers in the foreground, the wide view was the same as it had been when Elizabeth was a girl. *How have we grown so old,* she wondered. *How have we grown so that so little matters any more?* She turned her back on the beach and the bay, and bent to tear the dead heads off her flowers.

It was a hot day. Corn-weather, as Aaron and Hannah might have called it. The sea was a restless plate of ripples and the beach stones and sand were baked dry by the sun. At the southern end of the beach there were clusters of sunbathers on spread towels, lying between their encampments of picnic baskets, sand toys and rubber inflatables. Children ran into the waves, kicking up arcs of spray. The families from the five houses were out too. John Duhane was walking the low-water line with a panama hat pushed down on his head. Ivy lounged in her bikini, using Lucas's bent knees as a backrest. Beam children and friends leapt and shouted on either side of a volleyball net, and Judith Stiegel sat reading in a low chair with Justine in a basket beneath a parasol. A shadow fell across

Judith's book and she looked up at Marty. The camera was at his eye again and she grinned into the lens, a lazy, barefaced smile that made him lower it without clicking the shutter. He bent over and kissed her instead, his hand cupping the rounded mass of her naked shoulder. Her skin was warm and slick with sun cream.

'Where've you been?' she asked him.

'Visiting the three witches.'

'Mart. Pancakes?'

'Hole in one. Justine had her feed? Can I get you something? Otherwise I thought I might play volleyball with the kids for half an hour.'

She nodded her agreement, made complacent by the sun and his deference to her.

Leonie was sitting twenty yards away with Tom at her side. He didn't often sit on the beach doing nothing, but he had already done his run to Pittsharbor and back, and there wasn't enough wind for sailing. She watched Marty saunter over to the volleyball and saw Judith settle again to her book. The busy details of the beach, the specks of colour against the sea and sky, and the air's relentless clarity made her feel as if she were in a Victorian picture. One of the minor English pre-Raphaelites perhaps, painstakingly observed but lacking in emotion. It was not a comfortable feeling. She longed to make something happen, some undisciplined smear of brilliance in the centre of the canvas, and at the same time she dreaded the impulse.

Tom folded the *Wall Street Journal* vertically into

160

three. Leonie realised her arms were wrapped so tightly around her knees that the muscles of her shoulders were burning. She dropped her hands and kneaded fistfuls of warm dry sand instead. 'I've hardly seen you this vacation,' she said.

He looked up for a second, not quite audibly sighing. 'You know how it is in the restaurants. This summer more than ever.'

'Tom, are you seeing someone else?' The question came out of nowhere. Once it was spilt it was like a drop of acid, smoking, then burning a hole in the sheet of their tolerance.

'No.'

She saw that it was the truth. Or at least near enough to the truth to allow his face to blaze with indignation. 'Are you?' he countered.

Leonie shook her head. It was the same. Technically innocent, but the smooth surface of honesty was so undermined with the burrowings of despair and dissatisfaction that it must soon collapse.

'That's okay, then.'

He was going to turn back to his paper, but she wouldn't let him. Not now there was a blur right in the middle of the day's pretty canvas. 'Do you feel like a walk?' Leonie suggested.

He considered. 'I'll come with you.'

Not *I'd like to*, she noticed. But doing her a favour.

They skirted the edge of the water, walking with a space of solid air between them. Leonie wondered if John Duhane had turned to watch from under the brim of his panama hat. The dull weight of unhappiness made her hunch her shoulders with self-dislike. There was no reason for this misery, she thought. Or only the old reason that couldn't be discussed any longer and therefore apparently did not exist. The fact that she couldn't be happy with all she had was turning her life rancid. And Tom's, too; the blight was not limited to herself.

They were following the route of the walk she had taken with John. Leonie didn't want to retrace those comfortable steps in ugly silence. When they had rounded the first headland they came to a narrow inlet lined with rock and pungent with steaming rockweed. At the head was a gritty tongue of sand choked with the grey skeletons of dead trees. She sat down suddenly on the sand. With one hand she gathered some stones and pitched them one by one into the slapping water. Tom hovered behind her for a moment, then sat down a few feet away.

When they had first known each other, their earliest summer together, Tom and Leonie had sometimes taken a walk this way to escape from the rest of the family. Once or twice they had slipped deeper into the spruce wood and found a bed of moss to lie on. They had clung to one another, laughing and whispering like conspirators.

Leonie frowned now, trying to recall exactly how love had felt. A state of greedy inclusion.

She looked sideways at Tom. His face was set in the expression she was too familiar with – unyielding, with the corners of his mouth drawing sharp lines down his cheeks. Sadness and sympathy for him suddenly took hold of her and on an impulse she reached out and put her hand on his arm. He didn't acknowledge her touch. 'Do you remember we used to make love in the woods?' she asked.

'I remember you saying you felt overheard in our bedroom.'

It was true, but it pricked her that he chose to make it a criticism.

Marian had not put them in Tom's old childhood bedroom. She had told them that his was too shabby, too cramped to be shared with Leonie, but the new room was also much closer to hers. As if it were as near as she could get to insinuating herself between them.

'Anyway. It was lovely up here,' Leonie said lamely, drawing back her hand. She had wanted to be Tom's wife, but she had ended up in unequal partnership with his mother and his siblings and his businesses.

Tom didn't answer. He was staring at the sea.

A wave of anger broke and washed over the swell of Leonie's sympathy. Her husband was mean-spirited and neglectful. If there was guilt it was his, not hers.

So far, she thought with a little shudder of black excitement. *So far*. 'What are we going to do?' She made it clear that she wasn't asking about tennis versus sailing.

Tom still didn't look at her. *Why*? she wanted to shout at him. *Just because I can't grow us a baby, do you have to cut me off altogether?*

After a long interval, he answered, 'Nothing.'

She thought she knew him well, but even so she was shocked by the extent of his withdrawal. Then, just as

163

she had understood over a plate of cherries in Sandy's Bar that she and Tom didn't love each other any more, another huge truth dawned on her.

Tom wouldn't initiate any split between them. He wouldn't be the cause of it, or even a collaborator. He would not demonise himself in the eyes of his family by dismembering even such a rudimentary and unblessed union as his with Leonie. She would have to be the villain.

The simplicity of it caused her to nod her head, even though her eyes burned.

He wouldn't even fight properly with her now. They had escaped from the beach to the seclusion of the woods, not for sex any more, but they couldn't even take the opportunity to yell at each other. A longing for a real war swelled in her throat, a vicious one that would rip their separate protective layers and expose the flesh, after which there could be a truce and maybe a reconciliation. 'Nothing?' She began to shout: 'Jesus, Tom, what are you? It's like living with some fucking rock formation. Don't you care what happens to us?'

His face was turned away from her.

Slowly, Leonie wiped her mouth with the back of her hand. 'Speak. Say something.'

He did look at her then. Articulating slowly, pushing out the words between his teeth, he said, 'You can't have a baby. You're not the only woman in the world to suffer it. Grow up, Leonie. Get on with your life.'

'I don't think it's just about babies any more,' she whispered. *Get on with my life. Is that really what he wants?*

164

When there was no response she tried, 'Can't we talk about adoption?'

'We have talked about it. I don't want to adopt.'

It was true. Through sleepless nights and dry-mouthed car journeys, and dinners that turned into a wasteland of crumbed table-cloths they had followed the same thread. Now they had wound their way into the heart of the labyrinth only to find there was no heart. There was only a blank wall and nowhere to go beyond it.

The desire for a fight had gone out of her. She was left with little except an aversion to the stink of rock-weed and the boneyard of dead trees. A fisherman in his lobster boat puttered across the middle distance, turning a furrow of white water as he rounded in on his floats. 'Okay,' she said flatly. As an ending it couldn't have been less of a whisper. 'I think I'll walk back now.'

Leonie stood up, straightening her back because sitting hunched over had put a crease in it. Above her she saw a woman steadily climbing the slope away from the shore. Her pale-coloured clothing showed like a shaft of light between the dark verticals of the spruce trunks. It was uncomfortable to think that she might have overheard them. 'There's someone up there. It must be one of the Kellys.' She remembered the name of the people who owned the isolated cottage set up on a ridge above the inlet.

Tom didn't look. 'No, the Kellys never come up here in August. They think it's too crowded.'

'They must have let the place, then.' The woman had moved out of sight now.

'If they have, it's the first time in living memory,' Tom said coldly, as if it was a matter of importance.

Leonie bent her head. After a minute she scrambled away from him up the ledges of rock and began the walk back to the beach.

There came a day not so long after the *Dolphin* crossed the Line when Captain Gunnell ordered the boats down. The look-out had sung out at the sighting of a pair of good whales, a cow and a calf, about a mile to leeward of the ship. It was a bright day with a good sea running and the oarsmen soon brought the boats to the spot where the cow had sounded.

Matthias Plant gave the order to his men to rest easy. At the prow the boat steerer was ready with his harpoon and all was silent as they waited upon the whale.

Of a sudden there came a great boiling of the water to the stern of the boat as she blew, and it seemed but a second after that her great head reared up and Matthias's boat was caught dead in her eye. Her jaws were open wide but Heggy Burris the boat steerer did not delay an instant in hurling the iron true to the flank, where it lodged fast. Some blood ran from the wound but the beast seemed not to feel it, for all her attention was fixed on the fate of her calf.

Another boat had got the calf fast and it thrashed pathetically enough in the swell, its head dipping beneath the water as its life faded and a great wash of its blood darkened the sea.

The sight launched the mother whale into a transport. Her back arched into a mountain standing proud of the water between the boats and the dying calf. Then Burris was forward with his second iron, thrown as true as the first and the lines made a great run as her flukes went up and beat the water into a torrent of spray, which left the men blinded for an instant.

Matthias shouted, 'Forward, forward all!'

The line begin to whip out of the tubs and the experienced hands knew for sure she was going away, an ugly whale that might lead them the dance of all their lives.

Then there was a scream that would sound in every man's dreams until his dying day, as the line fouled and a loop of it caught around the body of Martin the bowman as he bent over his oar.

In an instant he was snatched overboard, gone after her as the whale dived, and his companions were left in the boat staring like stone men at the smoking line about the loggerhead, until William Corder tremblingly cooled it with water from his bailing bucket as Mr Plant had reminded him to do a dozen times.

The whale plunged many fathoms, taking the bowman down with her and boat careening in their wake.

Heggy Burris began shouting like the devil, with his lance at the ready, 'Pull one, pull all, for here she comes again' and they readied themselves to haul on the line as their only chance of seeing Martin again. William bent to the frantic work like the others, giving the sum of his meagre strength to the task.

The whale broke the water not one hundred feet away and every man gave his all to bring the boat round to take her head and head.

It was this turn of direction that slackened the line for a brief moment, so releasing Martin from his terrible noose. He rolled up, to surface like a log and Matthias roared the order to row to his rescue. The men did not need to be told twice. Even as the craft flew across the width of water the whale went flukes up again and for all the two harpoons lodged deep in her side she was going at an even greater rate than before. The line flew out once more but there was yet enough in the tubs to allow them to reach Martin where he floated and to haul him over the stern and into the boat.

It was a terrible sight.

The line had bitten through coat, shirt and flesh alike, and was near to having cut the poor man clean in two. As it was, his chest was hacked open as if with a butcher's knife and the rib-bones laid bare. A mess of blood bubbled and welled out – it seemed to William's horrified eyes more than a man's veins could hold – and ran into the bottom of the boat to crimson all their feet. The poor fellow gave a cough and his eyelids fluttered, and Heggy Burris cried out, 'Dear God, he lives.'

But even as the words were spoken Martin's mouth opened and a groan and a great spout of blackened blood and sea-water spilled out of him together, and he lay still. He lived no longer.

William Corder watched all of this with staring eyes and the back of his hand pressed up to his mouth.

168

'Hold hard,' Matthias bellowed at him. There were other matters to attend to if they were not all to end up in the same way as Martin the bowman. The whale was still running away from them and they were fast being drawn from the other boats in the wake of this leviathan. The boat steerer was calling for the drags to slow her rush, and Matthias saw to it that William and the other two men worked the line regardless of the grim cargo they bore with them.

The whale flew on like an arrow and at such a speed that the water rose up in a wall on either side of the boat. The tubs would soon be empty of line and there was no other boat within reach to bend on with her own lines and help save them, and the fine whale.

William Corder cooled the flying line with water from his bucket, but his face had no more colour than the dead man's.

At length Matthias had the bitter choice between giving the order to cut the line and thus surrendering whale, whaleline and two harpoons, as well as his bowman, or to risk being dragged under, and losing the boat itself and the lives of five more men. He gave the command, the lines were cut and, freed of her tormentor at last, the vessel wallowed in the swell like a porpoise.

The *Dolphin* rode three miles off to their stern. It was a bitter hard row back to her, with Martin lying cut almost in half at their feet. The sight of William Corder's face touched some chord of pity buried deep in Matthias Plant's hardened heart and to hide it the mate let out a great bluster of rage. He cursed the boy

169

squarely for his softness, so that William bowed his head over his oar to conceal the shock and grief that racked him.

The men carried the body of their companion back on board the *Dolphin* and that night it was William Corder who sewed him into his sailcloth shroud. The last stitch was made through his nose, in the whalemen's way, to be sure that the man was truly dead. Yet no man could have lived an hour with wounds like Martin the bowman's. Before his body was given back to the sea William Corder tenderly kissed the cloth over the man's face. Matthias Plant was the only one of the men who witnessed this last tribute, and that because he was secretly watching the boy and wondering what had led such a tender-hearted creature into the cruel chase for whales.

Captain Gunnell read out the funeral service and the corpse was slipped over the side. William turned away from the rail as soon as the water closed over it and silently sought his bunk down in the forecastle.

May was sick of reading, sick of her bedroom, of every mute piece of furniture and spider crack in the walls, and when she left it and went outside she felt like a snail winkled out of its shell to perish in the heat. The beach was a place of glaring light and intrusive happy voices, and the house was full of shadows that frightened her because they were impenetrable. She crept restlessly from one place to the next, never finding a refuge in which to be comfortable.

The three books lay on the bedroom shelf. She didn't bother to replace Doone's diary in its hiding-place any longer. It refused to give up its secrets to her, so she retaliated by leaving it in the open. *Voyages of the Dolphin* was significant because it had been in Doone's possession, but she couldn't fathom what it meant or why it mattered. What she had read of it was gruesome or boring, in equal parts

The other book Hannah Fennymore had lent her, *In the Country of the Pointed Firs*, she had read in a couple of sittings. It was quite short and easier than the whaling book. There was a lot about picking wild herbs and going visiting, but two stories from it stuck in her mind even though she tried not to think about them.

One was about the grave of a young woman who had cut herself off from the world because of some secret sin, and had lived the rest of her life and died alone on one of the bay islands. The image of the deserted place and the grassed hump of ground in the corner of a field was too vivid in May's mind. One of the characters said of it, 'A growin' bush makes the best gravestone. I expect that wormwood always stood for somebody's solemn monument.' May had no idea what wormwood might be, but it spoke eerily of worms and coffin wood.

The other story was to do with a woman, quite an old woman herself, rowing out to visit her mother on some remote island. As soon as the boat drew near enough to be seen the ancient mother was at her cottage door, her handkerchief a white speck fluttering in the distance. The daughter smilingly said to her companion, 'There, you never get over bein' a child long's you have a mother to go to.'

The words had made May buckle with grief. Even when she thought about them now and about never having a mother to go to, her mouth stretched and saliva flooded her tongue.

She hadn't got past being a child, and now she was stopped dead, stuck in some midway place where nothing seemed to be within control nor ever to change. No talking to a tree, even one that reminded her of Alison, was going to help her. May was afraid and the worst of it was that she was frightened of herself, because she didn't understand what was happening to her.

She left the books again and walked out of the house. From the land side of the porch she could see across the gardens to a corner window at the rear of Elizabeth's house. Suddenly she remembered that she had told Elizabeth about the woman on the island and Elizabeth had responded with some embarrassing question about love, before telling a long story about sneaking out to meet some guy here in the Captain's House.

Listening to anything would be better than going round in circles alone.

'Hi,' May said, when Elizabeth opened her door. 'I, um, I thought I'd just, kind of, come by. Is it okay?'

Elizabeth thought how sad the child looked. Her chin and bottom lip jutted out, ready for a rejection, but her eyes were imploring. 'Come on in.'

The girl followed Elizabeth through the house. In the evening room she marched to the window and stared out at the garden. 'What's wormwood?' she asked abruptly.

'It's a plant. Artemisia is the botanical name. Why?'

'Does it grow on graves?'

'I don't know. I suppose it could do, but I've never heard of it. Look, there's a bush outside.'

It was a silvery white mound, dotted with yellow flowers. Just a garden plant, nothing more. May studied it in silence; then, without turning to look at Elizabeth, she said in a low voice, 'I want to know about the woman I saw on the island. I can't forget the way she looked at me. You know something about her, don't you?'

'Yes,' Elizabeth said. The softness of her voice made May shiver. 'I saw her fifty years ago.'

'But . . .'

'I can tell you the story, if you like.'

May did turn pleading eyes on her now. 'Do you have to make it a story? I'd kind of like to know about things for real.'

'How do we know what's real, May? Anyhow, I don't know any other way. I was told it as a story myself, by my grandmother, Elizabeth Page Freshett.'

May understood that she wasn't going to get any matter-of-fact explanations. This old woman with her milky eyes looking back into the past, and her forbears and their murky, staring portraits, were all a part of this place, wound up tight with it and she was delivering herself up just by being in the house with them. Daring a glance around the room she saw that everything in it was old, and looked as if it had sat in the same place for ever, regulated by the ticking of the clock and the crawl of sunlight across polished wood. The door of the room was shut tight. She thought the old woman might see her shiver. 'Go on, then,' she ordered in a loud voice.

'I told you how I fell in love,' Elizabeth began. She wasn't looking at May any longer, but away to one side, at a little army of photographs in silver frames, drawn up on the lid of the piano. 'I was unhappy because I couldn't marry him. I wanted to, and I should have gone ahead and done it, but I was a coward.

'I was going away to Europe for a year. I didn't often go out on the water, but I wanted to get to Moon Island and look back at the beach and the houses to get a picture in my mind, one that I could carry with me, do you understand?'

'I took my father's little rowboat. It was a misty day, not a regular fog but one of those light, silvery mists that lie in wreaths over the water. I drew the boat up and sat down on a rock. I don't think I can remember feeling such desolation before or since.'

There had been a seductive shimmer to the sea. The implacability of the water's fall and rise was soothing and Elizabeth watched until she felt she had become a part of it. Slowly, she had stood up and drifted to the water's edge. The bluff and her father's house looked a long way off, and the pain of her indecision receded too.

174

Dreamily she'd thought, *I could lie down in the water and let it carry me away.*

Her shoes were already wet, and her ankles.

Then the certainty that she was being watched had made her turn away from the hypnotic rolling of the waves.

A woman was standing at the edge of the trees. She had a pale oval face and her eyes were sunk deep in her head. Her hair was pulled cruelly back, so her skin seemed stretched over the bones. She was wearing wide trousers, which covered her feet, and a pale-coloured coarse shirt that hid the lines of her body. She was a stranger, Elizabeth knew she must be because she had never seen her before in seventeen summers, but she seemed to belong absolutely to the place. She had held up her hand and beckoned, and Elizabeth had begun to walk up the slope of shingle towards her, glancing back over her shoulder to the distant windows of her father's house and the dark Captain's House next to it.

When she'd looked up again the woman had gone. Elizabeth reached the spot where she had been standing and searched between the trees, even calling out *are you there?* but there was only the sound of her own voice, the sea-birds and the waves. Her feet and legs were soaking and the cold had made her shiver.

'That was her. That was the woman I saw,' May cried. Then she stopped short and chewed at the corner of her mouth as she took a reckoning. 'But I don't believe it. It was *fifty* years ago?'

175

Elizabeth understood that to May it was an aeon of time. She nodded her head.

May sneered bravely, 'So you're saying this woman is, like, a *ghost*, right? Like *The X-Files* or something?' Only she couldn't disguise the flash of fear in her eyes.

'The Passamaquoddy Indians believed that the island was haunted, or possessed. It was one of their sacred places. Then, in the nineteenth century the whalemen had a small settlement on the seaward side, just a few rough huts for shelter and a tavern. The only building here on the bluff in those days was yours. The Captain's House.'

'Yeah?' May shrugged. But she knew she was caught. She didn't want to be, she wished she could unlearn what she had already seen and discovered. But Doone and the white-faced woman were much too close to her now; she didn't know who would step which way, whether they would slip into her ordinary world or whether she would mistakenly break through a membrane and become part of theirs. The boundaries of normality were dissolving, fearfully, as if they were no more solid than a morning's fog. She wished with all her heart for them to be in place again.

Elizabeth Newton was waiting. Her chair was placed with its back to the light, so May couldn't see her face properly. She was afraid of Elizabeth, too, and of the other spectres of old age and resignation. She wanted to jump out of her tapestry armchair with its feet like claws and run out of the house, but she didn't move.

Instead, she sat still, listening to the clock ticking. 'What did you do after you saw the woman?'

176

'I asked my mother first of all. She was a very rational person, May. She believed in everyone and everything having their proper places in the world. If anyone had lived on the island after the whalers were gone she would have known about it. And she didn't know, therefore no such person existed.'

'And so you went to your grandmother, right? What was her name?'

'Elizabeth Page Freshett. I was named for her.'

'Yeah.'

'Come into the dining-room with me. I'll show you her picture.'

Reluctantly, May followed the old woman into the next room. The dining-room was a gloomy place with high-backed chairs ranged down a long table in expectation of guests who would never arrive.

'I think I told you that her husband was Senator Freshett, my paternal grandfather. That's his portrait above the sideboard.'

He was a frowning man with side-whiskers and a high collar. May glanced at him and looked away. There was a photograph of Elizabeth's son done up in academic dress on the sideboard. May reflected on how pleased with himself he seemed and the thought cheered her a little. Elizabeth held out another picture in an oval gilt frame.

The grandmother had a mass of dark hair arranged to crown her head with a miniature turret, a patient expression and a high-necked lace-throated white blouse. May nodded as politely as she could and handed her back.

'My grandfather bought this parcel of land when they were first married in the 1880s. He wanted her to have a summer cottage. She had a tendency to weakness in the chest and the sea air was believed to be good for her.'

May could imagine the dark-haired woman sitting propped up on some Victorian sofa, mournfully coughing. Boredom and impatience with Elizabeth's ancestors snagged with her deeper-seated anxiety. She found it difficult to breathe, and her skin crawled and itched so that she clawed at one forearm with blunt nails. Suddenly she thought of Lucas, flip-haired and sun-tanned, and how dismissive he would be of all this musty stuff. And of her childish fears and superstitions. She knew that she was childish, and May so much wanted to be adult, and with him and part of him, that she had to stop herself from groaning in despair.

Elizabeth was telling her about her grandparents building their cottage, and how old Mr Swayne had bought alongside and built the extravagant place with all its gables and gingerbread woodwork, and the widow's walk at the crown. '*Long* before Marian Beam's day,' she said.

May asked, 'When did Mr Fennymore build his house?'

Elizabeth's hand touched her throat. 'Oh, he put it up, let's see, it wasn't until just after the war. He went into the building business. His family were fishing people, always had been, but Aaron was different.'

Once she thought of it, May was surprised it hadn't occurred to her before. 'It was *him*, wasn't it?'

178

'What?'

'It was Mr Fennymore. The boy you fell in love with. And he was only a fisherman and your mother and father wouldn't let you marry him because your grandfather was a senator? So you went off to Europe and married Mr Newton, and the Fennymores married each other and he built his own house up here. Just kind of to show you that he could? Is that what he did?'

Elizabeth's mouth went white and she put her grandmother's picture back on the sideboard next to Spencer's.

'Sorry. It's none of my business,' May offered. She was trying not to remember what the old woman had told her at the Flying Fish, about sneaking off to the Captain's House and lying in the goose feathers having sex. With old Mr Fennymore. The thought of it disgusted her. It seemed that sex was all around her, oozing and creeping, contaminating what was supposed to be clean. Leonie Beam making eyes at her father. Ivy and Lucas in their hollow on the island. And another image: a shadowy room, lit by a single shaded lamp. Two people on a sofa, naked legs wound together, and a noise, the same sound, two voices. May squeezed her eyes shut, then forced them open again.

'Yes, it was,' Elizabeth said abruptly. 'It was long ago. It doesn't matter any more.'

Her voice and the sight of her face helped May to overcome her distaste. She took her arm and steered her to one of the straight-backed chairs. 'Can I get you something? Some, um, water or anything?'

179

'No, thank you. I'm quite all right. No one knows any of this, May. Do you understand?'

I don't want to know it either, May thought. *Why is it me, why should I have to?* 'Did Doone?'

Elizabeth looked startled. 'No. Of course not.'

That was something. It wasn't Doone who had fed the knowledge into her mind. She sat down at the table opposite Elizabeth, as if they were about to eat dinner together. 'I've forgotten it already,' May said. Alison had told her once that it was the right thing to say if you knew something that somebody would rather you didn't know.

'Thank you. You are a very nice and thoughtful young woman, May.'

'I wish that was true.'

Elizabeth only smiled. 'Do you want me to tell you about the Captain?'

'Um. Well, all right. Yeah, go on then.'

'The Captain was a whaleman. He was from Maine, not very far from here, and he went down to New Bedford to sign on a ship in the fleet there. He was brave and lucky, and in time he came to command his own ship. His wife, who was then his widow and an old woman, told my grandmother all this when she first came to live on the bluff.'

Seven

'You remember, May, I told you the Captain's was the first house here on the bluff. Then my grandfather bought a parcel of land next to it and built a summer cottage for his wife, and old Mr Swayne built what's now the Beams' place.'

It was a relief for Elizabeth to talk about land and history rather than to recall the other details of those long-ago summers. The girl had startled her by making such a shrewd guess, that was all, and it was unlucky that her own reaction to it had been so unguarded.

Her guess could be forgotten again, May had said so, yet Elizabeth had the sense that the ground was shivering beneath them both, that some seismic disturbance would expose what had been buried and believed to be obliterated. It was May's vulnerable age and the blindness of pain written in her face, and the crows' wings of secrets that even Elizabeth couldn't guess at that had set the tremors off. She was afraid that they wouldn't subside into stillness again. Carefully, deliberately therefore, she concentrated for this moment on what it was safe to remember.

Elizabeth could hear her grandmother's soft voice as clearly as if she were in the room instead of May. The old lady had loved to talk about the early days of her marriage, of the novelty of leaving Boston behind and travelling east to the coast to play at house in the cottage above the seashore. The blue and gold tea service had belonged to those times, and most of the heavy furniture that still filled the rooms, and the beginnings of the flower garden surrounding the house.

Even late in life the Senator's wife had been a dreamy, other-worldly creature, made almost ethereal by long years of invalidism and cosseting by her husband and servants. She had told the story relayed to her by the Captain's widow in languorous detail and the very words she used had stayed in Elizabeth's mind. They murmured and whispered around the image of the island woman. White, scraped face. *The poor, sad creature*. Eyes set deep in the staring bone. *A tragedy, and quite a mystery*.

Long ago when she was a young wife and mother, the Captain's wife had been sitting beside the window of the solid house her husband had built for her. It was within sight and sound of the sea that had made his fortune, but at the same time it turned its shoulder a little aside as if to emphasise that its hold on him had slackened now. It was a stormy evening, the last of the light just fading. The waves boiled and coalesced, and burst themselves on the shingle with furious energy. The young wife was musing on the desolation of the

182

world beyond the windows and on the comfort within, where the stove glowed and her husband was whistling softly as he bent to some task. Their new baby lay asleep on her lap. She dropped her eyes from the window to look at the rosy little features. Then she looked up again.

She saw a face staring in at her, so close that the features seemed almost flattened against the glass. The hollow eyes were wide and staring, and the mouth stretched open in a silent howl. The wet hair, a woman's long hair, stuck to the apparition's forehead and cheeks like coiled black snakes.

The Captain's wife screamed and swept the baby close to her heart. Her husband came running and looked where she pointed, but the face had already vanished. He ran out into the storm, leaving the door banging in the wind, but although he searched until the rain had soaked him to the skin there was no one to be found. He came back into the lamplight and tried to reassure his wife, telling her that what she had seen was only a trick of the light or a spectre conjured out of her own imagination. At last he was able to persuade her to follow him up the stairs to the safety of their bed and to lay the baby in her crib at the foot of it.

The storm wore itself out by the next morning. A day of stillness passed, then another and the Captain's wife began to believe that the face framed by the snakes of hair had after all been imaginary, just as her husband insisted.

On the third day, a fisherman was passing close by

the seaward side of the island. He noticed an unusual concentration of sea-birds lifting and circling around a point on the hillside above the shore, and growing more curious as he watched them he turned his boat and took it in to land. He made fast and climbed the slope to where the whalers' old stone tavern and refuge looked out to sea. In those days the cabin was already deserted and falling into disrepair because the few ships that still passed now made for Pittsharbor itself. The fisherman glanced in under the stone lintel, then walked out again into the sunlight. A cloud of birds rose with noisy cries from the trees behind the cabin and wheeled into the sky above his head. The man climbed slowly to see what it was that had drawn them in such numbers.

A woman's body hung from a branch of one of the trees. It slowly revolved on its rope, as if the buffeting of the wings and beaks had set it turning on itself.

When the poor body was cut down and the pockets searched for clues to the woman's identity, a piece of folded paper was found with the Captain's name scribbled on it. The words written beneath his name read, *I could not find it within myself to take the life of an infant's father. I take my own life in its place and I bequeath you the legacy of remembering what you have done. Sarah.*

Sarah was not a local woman and the enquiries that were made never revealed where she had come from nor why she had chosen to make such a sad end of herself. The Captain himself always steadfastly denied prior knowledge of her, or any of the details relating to her life and death. He had been, he said, to many strange places in his time and had seen many peculiar things that did not lend themselves to ordinary explanation. He was content to let mysteries lie. To his wife he insisted, 'She was some poor, deranged woman in the grip of a sad fixation which cannot now be explained. A decent burial is the best farewell we can give the poor soul.'

Sarah was buried on the island. Her lonely grave was within sight and sound of the sea and some of the fishermen's wives, who guessed at a history they would never know for sure, made it their duty to tend it. They planted herbs, which flourished in the broken ground, and at the beginning there were often fresh-cut flowers placed in a glass jar at the grave's head. But there was no name or stone to mark the place, and over the years the mullein and catnip ran wild around it and the low grassy hump sank back into the hillside once again. The suicide's grave was slowly forgotten, except when the Captain's old widow recalled the history of it for her new neighbour.

Elizabeth Page Freshett had listened to the widow's story with a shiver that made her want to forget what she had heard. She was waiting for the birth of her first child, and the image of a face staring in from the darkness at a mother and baby in the lamplight cruelly embedded itself in her imagination. There were often times after her son was born when she looked at the blank window glass as darkness fell and hurried to draw the curtains across it. But she never saw anything except a reflection of herself and the comfortable room behind her.

185

Her granddaughter was a different woman. The young Elizabeth was neither dreamy nor delicate and she was not especially susceptible to fears or morbid imaginings. But then she had fallen in love, and after the first delight the helplessness of her state seemed to peel her flesh raw and to leave her at the mercy of fierce influences that were not explicable by the steady rules that had governed her all her life.

And in this naked, elated and despairing condition she had seen the woman on the island.

She described her features and appearance to her grandmother, and the old woman lay back on her sofa and pleated her cashmere shawl between her ringed fingers. 'There were stories, some of the fishermen's wives used to whisper about a haunting. They always said in my young days that she only showed herself to other women. To young women in trouble, as a warning and a reminder.' The diamonds flashed as the fingers suddenly stopped their fidgeting with the soft shawl. 'Elizabeth, are you in trouble?'

'No. Of course not.' She knew that much, at least. Aaron wouldn't let that happen to her. Elizabeth kept her face and her voice as bright as she could, not knowing that all she achieved was a pain-filled parody of happiness which the old woman chose to ignore. 'I'm going to Europe, aren't I? I'm going to see all the sights and have experiences I will remember for the rest of my life.'

'Yes, my dear, you are and you will,' the Senator's widow had said.

*

Aaron and Elizabeth lay in their nest in the deserted Captain's House. In the house next door Elizabeth's steamer trunks were packed and her ticket for the *Carpathia* lay waiting for her. It was the last hour they would be able to steal together.

Elizabeth's head rested on her lover's chest. She could hear the steady pounding of his heart and when she moved her fingers she traced the outline of his mouth and the curve of his nose, knowing his features by touch as intimately as she knew her own. She was watching the window above their heads and the infinite gradations of pollen-yellow light that filtered through the salty glass.

'I knew there was a suicide's grave,' Aaron said.

His voice resonated within the arch of his rib-cage and Elizabeth moved her head a fraction, to press her ear closer to the sound. It was like hearing two voices, the inner and the outer. 'I saw her, standing there in the trees. I know it was Sarah and that she was watching me.'

Aaron would not deny what she had said. He lay in silence, sceptical and separate from her, listening to the contradiction of their joined breathing.

Elizabeth suddenly felt the tears running from the corners of her eyes.

'I'll come back,' she whispered. 'In a year I'll come back to you.'

'Is that it?' May demanded. She was rubbing the mosquito bites on her bare ankles where the raw patches wept like tiny red eyes. The room, the house

187

and Elizabeth's murmuring voice made her shudder with claustrophobia. Why had the passage in the book about the grave seemed to jump out at her, when there was just such a real grave, if it wasn't that Doone had read it before her? Angrily she pushed the thought out of her mind. She could stay real, if she concentrated hard enough. 'You're saying, like, this is a woman's ghost, which only appears to women and I'm in some kind of trouble so she's warning me just the same as she warned you when you were young?' She shook her head, not waiting for Elizabeth's answer, and gave a dismissive bark of laughter. The echo of it seemed to hang in the room.

'You asked me to tell you the history,' Elizabeth neutrally reminded her.

May jerked her head, gathering her forces, her mouth set in a hard line. Doone and her obsession, and Elizabeth and all the faded, musty business of regret and old age, and her own half-recollections and the spindrift of unease that rose from the island itself were like a gas threatening to choke her. She needed to jump away from the swirling cloud of it into fresh air. All she wanted was to be like Ivy, who was thin and impervious and desirable. 'It sounds like total garbage to me,' she snapped. Then, seeing the displeasure in Elizabeth's eyes, she had to redeem herself by saying something that was clever but still distancing: 'I mean, there's history and there's hysteria, isn't there?'

There was a moment's quiet. 'You may be right,' Elizabeth said softly.

188

May stood up and said that she would have to be getting back home.

The good weather still held. May walked through the stones and spikes of the Bennisons' Japanese garden to the top of the beach steps. The view unrolled beneath her, shimmering in the heat-haze, as if it had been set up by a director who wasn't afraid of using all the clichés to convey the perfection of a summer's day on the beach.

Ivy and the Beams were playing one of their endless games of volleyball. Her legs glimmered like smooth toffee as she leaped and punched, and Lucas's hair fanned around his face as he dived in response. His back was exactly the same colour as Ivy's legs. Out on the backdrop of water the handkerchief sails tacked thin wakes behind them.

Marian sat with her baby grandchildren crawling around her and three of her daughters-in-law within ordering distance. Richard Beam slept in a canvas chair with his hat tilted over his face and Marty Stiegel wandered at the lacy edge of the waves. He wore a camera and the baby in a sling across his chest.

Leonie lay back in another low chair not far from Richard. In the midst of the contented families she felt that she was no more than a brittle composition of long bones. John had unobtrusively drawn closer to her chair. He sat on a sweatshirt spread on the sand, his ankles crossed and the fingers of one hand circling the wrist of the other. He was looking out to sea, apparently watching Karyn and Elliot trying to catch

189

some wind in their dinghy sails. He wasn't an ally, Leonie was thinking, not as she had first imagined he would be, before the kiss in the car-park. Almost without their acknowledgement the issue between them had become bigger than that, and darker because it carried the threat that everything might change because of it.

Before she encountered John Duhane, before this vacation, Leonie had gone on with her life day by day. She had done her job because she enjoyed it and found a refuge in it, and she had been Tom's wife. The unhappy aspects of their relationship had been forced like a flower under glass by her failure to conceive, but the seeds had been there all along, and she had dutifully watered and tended the plant of their marriage because that was what she expected of herself. She hadn't looked beyond what she possessed except to long for a baby – a yearning that had soaked up all the desires she had and more.

But in the way that everything can change, irrevocably and absolutely without warning, Leonie knew that her life had taken a different direction now. She didn't want to drag the bulk of her unhappiness about with her any longer. The weight had become intolerable. If she had the choice simply to drop it and take a new direction – yes, that was the choice she wanted to make. It would have to be her choice. Tom would not do anything to ease the tension between the two of them; the more she thought about it the more certain she became that he would never make himself the villain. And John was inhibited by a debt of honour owed equally to his daughters and to her own married state; she didn't think he would make the first move, although he hovered close enough to it.

Uncertainty made time stretch and distort, like a long road shimmering in a heat-haze. These beach days of sunshine and waiting, and Marian's autocracy, seemed to dwindle into infinity behind and ahead of Leonie. She moved her bare feet in the sand, an impatient flurry of movement which made John turn his head and look at her. 'It's too hot out here, don't you think?' she said to him, the words dropping into a vacuum in which the waves and the gulls and the children's voices were suddenly silenced. 'Shall we go inside out of the sun?'

He unlinked his hands and stood up, as easy as if nothing significant were happening. They saw that May was walking in the thin strip of shadow at the foot of the beach wall, but as soon as she noticed they were watching her she veered sharply and arrived at the edge of the volleyball game.

'Come up and have a cold drink in my house,' John said.

They walked away from Marian and the encampment of baby toys and strollers. Leonie felt the eyes of her mother-in-law following her, but for once there was no call asking her to bring Sidonie's parasol or some bottled water when she came back down again. The shingle was cool underfoot, then the wooden steps burned her with their splintery heat. She hopped too fast and almost overbalanced, and John steadied her with one hand.

191

'Sorry. Should have some shoes on.'

They crossed the garden and climbed the shallow steps to the porch. Shade fell across Leonie's burning face like a blessing. John held open the door for her and she passed into the shadowy room. The dimness and the wintry smell of woodsmoke was momentarily confusing, and she looked around to regain her bearings. A Walkman and a scatter of tapes lay on the table, amid a litter of dirty plates and glasses. Sneakers and a baseball cap and a Coke bottle decorated the steep stairs.

John opened the old-fashioned refrigerator and took out ice and mineral water. He filled a glass and gave it to her, and Leonie drank and rolled the beaded coldness between her sweaty hands. It was the first time they had been alone together since their walk to Berry Island. 'I'm sorry,' she said again.

'Why do you keep saying that?'

'I suppose I'm just used to it.'

'That sounds like the answer of a weaker person than I think you are.'

He took her by the arms and while he was holding her looked carefully into her face. Instead of saying anything she waited, letting him discern whatever there was to see. 'What do you want?' he asked.

She knew what she wanted now, this minute, and the recognition made her skin burn. Beyond that she had no idea how to sort the longings into a sequence she could give voice to.

He slid his hands to her shoulders and drew her against him. There was still time, Leonie thought

192

wildly. Everything that had happened between them up to now – talk, lunch, kiss, walk – could be lightly dismissed or explained away. She could give a little regretful laugh or a rueful shrug, and step away from John Duhane and back into the dissemblance of her life. *I don't want to. I don't want to step back.* It was impossible for everything to go on being exactly the same. Whatever she did, it would have to mean change beginning at this moment.

Even as she hesitated Leonie was reflecting on damage, and how the instrument of her infidelity would almost certainly smash the last struts of her marriage and the remnants of Tom's affection for her – if there were any. There was John's life to consider also, and his daughters', and the complications that would be visited on all of them. But if there was no stepping back, all she could hope to do was walk forward. The thought was like a reprieve and it made a beat of happiness shiver through her. John saw the change in her eyes and bent his head as she lifted hers.

When they kissed the tape of guilt and self-admonition stopped running. It was natural to do what they were doing and the urgency of it amazed them both. Leonie gave herself up to him and he took the offering with pleasure. It was a long time before they moved apart again and even then he kept hold of her, as if he was afraid that otherwise he might lose her.

He was looking for words and at last he said, 'I've wanted to do that almost ever since I met you. But I don't want to cause pain, or do damage. I've experienced enough of that.'

193

His echoing of her feelings was so precise that she laughed in sudden surprise and touched his cheek with her fingers. *What scarred veterans we both are*, she thought. 'I knew you did, and I know what you don't want because I don't want exactly the same things. But neither do I want to turn my back –' she paused, reversing her palms upwards to reveal their emptiness '– on whatever chance we might have. Am I allowed to acknowledge that? Or is it misplaced?'

'No,' he said gently. 'Not misplaced as far as I am concerned. But I am free to say that because I'm not married or in any way attached. Except to my children, that is.'

Leonie nodded. 'There are some things I should tell you. I'd like to tell you, before anything else happens between us. If anything else is going to happen, of course.'

'Would a proper drink be a help?'

'Yes, it would.'

He found a bottle and poured whiskey for both of them. Leonie sat down on one of the battered chesterfields and let her head fall back luxuriously against the cushions. The bright sunlight squared behind the old windows made the whiskey taste dramatic and nocturnal. She blinked back the tears the first gulp brought to her eyes. 'The failure between Tom and me began a long time ago. Began and took its course. It's complete now. It was nothing to do with you, then or now, except that on the day we had lunch at Sandy's Bar I looked down at my plate and it dawned on me that Tom and I didn't love each other any more. And once I knew it I couldn't get rid of the knowledge.'

'I understand that.'

'I did that clumsy thing of kissing you in the car-park. It was in a kind of reckless *glee*, because of what I had just realised and because I knew that at least there would be a difference now, instead of the same old painful monotony.'

'And there was I thinking you kissed me because you wanted to kiss me.'

Leonie took another happy swallow of the whiskey. The rawness of it in her throat was fiercely pleasurable. She thought she could easily get drunk, letting all her locked-up feelings run sloppily loose, then climb into bed with John Duhane and never get up again. 'Oh, I did want to. And I wanted to give Spencer Newton something to think about, of course.'

'Of course.'

He wasn't touching her now. He was simply sitting beside her and listening, and the wholeness of his attention made her understand how isolated she had been. She basked in the comfort of his notice, resting her cheek against the glass she had just emptied. 'I think I'm an intimacy junkie.'

The idea was tangential enough to make her wonder if she was already drunk, but John didn't miss a beat. 'Yes, maybe we both are. And we're afraid of our addiction, so we shy away from what we long for.'

He was at least as lonely as she was, Leonie understood. She remembered what John had told her about Suzanne and the other stillborn relationships that had followed Alison's death. It wasn't just May and Ivy, then, who had pinched the bud before it flowered, but something in John himself. And what did that mean about him and Alison? 'Tell me about her,' she asked and waited, suddenly aware of the shadows in the room that remained out of reach of the sunlight, and the insistent murmur of the sea.

'Al was very . . . vivid. I told you. She could swing between euphoria and despair within a day, sometimes it seemed like within an hour. And she never saw anything wrong with that, she thought it was how life should be lived. She never made compromises about what she wanted or what she believed in. I always loved her, from the time we first met.'

'And she loved you.'

He took it as a question. 'Yes, in her way.'

'Were you faithful to each other.'

'I was.'

On the beach May pushed herself into the volleyball game. The bright sunlight made her frown but Kevin Beam sidestepped to allow her some space and she flashed him what she thought might be an Ivy smile. If she could penetrate this circle, she thought, and join up with the younger Beam brothers and their dumb games and be near Lucas, then she could get free of Doone. If she hung out with the other kids and smoked weed and giggled like Gail and Ivy and the others, then everything would be ordinary again. There would be no island woman and no grave overgrown with wild herbs and nothing to be afraid of.

The ball boomed over her head to the opposite side

of the net and Lucas swung his crossed wrists to connect sweetly with it. The ball soared again as a star-shaped image of brown limbs and torso and a face blurred with hair printed itself behind May's eyes. She planted her feet apart and bent from the hips, waiting for the ball as she had seen Ivy do, but she was too late and her eyes were still dazzled as it came out of nowhere and hit her on the shoulder.

'Hey, Maysy, that's some cool play. We want you on our team for Pittsharbor Day.'

She knew that Kevin and Joel were smirking behind her back. She twirled round to face them and forced another smile. 'Sure. You can count on me.'

'Thanks, man.'

'May!' Lucas was calling her. He punched the ball in her direction and as if she were pulled towards him on a thread May's head lifted in response and her back straightened. She jumped and her arms stretched out to meet the swelling black dot.

The blue air seemed to shimmer around her and gravity lost its hold as her feet left the ground. She knew she couldn't fail and sure enough her shoulder drove her fist through an immaculate arc and her knuckles connected with a jolt of pain that was also a stab of pleasure. The ball skimmed back over the net and Ivy missed it altogether.

'Yeah!' Lucas smiled and swept the hair back from his forehead. Ivy and Gail applauded, even though it was a half-ironic slow handclap.

In the unaccustomed perfection of the instant May was thin and strong, and confident of her powers. She

197

leapt once more in pure exultation and Marty Stiegel caught her in his camera lens. 'Good one,' he told her casually and lowered the camera again. He adjusted the sling tied to his chest and cupped his free hand protectively around the baby Justine's sun-bonneted head before he strolled on again.

'Five two,' Lucas called. He jerked a thumbs-up at May and she felt such a pinch of love for him that it crimped her chest and threatened to stop her breath. She bent double, pretending that it was the play that had winded her. After the game the players streamed down to the water's edge. Lucas and the other boys dived like seals under the glittering swell, while Ivy and Gail and Richard's daughters shrieked and danced in the shallows. Droplets of water starred their arms and shoulders with diamonds. May was sweaty and still scarlet from her moment of glory, but she was too self- conscious to wear her swimsuit. She hovered in her shorts and T-shirt until Joel sneaked behind her, planted his hands at the small of her back and propelled her into the water. She stumbled forward and lost her balance. A wave broke and she fell, hearing the shouts and laughter.

The water was icy. She gasped and a flood filled her mouth and nose. She came up coughing and blinded, humiliated by water that was not much more than knee-deep.

The next wave washed another body up beside her. Lucas jumped out of the surf and grabbed her wrists, then dipped and rolled his shoulders to hoist her on to his back. Only staggering a little under the burden he stood upright and lunged for the deeper water.

His back was slick and cold. May's mouth collided with his neck and she tasted salt and – with a shock of amazement – the unique flavour of his skin. He was gasping with laughter and still wading, drunkenly now because she was slipping from his grasp, and before it was too late she pressed a blind and desperate kiss against his shoulder.

Lucas tottered and they fell together. Even under the weight of water May thought she could hear his laughter, but when she surfaced again he was watching out for her. 'Swim,' he ordered, and obediently she rolled on her back and kicked towards the island. Immediately the world receded and there was nothing but the sun on her closed eyelids, and the fingers of the tide combing her hair, and the turbulence of Lucas swimming alongside her. Happiness made her buoyant. She forgot that she had been afraid of the rolling currents and the island with its dark spine of trees, even the omnipresent dark shadow of Doone.

They swam for fifty yards, then Lucas stopped and trod water. 'You okay?'

She nodded, speechless, wishing she could offer him something other than her awkwardness in return for the gift of his attention. In the end she just smiled at him. Lucas looked at her for perhaps half a second longer than he had ever done before.

Ivy was waiting on the beach. The double band of her silvery bikini gleamed as she half turned, hands resting on her hips and all her weight balanced on one leg.

'Time to head back,' Lucas said. He ducked under the water and when he surfaced he struck out with a powerful crawl. May paddled after him towards the beach. When she waded out he was already standing with Ivy, their heads close together as she rubbed his hair with her towel. 'Don't get cold, May,' Lucas called. 'Go put some dry clothes on.'

May's ears filled up with extraneous sound again. She heard the surf and the complaints of gulls, as well as Ivy's laughter. But she did exactly as Lucas told her. She picked up a dark-blue towel and swathed herself in it, before plodding up the shingle towards the beach steps and the Captain's House.

The light in the room had dimmed as the sun travelled westwards. It was the colour of dust now and the shadows in the corners were touched with violet. Leonie and John had talked for a long time, exchanging their histories in a conversation that seemed to her to have been more intimate than sex. They touched each other's hands and explored the contours of one another's faces, but it wasn't until the day receded and left them in the dusk that they stopped talking.

The whiskey bottle was half empty, but Leonie had never felt more clear-headed. 'It's getting dark,' she whispered.

'Not quite yet.'

The cushions of the chesterfield smelled of mildew and smoke. The timbers of the house seemed to shiver as Leonie and John wrapped themselves together.

There was a long, blind interval while they kissed again.

Then Leonie opened her eyes.

There was a face at the window, muffled to the throat in a dark wrap, looking in at them. The eyes were staring with horror in the white mask and the wet hair lay in ropes plastered to the skull.

May had no idea how long she stood frozen to the porch boards. In truth it was probably no more than two or three seconds. But she knew that the tableau of her father and Leonie Beam with their arms and legs entwined and their mouths greedily fastened together was already indelible. She would never be able to make it go away.

It bred another image out of itself.

Once again the other picture came swimming up out of a dark place. The pairs of legs and arms seemed to writhe and multiply, clothed and naked, and the intent unseeing faces fed on one another until they blurred and became one, and turned into everyone she knew and everything she feared.

May drew back her fist, just as she had prepared herself to punch the volleyball, with the same ecstasy of determination. But now she drove her arm straight through the window glass. There was a smash and a scream – she never knew whether it was hers or not – and a white-hot wire of pain ran up her arm and straight down to her heart.

The floor, the rugs and the mildewed cushions were splashed with blood. Leonie knelt in front of her with an armful of towels and over her shoulder May glimpsed the shocked crescent of her father's face.

'It's okay, it's okay,' Leonie was murmuring over and over. The towels were bloody too, but there wasn't as much of it as she had feared. 'John, bring me a bowl of water, some cottonwool, anything.'

May's fist was clenched and the curled fingers were mired with blood. Leonie swabbed at the lacerated knuckles and May bit the inside of her cheeks to stop herself moaning aloud.

'Look, see, you're okay. Open your fingers. Show me, May, please let me help.'

John came with a bowl of warm water and offered it up. Leonie rinsed out a cloth and swabbed the cuts clean. Gently she prised the curled fingers loose. The veined wrist was miraculously unscathed, the palm was sticky with blood but uncut. Leonie bowed her head with silent relief.

'May, do you know what you just did? Do you know what you could have done, severed an artery?' John's voice was loud and Leonie could hear the raw vibration of horror in it. He gasped for breath and the loss of control told Leonie more clearly than all their hours of talk how deeply he cared for his daughters. 'You could have bled to death.'

'John . . .' She tried to calm him but May sat upright.

'I don't care. I wouldn't care if I did die. Like Doone Bennison.'

John made a movement that was so quick and violent Leonie thought he was going to hit the child. Instead he enveloped her head in his big hands and

202

pulled her face against his chest. He tried to rock her, murmuring, 'No, no.'

Slowly Leonie stood up. She wanted to leave them alone and to spare herself from seeing this. But May snatched at her wrist with her undamaged hand. 'Stay,' she commanded.

She was so angry with her father for what she had just seen that she wouldn't be alone with him, even if it had to be Leonie who was the buffer between them.

Leonie hesitated and saw John unwillingly nod. 'I'll dress those fingers,' she said.

There was a first aid box in one of the cupboards. She fetched it, checked the lacerations for splinters of glass and swathed May's hand in bandages. May sat silent, uncomplaining. At the same time John swept up the broken glass and wrapped the jagged fragments in newspaper. He found a piece of a cardboard carton and cut it to fit over the hole in the window, then taped it securely in place.

At last May sat nursing her bandaged fist in her lap. Leonie made a cup of tea and gave it to her, and the child obediently drank it. Then she put the empty cup aside and stared through the window with its disfiguring patch of card at the velvety sky beyond. There was a bruised quiet.

John sat down on the chesterfield at May's side. 'Do you think we should talk about this? About what you saw happening between Leonie and me?'

May turned her head stiffly. She darted a look at Leonie, not her father. 'Not now. I don't want to.'

'Why did you try to hurt yourself?'

203

'I don't know. I just did it.'

Leonie sensed that it was the truth. Also that there were too many other things that May did not know or understand.

'You won't do it again,' John said.

'No,' May answered quietly. After a moment she added, 'I think I'll go upstairs now.'

They waited until they heard the door of her bedroom close and the faint creak of footsteps subside overhead.

John dropped his head into his hands. 'Jesus.'

'Yes.'

'I'm sorry she had to see what she did. But doesn't she have to learn to accept sooner or later that there's a world beyond her immediate wishes and concerns?'

'Yes. But I don't know how that happens.'

They sat in silence after that, occupied with their separate fears.

May felt calm, as if breaking the glass and shattering the image behind it had been a catharsis. She walked the thirteen steps across her room and back again, then touched the tips of her fingers to the door, checking that it was firmly closed. She turned again and saw the three books innocently lying in their place on the shelf.

Without thinking she picked one up and awkwardly flipped the pages with her bandaged hand. It was the whaling book and she looked with indifference at the heavy old-fashioned type until she noticed some pages near the end that were marked with pencil. Words were faintly underlined, not consecutive words, nor did they make any sense when she read them in order, but still some faint association nagged in her mind. She frowned at the brown-edged pages, then at the pencil marks themselves because they seemed to contain some familiarity that maddeningly swam just beneath the surface of her consciousness. She riffled through the pages in the opposite direction and found nothing. She was about to discard the book again when frustration made the connection for her.

She had flipped the pages of Doone's diary in this way and felt just the same baffled impatience with a secret she couldn't unlock. The skin at the back of May's neck suddenly prickled with cold.

She placed the whaling book open and face up on the top shelf, and picked up the red-and-black diary. Some of Doone's last entries, the coded ones scribbled with such heat that the groups of numbers were gouged into the underlying pages, were written in pencil. The same soft, blunt pencil.

May stared at the trios and pairs of numbers. She realised that her mouth was open and her breath snicked audibly in her chest. Eagerness fought with an impulse to throw the books aside and never look at them again. With exaggerated care she smoothed both sets of pages, glancing from one to the other.

Then she remembered the birthday present. It had been a gift from an English relative of Alison's when Ivy turned thirteen. The great-aunt hadn't seen Ivy or May for a long time and the present was much too young for Ivy, whose interests had long ago switched from toys to nail polish and sleep-over pyjamas. May had inherited the book. She remembered the laminated white board covers and bold title lettering quite clearly. It was *Great Games, Puzzles and Quizzes for Kids*. One of the pages was headed 'Secrets to Share: a simple book code'.

May licked her dry lips. That was what it was, of course, Doone's secret code. Simple, once you knew which book she had chosen. The trios of numbers were page, line and word. Where there were only pairs of numbers she had found the word she wanted on the same page.

May chose a group of numbers at random. Her bandaged fingers and the way her hand shook made it hard to turn the pages of the Dolphin book. The first set of three numbers – page, line and word, she murmured to herself as she laboriously counted them off – yielded *I*. The second gave her *followed* and the third, which she knew would be proof that her guess was right, was *him*.

I followed him.

Breathlessly she took the next chunk of numbers and slowly counted out their placings too. She was staring at it so intently that the book's sullen typeface began to blur in front of her eyes. It took her several minutes to decode Doone's words but at last she had *He turned around and saw me*.

She glanced up briefly at the bare room. There was the rug covering the burn mark in the haircord carpet, the faint outlines on the walls where Doone's posters had been taped, the French bed.

Now, May thought. *Now I'll know.*

206

Eight

By nine o'clock in the morning on Pittsharbor Day preparations in Main Street and on the green beside the church were in full swing. Flags and bunting strung between the Wigwam craft gallery and Sandy's Restaurant stirred in a gentle breeze off the sea. Main Street was closed to traffic for the day and store-keepers were laying out displays of goods on the sidewalk in front of their windows. The Wigwam's owner made a pyramid of native American baskets and arranged an armful of dried flowers on the top.

'Going to be a good one,' Alton Purrit remarked to Edie Clark in the Sunday Street Bakery.

'I don't know as it makes much odds,' Edie said with a touch of sourness. The home-bake stalls on the green took away more business than the day's extra visitors ever brought in.

'Well, there's no harm in getting the town talked about by the rest of the county,' Alton chuckled. The *Jenny Any* would be full all day long taking visitors on twelve-dollar trips around the bay and islands.

'Talk never cost anything, of course.' Edie had to

have the last word. She bundled his bread into a brown bag and folded the mouth with a sharp crease before handing it over. When Alton took it without a word she was afraid she might have been unfriendly and to make amends she nodded towards two people passing beyond the bakery window. 'Nice to see Aaron out and about.'

He was leaning heavily on Hannah's arm. They shuffled slowly down the sidewalk towards Main Street and the harbour.

'Mhm. He don't look too bright, though,' Alton said. 'Morning, Edie.' He tucked his bag inside his year-round windbreaker and headed out into the street.

Aaron stopped for breath on the corner of Sunday and Main. Glancing at his face, Hannah steered him to a bench in the shade in front of Howard's Hardware. They sat in silence for a minute between two pyramids of saucepans and shiny galvanised buckets, while Aaron sucked the mild air into his lungs. 'Just look at it,' he rasped, when he could speak again.

Hannah surveyed the flags and flowers and tables of goods for sale. 'It's only a day, what harm can it do? The visitors like it and so do the children.'

When she turned her head again she was pained to see that the seams in Aaron's cheeks were glistening with tears. She knew him perfectly, from so many years of watching and accepting his ways. It wasn't just the catchpenny street decorations, or the traders' determination to do as much selling as possible in the invented name of Pittsharbor Day that had made him

208

weep. They were only the outward signs of changes he could do nothing to prevent. Aaron was crying for a time and a place that he had lost, and for chances that would never offer themselves to him again.

Hannah understood too that he would despise his own grieving, because he would interpret it as weakness. She inclined her head so as to seem not to notice his tears. Her knee-bones stood out tiny and sharp under the folds of her skirt. Then she took Aaron's arm through hers. The back of his hand when she touched it felt as brittle as a dead leaf. 'Have you got your puffer?' she asked.

Aaron used an inhaler to help his exhausted lungs. 'Not using it out here,' he reprimanded her. There was a blue tinge to the skin around his lips and the rest of his face was stone grey.

A pair of dead leaves was exactly what they were, Hannah thought, still clinging to the branch while the fat spring buds pushed out all around them. Pittsharbor was putting out new foliage in gaudy colours and they hung on at the tip of their twig, waiting for the brutal wind to dispatch them. How cruel old age turns out to be, she reflected, and a twist of sympathy for Aaron that was all wound up with love and exasperation pulled at her heart. She felt a distaste suddenly equalling his for the new Pittsharbor with its gaudy decorations and artistic shops and hand-painted signs set out to catch the summer visitors' jaded attention.

The town that she and Aaron had grown up in had been a harsh but logical place. It was governed by the winter ice and short summer's heat, and by fishing and making do against the weather, and the other plain rules of survival. It had been the same way since the first houses were built around the harbour. There had been no pizza and subs, or quilt shops lining Main Street, or summer visitors in their rental cottages. Except for the Freshetts to begin with and the other families who had followed them out to the bluff. It didn't occur to Hannah that she might also let herself grieve for a way of life that was finished. She sat and held on to Aaron's arm instead, gazing expressionlessly ahead of her.

A red jeep swung down Sunday Street and braked noisily in front of the bakery. A young man in bermudas and sneakers leapt out and ran into the store, leaving music tinnily thumping from the jeep's speakers. Hannah knew him by sight. He came every year to stay at one of the cottages in the woods behind the bluff. The land had once belonged to Aaron, from a parcel he had bought for next to nothing right after the war. In time he had sold it again, using the money from the sale to extend and weatherproof the house where he and Hannah now lived. Over the years a series of boxy houses had been put up in clearings in the woods and the occupants' name-boards lined the access track that had once led only to a loggers' clearing. The young man sprinted out again and tossed a brown bag into the passenger seat. He reversed up to the top of the road and accelerated away.

As the din faded Hannah was thinking about Elizabeth Newton. If she had come home from Europe

210

and agreed to marry Aaron, against the Freshetts' wishes, would he be a happier man now? It seemed cruellest of all that there was no way of telling. The different paths their lives might have taken were as conclusively lost as the old Pittsharbor their possibilities had once inhabited.

'I'm ready to walk back now,' Aaron said.

Hannah had left the station-wagon at the other end of Sunday Street, not far from the church. Aaron had insisted that he wanted to walk down the town first thing to see what inanities were going on and that, of course, was what they had done.

They stood up and moved to where the sharp sun sliced across the sidewalk. With the warmth of it on his back Aaron put Hannah's arm aside. They walked slowly past Edie Clark's windows. 'Leave them all to it,' he said.

'That's right,' Hannah agreed.

Spencer saw the station-wagon with Aaron and Hannah inside as it turned into the Fennymores' entry from the road behind the five houses. He murmured to Alexander, 'I'll call on him now. I guess it's as good a time as any.'

He waited for a few minutes, then sauntered after the car. Hannah was coming down the steps from the porch. 'Good-morning, Mrs Fennymore. How are you?'

Spencer Newton had impeccable, slightly old-fashioned manners that went with his preppy clothes and air of unshakeable superiority. Spencer would

211

never be rude, or even abrupt. Like his mother he made Hannah feel wrong-footed from the moment he opened his mouth, but she held her ground on the bottom step. 'Thank you, Spencer. What can I do for you this morning?'

'Is Aaron at home?'

'He's resting. Can I help you?'

Spencer put his head on one side and smiled. 'I was hoping to discuss our proposition.'

'No.'

The smile only broadened. 'Mrs Fennymore, you can see the sense of it, surely? If Mr Fennymore agrees to sell the land to me it will give him – and you – a healthy capital sum that you can invest against medical expenses, nursing requirements, whatever you both may need in the future.'

Hannah said nothing, only watched him with her round bird's eyes.

'You both know me well. I belong to Pittsharbor and I love the beach as much as you do.' When Hannah made no response he corrected himself, 'Or almost as much. I wouldn't do anything or sanction any development over there that was in any way unsuitable or intrusive. I'd like to build a small house for myself, one or at the most two others, well screened, to cover my own outlay. . .' Spencer couldn't help glancing at the coveted ground as he spoke. It was the tongue of headland that backed the southern end of Moon Island Beach, from the side of the Fennymores' property to the curve of the bluff road as it wound towards Pittsharbor. It was prime seafront

212

land, ripe for development. Aaron had acquired it from old man Swayne forty years ago.

'No,' Hannah repeated.

Spencer had been wheedling and cajoling about the land for a long time. He had tried a dozen different tacks and none of them had brought him any closer. But Aaron was tired now and his grip was loosening. 'Why not, Mrs Fennymore? It's just a piece of ground. It sits there. It could be utilised, put to work for you . . .'

'No.'

Hannah was surprised at herself. Elizabeth was a part of all this, of course. The woman was probably lending her son the money for the deal. If she and Aaron gave way to what the Newtons wanted, a pincer movement would cut them off from the town and the space of the beach and the sea. There would be little grey shingled boxes and hammocks and barbecues under the trees, and their nearest neighbour on the town side would no longer be the shack that had turned into the Flying Fish.

The new Pittsharbor Aaron had seen this morning was swallowing up the old one and the greedy mouth of it was right here, mumbling against their own fences. Hannah saw it as only part of history's pattern that the offensive should come in the shape of Elizabeth and her son, because Elizabeth had always been there like a shadow. For all her married life Hannah had soothed and protected and defended Aaron, but she had never succeeded in blotting out the past.

She threw up her hands and pressed the flat palms

213

against Spencer's crisp shirt-front. If all she had ever been able to do was defend her husband, then she wouldn't give up the meagre role now. Her amazing strength propelled Spencer backwards, away from the house. He stumbled over his own polished loafers and his mouth gaped in an instant's disbelief. 'Go away. Go away right now, and don't ever come back here.'

Spencer took two more steps backwards and raised his hands in a gesture of submission. 'Yes. Of course not. I'm sorry you misunderstood me, I didn't . . .'

'It's not a misunderstanding. I'll say it again. Aaron won't sell our land to you so's you and your mother can build condos or whatever it is you've got planned. He may be ill but he won't weaken and even if he does you still have me to contend with.'

The declaration gave Hannah a novel thrill of power. She squared her shoulders and watched Spencer continue his retreat, until he had skirted May's tree and disappeared into the lane again.

When she turned round she saw that Aaron had come out on to the porch. He was leaning against one of the supports, steadying himself with one hand. He looked ill and very old. Hannah went to him at once.

'What did he want?'

'Nothing. Just giving me a message from Elizabeth about the bake stall.'

Alexander was sitting out on the deck reading Scott Turow. The glittering bay and the island were a perfect backdrop. He put his bookmark carefully in place when he saw Spencer. 'What happened?'

Spencer shrugged. 'Still a blank. But there's plenty of time.'

'Ah. Elizabeth was out here looking for you five minutes ago.'

'Thanks. I'll go and see what she wants.'

The house was cool with blinds drawn against the sun. The scent of baking led him to the kitchen where Elizabeth was setting out trays of blueberry muffins. She was wearing an apron over one of her old-fashioned afternoon dresses and a complex of associations made Spencer suddenly feel a child again. He stole a muffin from a corner of one of the trays and bit into it as his mother turned and asked him, 'What's wrong?'

'Nothing. Hannah and Aaron Fennymore still being obstructive about the sale.' He made a wry, appealing face.

The instant's unpeeling of the years affected Elizabeth too. She put down her oven glove and hugged Spencer as if he were a little boy again. They almost never touched each other nowadays and broke apart quickly, without speaking. 'I wanted you to drive me and the muffins up to the green, so I won't have to search for somewhere to park.'

'Of course I will.'

'Marian's already gone, so we'll have to be quick. I saw Leonie driving her.'

Spencer helped her out of her apron and folded it over a kitchen chair. 'Leonie?' he murmured, remembering something. 'What's going on there, I wonder?'

'What do you mean?'

'Guess what I saw?' He described the brief scene in the car-park. Spencer had an eye for telling details.

But instead of responding to the titbit of gossip Elizabeth only hesitated, frowning. 'Poor child,' she sighed in the end.

'Child? If Leonie Beam's not a grown woman I'm Bette Midler.'

'I meant the daughter. John Duhane's younger one.'

Spencer had barely noticed May's existence. 'Why would it be a problem for her? Didn't you say Duhane's wife was dead?'

Marian was presiding at the stall. The church green was already thronged with people although it wasn't quite noon and the Reverend Leavitt hadn't declared the fair officially open. There were families with young children and weighty, meandering older couples, most of them wearing bermudas and peaked caps against the bright sunshine. It was one of Pittsharbor's rare, truly hot days when even the breeze off the sea was stilled. Most of the younger visitors and townspeople were missing. There was a softball tournament starting up and a three-mile fun run was under way from Deer Hill to the finish point at the harbour car-park.

But May was there.

She hung in Marian Beam's shadow, watching without seeing as Marian briskly laid out the baked goods.

'You sure you know the price of everything, May?' A tray of moist, glazed blueberry pies from Hannah's kitchen took centre place. 'There's a list here, see, so

216

you can always check.' Marian rattled a canister with a secure lid. 'And you give change from here, we'll be needing a heap of quarters since Elizabeth insisted on pricing the pies at two seventy-five. Good, here's Marty at last.'

Marty and Lucas unloaded the gas barbecue from a borrowed pick-up and hauled it into position under Marian's directions. Unable even to look at Lucas, May stared dully at the grass. It was pocked with dusty hollows and coarsened with weeds.

'Hi.' His bare feet were planted in front of her. There were tiny tufts of bleached hairs glinting on each of his toes.

The diary. With the whaling book in her hand the sets of numbers had slowly but obediently yielded their meaning. 66 7 10, *He*. 146 12 2, *touched*. 67 10 9, *me*.

Doone's words about Lucas crept in May's blood-stream – or not the words themselves because they were so bare – but the thick, impassioned, glutinous intensity that was locked into the unravelled code.

Those coded parts of the diary were the most disturbing, yes, the *hottest* thing May had ever read. Once she had painstakingly picked them out she couldn't get them out of her head. 'Oh. Hi.'

'How's the hand?'

The knuckles were criss-crossed with surgical tape, but the shallow cuts were already healing. An accident, John had told everyone, even Ivy. May had tripped and stuck out a hand to save herself. *Do you want to talk about what's happening?* her father had asked her. May had answered flatly, *No.*

217

'Uh, it's okay.'

May felt rather than saw Lucas shrug and stroll away, and all the time Doone's obsession made her skin shiver as if she had a fever.

> He touched me. I knew he wanted to. All the time he wants to, but his hands move nearby in the air instead. But today, after we swam in the sea, he gave me my towel.

'Towel' was one of those words written plain, because Doone couldn't find it in the whale book.

> Nobody was there. He dried me and lifted a coil of my hair between his fingers. Touched my shoulder with his finger, his eyes shut. Both of us shaking.

The very clumsiness of the available words, the make-do of the language, stirred a response in May. She closed her eyes and the scene made itself vivid. She saw Lucas bending his head, intent on drying the beads of salt water from Doone's pale shoulders and the precise articulation of his finger joints as he played with the sticky curl of her hair. It wasn't the same Lucas who fooled on the beach with the rest of the Beams, nor even the version of him who fondled and necked with Ivy. She never even named him in the scribbled pages but he was Doone's alone, violently painted and coloured out of nothing with words that sometimes didn't even fit together. And mine, May thought. Mine, too, because of her.

She opened her eyes, realising that she had been

218

hugging herself so tightly that her finger-nails had dug into her upper arms.

Marty Stiegel was looking at her. 'You okay?'

There were already people standing in line for blueberry pancakes. A little girl held a balloon and her brother tried to grab it from her.

May nodded her head. 'Yes.'

The blur of burning gas wavered and fined down into little blue points as Marty fiddled with the controls. 'Right. We got customers, so let's make pancakes. You want to take the orders and set out plates for me?'

'Okay. Whatever you want.'

Marian was loudly giving instructions too, from behind the pies and muffins. It was very hot next to the barbecue and the crowd pressed all round them. Tom Beam was there and Elizabeth Newton in one of her ladylike dresses. May saw Leonie's pale face swim out of the sea of all the rest and turned sideways so that her shoulder partly blocked the unwelcome view. She hadn't seen her for two days, since the night of the broken glass. Lucas had gone, to play softball or to hang out with Ivy at the beach. She rubbed her forehead with her fist and tried to concentrate on what Marty was telling her to do.

Leonie thought May looked ill. It didn't escape her notice that the girl wouldn't meet her eyes.

Marian was rattling the tin of quarters to attract her attention and Tom moved to make room for his wife behind the makeshift counter. Leonie took her place obediently, with the heat of rebellion invisible inside

219

her. She was thinking that nothing tied her here, to Tom or her mother-in-law or the Pittsharbor Day bake stall, and she had been wrong to bend her head to their demands for so long. *If Tom and I loved each other*, she thought. *If we did, then Marian's intransigence would be funny, and I would be able to bear the closeness of my baby nieces and nephews, and Pittsharbor would be as precious to me as it is to them. But we don't love each other.*

Instead of sounding a knell, the truth began to offer her some hope of escape.

Elizabeth worked from the other end of the stall. She didn't recognise many of her customers for cookies and muffins. There were few local people in the line, or anywhere on the church green. At the height of summer Pittsharbor belonged to the visitors and she saw no harm in that. Tourists brought prosperity to a coastline that had once been frozen with poverty; she was a summer migrant herself, just like the Beams and the others, although Marian considered herself above the rental tide that flooded the coast every year. It was a shame Aaron and Hannah were so resistant to Spencer's proposition. The land was ripe for development.

Characteristically, Marty was a blur of energy. He juggled his two pans, flipping an unending series of pancakes out on to the paper plates May held for him. He even found time for good-humoured conversation. 'I got a great shot of you.'

'What?' Her sore hand wobbled and she almost

220

dropped a loaded plate before thrusting it into the outstretched hands of a waiting customer. 'Three dollars, please.'

'Down at the beach. When you were playing volleyball with the other kids. I'll show you tonight, if you want to come over before the party.'

'Party?'

'After the town fireworks. Just beer and barbecue, for the five houses and whatever kids are around. Maybe not the Fennymores. Are you and your dad and sister coming?'

May moistened her lips. 'I . . . I guess so. Although, I don't know.' A party for the bluff houses meant Leonie as well as Lucas. Darts of confusion shot through her. A hand clutching loose change opened under her nose. 'Miss? You gave me a dollar short.'

Marty had already turned back to his pancakes.

The afternoon grew hotter. The sky was a thunderous metallic blue and the sea seemed exhausted into stillness. The crowds that had thronged the green over lunch-time thinned out as people drifted down to the harbour and the beach. Karyn and Elliot arrived to relieve Marian, who swept the babies away to buy balloons. Tom took over the pancake-making and when Marty left May seized the opportunity to slip away too. A little later Richard and Shelly arrived with their children and suddenly there were more helpers than customers.

Leonie stood by her husband's shoulder. 'Is there something I can do?'

He flipped yet another pancake on to a paper plate and heaped it with sweet blueberries before folding and anointing it with sugar and cream. A woman who should have refused the temptation accepted the plate and dug a plastic spoon into the ooze. 'Nope. Thanks.'

Leonie knew well enough what Tom thought of her cooking, but the curtness of his dismissal made her head jerk up and her mouth fill with a retort. Before she uttered it she looked along the efficient line of Beams working the bake stall and turned away abruptly.

The churchyard was enclosed by a tidy white picket fence and a gate that led on to the green. Leonie clicked open the gate and stepped inside. Immediately the air felt cooler from the prospect of shade under the trees edging the plot. She put her hands in the pockets of her shorts and wandered along the path between the gravestones. Most of the inscriptions were familiar to her, but she let her eyes travel once more over the memorials to Purrits and Hanscoms and Deeveys.

What to do? she asked herself hotly and incoherently. *What to do for the best?*

In the farthest corner stood an old yew tree. When she reached it Leonie stopped in its green-black shelter, stroking the ribbed, fibrous bark with her fingertips.

To go or to stay. Those were her choices, without making John Duhane a factor in either of them. The other night after May had gone up to her bedroom they had sat together for a little while, mostly in silence. Then John had stood up and said he would see

222

her back to the Beams' house. They had flitted through the Japanese garden and descended the beach steps. Their footsteps mushed noisily on the shingle and the waves sucked at the tideline.

At the Beams' stairs John had stepped back, almost melting into the darkness. 'Good-night,' he'd said quietly.

An hour before, they had been locked in one another, then May's staring face had materialised at the window and the glass had shattered under her fist.

'Good-night,' Leonie had answered formally, as if they were strangers.

Since then they had only glimpsed each other in the distance.

'I always find it a good place for thinking.' The voice made Leonie spin round, a startled gasp catching in her throat. Elizabeth was kneeling beside one of the graves. 'I'm sorry. I didn't mean to startle you.' She motioned towards the headstone. 'I took the opportunity to come and do some tidying up. Have they finished with you at the bake stall too?'

Leonie moved out into the harsh sunlight and stood at Elizabeth's side. The plot was well-tended and there were fresh garden flowers in a marble urn. Screwing up her eyes against the brightness, she read the inscriptions and saw that it was the grave of Elizabeth's parents. 'Don't let me disturb you,' she murmured, but Elizabeth stood up and brushed at her skirt.

She dropped a pair of secateurs and a trowel into her raffia basket. 'I'm done here. Perhaps we could sit over there for five minutes.' There was a bench against

223

the fence, still in the tree's shade. A patch of scuffed earth in front of it and the scattering of cigarette butts suggested that it was one of the evening hang-outs of the town youth.

When they sat down Leonie groped in her pocket and brought out a pack of her own cigarettes. She had started smoking again in the last few days, ignoring Tom's disapproval. She lit up and exhaled fiercely. She was calculating that she must have known Elizabeth Newton for all the years she had been coming to the beach, but she couldn't remember ever exchanging more than polite commonplaces with her.

'My mother and father are here. But my husband is at St John's in Boston. Where should I be put when the time comes, I wonder?' Elizabeth spoke meditatively, as if to herself. 'In the end it will be Spencer who decides.'

'Won't he do what you tell him to?'

'I suppose he might.'

Leonie suddenly laughed. There was a sly humour in Elizabeth she had never noticed before.

'What I would really like', Elizabeth continued, 'is to be planted out on Moon Island, like Sarah. Now, that is a beautiful spot.'

'On the island? Sarah who?'

Elizabeth slowly turned her head. She examined Leonie's face in detail, searching for a sign. 'It's an old story. Haven't you ever heard it?'

The Pittsharbor Day noise from the green was a long way off as Leonie listened. But threading in and out of Elizabeth's low murmur she thought she could hear the counterpoint of Tom's voice and Marian calling, and the clamour of children. She frowned in concentration, following Elizabeth's narrative. The old woman was a good story-teller.

'Little May Duhane saw her ghost.'

Leonie straightened her back. The gravestones marched away from her across the grass, their shadows beginning to lengthen now. An uncomfortable association that she couldn't place scratched at her subconscious. 'I don't believe in ghosts,' she said. 'Or in supernatural warnings, whatever they might be. But I'm sure of one thing. May will be all right in the end, however difficult her life may be now. Her father loves her and he puts his children first, above everything else.' She paused, looking down at her hands resting in her lap. She twisted the wedding ring on her finger and stared away again over the gap-teeth of the gravestones. 'It's her age. The demons of adolescence. They'll let her go in the end. Don't you remember what it was like to be that age?'

'Yes, I remember.'

The tremor in the older woman's voice made Leonie turn to look at her. 'I didn't mean to dismiss the Sarah story.'

'You didn't dismiss it. You just said you didn't believe in one aspect of it.'

Leonie sighed. She gestured away to the green, where the buying and selling was beginning to wind down. Lucas Beam was reversing a pick-up truck too fast towards the grass. 'Pittsharbor's a mundane place. We spend muddled, ordinary times in it.'

'Do you wish for something more than that?'

'Yes, I do.'

'Are you in love with him?'

The question was so unlooked-for that Leonie found herself answering without calculation. 'Perhaps. Or I could be if I let it happen, which I won't.'

Of course Spencer had passed on what he had seen in the car-park that day. How is it, Leonie wondered, that there are any secrets at all in a place as small as this?

'It's none of my business, I'm sorry.'

'You're right.'

But Elizabeth was not deflected by the finality in Leonie's voice. 'Forgive an old woman's intrusion. At my age there isn't much to do but observe other people's lives and make presumptuous conclusions about how they should handle them. You aren't very happy, are you?'

There was no point in attempting a denial. The children were much closer now, running past the fence that separated the graveyard from the green and Leonie tilted her head to watch them as Elizabeth talked.

'Don't pass up the chance of happiness, if you think it might be within your reach. When it's gone you will never stop regretting its loss.'

'It sounds as though you speak from experience.'

'I do,' Elizabeth said. Leonie waited with interest and the beginnings of sympathy, but the older woman didn't say any more. Instead she added, 'I saw the ghost too, when I was not much older than May. I

226

asked who she was and my grandmother told me the story.' Elizabeth's hands opened as they lay in her lap. Her wedding and engagement rings were worn to thin gold hoops and they were loose on her finger. 'It's like a duty, a piece and a part of belonging to the beach, to hand on the history. Keeping the thread running.'

'To hand it on to May and me? I don't feel that I belong here. The opposite, in fact. I wouldn't know about May.'

'You remind me of each other. You're alike.'

The incongruity of the idea made Leonie hesitate, then suddenly she thought, *yes. Maybe we are. Maybe that's why we mistrust each other.* 'And you too,' she said with conviction. The idea comforted her. 'What do you think I should do, Elizabeth?' Using her name was a token of friendship.

'I can't tell you what to do. All I know is that I didn't take a chance, a gamble, a long time ago. I was sorry for it afterwards.'

'I see. Thank you,' Leonie said.

Ivy and Lucas were with a crowd of young people at the Seafood Shack down on the harbour. Lucas had been playing softball all afternoon and Ivy was angry with him for neglecting her. She sat sideways at the table where Lucas was eating a double crab roll, with one smooth thigh touching the leg of Sam Deevey's jeans. Sam was one of the locals and a bit of a hick, she thought, but not at all bad-looking in an Antonio Banderas kind of way.

227

'You coming down to the beach tonight?' Lucas asked her, his mouth full of crab and mayo.

Ivy barely turned her head. 'I'm going to watch the fireworks with Sam. Maybe afterwards.'

'Sure,' Lucas said uncertainly. He wasn't used to rejection, even by someone as gorgeous as Ivy. The evening in prospect was uninviting without her.

May waded out of the sea and shook the drops off her hair and skin like a dog. It had been so hot that for once the cold shock of the water was welcome and she was glad there was no one about to see her in her swimsuit. She stood with her back to the houses and the deserted beach, rubbing her chin with the corner of her towel. The sea was flat and milky pale, reflecting the mild early-evening sky. The island's hunched back bristled against the colourless horizon. Then she heard confident footsteps treading the shingle behind her.

'Hi,' Marty called to her in his friendly way. Judith and he were younger than most of the other beach adults and he liked to make his social moves between the generations of parents and teenagers, seeming to belong with equal ease to both groups. 'Are you all on your own? Want to come up and have a Coke or something with Judith and me?'

'Okay,' May said. She pulled a wrap over herself.

There was baby stuff spread all over the Stiegels' floor and Judith sitting in the middle of it with Justine on a diaper across her broad knees. May loitered awkwardly, wishing she hadn't come, while Marty fetched drinks for them.

228

'Are you having a good time up here?' Judith asked. She was so big, with her solid shoulders and upper arms rounded like boulders on the beach.

May knew she was a sculptor and thought she looked a bit like a sculpture herself. One of those massive, immoveable pieces of work that sit on lawns outside public buildings. 'Yes, thank you.'

Once the baby was parcelled up in a stretchy sleeping suit Judith calmly hoisted her shirt and undid her bra. A vast white breast spilled out and Judith took the nipple between thumb and forefinger and pressed it to the baby's mouth. Its gums clamped and it began noisily sucking. *How disgusting*, May thought giddily. Never. I'll never do that.

Marty came back and she gratefully took the Coke and drank with pretended thirst, not even asking if it was a Diet one. 'Come through here.' He beckoned.

There was a small room off the main one, obviously used as a study. There were a desk and a laptop computer and a fax machine, and a scatter of folders and notepads. Marty busily opened an envelope file and May saw that it was bulging with black-and-white photographs.

'You take a lot of pictures.'

'Uh? Yeah. I'm lucky. My work is my hobby.' She remembered now that he was a photographer in the city, taking the pictures for ads. 'Here they are.'

He fanned a handful of the photographs expertly in front of her. It was the volleyball day. There was Lucas, with his hair swinging up from his forehead. And Ivy and Gail, clapping hands. Marty found the shot he was looking for. May was leaping high in the air. All the picture's huge energy was driving through her arm and clenched fist. Seeing it brought back to her the power and exhilaration of the moment. She looked like someone else, perhaps in a Nike ad, not herself at all. 'Oh,' she breathed. She turned her lit-up face to Marty. 'It's good, isn't it?'

He patted her shoulder. 'I was pretty pleased with it. I'll get you a copy.'

The photograph gave May an unfamiliar feeling of warmth. She put it down with reluctance. 'Thank you. I'd love that.'

She cocked her head to one side to examine the other pictures in the sheaf. There was one of Elizabeth with Mrs Beam and Mrs Fennymore, standing at the top of some steps. The picture had been taken from an angle below them so they loomed grotesquely. Their contrasting features were sharply delineated, but something in the patina of old age made them seem three different versions of the same witchy old woman. Alarmed, May looked away quickly.

'Marty?' Judith called from the adjoining room. 'She's spat up. Can you pass me the towel from her bag?'

He hurried away and May could hear them dealing with the baby emergency. Idly she poked at the concertina openings of the picture folder. One of the sections held a squared wad of pictures tied with a piece of braid. Without thinking May picked out the package and looked at the uppermost photograph.

It was of a girl sitting on a rock. Her arms were

wrapped around her drawn-up knees, but there was movement in all the lines of her body, as if the photographer had unexpectedly called her name and she had turned happily to see him. Her face was solemn but it was about to break into a delighted smile. Her eyes were locked straight into the lens.

May was gazing at the picture when Marty came back. She fumbled and almost dropped it, ashamed she had been caught snooping into his folder. She held out the little package, but he didn't take it from her. 'Who is she?' May asked, already knowing the answer.

Marty said, 'Doone Bennison. Would you like to look at them?'

'Yes, please.'

She undid the tie. There were a dozen photographs, all of Doone alone. In a windbreaker, a polo shirt and in one case a lifejacket with the wind whipping her hair across her cheeks. She had a heavy, rather pasty face with thick eyebrows and a wide mouth, but her smile was transfiguring.

May gazed at her and her eyes fastened on Doone's as if they were meeting in the flesh. But she was looking at a stranger. Nothing about Doone's features was familiar, or even remarkable, except for her smile. May was amazed at how happy she looked. 'She looks . . . she looks ordinary. Like any girl.' A stupid thing to say, May thought, as soon as it was out. It was only her deadness that made her any different and the diary of her love.

Marty was standing at her shoulder, solid and self-assured and detached from all the whispering undercurrents that washed the beach, in the adult way that her father was and the other men from the five houses, except for Lucas. May suddenly felt reproached by his normality. She was clumsy and intrusive, like a voyeur with Doone's pictures in her hand. She folded them together abruptly and handed them back. 'I'm sorry, I didn't mean to be snooping. It must have been terrible when she drowned.'

'It was. For everyone at the beach.'

Of course she was still here in their memories, her life and her death. They were all back for the next summer, enjoying their vacations because that was what you did, you carried on with living. Just like she and John and Ivy were doing, even though Alison had died. But Doone would still inhabit the place for the Beams and the Stiegels and the rest. They would remember seeing her on the rocks where Marty had taken her picture and on a towel on the sand, and in the sea that had taken her away. She was there even for May, who had never seen her face until today.

May shivered. Only the thinnest membrane separated the beach people from another multitude that held Doone and Alison and the island woman. The divider was as opaque as a Pittsharbor mist and as insubstantial. Any of them could slip through it. Maybe without even knowing it.

The telephone rang shrilly on the desk. The edge of a startled scream came out of May's mouth but she pressed her hands over it. Marty's eyebrows lifted as he answered. After a few words he handed her the receiver. 'It's for you. Your father.'

'Yeah? Hi. Yes, I'm here. How did you know?'

He had been reading on the deck and had seen her going up to the house with Marty, nothing more complicated than that.

John wanted to know if May was going to the harbour with him to watch the Pittsharbor Day fireworks. He made regular overtures of the same kind, giving her the opportunity to talk to him if she wanted to. It left May feeling cornered, keeping the refuge of her silence. 'I've got to go, he wants me,' she mumbled to Marty.

'You okay?'

Why were people always asking her that? 'Yeah, thanks. Thank you for the drink. And letting me see the photos.'

The pictures of Doone were already tucked away again.

After the loss of Martin the bowman from the third mate's boat, the *Dolphin*'s days at sea took on a heaviness and a monotony that the lack of wind and whales did nothing to dispel.

A sombre mood possessed every man among the officers and crew, but the worst affected of them all was William Corder. On more than one occasion good-natured Matthias Plant sought him out wherever it was he hid himself, behind the thin curtain of his bunk or up in some sheltered corner of the deck, and tried to raise the boy's spirits by joking with him, or at the least by persuading him to share the reason for his

233

melancholy. The mate had seen enough deaths in his years of seafaring to be by rights almost immune to tragedy, but still he was enough of a man of feeling to remember how he himself had been affected the first time he had witnessed such a loss. Yet it seemed to Matthias that the boy was overtaken by deeper sadness and anxiety than could be explained even by the terrible death of his shipmate. But whatever method of coaxing Matthias employed on him, William begged only to be left alone and retreated into the silent sanctuary of his own thoughts.

At length Captain Gunnell despaired of the poor hunting around the Congo basin and the whaling grounds of the southern Atlantic sea. He gave orders to his officers to set the *Dolphin*'s course westwards for the islands of Fernando de Naronha, to the north-east of Brazil. At first a fair wind seemed to promise better fortune, but after not many days the breeze died to a whisper, then failed altogether. A cruel heat descended on the ship and pinned it like an expiring insect to the harsh mirror of the sea. The foul smells and vermin bred by the heat below decks were a torture even to the experienced men, and the lack of fresh food and sweet water began to take their toll on the health of the crew.

William Corder fell ill of a fever. After insisting for two days and a night that he could stand his watch with anyone, he collapsed in a dead faint one morning while kneeling to the task of scrubbing the ship's decks. The officer of the watch ordered him to be carried below and he was placed in his bunk to recover.

Matthias Plant was the officer of the middle watch on that same night. The sea was dead calm with not so much as a breath of wind stirring and Matthias wearily stretched out his arms on the rail, praying for a wind or at least for some thought of action that would keep his eyes from falling shut in sleep.

One of the men from the watch on deck ducked below, with the intention of lighting up his tobacco pipe at the lamp in the forecastle. A moment later there came a great shout, enough to have roused the whole ship if the sleepers had not been so drugged with heat and lassitude. The man who had gone below burst out of the forecastle scuttle. Matthias could at first make no sense of his babble of words. 'That young fellow,' the sailor raved. 'The one that's sick and lying below.'

'What of him?' Matthias shouted back, fearful that poor William had taken a turn for the worse. 'Come, out with it. Are you an idiot or a native, that you can't speak properly?' For indeed the man was gibbering, hardly able to form his words in a manner to allow understanding. The mate took him by the throat and shook him like a dog with a rat, for his sudden anxiety for William Corder overwhelmed his habitual reason.

At last the sailor found words that could be understood. 'That young fellow is a woman, sir.'

Matthias gaped at him like a fish, the first time in many years that he had been silenced by one of his own men.

'Come below,' the man exhorted him, tugging at his arm. 'Come below if you will not believe me, and see for yourself.'

Matthias followed him at once. It was all quiet below decks save for the faint creaking of the timbers as the ship made slow headway over the flat water. The young creature they had known as William Corder lay in his bunk, with the lamp shining in on him. In the stifling heat of the night and with the burning of his fever he had thrown off his clothes, and now lay exposed to the eyes of his rough companions as a perfect and beautifully made young woman. She was lying there in restless sleep with the sheen of sweat upon her white skin.

The commotion on the deck had drawn the rest of the watch crowding into the forecastle and the watch below was stirring drowsily in their places.

Matthias swiftly pulled the curtain to shield the woman. He dispatched one of the men to rouse the Captain and sent the others back to their places in short order. He bent over the young woman and drew the tumbled bed-things over her body. Her eyelids were already fluttering, and she gave a low moan and came fully awake. Her eyes fixed on Matthias's face with a flash of terror, then such speechless pleading that it brought a pang to his heart the like of which he had not felt since he was a young man newly in love. 'Come,' he said, almost adding *William*. 'Your secret is discovered. This is no place for you. You must make yourself respectable and come with me to the Captain, who will see what should be done to help you.' And all the time his mind was running over the almost incredible fact that this young woman had spent so many weeks living alongside the coarsest creatures who inhabit the forecastle of a whaling ship. What she must have seen and suffered overwhelmed him with pity.

Her eyes filled with tears at the mate's words and she whispered, 'I am glad I am found out, because I do not think I could have borne this life for many more days. What will happen to me, Matthias?'

He told her, 'That is for the Captain to decide. But he is a good man, as you well know, and he will see that you come to no further harm.'

While he waited with his back turned and his eyes sternly fixed on the other astonished occupants of the forecastle, she hurried into some clothes without leaving the shelter of her bunk. Then she slipped upright and, seeing the size of her and the fragile curve of her arm and shoulder, Matthias wondered how he had ever been blind enough to have taken her for a man.

The Captain was waiting in his cabin. Shock and disbelief made his mien sterner than was usual and the poor sick girl began to shiver with fright as well as fever. 'Sit down,' he said, indicating the chair opposite his. 'And you had better stay here, Mr Plant.' Seeing her shivering Mr Gunnell took the rum bottle from its resting place and poured her a good measure. 'Drink this. It is hardly the refreshment to offer to a lady, but I suppose you are used to it by this time.'

She took the tot and downed it, and they saw that her hands were well shaped, although badly roughened by the heavy work she had been doing for so many weeks.

237

'What is your name?'

'Sarah. Sarah Corder, sir.'

'Well then, Sarah, you had better tell Mr Plant and myself what you are doing aboard my ship disguised as a green hand.'

'I did my work as well as I could, sir, and as well as any of the others. Matthias . . . Mr Plant . . . will tell you that.'

She turned her face in supplication, looking to Matthias as her friend.

'It's true, Captain.'

'I have no doubt. But you must tell us how you come to be here in the first place.'

Sarah took a deep breath. As she began her explanation they could see it was a relief to tell her story to listening ears that were at least half sympathetic.

It was a sad tale, but in the end the two mariners were not so very surprised by it. It was only Sarah's bravery and determination that left them wondering.

She was a young woman of good family, from Portsmouth, Massachusetts. Her mother had died when she was a child, and she had been brought up by her elderly and somewhat strict father. When Sarah was eighteen she went to stay with some relatives of her mother's who lived up at Portland on the sea coast of Maine. While there, she met a young man. He was a friend of a friend of the son of the family and had therefore been introduced into their circle without anyone having much knowledge of his history or connections. He was an attractive and lively young fellow, and his manners were plausible enough, so he was made welcome as such men often are when there is a need for dancing partners.

Sarah and Robert Hanner soon fell deeply in love. He begged Sarah to marry him, but he also explained that he was waiting to inherit some money from an ancient and infirm relative who lived in New York. The bequest was dependent on Robert appearing to remain just as he was, an attentive and dutiful bachelor with a care for his ailing great-aunt. Notwithstanding this, however, Robert claimed he could not live without his love. Even though they would not be able to marry just yet, for a matter of but a few weeks because it was certain that the great-aunt could not survive beyond that, he begged Sarah to accompany him when the time came for him to leave Maine and return to the city.

'I know now that I was a fool,' Sarah told her audience across the Captain's polished table. 'But I loved him and I believed what he told me with all my heart.'

The young couple ran away to New York together. No more was heard of the elderly relative. Robert Hanner did not marry Sarah, and within a matter of weeks he abandoned her and disappeared. Sarah's father and family had cut her off, and she was alone in the world. She had a very little money of her own, and used it to try to find her lover. In the end she had hired a private detective, who traced Hanner to a shipping office where he had declared himself ready to go a-whaling.

The Captain and Matthias Plant gravely nodded their heads. In their time they had encountered many a blackguard who had taken to sea as a way of evading enemies and creditors too numerous or too troublesome to escape by a less demanding route.

'And then?' asked Captain Gunnell.

Her voice was soft when she answered but from the flash in her eyes neither of the two men was left in any doubt of the steel beneath Sarah's tender skin. 'Why, I determined that I would follow him to whichever end of the earth he had chosen. And when I found him I would make him marry me, because for all that I am a fool and a lost woman I have my strength and my wits to depend upon. God help me but I still love him, and I believe that we would make a good partnership.' It was only at the last words that her voice wavered and the tears started to her eyes once more.

'I am sorry for you,' said the Captain gently.

Sarah had travelled homewards again from New York, but only as far as Nantucket, from where she was advised by the shipping office that Robert Hanner had embarked. 'I thought that once I was in Nantucket it would be easy to find him, or to discover which ship he had signed to. But I had no idea there were so many whaling ships and such crowds of sailors, or that the life they lived would be so rough and dangerous. By this time I had no money left nor anywhere to go, and so it seemed that my only course and the sole hope of finding him was to disguise myself as a man and follow the whales, just as Robert was doing. Even when this ship set sail I thought

240

somehow our paths would cross, but I see now that I was mistaken.'

Matthias at last understood why she always scanned the faces of the crews when the *Dolphin* lay near other whalers and the reason for the deep sadness that had recently overtaken her. It was no brother she had been searching for. 'But this is a bitter, cruel life,' she added piteously. 'I had determined that when we reached the next port I would slip away and try to make my way home again. Then I fell ill and you discovered me.'

From the manner in which Captain Gunnell cleared his throat before speaking Matthias knew that he was as affected as he himself had been by Sarah Corder's story. 'A whaling ship is indeed no place for a lady,' he declared. 'And I must put you ashore as soon as I can. My plan is to put in to port to take on water and supplies, then I shall place you in the care of the Consul at Rio de Janeiro. It is my only course of action, Miss Corder.'

'I understand,' she softly answered.

It happened that there was an empty stateroom next to the Captain's quarters. On his orders it was rapidly cleared, a pair of his own sheets were placed on the bed and the young woman was allowed to rest there in some measure of comfort and privacy. The officers of the *Dolphin* saw to it that she was provided with what nourishing food their limited supplies permitted and were rewarded by her almost hourly improvement.

When she was somewhat recovered she thanked them with proper warmth. 'The officers of this ship are true gentlemen and I am in your debt for ever.'

241

She had a pretty smile and modest ways, and soon the other men were as much under her spell as Matthias Plant.

The weather changed within a day of Sarah's secret being revealed. A strong north-easter helped the *Dolphin* to landfall at Fernando de Naronha, where much-needed water and fresh food were taken on board, then a course was set for the mainland. For most of this time Sarah kept to her cabin, but from time to time she was persuaded to take the air up on the deck. Her behaviour when she met her erstwhile forecastle companions was a picture of modest goodwill.

Sometimes when Matthias had a spare hour they would pass it together in talk, for the good mate had no doubt that she was lonely. He learned much about her childhood and the friends and companions of those early days, but she would almost never speak of Robert Hanner. Yet notwithstanding her reticence, Matthias did not believe he was ever out of her mind for more than a minute at a time. He would come upon her when she was staring out to sea or down at the ruined skin of her hands, and she would be so lost in thought that his voice would startle her. He knew then that she was thinking of her betrayer and most likely still planning how she might discover him again. Matthias felt a dreadful weight of fear and anxiety on her behalf, yet there was determination and an iron will in Sarah, as strong as or stronger than any man's, that in some way only heightened her very womanliness.

At Rio de Janeiro the Captain sent word to the Consul, and he soon received assurance that that gentleman and his wife would receive Sarah into their own home until such time as a passage home could be arranged for her.

The day came for her to leave the *Dolphin*. Her share of the oil taken amounted to some sixty dollars and this money the Captain arranged for her to have, together with a similar sum collected for her by the other officers and men, so she was at least not quite penniless. For his own part Matthias gave her his gold watch, and she put her arm around his neck and kissed him and sobbed that he had been kinder to her than any father or brother.

One of the boat steerers who was of similar height had given Sarah a white cotton shirt with a wide blue collar, and a pair of black broadcloth sailor's pants, which fell smoothly to cover her low shoes. She had a broad-brimmed straw hat, tied with a black ribbon. She did not look like a lady of fashion, but she was neat and pretty in her makeshift clothes. The crew had gathered on the deck to see her off, and as the boat that was to row her ashore was lowered she shook the hand of each of them and whispered her thanks. Matthias waited until the last, except for Captain Gunnell.

When it came to his turn to say farewell he took her small hand between both of his great calloused ones. 'Sarah, if you do find who you are searching for, what do you truly believe will happen?'

'I will make him marry me.'

'And if he will not? Or cannot?'

Her wide eyes never wavered. Matthias felt a shiver touch him like the first intimation of a fever. 'Then I will kill him like a venomous snake.' Her hand slid from his grasp and she was smiling. 'Good Matthias, you must not be anxious on my behalf. I am truly grateful for your kindness and I will always be your friend. Goodbye.'

So saying, she kissed his cheek for the last time and turned to Captain Gunnell at the taff-rail.

The men stood together watching as the boat carried her towards the shore.

'Do you imagine that she will find him?' Matthias musingly asked.

'I am certain she will.'

'And then?'

'I would not be in that man's shoes for any money.'

News of the woman who had disguised herself in men's clothing and sailed on the *Dolphin* had travelled fast. A crowd of people were gathered on the dock, all waiting to catch a glimpse of her. Sarah stepped out on to dry land, handed up by her boatman, and the press of people immediately closed around her.

She turned once to look back at the old *Dolphin*. She took off her straw hat and waved it, the black ribbons fluttering on the crowded dock.

That was the last glimpse they had of her.

May yawned and scratched the mosquito bites on her ankle. She liked books and she was quite interested in

244

the sad and gory whaling stories, because of the remote connection with the history of Moon Island, but she couldn't imagine that Doone would have read much of them by choice. From the plain sections of the diary she knew Doone didn't exactly have broad literary or historical interests. Maybe Hannah Fennymore had offered to lend her the books and Doone had accepted out of politeness. Perhaps there had been no other suitable book to hand, so Doone had used the Dolphin book as the base for her code.

May flipped idly to the front and scanned the introductory pages that she hadn't bothered to read before. She learned that the book's narrative was based on Matthias Plant's journals. The old whaleman had continued writing his journal for the rest of the Sarah Corder voyage and the three voyages that followed it, until he retired at last in 1848. Finally, in old age he set up home with his wife in the village of Wellfleet on Cape Cod, to be near one of his married daughters. After his death his books and papers were stored with the rest of his keepsakes in a tin trunk, and there they stayed until they were disinterred in 1902 by his grandson.

This young man read the whaling diaries with the utmost fascination and passed them to a college friend who worked as an editor for a New York firm of publishers. So it happened that more than fifty years after they were written, the story told in Matthias's memoirs was published by Charles Scribner & Sons under the title *Voyages of the Dolphin*. When she looked at the front of the book again, May saw that Hannah's book was the second reprint, dated 1909. Hannah must have owned the book for a long time. Or perhaps, May thought, she had found it on the second-hand shelves of the Bookhouse, Pittsharbor's only bookshop. Her name was written on the blank first page in blue ink, but there was no date.

'May?' She looked up. John was calling her from the foot of the stairs. 'Are you coming to watch the fireworks?'

May swung her legs off the bed, noticing as she always did the ugly way the flesh quivered inside the loop of her shorts legs. 'Yeah, okay.'

John and May walked down the Pittsharbor road together. They hadn't even waited for Ivy to materialise, knowing that she would have her own plans for the evening.

'It's a wonderful evening. We're lucky,' John said. Darkness was settling over the bluff and the first stars pricked the sky.

May wrestled with what she should say. The image of her father on the sofa with Leonie Beam remained obstinately stuck in her head. It jarred like a mis-shapen jigsaw piece with other graphic sexual images. A scene from a video she had seen long ago with Ivy. Ivy herself with Lucas. The old people, Elizabeth and Aaron long ago in the Captain's House. Doone's numbered words conjuring thick passion out of the pages of an old-fashioned book. They were images she didn't want to see but they attacked all her senses. Sex was everywhere, roping around everyone but herself.

It was impossible to tell her father any of this. Disgust and shapeless longing possessed her in equal parts. 'Yes.'

After a moment's hesitation John asked, 'Can we talk about the other evening?'

The cuts on her hand were healing. The new tissue puckered and crawled under the antiseptic tape. 'No.' She heard how her blank monosyllable disconcerted him. Miserably she added, 'Can't we just forget about it? I'd rather we did. Truly.'

'It's just . . .'

'*Please,*' May begged.

Her desperation silenced him. 'If that's what you really want,' John murmured. They walked on to the harbour without speaking.

At the moment of their arrival the first firework exploded overhead in a mushroom of sparks and a cascade of blue and emerald fireballs. The sparks drifted down, turning scarlet until they were blotted out in the sea, and another rocket streaked upwards.

Ivy was in the crowd, with her arm draped around the shoulders of Sam Deevey. She waved when she saw them. Leonie Beam was there too, with Sidonie on her shoulders. The bursting rocket illuminated her profile for an instant and May knew that her father's eyes stayed on her.

Lucas came out of a group and greeted them. It was clear that he had been drinking. 'Hi, Maysy. Happy Pittsharbor Day, guys.'

Nine

The driftwood fire on the beach facing Moon Island held a core of pure red heat within a cage of branches. Every so often part of the latticework collapsed and a column of sparks went shooting upwards like a tiny echo of the Pittsharbor fireworks. Even now from the direction of the harbour an occasional rocket streaked into the darkness, followed by the peppery explosions of firecrackers. Freelance celebrations were continuing in the town long after the official ones had ended.

Food had been barbecued and eaten around the bonfire by the bluff families and a loose group of guests, mostly friends of the Beam children. Everyone had drunk wine or beer, and a fragile gloss of cordiality slicked over an undercurrent of tension, which seemed to dull the fire and thicken the already stifling air.

In an effort to lighten the atmosphere Marian and Marty had talked too much from opposite sides of the group. Now one of the boys was picking at a guitar and an uneasy calm settled. Figures moved in the firelight,

248

to pick up a bottle of wine or fetch more wood, and an umber glow halved their silhouettes.

Murmurs of conversation threaded the groups; the evening had reached the point where the young people would begin to drift away and the older ones might safely collect up the debris of the barbecue and move towards home.

Ivy was still sitting hip to hip with Sam Deevey, her lovely neck bent so she could whisper into his ear. The shifting of her favours was obvious, but no one had audibly remarked on it. John frowned a warning at her but she ignored him and Marian's displeasure was only revealed in sharp glances. Lucas merely looked on in silence and tipped his head back to swallow another drink.

Leonie had reorganised the plate of food Marian had pressed on her, but had eaten none of it. She could only think how her way ahead had narrowed to the vanishing point where there was no possibility but to leave. She wrestled in her mind with the question of where to go. Not back to the apartment in Boston, filled with the possessions Tom and she had accumulated together over the years.

But if not there, then where else? To rent some-where, that would be the answer, but the practical difficulties of doing even that seemed all but insur-mountable. Leonie knew it was unhappiness that was disabling her. She must move, before the paralysis became complete.

Tom was sitting on the opposite side of the fire, with Judith Stiegel and Spencer and Alexander. They were talking, but Leonie couldn't hear what they were saying because the low murmur of the sea amplified itself in her ears. The firelight shone on her husband's face, casting unexpected shadows, turning him into a stranger.

Marian's bulk interposed itself. 'Do you suppose anyone would like more blueberry pie?'

There was a surplus from the bake stall.

In translation the question meant *get up and offer second helpings*, but Leonie disregarded it. 'If they do I expect they'll manage to help themselves.'

A corner of gipsy skirt whipped her knee as Marian swept on by. I'll pay for that, Leonie told herself, then remembered that she wouldn't have to because she would be gone. The idea of such an upside made her mouth curve in a sudden smile and she saw that John was watching her.

Aaron and Hannah had not come down to the beach and their house at the end of the bluff was in darkness. Elizabeth had joined the party only for an hour. Spencer jumped up to escort her when she stood up to leave. She was relieved that Pittsharbor Day was at last over and she had done all that could possibly have been expected of her. On her way around the circle she thanked Marian, although there was no reason for Marian to have appointed herself hostess of the evening.

The last person Elizabeth came to in her circuit was May. She was attached to the group of teenagers without in any way being a part of it. Elizabeth patted her shoulder and wordlessly May took hold of her wrist.

250

Her hand was burning. For a moment Elizabeth felt that there were wires criss-crossed tight between too many people in this circle, red-hot where they passed through the heart of the fire, cold and invisible on the margins.

May's fingers dropped away. 'Good-night,' she said.

Ivy and Sam and Gail and the others were also making ready to go. The boy stopped strumming his guitar and pulled Gail to her feet. She gave a mock stagger and almost fell into his arms.

Ivy stood in front of Lucas. 'You coming?'

'Nope.'

'Right.' She walked off without a backward glance, with Sam close behind her.

The rest of them stood up too, hoisting bags on their shoulders and murmuring their thanks in Marian's direction, before melting away across the crescent of sand. May knew they were making for a more secluded part of the beach, or maybe someone's bedroom where they would not be interrupted. They would drink and smoke some more draw, and talk and snigger, and while she longed to be included she despised them at the same time for the repetitive dullness of their pleasures.

The young people moved away in a dark mass. The diminished group of eleven adults remained, plus Lucas, sitting alone. May shot a glance at him. His arms were wrapped around his knees and he stared into the fire. *Now*, May thought, *if I am ever going to*.

She had drunk two bottles of beer and she couldn't remember how much red wine, covertly, while her father's attention was turned elsewhere. The mixture lay uneasily in her stomach, but it had the effect of dividing her thoughts from the rest of her weighty self. She felt clear in the head and quite untroubled, with the knowledge that whatever she did or whatever happened wouldn't matter much. Not enough to worry about. Not enough to care about.

She slid across the sand to Lucas's side. 'Hi.'

He rolled his head on his knees to look at her. 'Oh. Hi.'

She waited a minute or two, giving him a chance to get used to her being there. No one else was looking at them. 'She can be like that you know. She doesn't mean to hurt people, not really. It's like just sometimes she has to be a bitch. Kind of a power thing.'

The fire was dying into dull crimson embers. Flakes of ash twirled like snowflakes and settled on the sand. May raked and sifted sand through her fingers, looking anywhere but at his face.

At last Lucas sniffed and rubbed his cheek with the flat of one hand. 'You want to come for a walk or something?' he asked. 'I feel like getting away from here.'

May waited a decent interval before she said, 'Okay. If you like.'

They skirted the edge of the water where ink-black ripples subsided into the shingle. May walked boldly at Lucas's side instead of drifting in his wake. They passed the Captain's House and climbed northwards on to the headland. When she looked back she saw her father making his way towards the beach steps and felt a mean little beat of relief that he was alone.

It was difficult climbing upwards in the dark. Roots and brambles snagged May's bare ankles but she let them tear at her because she was too conscious that a swerve might bring her into contact with Lucas's arm and shoulder. A prickie of heat ran down her side at the thought and her scalp tightened over her skull.

Then Lucas tripped over a branch, and he stumbled and swore. 'I can't see a thing. Let's stop.'

The headland rose on one side, a black sweep of trees. On the other was the sea, invisible but always audible. Tonight it made a low murmur like a chorus of close-matched voices. There was a dip in the ground, not much more than a shallow saucer but still a shelter of sorts, on the landward side of the path. Lucas sat down with his back against a tree stump and with only a second's hesitation May took her place beside him. There was a lightness inside her head now that allowed her to do what would have seemed impossible a day ago. She eased herself back against the stump, stretched out her legs next to his. They sat and listened to the sea.

A year ago, May thought. The last night of Doone's life. She had drowned the morning after Pittsharbor Day. All the other people gathered on the beach this evening must have remembered it, even though none of them had spoken her name. But she was always there, she must be, on the other side of the invisible membrane.

'You okay?' Lucas asked and she nodded wordlessly. She put her head on his shoulder and he shifted his position to fold his arm around her. She felt a jolt

253

when he touched her and she had to look down dizzily at her folded hands, at the thickness of her own thighs, to assure herself that she was still May – that she hadn't slipped sideways through the same membrane that seemed to grow thinner, almost to have dissolved into nothingness.

The hands were hers. But Doone was close, it was her breath in May's hair, not the breeze off the sea. The sea's voices were louder.

Time and space were shifting. Had Lucas brought Doone up here a year ago? Was she living this night now, or the other one, which had somehow swum back again to engulf them all?

The entries she had decoded from the diary whispered in May's ears. Hot, heavy words that made her feel loose and restless.

He slipped down beside me. We kissed for a long time. I touched him, I made him touch me. Everywhere, and there. I don't care, I don't care about anything else.

I love him.

Those three words, over and over, written with such passion that they scored the underlying pages.

Lucas was probably drunk, May knew that. She was certainly drunk herself. None of it mattered. Behind his head, where the glimmer of his hair bisected the sky, she could see an arc of cold stars. May closed her eyes to shut them out. She leaned forward, dipping into space, swimming through nowhere until her mouth connected with his. Warm, solid and a surprised hiss of indrawn breath. She pressed closer, willing him with all of herself not to recoil.

There was a surge of delight when he began to kiss her back. She sucked the inside of her cheeks to stop her lips curving in triumph. It was not a matter of scraped mouths and clashing teeth, which was all she had known of kissing before. It became simple and imperative, like drinking when you were thirsty. Only it made you thirstier still. It wouldn't be enough, even if you drank until the water ran out of your mouth.

Lucas stretched himself on the ground in the shelter of the hollow and drew May down in the circle of his arms. She measured herself against him, gleefully registering soft and hard. His hand found a breast. 'How old did you say you were?'

'Uh, fifteen, nearly sixteen.' He had forgotten; she had told him the truth once before.

'Jesus.' He breathed the word into her mouth but he didn't lift his hand. His fingers teased in a slow circle so that her back arched upwards to meet him as he leaned over her.

She opened her eyes and saw the stars again. Don't move, she warned them. Stay frozen like this for ever.

Lucas's long leg rested over her hip now. His hand was in her hair, she was fastened to him. There was a trace of sourness in his mouth. His fingers were busy at her shirt front.

I touched him everywhere, and there.

May knew what she should do. Lightly, with her breath locked in her chest, she trailed her fingers down to the belt of his jeans. *Don't let me fumble*, she prayed.

Was this what Doone had done?

The leather tongue was awkward, clamped in the buckle's ridges. One-handed, Lucas undid it for her. A minute's exploration yielded folds of cloth, then what she had expected to find. Only more solid than in her imaginings and somehow more brutal.

She didn't know what to do now. She had forgotten how to breathe and her stomach was churning. Her mouth dried and she drew her head back a fraction. Out of the corner of her eye she saw a movement between the trees. She struggled to sit upright as words broke out of her mouth. 'There's someone there.'

Lucas lifted himself on one elbow and scanned the silent woodland. 'No, there isn't. There's nobody.'

'Someone was watching us.'

The note in her voice made him shield her with his arms. He found that she was shivering. 'It's okay. C'mon, look. We shouldn't be doing this, anyway. I'm really sorry.'

Whatever it was must have been in her imagination. May threw herself down again into the mould-scents of dead leaves, knowing the thread was broken, torn between despair and relief. Lucas lay back too and held her against him. He had done up his jeans and now he began to button her shirt for her.

'Don't be kind,' she begged. 'I don't want you to be *kind*.'

A door had opened on to a new landscape and had

256

slammed shut again before she had a chance to take in the view.

He smoothed her hair, tidying strands of it away from her open mouth, the embodiment of kindness. 'Why not? You're really nice, aren't you? Much nicer than your sister.'

The clarity had all gone. Her face felt swollen and a tide of nausea and longing and revulsion swelled inside her. She lay still in order to contain it, and made herself listen to the sea and the minute crackling and sighing of the woodland. She was wrung out by this confusion of the explicable and the unknown. After a while Lucas's hand faltered, then stopped in mid-stroke of her hair. From the rhythm of his breathing she could tell he was falling asleep. 'Talk to me. Tell me about something.'

'Sure.' His voice was blurred. 'Tell you about what?'

'Last year.'

'Uh. What about it?' He was yawning under his breath. There was no shadow, no weight pressing on him – there couldn't be.

'Doone. Will you tell me what she was like?'

They were lying so close that his twitch of surprise passed straight into her. 'Doone, why? She was kind of just a kid. I didn't really know her. It was sad when she drowned but – you know, it was an accident. It was exactly a year ago, come to think of it.'

'I know,' May said.

I made him touch me. Everywhere, and there.

Only now she understood that somewhere along the

257

way, somehow, she must have made a miscalculation. Lucas wasn't hiding anything, he couldn't be. He wasn't clever enough to act so convincingly. His detachment was genuine. Whoever *he* had been for Doone, it couldn't have been Lucas.

The certainty made her feel suddenly lighter. They were separate after all, the two of them – what she knew now wasn't what Doone had also known. Perhaps none of it was significant, none of Elizabeth's disturbing old stories, the island, the pale-faced woman. Lying down with Lucas it was easy to dispel the thoughts of them. What was real and yet fantastical was here and now. The ribbed collar of his faded sweatshirt that curled under her cheek. The rivets on the pockets of his jeans revealed to her fingertips, the faint grease scent of his hair. Finding herself in Ivy's place. Love lodged itself uncomfortably beneath May's breastbone like a lump of undigested dough. 'What did you do a year ago tonight?'

'Pittsharbor Day? Let's think. Softball, like today, and the girl I was with didn't get in a snit about it like your sister. We swam, I think, and drove over to the Star Bar for a burger. Yeah, that's right, I remember Beth got carded. There were a bunch of people over there, it was a good night.'

'Did you see Doone?'

'No, of course not. In the afternoon I saw her on the church green, when I went up there for half an hour. I didn't speak to her or anything and I only remember seeing her then because of what happened the next day. What is all of this?'

There was the choice of telling him, or keeping it zipped within herself. Either he would think she was nuts, with her diaries and codes and fears of slipping out of herself and into someone who was *dead,* or else she was normal, like everyone else. Or maybe even better than that, in the way Ivy always managed to be. 'Nothing,' she managed to say. 'I just feel sad about her. You know I'm sleeping in her bedroom?'

'No, I didn't know that.'

She pressed on, knowing that she should be quiet. 'I wondered if people, all of you who were at the beach last summer, can still see her in your memories? Like today, if remembering the way she was last year somehow gets overlaid on this day that's empty of her, so it seems like she is still here?'

Lucas thought about it, but not for very long. He sounded bored. 'I guess if you knew her at all, you might feel something like that.' And beneath May's cheek his shoulder twitched in dismissal. She felt a tiny flake break loose from the block of her admiration for him and drift away into a space of disappointment.

The recklessness that had come after the wine was diminishing too. There was a cramp in the arm that lay buckled underneath her and she didn't want to move her legs in case it made him let go of her. She forced herself to lie completely still instead, thinking, *I can make him go back to where we were. Ivy would, in her cool, self-sure way.*

Everywhere and there, only what happened now wasn't dictated by Doone. It was between herself and Lucas.

She moved her free hand, sliding it over his hip to rest in the hollow of his waist. If he had been drifting into sleep again the movement reawakened him. He rolled half on to his back and stared up at the sky. Awkwardly May bumped herself closer and hooked her knee over his leg. When he didn't respond she hoisted herself higher, almost to lie on top of him, and nuzzled his jaw with her mouth. Even as she did it she knew it was all wrong.

Instead of drawing back she rolled further across him and tried to reconnect the thirsty kiss. There was a weightless second in which he might have responded. But instead he sat up abruptly and May sprawled sideways. Her teeth snapped on a sliver of skin inside her lip and the pain of it made tears sting in her eyes.

'Hey, I'm sorry. Are you okay?'

'Yes.'

His voice had changed, back to the way it had been when he told her on the beach to fetch a towel and keep warm. 'May?'

'*What*.'

'I shouldn't have done that, before. It was dumb of me, I wasn't thinking.' He touched her shoulder, tried to turn her head so he could see her face, but she kept her neck rigid. 'You're really nice, May. Too good to be treated like that. I'm sorry.'

'What for? It's nothing.' Humiliation almost choked her, tasting like acid in the back of her throat. She wanted to bury herself under the blanket of leaves, burrowing down into rotten blackness.

260

'Are you sure?'

Blood roared in May's ears, much louder than the sea had ever sounded. She nodded hard, thinking that she had to get away from him immediately before any more shame descended on her.

He said, so kindly that she flinched under another stab of misery, 'Come back to the beach.'

'No. You go and find Ivy. She'll want you to.'

'Perhaps. I'm not sure I want it.'

Yes you do, it's all you do want. 'Go on. I'm just going to sit here for a bit.'

'I can't leave you on your own in the dark.'

May scrambled to her feet and spat at him, 'Just *go*, will you.'

The shrill words vibrated endlessly until the salt air at last damped them into silence. Lucas was as embarrassed as she was. 'Okay, if that's what you want.'

He turned abruptly and crashed down the path towards the beach.

When she couldn't hear him any more May sank down again into the leaves. She lay back, but immediately the branches over her head knitted together and began a whirling that made her stomach heave. She sat up and concentrated on not being sick. As the ground levelled again and the trees slowed in their rotation May remembered the movement she had seen between the black pillars of the trunks. It had been no more than an instant's flicker like a pale flame, but without Lucas's protection fear expanded in her chest and rose into her mouth, more stifling than any nausea. She saw the island woman's face

261

again but now the eyes stared wide and the jaw hung open.

A scream began inside May but it died before it reached her throat. Unsteadily she hoisted herself on to her feet and looked dazedly around her for the way home. She couldn't remember which way to go and she staggered for a dozen yards uphill before turning and running wildly down the path. Long before she reached the beach she was gasping and sobbing, and her ankles and calves were ripped with thorns. At last she burst out on to the slope of shingle and her terrified rush slowed to a stumble before she stopped and hung her head, panting for breath and soaked in a clammy sweat. She had rushed almost to the water's edge and now a wave gathered itself and broke over her feet. She hardly noticed that her shoes were filled with water.

The moon had risen and it laid a silvery streak across the water. In its light the beach was empty and unthreatening. The Beams' sailboat swung gently at its mooring and the light wind teased out a metallic rattle from the mast. Beyond it the island was a featureless black hump.

May shivered. Turning to look at the houses she saw that there were cosy lights in all of them now, including the upstairs windows of the Fennymores'.

Her terror slowly drained away. In its place a lumpen misery remained.

In the Captain's House John would be sitting on one of the chesterfields, reading his book. May found she couldn't bear the idea of going in to face him, or Ivy's inevitable absence. She moved back out of the range of the wavelets and flopped down on the stones. All her undigested love for Lucas had turned to a knot of disgust with herself. She drew up her knees and resting her chin on them she let the tears run.

Even Doone, her alter ego, had deserted her tonight.

In the grip of her loneliness May understood how much of an eerie companion she had made of the dead girl.

She didn't hear the footsteps behind her until they stopped a yard from her shoulder. Then she spun round and saw Marty Stiegel. He was breathing hard as if he had been running and his face in the moonlight looked pale and sweaty. 'May. It's you.'

He didn't sound as he usually did, one of the knit-together group of adults who played tennis and grilled shrimp on beach barbecues.

'Who did you think?'

Marty shook his head, then looked more closely at her. 'Is something wrong?'

'No. Nothing. Just, you know.'

It would be such a luxury to talk to someone. Marty was friendly and he had been kind to her; May valued that.

'I'll walk you back up to your house,' he offered.

'Can I come up and have a drink with you? Like I did the other day?'

Marty hesitated but she hurried on, extemporising, 'There's been a fight. Family stuff. I'd kind of like to be out of the house for a while.'

'Sure. Okay. I remember fights with my mom and

old man like you wouldn't believe, when I was just about your age. But we got over them, you know. We're good friends now, and you and your dad and sister will be too.'

'Do you think so?'

'I know so.'

They crossed the beach in front of the Beams' house and climbed the Stiegels' steps. Justine's stroller lay folded in the seagrass at the top of the wall and Marty picked it up and carried it like a shield.

The room was empty although the door on to the deck stood open and all the lights were on, as if Marty had hurried out on to the beach without a backward glance.

He told her that Judith and Justine were asleep, that he must go up himself in a minute. But at the same time he moved around the room, turning off some of the lights, switching on some music that sighed in the background. He heated some coffee for May and poured wine for himself. Then they sat at opposite ends of the sofa. Through the half-open doorway May could see the room he used as his study, where the sheaf of photographs of Doone rested neatly squared in the concertina folder.

'I got a copy made of the volleyball picture for you.'

'Thank you.'

May drank her coffee, letting it warm her. She didn't feel any longer that she might be sick at any moment, but a blunt finger of pain prodded behind her eyes.

'What happened to your mouth? Here?'

Marty leaned forward and dabbed it with a Kleenex. She winced at the pressure where she had bitten the inside of her lip. He showed her the red-brown blood-stain on the pink tissue and at the same time glanced at the Elastoplast on her hand.

'Oh, no, it's nothing. I climbed up on the headland and fell over a log or something. Bit the inside of my mouth. Dumb.'

Now a silence grew in the room. It spread, lapping into the corners like an incoming tide until May shifted against the cushions. Then Marty asked gently, 'Do you want to tell me what's wrong? I'm a good listener. There is something, isn't there?'

'I guess there is,' May whispered.

She rested her aching head against the high back of the sofa. Instead of closing her eyes she began to talk in a low whisper.

She told Marty about not wanting to come on the family vacation to Pittsharbor with her father and sister, because they were only pretending to be a family nowadays. She told him about the bedroom in the Captain's House and the French bed, and the way she sometimes felt safe and sometimes trapped in there.

Tentatively at first, then in a stream of words so fast they tangled themselves in her mouth she told him about the woman on the island and Elizabeth's story about her, and about her fear, and her conviction that Doone was separated from all of them only by the thinnest dimensions of time and space, which shivered and paled, and threatened to dissolve.

Marty was right, he was an excellent listener. He

265

took in the flood without moving or interrupting, watching May's face.

'I thought I saw something moving in the trees up there.'

He nodded. 'I understand exactly. I feel the same, sometimes. In fact I thought I saw Doone on the beach tonight,' he murmured. 'But it was you. Moonlight plays tricks.'

A tremor passed through May. Marty took hold of her hand and patted it in reassurance. 'Imagination is a powerful force, especially in a place like this, which is governed by tide and wind and fog. Of course it works to shift reality into a different dimension. The effects of a vivid imagination like yours or mine can be fearful or delightful. Or both.'

It was only imagination working. That was better to hear than Elizabeth's unsettling bits of history and personal experience. 'Can I tell you what I was really afraid of?'

He came closer. 'Go ahead.'

Here in the pleasant room, with Justine's baby toys in a basket and the music playing, it was almost easy to admit to it. May half smiled at herself. 'I thought . . . I was afraid that somehow I was becoming Doone. That the differences between what we are and what we did were so blurred that she was taking me over. I thought, you know, that I liked Lucas because she had done. I thought everything was connected together and I started worrying about what was going to happen to me in the end.'

Marty was smiling too. 'You're nothing like her.'

266

The reassurance was welcome even though she had heard it before. She sighed with the relief of having confessed her fears and in doing so making them seem small and irrational. Her headache made her roll her head sideways and Marty helped her to cushion it on his shoulder. May let the comfort of his attention wash over her. He was like her father, without the collisions and misunderstandings that governed her relationship with John.

May said, 'I found her diary hidden in our bedroom.'

Marty settled his chin against her hair. She heard the gentle exhalation of his breath. 'Did you?'

'It was hidden in a hole in the wall.'

'Did you read it?'

'Yes. After I'd tried not to for a couple of days. That was when it began, when I started feeling that she was too close to me.'

'Why was that, do you think?'

'Half of it was stuff about school and friends, and her mother. Just like I'd write if I kept a diary. Except about my mother. But the rest of it was different. She was in love and she wrote about it so weirdly. For her it was either despair or wild happiness. I thought the guy *must* be Lucas.'

'But didn't she say so?'

Marty was so close that his breath was warm and moist on her cheek. The comfortable feeling left her, replaced by a tingle of unease. She lifted her head and edged away, and at the same time she heard a floorboard creak overhead.

'No. Quite a lot of what she wrote was in code.'

'Go on,' he said softly.

'There isn't any more to tell.' May folded her arms.

Marty moved back to the opposite corner of the sofa. He lifted his glass to his mouth, but put it down again without drinking. Upstairs, Justine began to wail. 'I've got to go up,' he said. His expression had become both eager and submissive in a way that intensified May's uneasiness. She had a sense that there were fetid adult concerns here, which were at the same time too close to her. The hairs at the nape of her neck prickled, recalling the different sensations Lucas had stirred up.

Justine's wail became a louder cry.

'I'm going,' May assured him. 'I'll go the front way, along the lane.' Marty was barring her way. 'I'll be okay. It's only a couple of steps,' she promised.

'Does anyone else know about what you found?'

'No.'

'Don't let it upset you, May.'

'I won't,' she breathed. Marty was already on his way to Justine. May said good-night and let herself out in the opposite direction from where she had come, through the door that faced towards the Pittsharbor road.

As she slipped past the Stiegels' black Lexus she saw through the tangle of hedge that there were lights and people outside the Fennymores' house. She reached the lane and looked past the tree where Aaron had once surprised her.

An ambulance was drawn up at the porch steps and

paramedics in blue coveralls were lifting a loaded stretcher into the back. Hannah hurried out in her brown coat and climbed in beside it. One of the men secured the doors and took his place in the seat at the front. The engine started up and the headlamps swung over the ragged grass, so May instinctively ducked out of sight behind the hedge. She shrank further when the ambulance had rolled past her. Someone else was coming out of the house, stopping to lock the door and hurrying towards the lane.

It was Marian. She fled unseeingly past May but May saw her clearly and she was weeping helplessly.

John was reading in the shadowy room, but he threw his magazine aside as soon as May came in. 'Where have you been? I was about to come out looking for you.'

'I just went for a walk.'

'Why didn't you tell me you were going to be out for hours?' He came across to her and tilted her face towards the light.

May pulled away from him. There had been too much touching tonight and her skin felt bruised by it, although it wasn't the kind of damage that her father would be able to see. She hid her bitten lip behind her hand. 'So, where's Ivy?'

'That's not the point. Ivy's adult and you aren't, not yet. May, why can't you talk to me?'

There was accusation in his eyes and pleading, when she didn't want to see either. She wanted reassurance. If she were still a little girl she wouldn't have to understand any of the things that had happened to her tonight. But John was failing her. Even though he insisted she was a child he couldn't make anything right for her and wasn't that what fathers were supposed to do for their children?

She had seen him through this window, which now admitted black sky into the room, except for the pane that was blank with cardboard. His arms wound around Leonie Beam and his face different, distorted and remote. Even the thought of it made her feel sick. And it gave her the old crawling sense within her head, in some dark cavity, that there was something connected but even worse. She would do anything, violent or craven, so long as she didn't have to turn round and see what it was.

John hadn't kept Ali safe, had he? How could he shield her either, from anything, when all the time she could read his weakness in his eyes? He wanted things from her, to know that she was all right, when it should be the other way round.

Dr Metz had told her that it was okay to be angry and it was anger that made her say coldly, 'I don't know. Talk about what? I just went for a walk, that's all.'

He tried to make her look at him, to hold her eyes, but she slid herself away.

'I saw them taking Mr Fennymore off in an ambulance.'

'When?'

'Just a few minutes ago.'

'Poor Mr Fennymore.'

The telephone began to ring and over the insistent noise May said she was going up to her room. Her foot was on the bottom stair when she heard her father answering. After the first hello his voice changed. It was Leonie, obviously.

In the bathroom she ran the bath water at full velocity to block out all possible sound and stripped off her clothes. With one foot she nudged the crumpled heap into a corner. Her body felt polluted and ingrained with dirt. When the bath was full to over-flowing she reluctantly turned off the taps. There was silence from downstairs.

She stepped into the hot water and slowly lay down. It crept over her skin until it engulfed her. May let her head sink back until her face swam beneath the surface and her hair fanned out like seaweed. She let out a sigh of bubbles from between her lips.

Ten

It would be another hot day, but as yet there was a whitish mist blotting out the sky and sea. The horizon quivered between the two in parallel pale lines of grey and pearl, and the unmoving air was thick with salt. The gulls on the beach stalked and pecked at their wavering reflections in the low-water pools but Leonie stared beyond them at the confines of the bay.

She saw a lobster boat drawing a diagonal line from the headland to the corner of Moon Island. It slid out of her sight behind the outlying rocks but the pulse of the outboard, more subcutaneous vibration than sound, stayed with her for a long minute afterwards. It was a year ago this morning that she had stood with a brown bag of shopping in her arms, watching Doug Hanscom's boat bring Doone ashore.

A jogger down on the beach reached the steps at the southern end and began the climb upwards. It was Tom, on his morning way into Pittsharbor.

Leonie opened the screen door from the porch, closed it behind her and stood looking into the centre of the house. The wide, shallow stairway with scuffed matting led up from the big hall. On either side two tall, foursquare rooms were filled with white morning light. It was a good house, solid and benign, and untidily comfortable with the well-used and unfussy things that Marian had filled it with. And Leonie was thinking as she walked through the quiet space that she felt about it just as she felt about Marian herself. She could appreciate all the qualities, but she had never been able to make appreciation warm into affection.

In the kitchen she toasted an English muffin and spread it with cranberry jelly. The sunlight cut through the jelly on the blade of the knife to make it shine like a jewel, and it warmed the yellow Formica of the worktops with their edges eroded like a geological formation to reveal the brown and white strata within. Leonie touched everything gently, the handle of the knife, the ridged knobs of the cupboard doors and the taps over the old sink. In Tom's absence, in his continued and unbroken absence even though they had slept side by side, she was saying goodbye.

She sat down at the kitchen table to eat her muffin and watched the sky beyond the windows. The peace didn't last long.

Elliot came down the stairs with Ashton in his arms and Sidonie skipping in front of him. 'You're up early,' he said.

Sidonie squirmed up on to a chair and turned a radiant smile on Leonie. 'Banana me,' she wheedled.

'D'you mind, Leonie?' Elliot asked over his shoulder.

'Of course not.'

When did I ever mind? I am Aunt Leonie, infertile but obedient.

As Elliot put the baby into his seat Leonie mashed a banana in a saucer. She put a spoon into Sidonie's fist, breathing in her early-morning unwashed smell of innocent sleep. Sidonie began to eat and the intensity of childish concentration moved Leonie as it always did. Out of Elliot's sight, under the table, she clenched her empty hands.

Richard was the next to appear, yawning in his bathrobe. 'Tom gone running?'

'Yes.' The question was superfluous. When did Tom ever relax his rigid routines?

The smell of coffee brought Karyn and Shelly downstairs, and two of the younger children who argued about tennis games over their bowls of Cheerios. The noise level rose and Leonie sat within her bubble of isolation and let it break over her. At home in Boston she always ate breakfast alone and in silence. Tom usually stayed in bed longer because he left later for work.

It seemed inconceivable now that she had ever tried to be one of the Beams, let alone kept on trying for so long. Determination was crystallising inside her. It tasted like elation salted with fear.

Usually none of the older children appeared until long after breakfast, but this morning Lucas slouched in in his shorts and creased T-shirt. His hair hung down around his face and when he leant over Leonie for the milk he gave off a powerful waft of sweat and

274

stale alcohol. He yawned. 'Is Grammer all right after last night?'

Karyn scraped a ribbon of yoghurt from Ashton's chin. 'What d'you mean? What happened last night?'

'I thought I was the last one in but Grammer came back a few minutes after me. Mrs Fennymore had called up to ask for some help. The old man was taken ill. They hauled him off to the hospital.'

'I didn't know,' Karyn said. 'That's really tough.'

They heard Marian coming down the stairs and fell silent as they waited for her, all of them looking at the door. She appeared in a torn silk kimono with her hair standing out in a thick mass of grey and silver coils. Her face was marked with creases and there were dark pouches under her eyes.

Her children made themselves busy around her and even the grandchildren paused for a second in their intake of breakfast. Marian was irritable and rejected the coffee Shelly gave her as too weak. She rebuked Lucas for being only half dressed, before settling at the table in the place she always occupied. She answered their questions about Aaron in a sharp voice.

He had had severe breathing difficulties, and had become ill and distressed. Hannah had called for an ambulance, then telephoned Marian. 'She was distressed herself. I went to help, that's all. There wasn't much I could do.'

Leonie watched her. There was a difference in Marian this morning that she couldn't quite place. The kitchen was too full, there was too much light and noise and talk. Marian drank her coffee and pulled her kimono more securely around her bulk. After she had finished she went to the telephone, but there was no reply from the Fennymores.

'Hannah must be still at the hospital.'

She brushed aside the questions and went out of the porch door, leaving her children mutely raising eyebrows at each other.

Leonie dutifully loaded plates and knives into the dishwasher and swept crumbs off the Formica into her cupped hand. Each small action took on significance for being the last time she would do it here. Today she would have to leave. She felt the potential energy spring-loaded inside her, surely just enough of it to carry her away and out of the gravitational field of Pittsharbor. Beyond that, she had no idea.

She found Marian sitting alone on the cluttered porch. The old wicker chair with a beard of broken cane hanging beneath the seat was her favourite. Marian's eyes were fixed on the sea and her arms hung heavily over the chair arms, with the dirty diamonds of her rings looking like marine encrustations on the bay rocks. She didn't hear Leonie approaching, or see her stop and lean against one of the porch pillars with her arms folded.

Although she had followed her mother-in-law out to the secluded corner, Leonie didn't know what she wanted to say to her, exactly. It was just that there should be at least some acknowledgement between them of the decline and wastage of her marriage, some honest transaction made and recorded for the future.

276

I wanted a baby. I didn't try on purpose to have this ache and a crater in my belly, did I? Do you think it's worse for you, or for me, maybe? It wasn't to Tom she wanted to say this, not any longer, but to his mother who had never loosened her grip on him.

At length Marian turned her head.

In the unguarded moment before their eyes connected Leonie saw what it was in Marian that was different this morning and the recognition of it arrested the momentum of bitterness in her.

Marian was transfigured by grief. It washed the hauteur out of her face and left it loose and vulnerable.

An uncalculated movement of sympathy started up in Leonie. She found herself kneeling down beside Marian's chair and taking hold of her meaty hand. She squeezed it tight until the big diamonds of Dickson's old-fashioned tributes bit into her clenched fingers. 'Is Aaron dead?'

'No. Not so far as I know.'

Marian didn't yield an inch. But Leonie could still imagine why such a chord of sorrow was sounding within her. The Beams and the Fennymores had lived side by side on the bluff for many years. They hadn't been close friends, or at least Leonie had never detected any signs of particular friendship, but surely Marian would look back on the summers of her own life lived in parallel with Aaron's and Hannah's? The probability of Aaron's death would make her think of Dickson's and her own. The grief in her face must be for losses Leonie could only guess at.

It was the *place* that affected them all. The beach

277

reverberated with sadness. *Why did I never recognise it before?*

Sadness was thick like the sea-salt in the air, and as blind and all-pervasive as the endless fogs. The peculiar taint of it clung to the Fennymores and Elizabeth, and it crept through her own tissues like a disease. Now she saw the ravages of it even in the invincible Marian. Under the bright, healthy skin of all their summers, the swimming and sailing and barbecue parties and tennis games, lay the invisible cancer of sadness. The spirit of the place.

Leonie tried to dispel it, to rub some warmth back into Marian's hand. 'Can I do anything?' she whispered.

Marian inclined her head. The possibility of a connection stirred between them. Marian felt it too, it was obvious that she did. Leonie thought, *maybe it's not too late. Maybe we can talk to each other. I haven't tried very hard. I will if she'll let me.* The beginnings of a smile twitched at the corners of her eyes and mouth.

Marian's head lifted again and she stared at Leonie. 'Do anything? No, I don't think so.'

The possibility had been there, lying in the no man's land between them, and she had seen it and chosen not to pick it up. Not only was it too late, the entire night had passed and now the day was coming round again.

Slowly Leonie let go of her hand. She sat back on her heels with cramp twisting her leg muscles and shook her head as if to clear it after a ringing slap. 'You never liked me, did you?'

Sidonie had wandered on to the porch. She stood at the top of the steps looking out over the water in her pink dress and jelly shoes. One fist twisted up the hem of the frock, showing her pants underneath. The jet-black spirals on her forehead lifted a little. A breeze had sprung up off the sea and the tentative white mist would soon be gone.

Marian had the grace to look startled. 'You're Tom's wife. Of course I like you, Leonie. It goes much deeper than that, you're family.'

'I don't think so.' Leonie stood up, looking down on the fuzzy grey circle at the crown of Marian's head, all the sympathy gone out of her. 'I think you and I disliked each other from the beginning. The shame is that neither of us ever had the guts or the wit to own up to it. If we had done we might have fought about it, or even laughed at ourselves.'

Richard wandered out with his coffee cup, and Karyn appeared, scooped up Sidonie and ran inside again. 'What's happening?' Richard asked, without much interest.

'Leonie's upset.'

'I'm not upset,' she answered. The stored-up energy was suddenly released. It carried her along in a seductive rush. 'In fact, I'm happy. I'm very happy because I'm going to walk out of here right now and I'm never coming back to this place again. I've had it with family parties and being an auntie, and a good daughter-in-law. I'm a failure at all of that and at being Tom's wife as well, although God knows I've tried hard enough.'

279

Marian's face contained three perfect circles of shock and amazement, and when she looked at him Leonie saw that Richard's expression mirrored his mother's exactly. They were so alike, they were so fucking *identical*, all the Beams.

Enough. In her outburst she had sounded just as petulant as Gail or one of the even younger ones. It was time to go, before the Beams or the beach itself finished her off. She half turned in the stunned silence and saw an arrangement of helmet crab and conch shells against the porch rail. She had always hated the beachiness of them, and now she picked up a shell in each hand and hurled them one after another in a curving trajectory towards the edge of the bluff. As if to smash the mirror of the sea. Of course, they fell far short even of the drop down to the beach. They bounced and rolled harmlessly in the seagrass.

A tide of elation and cathartic fury carried Leonie the few steps to the porch door. She opened it and closed it behind her with elaborate care. In the kitchen there was another silence, with adults and children frozen in their places. They couldn't have heard from here what had actually happened outside, but the atmospheric shock waves had rippled a warning all through the house.

Leonie picked up Tom's car keys from the counter top. Her own car was back in Boston. He always insisted it was pointless to have two cars up at the beach, even though when he went on one of his trips back to the city it left her without independent transport. Her handbag, luckily, was where she had left it yesterday on a chair on top of a pile of magazines. She dropped the keys inside and swung the strap of the bag over her shoulder.

'Leonie . . .' began Shelly, who was not a Beam and therefore might have been an ally, but still managed not to be.

Leonie didn't wait to hear her. She went out again into the high hallway and looked up the stairs towards their bedroom, *Tom*'s bedroom as it had always properly been, thinking about clothes and a suitcase. But then, through the narrow glass panes of the front door, she saw Tom himself coming between the dogwood bushes towards the house. The sight gave her a slight shock, as though she had already placed him somewhere else.

He opened the door, one arm crooked around a bag of croissants and the newspaper.

'Good run?' she asked.

She was blocking his way but he side-stepped around her, already moving towards the kitchen. 'Yes, thanks.'

'They're all in there. Everyone's in the kitchen except Marian and Richard, who are out on the porch.'

He hadn't even looked at her. But even if he had done, if he had faced her properly and taken account of her it would have been too late. The sweet stream of liberation was running too strongly.

'Are you going out?'

'Yes, Tom. I'm going out.'

And with that she left the house. In the sunlight,

which had now grown strong, she passed the rusting cage of the tennis court and the bushes that separated the garden from Elizabeth Newton's. Each successive footstep was lighter and faster. Tom's elderly Saab was parked nearest to the lane. She slid into the driver's seat and adjusted the incline and the rear-view mirror to make it hers. As she reversed, then nosed forward into the road, she looked back at the house; the door was firmly closed and no one had come outside to follow her or try to stop her. Leonie realised she was panting for breath as if she had been running.

She drove down the lane, away from Tom and Marian, and the Captain's House, and the malign curve of the beach with the hungry glitter of sea-water beyond it. She slowed as she passed the Fennymores', but there was no one to be seen there either.

She took the south-westerly road out of Pittsharbor. When she had put five miles between herself and the beach she relaxed the tension in her braced arms and let her shoulders rest against the seat back. She waited for the undertow of guilt and anxiety, but nothing came. There was only relief.

After another five miles she turned on the radio and searched across the local news and country music stations and weather reports until she came across the voice of Alanis Morissette. Leonie drove on, singing softly, with no idea where she was heading.

The first sign for the upcoming freeway startled her. She had automatically followed the route home – not *home* any longer, but towards Boston.

She didn't in the least want to go back there. She

braked suddenly and swung in to the side of the road, causing the Ford station-wagon behind her to sweep by in an angry diminuendo of hooting. In the past she might have reddened in belated apology, but now she merely shrugged and wound the wheel in the opposite direction. She took the next turning at random, then another, driving deeper into countryside she had never penetrated before until she had no idea even whether she was headed north or south. The fuel gauge blinked an amber light at her and she frowned back at it, unwilling to have her shapeless reverie broken.

A sign ahead indicated that she was coming to the town of Haselboro. She had never heard of it, and it looked a small, sleepy place as she drove past the neat lawns and white gates of the outlying houses. Although she had eaten the muffin and cranberry jelly for breakfast she realised suddenly that she was ravenously hungry.

Haselboro didn't have much of a centre. There was a dingy supermarket down a slip road and a garage opposite it across a wider section of the through road. Leonie pulled into the garage forecourt beside the gas pumps and a boy in blue coveralls emerged at once. 'Fill it up.' She smiled at him. He had longish hair the same colour as Lucas's and a face buckled with shyness. Leonie rummaged in her bag and brought out her wallet. There were only fifteen dollars in cash, but she had her credit cards and bank book.

'Going far?' the boy asked, not quite looking up from the fuel nozzle.

'Yes. Well, no. Not really. I'm not quite sure where I am.'

He did squint round at her then. 'Got a map, have you?'

'No, actually.'

'There's one in there, if you want to have a look. I can't give it to you, it's not mine.' He pointed towards the shop door.

'Just a glance would be a help.'

The map lay on a counter near the cash till, with a half-eaten hot-dog oozing ketchup into a paper napkin alongside it. Leonie looked longingly at the bitten frankfurter as she flipped the map open. She fumbled the route from Pittsharbor with her forefinger, trying to trace the roads she must have followed in her meander. At length she located Haselboro. To her surprise it was only a couple of miles from the coast. She had driven a sprawling U north-eastwards from Pittsharbor.

The boy materialised at her shoulder.

'I'm sorry, I interrupted your lunch.'

'It's okay.' He blushed as he busied himself with her credit card.

'Where can I get one of those?'

'Huh?'

'A hot-dog.'

'Oh, there's a store down the next street. It's more of a grocery store, they don't really sell hot-dogs but I'm sure they'd fix you one if you asked. It's my mom working there. Say I told you to come by.'

'Well, thank you, um . . .'

'Roger.'

'Pleased to meet you, Roger.'

'And you, ma'am.'

Leonie went out again into the sunshine and found that she was smiling.

The store was on a corner at the intersection of two streets. Traffic lights blinked at an empty road each direction and a large yellow dog lay panting in the shade of the store awning. There was a public telephone against the outside wall. Leonie glanced at it and hurried into the store.

A pleasant-looking woman was stacking cans behind a glass-fronted display case. She had the same shyly indirect gaze as Roger. 'I guess I can,' she agreed, when Leonie had blurted out her request. 'It'll just take a couple of minutes out back.'

While she waited Leonie idly read the local ads on cards pinned beside the door. Laurel Jackson had lost her progressive bifocals, brown steel-rimmed, some time after the first week in August. There was to be a colossal yard sale at Kingdom Road, and a grey and white cat, four white paws, very friendly, had gone missing from home. And under the heading Summer Rental was a snapshot of an uncompromisingly plain grey-boarded box of a cottage, one square window on either side of a tight front door, set in a pretty woodland clearing.

Leonie read the details twice. Suddenly available for short summer rental. One bedroom, fully furnished, $280 per month, plus utilities. No pets, no children, no smokers. There was a name and a telephone number at the foot of the card.

She became aware that Roger's mother was at her elbow, holding out the hot-dog in a folded paper napkin. 'Ketchup or mustard?'

Leonie paid, then propped herself against the hood of Tom's car while she ate, eyed by the yellow dog. The peace and emptiness of Haselboro was soothing. An idea was turning over in her mind and before the last mouthful of frankfurter it had turned into a decision. If not Boston, where she didn't yet want the company of friends or their inevitable questions, then why not here rather than anywhere else?

It was far enough from the sight and sound of the sea.

In a cottage in the woods she would take a spell of solitude and reflection. Such a place would give her the privacy she needed and the independence, much more than a hotel or a bed and breakfast. There were still almost two weeks of her summer vacation remaining and she could spend that time alone, thinking, and walking and making some plans for the future. At the end of it she would have to go back to Boston, to the job that she now needed more than ever, but maybe, Leonie thought, her mind running ahead, if she kept a cottage she could come back to it when she needed to. It would be her own place, not permanent enough to be a tie but still somewhere she could depend on. Somewhere that was neither Boston nor Pittsharbor and so free of all the associations that clung to the familiar places.

'Was that hot-dog good?'

'Better than good. Mrs . . . ?'

'Brownlow.'

'Mrs Brownlow, I'm looking for a rental cottage. Not for too long, maybe only a couple of weeks while I sort some things out. Do you know if this one is still available?'

She looked doubtful. 'Jim Whitsey's place? It's a ways out of town, I wouldn't know who's up there right now. But you could give Jim a call, he's generally at home in the day since he retired. Phone's right out there on the front wall.'

Two hours later, after a series of wrong turnings on the woodland roads, Leonie sat in the sun on the cottage step waiting for Jim Whitsey. Goldenrod and magenta spikes of loosestrife grew in the long grass at her feet. There was plenty of light in the clearing and the mixed woodland encircling it danced with shafts of pale green and gold. It seemed welcoming after the forbidding spruce stands of the Pittsharbor shore.

Mr Whitsey bumped up the track in a Chevy pick-up. He shook hands and unlocked the cottage door, stepping aside to let Leonie walk in. He was a man of few words.

There was a woodburner in the main room and the ingrained scent of woodsmoke caught in Leonie's throat with a reminder of the shadowy room in the Captain's House. The kitchen was in a corner of the same room, with the bedroom leading off it. The only other room was a tacked-on bathroom at the rear, with an old water-heater and a green-stained bath. A large spider was stranded in the bottom. Leonie opened the window and carefully deposited it outside. 'I'll take it.'

'Two weeks in advance. Cash.'

'I'll have to drive back into town to the bank.'

'Yup.'

But when he secured the door again behind the two of them he extracted the key from the lock and dropped it into Leonie's hand. 'You enjoy yourself here. I'll call by later for the money, if that suits.'

Leonie smiled at him in the sunlight, wondering why she felt so cheerful when she had just turned her back on her whole life. 'Thanks. I'll be here.'

After Jim's pick-up had bumped away she took her seat again on the step. Back into her mind's eye came the picture of Marian's crab and conch shells spinning in crooked arcs over the porch rail. Anger had disabled her to the point where she couldn't even throw straight. Leonie dropped her head into her hands and laughed out loud at the memory.

There was no one on the beach. At the public end were the usual families and groups of kids, but in front of the five houses the glitter of sand and shingle was unbroken.

May paced her way slowly along the tideline. Fragments of twine and polystyrene granules and crustacea shells were caught up with the bladder wrack. The harsh sun burned on her head and drew an unhealthy stink of decaying fish out of the debris at her feet.

The Beams' porch was empty, not even Sidonie or Ashton was about. Their bright-coloured toys lay scattered around. May looked sidelong, in fear of seeing Lucas, but also willing him to be there.

The breeze had died away and the air was motionless. She shaded her eyes and looked in the opposite direction, out to the island. Its ridge of black trees looked like the spines of some fantastic creature. She thought the whole island might shudder and heave, then dive slowly beneath the water.

A year ago, Doone was already dead.

When she turned to the beach again she saw that Ivy had suddenly appeared. She picked her way over the stones at the base of the beach wall, gold-skinned against the faded green wood of the breakwater. When she reached a patch of sand she spread out her beach towel. Even at this distance May could see the minute crescents of pallor exposed beneath her buttocks as she bent over. Ivy arranged herself on the towel and bent her neat head over a book.

May went on walking aimlessly but all the time her path tended itself towards Ivy. At length she came obliquely to a point within talking distance.

Ivy glared at her. 'Don't hang around me. Come over and sit down if that's what you want.'

May sat down a yard away, looking straight out to sea. Ivy was always so dismissive. May wanted her sister's attention and she wanted to challenge her too. 'Where's Lucas?'

'How should I know?'

'Where did you go last night?'

289

'Oh, just to the Star Bar with Sam and some of the others. It was okay. Not that thrilling.'

'Yeah? I went for a long walk with Lucas.' She had Ivy's full attention now. She could feel her eyes drilling into the side of her head.

'So what happened?'

May shrugged hotly. She wanted to lay out the details, to have the scald taken out of them by shared exchange and to be reassured she wasn't a freak, that it was how it sometimes happened with the right person but so disturbingly in the wrong place at the wrong time. But neither could she resist the chance to taunt Ivy just for once. 'Oh, uh, you know. He was really nice.' She sensed but couldn't see the glare of jealous disbelief and enjoyed it like a sip of iced water cooling her parched throat.

Then Ivy gave her low, disbelieving laugh. 'Was he? With you and your braces? Well, there's no accounting for tastes.'

May bowed her head. The taunt made her mouth fill with metallic saliva and puffed the flesh of her thighs and belly into hateful cushions within her tight clothes. That was how they did it, of course, Ivy and the handful of thin girls like her whom every boy in every school wanted to date. They promoted themselves with an effortless armoury of ridicule and superiority. Under the claustrophobic skin of the day a flood of hatred pulsed through May and directed itself at Ivy. 'Why are you such a bitch?'

'Why are you such a baby?' Her voice was cool and bored as she turned back to her book.

Effortfully May stood up. The memories of the night before were too vivid and unresolved in her mind. They became a series of jerky tableaux, grotesquely overlit figures superimposed on blackness. How hot the sun felt on her head.

Inside the Captain's House it was at least cool. With the clockwork force of habit May opened the refrigerator and quickly closed it again. The sight of margarine tubs and dribbled mayonnaise bottles was disgusting.

Upstairs, her bedroom held the sound of the sea within it like a conch shell.

The diary lay in its place next to Hannah's books. May dusted the tips of her fingers over the black cover.

Marian sat in unaccustomed stillness. Making considerate detours around her, Shelly and Karyn prepared lunch once the babies had been put down to nap. The younger generation from Lucas downwards, for once aware of concerns beyond their own immediate circle, had taken themselves off for the day to another beach. The telephone rang once and Marian made a heavy movement towards it, but Tom was too quick for her. It was only a girl calling for Joel.

The adults sat down to eat at the kitchen table. It was most unusual for the food not to be laid out on the shady porch overlooking the sea. A fly buzzed drearily against the screened window, and knives and forks clinked in the silence.

'Will she have gone back to Boston, do you think?' Karyn asked.

There was a whitish, pinched area of skin around Tom's mouth. 'I've no idea where she's gone.'

'You must go after her,' Marian said.

'I think she'll come back when she's ready.'

'You must go and bring her back.'

Tom put down his knife and fork, neatly positioning them. 'Leonie is an adult. And so am I. We can make our own decisions.'

There had been so many meals, so many variations on this same rigid theme of family gatherings and advice dispensed. Each of them was used to it, familiar with his or her place in the scheme.

Marian's lips drew together. 'I'm not convinced of that, on the evidence.'

Karyn reached out a restraining hand but her mother shook it off.

'Do you love her? Do you still love each other? Because if you do you'd be a fool not to go after her right now. *This* is what matters.' She made a gesture that took in the circumference of the table and the ring of faces.

'No.' The crash of Tom's chair shook them all. He was on his feet, pushing himself away from the litter of plates and broken bread. 'No,' he repeated. He turned from the table and left them staring after him.

Marian's face collapsed inwards, a network of lines meshing her mouth and eyes. She covered the lower half of it with her hand. 'What does he know about anything?' she whispered.

*

Elizabeth sat in her evening room, where the tendrils of a creeper made a minute scraping against the window glass. The irregular sound competed with the metronome ticking of the clock. Spencer had brought her the news that Aaron had been taken to the hospital. She had telephoned once and had been told that Mr Fennymore was stable. Beyond that there was nothing to do but wait.

When she came back from Europe, with her trunks of new clothes and her albums of photographs of Paris and England, and her taste for French cigarettes, it was Aaron who had been waiting.

The Captain's House was now owned by some people from Bangor, Elizabeth's mother had told her that in one of the regular letters from home, so there could be no more meeting in the empty dust-barred rooms where feathers waltzed in the breeze of their passing. Instead there had been a chance encounter on Main Street on an afternoon when summer had faded into the smoky chill of late September. Elizabeth had already been back in Boston for almost a month; there had been some parties she had wanted to go to, so she had not made the journey up to Pittsharbor right away. At one of the parties, the engagement celebration of a girl she had been at school with, she had been introduced to a lawyer called Andrew Newton. He was almost thirty, more than ten years older than Elizabeth herself. But she had liked his dry sense of humour and his slightly formal manners because they reminded her of some of the Englishmen she had met on her travels.

'Newton? Newton?' Grandfather Freshett had mused. 'Randwyck Newton's boy?'

'I think he must be,' EIizabeth's mother responded. 'Randwyck married Dorothy Irvine, didn't he?'

'That's right.'

Elizabeth would once have felt impatient with this exchange, but now she found that she listened with a flicker of interest and even understanding.

In Pittsharbor, when she did come back to it at last, nothing seemed to have changed. Except, she thought, that the houses looked smaller and Main Street was narrower and more old-fashioned than she remembered. In Purrit's Dry Goods the very same sacks and cans were arranged behind the salty window glass. And for a night and a day after her arrival she had looked out for Aaron Fennymore with almost the same breathlessness as when she was a girl, eager to slip away with him to the Captain's House. She had watched the tides and the movements of the fishing fleet, and had wondered when she would hear the signal of his low whistle.

They had written no letters to one another in all the months of her absence. At the beginning of their separation Elizabeth had believed that their love was enough to bind them together without needing translation into the pale medium of words and she also feared that in any case her lover would be no letter-writer. Then, as the months passed, she had been reluctantly and gradually more eagerly taken up in the new world of Europe. Pittsharbor and Aaron had settled deep inside her, precious but untouched. Now

294

that she was back, with the murmur of the sea in her ears and the tiny prickling of salt crystals on the skin of her arms, she was filled equally with longing for Aaron and with apprehension.

When she first caught sight of him, swinging down Main Street with a sacking bag slung over his shoulder, her immediate and terrible instinct had been to duck away and hide from him. There was an arrogance in his bearing and a rough look about him that made a poor contrast with European poise, even with Andrew Newton back in Boston. As soon as she recognised her betrayal her face crimsoned with shame and she was rooted in place like a tongue-tied schoolgirl.

Aaron had seen her. He didn't change his pace, but came straight towards her. He stood foursquare on the sidewalk, blocking her path, and dropped the sack on the ground between them. It smelt powerfully of fish. 'So you're here, then?'

'Just. Yesterday.'

'I hear you were back in Boston a month ago.'

He had changed. There was a directness in him now that seemed almost brutal and the way he stared into her face was momentarily frightening.

'I . . .' She wouldn't let him accuse her. 'I had some things I wanted to do.'

'*Things*?' There was a sneer in his voice that was new, too.

'That's right,' Elizabeth said coolly. She was regaining her self-possession now, but the look of him and the sound of his voice still made her want to step into his arms and never move out of his reach again.

'You promised to marry me,' Aaron said. 'And you are old enough to know your own mind now. I've been waiting all this time for you.' He put his hand out as he spoke and took hold of her upper arm.

Elizabeth was wearing a lawn blouse with hand-sewn tucks and her good wool coat because the afternoon wind was cool. She faced up to him, aware of the looks of the passers-by and shopkeepers. She thought he was rude. 'Take your hand off me,' she said in a low voice.

His arm dropped at once. 'I'm sorry.' He made no effort to speak quietly. He didn't seem to care who heard or saw them, and Elizabeth felt herself turning hot with shame. It was only later, much too late, that she realised it was passion that made his face burn and anger that made him sound rough. She wasn't used to naked feelings, only to dances and mild flirtations in taxis and Andrew Newton's courtly manners.

Aaron bent down and shouldered his bag again. 'Well, then,' he said. 'I'm glad you're back safely. But it doesn't seem that all your wandering has taught you any sense.' He left her standing on the sidewalk.

'Aaron . . .' she called, just once. He never turned back, and she was too conscious of what her mother's neighbours might think or say to do what she wanted and run after him.

After that, they saw each other in Pittsharbor often enough. They met, even, once or twice in private, and tried to repair the damage. They kissed once, awkwardly, as if they were tasting a dish they had once overindulged in. But Elizabeth couldn't forget that she had wanted to run and hide, and Aaron had seen that urge so clearly in her face.

In the years afterwards they both thought separately that they might have tried harder and understood each other again. But circumstances were against them; the Freshetts were pleased with the idea of a match between Elizabeth and Andrew Newton, and Hannah had presented herself to Aaron.

On the night before her engagement party Elizabeth and Aaron met again, on the beach looking out to the island. It was February and the bay was a ring of ice, so they had to walk briskly over the crackling shingle.

EIizabeth held her furs tight against her throat, but Aaron pulled them aside and put his mouth to the warmth of her skin. 'It isn't too late,' he whispered.

Elizabeth thought of her diamond ring and the announcements in the Boston newspapers, and the house on Beacon Hill, which had already been bought. She knew she was a coward and despised herself for her weakness as she answered, 'It is. It was too late when I left for England.'

Three months later she became Mrs Andrew Newton, and within a year Aaron married Hannah and began his buying up of the land on the bluff.

What a waste, Elizabeth thought in the quiet of her evening room. What a long and colourless waste of a life.

Aaron lay on his back with his arms at his side. Beside the head of the bed was an oxygen cylinder on wheels with a mask attached to the hose.

Hannah sat in a chair, dozing with her head bent. He had tried insisting that she went home, but she had refused even to listen to him. His breathing was stronger and easier now, and the grey-blue tinge had faded from his lips. Footsteps approached and receded in the corridor outside.

Suddenly Aaron said loudly, 'I'm ready to go now.'

Her head jerked up again and she leaned forward to catch at his hand.

'Did you hear me Hannah? I'm ready to go.'

Her mouth worked but she couldn't make words come. She put her fingers on his forehead, bending closer over him.

He struggled to sit upright, weakly fighting her off. 'Where are my clothes?'

'Aaron, lie still.' She looked over her shoulder in the direction from which help might come.

'Bring me my *clothes*. I want to go home.'

'Hush. Keep still now. Bobby's coming from Cleveland and Angela . . .'

'It's not necessary. I'm not dying.'

'Of course you are not.'

'I want to go home. I want . . .'

She soothed him, 'I know, I know you do. In a few days, maybe . . .'

He looked past her to the window. The strength he had summoned for the brief outburst was already spent. 'I want to smell the sea,' he whispered.

Leonie waved and smiled at Mrs Brownlow as she loaded her purchases into the Saab. She had bought supplies of food and drink, although the stores in Haselboro hadn't offered much choice in either, and withdrawn Jim Whitsey's rental deposit from the bank. She could be self-sufficient for a few days now, except that she had nothing to read. There was no bookshop in town and the *Haselboro Compass and Advertiser* would not hold her attention for very long. She glanced again at the telephone on the wall of the store and this time walked towards it without hesitation.

It was May who answered.

'May, hi. This is Leonie Beam. How are you?'

'I'm, uh, okay.' Her voice was thickened, as if she had been asleep or perhaps crying.

'Are you sure?'

'Of course I am.' Hostility blanked out the moment of uncertainty and Leonie thought, *she is all right, or as much as she ever was.* 'May I speak to your father? Is he there?'

'Yeah, I guess, I think he's outside somewhere. I'll get him, if you want.'

I do want, Leonie mouthed. There was the sound of the receiver being dropped and footsteps scuffing away.

The yellow dog had roused itself from its spot in the shade. It came across now and sniffed at Leonie's ankles.

'Leonie?'

She smiled at the sound of his voice. 'Yes.'

'Where are you? Are you at home?'

Home? 'No. Well, in a way. I'm at a place called Haselboro. John, I've left him. I walked out this morning. I just drove here and rented a place.'

There was a silence while he digested this. 'And last night you said you had no idea what you were going to do.'

It seemed a very long time ago. It had been a bad telephone conversation; she had felt in despair. In comparison with that, this airy freedom was entrancing, and the mundane small-town street with its white fences and shade trees and slow-moving cars was poignantly beautiful.

'Leonie? Are you still there?'

'Yes. John, will you come and bring me some books? Just a visit, between friends. A glass of wine and some talk. I've got a jug of Napa Valley Chardonnay right here in the car.'

He asked for directions and she gave them. 'I'll be there in an hour or so.'

'Will it be all right for you to leave your girls, just for the evening?'

'Ivy is grown-up now,' he answered. 'And May is . . . well, May will be fine for one evening. I'll be there soon, okay?'

'Do you have to go?' May asked him in her most sullen way. She hated the thought of being left alone, yet could not acknowledge it. 'Where's she gone, anyway?'

'Just up the coast a way. I'm going to lend her a couple of books. Leonie needs someone to talk to right now. Do you want to come up there with me?'

May ignored the suggestion. 'She wants you, doesn't she? Isn't having a husband enough for her, she has to grab you as well?'

'It isn't quite like that.'

'No? What is it like, then?'

John sighed, caught between irritation and the knowledge that he should stay this evening and try to explain himself to May. She had sabotaged his relationship with Suzanne; maybe more honesty would help them all this time.

He hesitated, then remembered that Leonie had called him from a public phone. He couldn't get back to her to change anything now. May was planted in front of him with her fists balled in the pockets of her jeans. 'I have a life to live too, May,' he said quietly. 'Each of us does. Breaking windows and cutting your hands won't change the fact; all it does is hurt you and fill me with fear. I love you and Ivy . . .'

He saw her look away, as if to hide the unwilling pleasure his assurance gave her. He thought, I haven't talked enough, I haven't given her the love she needs, the way Ali would have done. 'And you mean more to me than all the rest of the world. But there are other kinds of wanting and loving as well as *this* kind.'

He tried to put his hands on her arms and turn her to face him but she stepped aside, round-shouldered. John sighed. 'Can we talk about all this tomorrow?'

'I suppose so.'

'Where's Ivy, anyway?' he asked.

'How should I know?'

'I'll see you later. Watch some TV or something, then both of you have some dinner.'

He tried to kiss her but May jerked away suddenly and the connection became more a blow than a kiss.

Then he was on his way out of the door with some paperbacks under his arm.

May watched him drive away. 'I hate you,' she yelled into the space he left behind.

Ivy came in later from the beach, in a black mood because Lucas and all the others had been missing for the whole day. May was huddled with her feet on the chesterfield cushions, staring at the television. Hostility crackled between them, low-key at first as they bickered about supper and the division of chores. The sky outside was turning lead-coloured as the light faded.

'Where's Dad gone, anyway?' Ivy demanded.

May told her, gracelessly.

Ivy adopted her dropped-hip pose, all her slight weight prettily angled. She pointed the tip of the bread-knife at May. 'You know, why don't you back off a bit? Why shouldn't he go see her if that's what he wants to do?'

'Don't point that at me. Because she's married to someone else, for starters. I came up here the other night and saw them . . . saw them through the window . . . it was . . .' her voice blurred in her throat, then came out too high and hard. 'It was disgusting.'

Ivy was staring at her.

The membrane was stretching, thinning. Losing its opacity. 'I mean, she's someone's . . . Tom's wife. I mean, how would it have been if Mom had. Had been with . . .' May's voice faltered and died altogether.

Out of the box in which she had kept it jumped the

302

memory. Suddenly and without warning it was there, and she knew what it meant and was amazed by its sharp completeness.

She had been perhaps six or seven years old.

She had woken up in the night, surprised because it seemed that at one minute she had been asleep and the next she was as wide awake as if it were the middle of the day. She was hot and her throat burned with thirst. Usually there was a cup of water beside her bed, but tonight Mom must have forgotten to put it there. She pushed the covers aside and climbed out of her bed. The apartment was quiet but the dim light burned in the hall outside, just as it always did.

She padded out and crossed over to the room where her parents slept. The door was ajar. The room beyond was in darkness and the big bed was flat and empty under its smooth cover. May went on down the hall, remembering that John was away somewhere doing his work.

There were lights in the big room where the TV was. Soft yellow light, from the big cream-shaded lamp on the corner table. Silently she pushed the door wider open.

Her mother and a man were lying together on the sofa. Their legs were bare and twisted together. Her mother's head was thrown back and she looked as if she was screaming. Only more terrifying than terror itself, there was no scream coming out of her mouth, but a little squeak, soft-sounding, like a kitten's cry. The man's breath was rasping. Then he began to moan too. He was saying her name over and over, 'Ali, Ali, Ali.'

May turned and ran away. She dashed back to her room, pulled the covers over her head and pressed her hands to her ears. She didn't know how she slept, but she must have done. In the morning she had a temperature. Ali was her mother again, cool and reassuring. She kept her home from school and sent a note to her teacher saying that May had a feverish cold.

She had forgotten it all because she had made herself forget. She had buried it away.

Ivy was still staring at her and she knew that Ivy knew, and now Ivy knew that she knew too.

Ivy gave her little shrug, prodded a bagel with her bread-knife. 'Jack O'Donnell,' she said.

May recalled a big, friendly man who had come to the apartment sometimes, no more or less memorable than any other member of her parents' big group of friends. Ali and John were sociable, they gave lots of noisy parties and big, relaxed lunches on winter weekends, which spilled on into evening drinks. Jack O'Donnell's had just been one of those faces.

'You knew about it?'

The shrug again: a twist of her sun-tanned shoulder and a downward pull of the mouth. Ivy was affecting adult knowingness. 'It happens. It's not exactly an original story, is it? People do these things, good or bad. You'll learn that.'

May thought of the night before. Lucas and Marty

Stiegel. People do these things. . . . *I made him touch me. There and everywhere*. Her own collusion in the stew of sex made her feel sick again. 'Was it, was it just once, Mum and him?'

Ivy laughed out loud. 'Of course not.' Her sneer took on a life of its own. It ballooned out of her mouth and swayed in the air between them, greasy and coloured, so that May put up her fists to bat it away from her, and she saw how Ivy flinched at the movement in the fear that May was going to hit her.

The idea lit up in May like power itself. The balloon sneer vanished and instead the space between the two girls was shimmering and splintering with threat. May clenched her fist and punched, and it was like the instant of hitting the volleyball, clean and pure, except that she slammed her knuckles into her sister's face instead.

Ivy staggered backwards with the bread-knife still in her grasp. It came up in a silvery arc through the glimmering air and came to rest against May's throat. Ivy was gasping with shock and a red blaze burned on her cheek. The knife blade vibrated against white skin. 'You fucking little bitch,' Ivy whispered. But her eyes widened when she saw what her own hand was doing. The fingers opened and the knife fell with a clatter. She put her hand up to cradle her cheek. Slowly they stepped apart, their eyes still locked together.

'You should be careful what you say,' May breathed. 'What filthy things you say about our mother.' But even as she said it she knew that her world view was askew; it was and had been balanced on the wrong

305

fulcrum. Without thinking she took her eyes off Ivy, looked round to find John and only then remembered he had already gone to Leonie.

With the contact between them broken Ivy bent stiffly and picked up the knife. She replaced it on the counter top and with her back turned mumbled, 'I shouldn't have said anything.'

'I suppose I knew already. I'd just forgotten.'

The telephone began to ring and Ivy picked it up at once. The change in her face told May it was Lucas. May knew how it was, she had seen and heard it so many times before. He was saying he was sorry, when it should have been Ivy saying it to him. 'Okay,' she murmured, sweetly grudging. 'Well, okay then. If you want.'

May went up the stairs. She opened and closed the door of her room but waited outside it, eavesdropping.

Ivy was agreeing to go out and meet him. There were endearments and a little curl of laughter like a feather settling on still water. Afterwards Ivy called up the stairs, 'May? I'm going down to meet Lucas on the beach. We won't be far away. We might go across to the island or something.'

For privacy, to their hollow behind the sandy crescent. *Everywhere, and there*.

When Ivy had gone the house settled around May into shadow and silence.

Eleven

There was not much Leonie could do to make the cottage living-room look welcoming. The chairs on either side of a brown shagpile rug were mismatched and hollow-seated, and the dim overhead bulb was dimmed still further by being encased in a cylindrical green shade. She put the jug of wine in the refrigerator, which looked as if it had stood in the same spot on the dented kitchen tiles for the past thirty years. She was humming as she went out into the dusk and picked some spikes of goldenrod from the clump beside the cottage door and arranged the flowers in a chipped earthenware jug from one of the cupboards. A pair of thick, velvety moths swirled through the open door and began a competitive dance around the lampshade. The silence of the woodland clearing and the damp pungency of the evening air soothed Leonie's spirit.

It was after nine o'clock when she heard the car coming up the track. She stood framed in the doorway and the headlamps swept over her before John extinguished them. A moment later he came in, bringing the outside world into the bleak room. He put paperback novels and a liquor store brown bag on the scarred coffee table.

'Thank you,' Leonie said. It was different to see him away from the beach. To be alone together in these bare, banal surroundings was intimate, but at the same time they had slipped out of the beginnings of easiness with one another and back into a kind of anxious formality.

'Shall I?' He gestured at the wine he had brought.

'I've got some chilled.' She poured it into ugly glasses and handed one to John.

He was looking at the chairs and the rug, and in the quietness the moths batted against the lampshade. 'What are you doing in this place?' he asked in clear bewilderment.

She looked at him before answering, trying to fit together the impression she had built of him with the reality of this big, greying man, who had brought awkwardness into her cottage. At the same time she caught a glimpse of her own desperation, which now seemed to fade like a shadow behind her. Had it only taken the day's one conclusive step to dispel it? 'I'm thinking. Marshalling myself, I suppose.'

She told him about stopping in Haselboro and the connections that had brought her to rest here.

'It's a pretty horrible little place.'

'Is it?' She was genuinely surprised at his vehemence. It was the bareness and simplicity of the cottage that had appealed to her; a place for people without much money to spare, which was still a shelter

308

and hiding-place in the woods. 'Well, whatever. I suppose you're right.'

'How long will you stay?'

The way he wanted to impose limits and horizons surprised her too. 'I don't know. Maybe I'll take some unpaid leave from my job and stay on for a while. Or perhaps I'll just go back to Boston in a couple of days or a week and do what has to be done.'

'Have you left him?'

She nodded her head. That much at least was certain. 'Yes.'

'Does he know?'

'I think even Tom will probably have registered my absence by this time.'

'I meant, does he think you've just flounced out and will come sliding back home in a day or so?'

'Maybe. But I made quite an exit. I threw Marian's shells over the porch.' He didn't know why she was laughing, she realised. 'I'm not going back. Whatever happens from tonight onwards, I'm never going back to live with Tom.'

She picked up the wine jug and tilted it towards John's glass but he half covered it with the palm of his hand. Leonie refilled her own glass instead and drank from it. 'I'm glad to have something to read.'

'I didn't know what else I could bring you. If I had known . . .' He couldn't stop himself taking another look around the confines of the room.

'I don't need anything else.'

'No. It seems extraordinary but I don't believe you do.'

They smiled at each other then, the first time since his arrival.

'I can even offer you dinner, of a kind.'

On the table in the kitchen Leonie laid out the cheese and fruit she had bought from Roger's mother, and they sat down facing each other. In both of their minds was the temporary picture of domesticity they made together, and the questions and possibilities that spread out from it now into an unreadable future, like roots burrowing under the ground. Leonie found she was closing out the questions, deliberately pinching off the growths. This distance had been far enough to come for one day.

She leaned across the table instead, pouring the wine, making John talk as they ate. She wanted to listen to him and he obligingly answered the need, first with generalities, then by answering her questions with more telling details about his life and his children. It seemed he lived a self-contained existence now, even though he liked the company of women. Leonie warmed to his independence and to the streak of resilience that she understood was hidden by his pliant exterior. He told her about May not wanting him to come out to Haselboro.

'I can understand why,' Leonie said. 'She wouldn't want to share you, would she?'

There was a small silence. Then John covered her hand with his. Leonie remembered their lunch at Sandy's, and the plate of cherries and the moment when she knew she didn't love her husband any longer. This was just as much a crossing place, she realised, although she didn't yet know quite what she should make of it.

'Is it a question of sharing me?' he asked her.

She gazed down at their joined hands, knowing that he deserved at least an attempt at an answer. And at the same time there was the old shadow of her despair slipping out of the periphery of her vision and disappearing. The way ahead looked suddenly bright and bare. 'Maybe not yet.'

'I see.'

They had finished eating. Leonie pushed back her chair and went around the table to take hold of him. 'Come and lie down with me.'

He stood up but made no other move. A space yawned between them. 'What does that mean?'

'I know it's a confusing message. It means I want to hold you and be close to you.'

'We can try it.'

The bed had a wooden head and footboard, and a thin green cotton cover. The centre of the mattress seemed to contain the impression of a single large body. They were both smiling at the incongruity of it all as they lay down in one another's arms. John put his mouth against her hair and she felt the warmth of his breath on her scalp when he whispered, 'I couldn't have dreamt of a more romantic setting.'

'I thought not.'

They hugged the bubble of laughter between them and Leonie thought dizzily, *today I left my husband. Tomorrow I don't know what will happen.* To be happy was a sensation she had almost forgotten,

311

but for all its inappropriateness it was what she did feel.

The bedroom window was a black eye staring at them. Leonie sat suddenly upright and swung out of bed to pull the dingy curtain across and block out the night. When she lay down again John held her and stroked her hair, and her neck beneath the veil of it. The comfort was all-enveloping. Leonie rested her head, letting her bones slowly sink into stillness. His warmth and the smell of him were benign, his breathing a steady rhythm against her heart. She sighed with satisfaction. 'That is so good.'

'Yes.' A movement of his shoulder settled her face closer to his.

'Can we just lie like this?'

'Of course.'

The pure silence from beyond the cottage filled the dingy rooms and seemed to cleanse them. Leonie realised that the comfort it gave her was in the absence of the sea's monotonous mumbling.

They lay in one another's arms without the need for talk. The awkwardness of John's arrival had all gone and the minutes slipped past them without being marked or counted. Leonie thought about the last time they had held each other, back in the Captain's House, before the shock waves of shattering glass cut out the sound of the sea. Dreamily she envisaged sex as a hurtling meteorite, a nugget of inexplicable rock red-hot from its passage through the atmosphere between them. It was separate from each of them and belonged to neither, but it would gouge a crater far

312

bigger than itself wherever it plunged to rest. Whereas this gentler intimacy suffused with silence was infinite. It was space itself.

Physical desire had left her. Sex had become associated with her inability to conceive and had been one of the garments that clothed her unhappiness. She had been so unhappy the other night. And without warning May's face upturned from her bleeding hand came back to her, with the same mute but fully legible lines of misery cut into it.

Is it a question of sharing me? John had asked.

Maybe not yet.

He should go home first to his children. It was already very late.

John's eyes were open, studying her face. Leonie shifted her position and he misread her intention. He found her mouth with his and busily kissed her. The kiss was half answered, then it shrivelled between them.

'Is this all wrong?' he asked. 'If you want me to walk away you must tell me and I'll do it. I know how that's done – it's moving in the other direction I've forgotten about. Only I don't want to be an instrument in the break-up of your marriage and I won't offer you myself in exchange for Tom because in time you'll come to resent the terms of the exchange even if they seem favourable now.'

'So what do you want?'

'I would like – yeah, I'd like to haul you off and make you mine in a cabin in the woods. A better one than this. I'd cut wood and draw water for you. Shoot

313

bears, spear fish. Forget about business mail and art history books. How does that sound?'

'Short or long term?'

'Uh, long. Whatever that means,' he corrected himself. 'You know what the bear and fish world can be like.'

Leonie smiled. His deliberate conjuring of a fantasy world made his intentions as opaque as hers. And that was perfectly fair, she thought. Lightly she asked, 'Can I get back to you?'

He took her face between his hands. 'Is that what we're saying? Not now, but maybe some time?'

'Yes. That's what I'm saying, at least.'

The creases at the corners of his eyes deepened. 'I think that's the right answer.'

He kissed her again. Then he unwrapped his arms and stood up, easing his shoulders and back, his height making him seem oversized in the cramped bedroom. Leonie wished for a moment that she had chosen now rather than some time. Instead she followed him out into the night, said goodbye and watched until the receding lights of the car had been swallowed up by the woodland.

When she was alone once more she experimentally turned off all the lights in the cabin. The instant darkness made flowers of retinal colour explode within her eyelids, but there was no menace in the star-shapes nor any threat in the night's mossy silence.

In the Captain's House after Ivy had gone May forced herself to process through the rooms, throwing open

314

the doors and staring in at the unmoving shapes of chairs and tables. There was nothing here, nothing to be afraid of, but still she shivered with currents of fear. Being alone made her think of Doone and the pale face of the island woman.

When she came back again into the downstairs room she pressed her face against the window with its broken pane and tried to see into the night. Then it came to her that her outline would be thrown up in sharp relief against the yellow lamplight and that all the house would be punctured with a collage of window squares. Quickly she retreated and flicked the wall switches that brought the dark inside.

When her eyes accommodated themselves she could see clearly enough to move around. She switched on the television. Immediately nodding heads with wide mouths filled the screen, and a babble of laughter and applause assaulted her ears. She found the remote control and aimed it at the noise so that it faded at once into silence, although her ears still rang with it. For a minute or two she gazed uncomprehendingly at the overanimated faces. The colour balance was off and the skins were greenish, the lips orange and puckered like weird specimens of marine life.

Oily waves of disgust heaved beneath May's breastbone.

Colour bled out from the screen and lent the darkness an eerie glow.

She pointed the remote like a weapon again and the set clicked off. Now the refrigerator started into life

315

with a low hum. Her ears were painfully over-attuned to the small noises of the house. There were the creaks of wooden boards and a tiny clinking, which might have been two pieces of crockery vibrating in harmony with the refrigerator motor.

May slipped to the stairs and crept upwards, setting her feet silently on each tread. The house was all in darkness now. She receded into her room and set the door open by the smallest crack, not wanting to shut herself in. At first there was no differential in the blacknesses contained by the hair's breadth of space looking out into the hallway and within the room itself. But as she sat on her bed with her spine drawn rigid she was able gradually to pick out the chest that held her clothes and the bookshelves where Doone's book lay in its place.

She reached out for it and held it. The red binding of the spine was peeling a little at one corner.

She knew by heart the last words Doone had written. She had been unable to forget them, ever since she had unlocked them with the help of Hannah Fennymore's whaling story.

I feel so sick with myself and the world.
I love him, every bone in me loves him, and I will never have him.
I want to die. It would be best for me to die.

The sea fretted and whispered bneath the window. In May's sharpened hearing the murmur grew louder and louder, swelling as if her head were empty except for the pearly whorls of a giant shell. Her legs were

316

unsteady when she stood up and the floor dipped beneath her like the deck of a ship under way. It was a long way to the window, much futher than the thirteen steps she knew it to be.

She looked out at the island. It was a black hump rising out of the silvery water but tonight there were lights on the crescent beach. There was a reddish glow near the waterline, a driftwood fire that would be sending bright sparks up into the salt air. There were smaller, dancing pinpoints round about that looked like torches. It was Ivy and Lucas and the others, Gail and Kevin and Joel and the rest of the cousins, and some of the kids from Pittsharbor. They had all gone out to the island and they were having a party.

May could hear their voices and meaningless laughter rising and falling within the sea-washed shell of her head. 'Hey Kevin. Just chill, willya? This grass is like, amazing. Whoo, unreal.'

And there was Lucas, with Ivy, their arms for-givingly wound around each other. Even now the physical imprint of him seemed burnt into May's skin, and she shivered with the confusion of absence and jealousy.

I love him, every bone in me loves him.

The impoverished and eloquent second-hand words of Doone's lament twined and echoed with the other voices.

Yet it wasn't *Lucas* Doone had loved so tragically.

I'm not her, May whispered to herself – I don't, I don't have to submerge myself like Doone did – if only the sea were not so loud and the house so silent and shadowed. Lucas was beautiful but he was ordinary, too, a chip of reality; the sweaty scent of him stayed in the back of her throat and she knew for certain that he was unconnected with any of this mess of darkness and water.

But if Lucas had never been Doone's fatal love, then who was it whose name she could never write even in her private diary?

Gently May laid the red-and-black book back in its place on the shelf.

She was standing at the window looking across the silver sheet of water towards the island when she heard the first soft footstep crossing the downstairs room. The old floor-boards creaked under an invisible weight. There was another step and then another, measured and unhurried. But no one had come into the house; she would have heard Ivy come in through the porch doors and John's car hadn't pulled up at the front of the house. The footsteps stopped and their hesitation froze her heart so that its beat faltered.

Something was coming for her, searching for her.

A liquid wash of terror poured through May. She couldn't allow herself to be trapped here in Doone's bedroom. Sometimes the door wouldn't open, as though an invisible shoulder held it tight, but it was open by a hair's breadth now, just as she had left it. She forced herself into motion, although fear locked her limbs. Her mouth dried with wordless gratitude for being barefoot as she slipped out of the room. The house itself had become a listening shell, the silence

318

noisy with whispers and sighs. May hung for an instant in the black hallway, motionless as a suit of clothes in a wardrobe, all her being trying to focus on what the threat might be. There was someone near, she could feel it in the tiny currents that electrified her skin.

As silently as a moving shadow she flitted across the stairhead. She could see no one in the narrow segment of the room visible at the foot.

John's bedroom door stood wide open. She melted into the blackness behind it and with her chest bursting and blood hammering in her head took the first breath since the footsteps had halted. They were moving again now. They came unhurriedly across the room to the foot of the stairs.

May retreated step by step until her knees came into contact with the edge of her father's bed. The steps advancing up the stairs now sounded as loud as a drumbeat. There was a shaft of light, lapping up the walls outside and sending a moving slice of visibility around the angle of the open door and across a wedge of floor. She stared in mute horror at the pattern revealed in the rug, then like a leaf falling she crumpled sideways into the bedcovers. She drew her knees up to her chest and pulled a blanket over her head. Her eyes squeezed shut and her breath stopped in her chest as she lay and waited to be found.

The bedclothes next to her face smelled of her father's body. When she was little she used to run into her parents' bedroom and climb into the warm hollow between them. She remembered that her father's smell was always strong but good, like hay or sawn wood. It came back to her now, and the memory of safety and security with it like a glimpse of a lost world.

The footsteps passed into Doone's bedroom and the light swept away with them.

At the back of the house where May lay huddled the sound of the sea was muffled. The tiny noises that reached her from across the hallway were much louder. She heard a soft swish like clothing brushing against furniture and the bump of small objects being moved around. That these sounds were audible and yet inexplicable made fear tighten its tourniquet grip on her. She was locked into immobility, but she could feel the bubbles of a scream or a sob forcing their way up into her throat. She closed her eyes tighter and bit the inside of her mouth to contain it.

Suddenly there was a snap. A second later the steps were coming back again, much louder and firmer.

It would find her now, whatever it was.

She hunched and waited. But the steps passed her father's door and trod down the stairs. They went across the living-room beneath, then she couldn't hear them any more, nor anything else except the endless voice of the sea.

She had no idea how long she lay in the same position. It was a long time, because when she did try to move hot wires of pain shot through her joints. She dared to push back the blanket and lifted her head to look around. There was nothing, except the darkened room.

After some more long minutes she found the courage to roll sideways and put her feet to the floor.

They were numb with cold and cramp in her legs almost made her stumble. May crept across to Doone's bedroom and with a brave sweep of her hand she clicked on the light. The brightness of it burned her eyes, but even so she saw at once that the diary was missing from its place.

A cold hand touched the back of her neck. She spun round, gasping, but there was nothing there.

From the window May saw that there were lights still moving on Moon Island. She could run out of this house with its echoes and footfalls, and simply row across to find the others. Kevin and Joel, mumbling about how stoned they were. Gail, and Lucas and Ivy. The moment she thought of it she was overcome by a longing to get to Ivy. Bold, sarcastic Ivy would pinch out this fear for her like an ant between her silver finger-nails. To *go to Ivy*, that was what she must do.

She ran down the stairs, her breath snicking in her chest. The room was empty, just as she had left it, the television remote dropped on the counter. She threw open the porch door and ran across the strip of garden to the beach steps. Across the shingle she ran faster, even though the stones hurt her bare feet. A rowing dinghy, one of the Beams' that they used to reach the sailboat at high water, was moored to a little white buoy. The oars were revealed neatly shipped inside when she tore back the tarpaulin cover.

May undid the mooring line and at a run pushed the dinghy away from the beach. She threw herself over the side and fell into the bottom. She was soaked to the waist, but hardly even noticed it. Her sister, she must get to her sister. A mixture of love and anticipatory relief made her sob, and there were tears on her cheeks as she fitted the lightweight oars and began to row. The boat skimmed over the flat water. The moon was up and the wake lapped behind the transom like molten pewter.

May looked back over her shoulder only once to check her progress towards the island. Then the prow of the boat ran into the beach with a soft judder and she let her head fall forward for one second in relief. Sweat from the effort of rowing so hard almost blinded her. She stumbled out of the boat and made the motion of pulling it further up into the sand. She realised then that there were no other boats beached anywhere along the glimmering crescent. The houses across on the bluff looked dark and gaunt. May had no idea what time it was.

On the beach she found the ashes of the bonfire. There were no embers left glowing at the heart of it but when she knelt down to touch it she felt the residue of heat. Glancing up from where she knelt she saw the lights again. They had receded into the trees. There was a pale glow, which wavered between the black boles of the spruces. 'Ivy?' she called out.

Her voice sounded weak and flat, and the salt-heavy air damped it into nothing. The tiny ripples breaking a yard away made an endless whisper. 'Ivy?'

There was no answer. May thought suddenly of Doone's sailboat gliding over the bay and the green skin of water closing over her body. The sea at her back seemed to pull at her, enticing her back to its innocent lacy edge and into the chilly beaten-silver oblivion beyond. Her soaking clothes were clammy against her legs.

May began to run. She pounded up the slope of sand away from the sea and over the lip of earth, where vegetation matted the margins of the beach. She stumbled across roots and brambles until she reached the black canopy of trees, then threw herself in among them. The light above and ahead tantalised her; it was further away, growing fainter. 'Ivy,' she screamed. 'Wait for me.'

All around her was the shiver and rustle of woodland. She began to run again, clawing her way up the slope. Once the ground seemed to give way beneath her and she looked down into the hollow where she had once seen Lucas and Ivy together. She remembered the pallor of Ivy's skin.

She was crying and gasping for breath as she scrambled on upwards. She had all but forgotten that there was no reason for her climb; all she could think of was setting a distance between herself and the cold beckoning of the sea. Ivy must be here somewhere. She had to reach her.

After another hundred yards, with her lungs threatening to burst inside her, May realised that she was plunging downhill. She must have crested the spine of the island and now she was running out of control towards the open sea. She crashed to a stop and looked around wildly, her breath as loud as tidal surges in her ears.

Over her head a huge oak tree spread its branches

like veins against the sky. They seemed to toss with the wind, although it was a still night. May put her hands up to her hair and found it wet. Slick strands of it clung to her skull and her neck, and there was salt in her mouth and on her tongue.

She took one step backwards and another, away from the great tree. The melancholy and doom that hung about it reached out to clutch at her, as strong as gripping hands. Weakly she staggered another few yards. Ivy wasn't here; she couldn't be anywhere near this place.

There was a darker mass ahead of her, more solid than the woven trees and branches. A sweet-sharp smell of crushed juniper caught in her nostrils and wrist-thick tree roots caught her foot. The island was alive with footsteps, with the swish of bodies steadily advancing on her through the foliage. She froze into stillness, knowing that there was nowhere to run, her ears filling with the pin-sharp signals of threat as they closed in on her.

Her innards loosened as she shrank backwards, one step.

It was a fine house that he had built for himself, she saw that immediately she began the walk towards it over the headland. Robert Hanner had always liked the best and it had never been his habit to forgo what he wanted or imagined to be his due.

The house was positioned on a vantage point that gave a commanding view of the serene bay and its islands, but it was set somewhat at an angle so that the occupants might not always have to gaze directly at the restless waves. After the months she had spent aboard the *Dolphin*, more than three years ago now but still present in her mind and in her dreams, Sarah fully understood the reasons why Robert might not always wish to have the sea before his eyes.

There was a grey curl of smoke rising from one of the chimneys. As Sarah drew slowly closer the sturdy clapboard walls and the secure shingle of the roof told her this was a safe haven for the people within. There were dainty lace curtains looped at the lower windows and a tidy pile of split logs was stored under a lean-to at the side.

After her long search and the journey that had led her here she was in no great hurry nor, knowing what she now knew, was there any longer the pounding of hope and anticipation in her heart. Instead there was a bitter determination to finish the course she had begun and to have done with it at last. She slipped a hand into the deep pocket at her side and closed her fingers around the smooth handle of the knife. She had carried the weapon about with her for so long that it felt like her trusted companion, the only certain ally she could claim in the world.

When she reached the shelter of a clump of bushes Sarah sank down on a rock so that she was hidden from the windows of the house. She rested for a moment, drawing her loose coat around her, although the fading afternoon had not yet turned cool.

It seemed that Robert had chosen one of the

sweetest spots imaginable to make his own. As it sank between bars of cloud the sun glittered on the sea and silvered the lines of breakers. The island in the bay's shelter was a handsome crescent of rock and sand crowned with a proud ridge of dark pointed firs, and on this distant beach another fringe of smaller waves was breaking. The light was as clear as spring water, and the air was fresh with salt and the scent of thyme and juniper.

'The Captain's House,' the woman at the lodging house in Pittsharbor had called it, although Sarah knew well enough that Robert Hanner was no retired sea-captain. Wherever and from whom his money had been stolen or extorted, it was not aboard a whaling ship, neither in the captain's cabin nor the forecastle. Robert had completed only one thirteen-month voyage aboard the whaler out of Nantucket before signing himself off. Once she herself had made the long voyage home from South America, Sarah's investigations at the shipping agents had revealed that much, if little else, about her one-time lover who was now her quarry.

After that there had been a long, weary time, which had yielded no information as to his whereabouts, and Sarah had come to understand that her task was beyond daunting. Robert Hanner had simply left Nantucket and vanished into the great continent of America, taking his name and his history, and Sarah Corder's life and hopes with him.

Once the small notoriety surrounding the return of the young woman who had disguised herself as a sailor

326

had died down, Sarah devoted herself to becoming invisible. It was not a difficult achievement. While her little store of money lasted she travelled the Massachusetts seaboard, staying wherever she could find a cheap bed, then moving on and always searching. Robert was a New Englander. Her belief and most fervent hope was that after all he would not have strayed too far from the familiar horizons of home. She scanned every face she passed in every street, eavesdropped on every conversation she could approach, read all the columns in each local newspaper. There was never any trace of him.

When her money was used up Sarah found employment as a scullery maid in the house of a Boston merchant. She slept in a curtained cubbyhole off the cavernous basement kitchen, and nursed her implacable resolve through the hard and monotonous days like a tender mother with a baby. Her meagre wages and few lonely hours off were all spent in searching the nameless crowds for Robert. When Boston yielded nothing of him she moved again, with a reference grudgingly supplied by the mistress of the house, to Portland and after a few months more to Rockport on Penobscot Bay. She allowed her instincts to guide her because she had no other inspiration. The daily sight of the sea was a reminder of what she had suffered aboard the *Dolphin* and served to firm her intentions, if any such reinforcement were necessary. Sarah had become a grim and melancholy version of the lost young woman to whom Matthias Plant had been drawn so tenderly.

At Rockport she found Robert Hanner. Or rather she stumbled across his name and whereabouts.

One evening, after she had completed her work, she was sitting beside the kitchen range with her weekly diet of the local newspapers. The light was dim and she hunched forward in her chair, turning the smudged columns of newsprint, frowning in concentration as she read. Turning to the Announcements section of the *Advertiser of Eastern Maine* the name she had sought for so long suddenly leapt out at her.

> At Pittsharbor on 22 July,
> to Robert and Charlotte Hanner,
> the gift of a healthy daughter.

Sarah let the paper fall into her lap and stared at the fire within its iron cage. She saw her handsome lover in the red heart of it as clearly as on the day he had abandoned her. Robert had not even changed his name, so he did not believe he had anything to fear. There would be no forcing him to marry her; he was already married and a father.

The fire crimsoned one side of Sarah's impassive face. The other cheek was as pale and cold as marble.

Within two days she had left the Rockport house and begun the journey north-eastwards to the fishing village of Pittsharbor. Part of the way she travelled with a local carrier who was transporting iron-mongery for delivery to general storekeepers along the route. There were certain favours he required of her in return and these Sarah performed mechanically, as if her mind and heart were entirely

328

disconnected from her body. The last fifteen miles she walked.

Two miles short of her destination she came to a rough inn and lodging house frequented by carriers and drovers, and the salesmen who brought commodities of all kinds to the remote communities of the area. Caring nothing for the speculative glances and bold invitations of her fellow guests, she took a room for the night and stayed within it until the middle of the following afternoon. If any one of the other travellers had been able to look in on her they would have seen her sitting motionless on the frowsy bed, hour after hour, her head bent in thought.

In the afternoon of the next day she emerged.

She called on the innkeeper's wife for some bread and cheese, and ate a little of the food when it was brought to her. She also drank a glass of rum and water. The woman of the house was a coarse creature who showed a ready tendency to talk once Sarah had explained that she was searching for a distant relative of hers. As a Christian gentleman, Sarah whispered, he might be willing to help her in some trouble that had befallen her.

The woman knowingly pursed her lips. 'And what might this gentleman's name be?'

Sarah uttered it.

'Why, yes. Captain Hanner, indeed. There ain't a better man in Pittsharbor, I believe, although I don't know him personal. Came up here two years ago, he did, from somewhere west. Married Charlotte Day within six month and built her a house on the bluff, out the other side of the harbour. Folk say he has a right nice little business started up, bringing ladies' dress lengths and bits of finery up from Boston to please those as have the money for such stuff. I wouldn't know a thing about *that*. Seems a strange manner o'work for a sea captain, although his wife's father is a draper with a good old store over in Belfast. But there, you'll know all this since he's a relation o'yours.'

The woman studied her, hard-eyed and appraising.

'How might I find the house?' Sarah asked softly.

'You take the Pittsharbor road and follow it on past the town and the harbour. You'll see the headland and the place he's built out there. Can't miss it, if you keep within sight of the sea.'

Sarah paid for her food and lodging, and picked up the small carpet-bag containing her few belongings. She slipped her hand once into her deep pocket, making sure her ally was still at her side, then set out along the Pittsharbor road.

Once on the headland within sight of Robert Hanner's house, Sarah waited impassively behind her screen of bushes until darkness fell. It was late September and the threat of ice already shivered the air. She saw the lamps lit in the windows of the house and stepped out of her shelter, leaving her carpet-bag behind her. She made her way silent-footed between the boxberry plants until she came close up to the house. Then, shadow-like, she melted into the deeper shadows beside the head-high pile of logs that had been providently stacked against the winter. She put her hand into her pocket and took out the long-bladed knife. The steel blinked its cold eye at her as she waited.

It was a weary interval before she heard the catch of the door undone and the creak of hinges. Sarah hefted the knife in her hand. She knew the weight and thrust of it too well from the work of stripping blubber off the stinking carcasses of whales.

Robert Hanner came out to the log-pile.

He was in his shirt-sleeves and with him came the scent of good food cooking and the warmth of a fireside. He bent to gather up the wood.

Sarah knew where to drive in the blade. She must guide it between the ribs and up, up into the tissue of the lung. Her arm, her whole body twitched violently with the anticipated thrust, but she could not make it come. Instead, she saw the body of poor Martin the bowman. He lay in the bottom of the whaleboat, his clothing ripped from him and his chest torn open by the line. She saw the bluish-white splintered ruin of his rib-age and the crimson pulp within that pulsed with the dying rhythm of his heart. It was an image that still visited her dreams. At the same time she heard the steady voice of good Matthias Plant. His fatherly kindness was a long time ago, but it was almost the last she had known.

The hand that held the knife hung paralysed at her side.

Robert Hanner gathered up the logs and all unknowing turned back to his family fireside.

She left the Captain's House and the headland, and carried her bag down to the silent harbour.

Moored to one of the jetty posts she found a dory and a stout pair of oars stowed within it. Her one thought was to remove herself, to retreat like a nocturnal animal beyond the reach of light and humanity. She unhitched the boat and bent to the oars. After the weight and speed of the whaleboat the little craft seemed no more substantial than an eggshell as she drove it through the swell.

Sarah rowed herself across the bay and out where the current ran between the island and the rocky promontory that jutted from the headland. Pittsharbor town nestled safely in its hollow, as far out of her reach as the moon.

Her first thought had been to row on to the horizon, until either weariness or the waves extinguished her. But some small flame of self-preservation still burned in Sarah, and the flicker of it made her turn her practised oar so that the dory drew broadside to the island and the shoreline that faced the open sea. She paddled through the surf and the prow of the boat grated on the shingle. With strength that she did not know she possessed she hauled it up out of reach of the greedy tide.

Above the beach she climbed upwards through the puckerbrush. The wind was rising and the first raindrops needled her face.

There was a shelter at the crest of the first ridge. She almost fell against the primitive structure of wood and rough stone, and the door creaked open at her touch. Inside nothing was visible in the intense blackness, but it was at least a protection from the rising storm. She reached out and followed the line of the wall with her chilled hand until she found the cobwebbed corner. She sank down on to her haunches, then to the bare earth floor. Out of her soaked bag she took a shawl and wrapped it around her shoulders. Only then did she allow her head to sink on to her knees and the hopeless tears to run out of her eyes.

The wind rose to a shriek, and rain and salt spray battered the walls of the hut. The storm raged all through the night and into the next day.

When the morning light began to thin the gloom Sarah was able to look around her. The few articles left inside the shelter were instantly familiar. There was a long-handled spade whose once-sharp blade was now rusty with disuse and a wooden bucket. The spade would have been used for severing the tendons of a whale's flukes, and for cutting deep incisions in the blubber by which the creature could be roped and towed back to the whaling ship for dismemberment, and the bucket was just the same as the one she had used for bailing sea water at Matthias's shouted command. From a peg on the wall looped a coil of whale line and on a shelf above it stood a brave row of pewter tankards.

The shelter into which she had stumbled was a whalers' refuge, a rough tavern for the crews of the small boats seeking to capture those whales which came close in to the shore. Their business must have been a disappointment because the place had been abandoned. But the irony at having fetched up in such a resort made Sarah's mouth twist in a bitter smile.

333

She waited out the daylight in the ruined tavern, venturing out into the wind-tossed open only once, to drink a mouthful of water from a brackish spring and gather a stained handful of wild berries to eat.

When night fell once more the wind dropped at last, but huge seas still battered the growling shingle. Sarah knew there could be no waiting for the waves to subside; she must row back to the mainland and do the deed that was waiting for her. She slipped through the trees and over the rocks to the beach, where the dory lay waiting for her. No fishermen from Pittsharbor had put to sea today.

Somehow she found the strength to propel the boat through the swell and spume to the bay shore. Drenched to the skin and light-headed with thirst and hunger she staggered across the shingle and climbed the rocks of the bluff. The soft lamplight shone from the windows of Robert and Charlotte Hanner's house.

Tonight she lacked even the cunning to try to conceal herself. She dragged herself to the nearest window and pressed her numb face to it.

A young woman sat within, dark-haired and dark-browed, with her head bowed in tender contemplation of the infant in her lap. In the background her husband busied himself with some small domestic business. The three of them were bathed in light and warmth, with the baby helpless and soft-limbed at the centre of the tableau.

Sarah's mouth stretched wide in a silent howl. She knew she could not murder Robert Hanner. The determination she had nourished melted away like

334

icicles in May and left her with nothing. The emptiness in her heart was worse than hatred; it was resignation and death itself.

The young wife looked up and saw the face at the window. Her scream as she snatched the child to her breast was so shrill that its echoes cut through the boiling of the waves and silenced them. Sarah turned and ran from the world for the last time.

She took the dory out once more and rowed through the wicked surf to the island. She waded the last few steps with the undertow ravenous at her legs and fell in exhaustion on to the bay shore. The boat tossed in the breakers and was carried away from her.

Somehow Sarah found her way over the island's crest to her last shelter. She spent one more long night huddled in the tavern corner and when the dirty light of morning crept around her once again she stood upright. She wrote some lines on a piece of paper from her pocketbook and printed the man's name on the folded sheet, before tucking it securely into her clothing. Then she picked up her bag with the few belongings and the knife that had lain on the earth floor beside her. She carried both of them down to the shore and dropped the bag into the sea. It wallowed at her feet for a moment, a waterlogged torso, then the current sucked it away. The knife she threw after it. It made a cold arc as it flew through the air.

She went slowly back to the whalers' hut and took the line down from its peg. Whaleline was both strong and light, the finest exemplar of the ropemaker's art. The best hemp was impregnated with tar vapour and three strands of seventeen yarns each were woven together, every one of those strands separately tested to sustain a burden of one hundred and twelve pounds. Her own meagre weight would make no impression on such a piece of line.

Above the shelter there was a sturdy oak tree with a convenient branch some seven feet from the ground. She climbed into the tree and tied one end of the line to a branch over her head. She lowered the free end and measured the drop with her eye. Then, using the boatman's hitches that Matthias Plant had taught her aboard the *Dolphin*, she fashioned the noose.

She did not sit long on her perch with the sea's merciless chorus loud in her ears. She closed her eyes and dropped into silent space.

Twelve

They stood at the doorway looking in. Ivy peered past her father's shoulder, twisting a strand of night-tousled hair across her mouth. May's bedroom was empty. It smelt unused.

'I don't know,' she muttered in answer to John's sharp question. 'Last night some time. Before I went out. I don't *know* what time I saw her.'

John pushed into the room. He patted the smooth bedclothes as if he might be able to detect the warmth of her body, rattled the catch of the window and ran through the line of clothes in the closet. Then he turned back to Ivy and his face reflected the fear within him as it ran and leaped into the recesses of his imagination. 'She must have been out all night.'

But when he had come in from Haselboro, from lying in a maze of indecision with Leonie in his arms, he had found his own bedclothes twisted and pushed aside. For reasons he couldn't begin to fathom some-one had tried to sleep in his bed. He had seen the evidence, but had let it lie in the back of his mind because his thoughts were busy with Leonie. The girls' bedroom doors were closed, the house lights were off and he had assumed they were both safe in their beds. He had taken his own concerns to sleep with him and had not missed May until she failed to appear for breakfast. He was standing at the window watching the crinkled skin of the sea when a shiver of disquiet made him turn back to look at the stairs. The leaf and flower carvings decorating the banister glinted with static menace.

He ran up the stairs two at a time. In May's room the bed was empty and the covers undisturbed.

He dragged Ivy out of her own bed, and now they stood with the backwash of disbelief and sudden anxiety slapping between them.

'She won't be far away,' Ivy muttered. 'She's probably only gone, only . . .' and her voice trailed away as she tried to come up with an explanation for her absence. May didn't have friends, not up here. She mooched around the house or the beach, or drifted irritatingly in the wake of everyone else. John's fear stirred an answering apprehension in Ivy. 'I don't know where she can be,' she whispered. 'I saw her, like, before I went out to meet Lucas last night. I left her here, watching TV or something. Lucas and me and the others went out to the island for a bit, just an hour or something. We lit a fire and hung out, but it was sort of cold over there, you know, and there wasn't much happening. So we just came back and I went off with Lucas for a bit, not back to his place because it's kind of heavy there right now.'

They were boxed in by truths that it had been easier

338

not to confront and now by unthinkable new possibilities. Ivy took a breath and launched herself at them. 'It's heavy because Leonie has left Tom, okay, and there's family stuff going on. But you know about all that, don't you? Maybe May going off has got something to do with it.'

'Why?'

'She was upset last night. We were talking about the old days, you know? Like, before Mom died.'

John walked the confined width of the room and back again. He pressed his hands together to try to ease the tension that twisted his sinews. He could hear breaking glass, the tapping of rain in the night and the predatory sea, and his mind raced ahead of of him, breaking out of reason. 'What did you say?'

'Something about Jack O'Donnell.'

'What about him?'

'She knew.' Ivy shrugged, but her dismissiveness was splitting, shredding into fragments. Her eyes reddened with sudden tears.

'I didn't know that. How could she? She was only small.'

There was a tragedy for both of them in this. For May, Alison had remained perfect and intact. And her preservation of her mother's inviolability had been a way for them to preserve it in part for themselves.

'Well, she did. And I . . . I laughed at her a bit for being upset by the memory. It's so long ago and Mom's dead, isn't she?'

John didn't answer. It seemed that he was looking into his own memories for the spectres that hid there.

'Wait a minute. She asked me if it was just once and I said no, of course not. She must have seen something, I guess. And not understood what was happening.' Ivy rubbed her face with the back of her hand, an uncharacteristic savage gesture. The ligaments joining history and today were thick and ugly, and too strong to be severed. May's awkward anger and her irritating needs and hurts made more sense when they were connected up to Ali and John. It was the same tangle that caught her, too, Ivy supposed, only she dealt with it in a different way. With Lucas and the others she proved to herself that it was no big deal, sex, or love if that was what it was supposed to be. 'We had a quarrel. She punched me in the face and I took the bread-knife to her. Just in self-defence, I . . . never touched her. It was over as quickly as it started, I *swear*.' Her voice dropped suddenly. 'God. What can have happened? How can we find out where she's gone?'

'We'll find her,' John said grimly. 'What about her things? Has she taken anything with her?'

They hunted through the room, trying not to think that they might only be the first to search it for clues to where May could have gone.

It didn't take long. Her clothes were all there, down to a knotted pair of shorts left damp and sandy on the floor. Her comb lay on the top of the dresser with a couple of dark, wiry hairs caught in the teeth. Her Walkman was on a shelf, pushed almost off the edge so that the wires and earphones trailed on the floor. There was an Anne Rice novel beside the bed, her place marked with a postcard view of Pittsharbor, and two other old books neither of them had seen before. In the bathroom her toothbrush, toiletries and cosmetics were undisturbed.

'She hasn't taken a thing. Nothing,' Ivy cried.

'All right. First we ask everyone else on the beach if they've seen her. We call a couple of people in New York, her friends, in case she was planning to run back there. Maybe they'll know other places she might have gone. Can you think of anywhere?'

Ivy shook her head. Looking back at it across the gulf of the morning May's life seemed dull and predictable, only now with the skew of loneliness. She hadn't wanted to consider the possibility of her sister's unhappiness before. The effort of keeping back tears made Ivy glare.

'After that, if we don't find her, it's the police.'

'Yeah.'

'Have you told me everything, Ivy?'

It was a shock when their eyes met because it happened so rarely. He thought, *I haven't seen either of them properly for so long. I've seen a collision of reproach and guilt and disability, not my children at all. And now, if it's too late, how will that be?*

'Yes, I have.'

Her glare dissolved for a second and he put his arms around her shoulders. 'We'll find her, wherever she's gone,' he promised emptily.

Ivy scrubbed her face again and twisted away to look out of the window.

John telephoned the other houses. The news of

341

May's disappearance caught everyone and slowed the stream of time so it seemed they were moving backwards, sliding in reverse into a day that had already gone.

'I don't believe it,' Karyn Beam said after she told the others. She lifted Sidonie and held her so tightly that the child squirmed and yelled to be put down. No one had seen May since the afternoon before.

Tom had come back from his run and was sitting with Marian on the porch. Shelly had whispered to Richard that she couldn't understand why Tom still had to go running when his wife had just left him, but Richard had only said that he supposed Tom couldn't think what else to do with himself. Marian looked tired and confused. There were no silver or tortoiseshell combs or jaunty scarf in her hair and the mad tousled sheaf of it made her look suddenly like a long-stay inmate of a hospital or a residential home.

'What's happening up here?' Marian kept asking. 'What's going wrong with everything?'

No one could answer her.

'Is John going to start a search? Does he need help?' Richard demanded. Karyn said John would call as soon as he had a plan or any more news.

They sat waiting on the porch. A little gnawing wind rustled off the sea. In the lulls of it they could hear the voices of Lucas and the younger children out on the tennis court.

When the telephone rang again Karyn ran to it. She came back and said to Tom, 'It's Leonie.'

He closed the door behind him so no one could overhear. 'Hello?' he said into the mouthpiece.

'Hello,' she answered, a statement not a greeting.

'Where are you? When are you coming back?'

'It doesn't matter where I am. Tom, I'm not coming back.'

'What do you mean?'

'Don't you understand the words?'

'Yes. I don't follow the reasoning.'

Leaning against the sheltered store wall in Haselboro and listening to the passing traffic, Leonie thought herself back to the bluff. There were the gulls' cries and the scrape of water, and the layers of voices and questions and family commandments from which she had removed herself into silence. By rights she supposed she should feel like a solitary separated wife, a dry husk winnowed out of the corn. She spread the fingers of one hand over her belly in a gesture of consolation. She felt a leap and twist within it, as if her womb had suddenly sprung to life. 'I've left you. I don't want to come back. I want to talk about a separation.'

'Why now? Why so sudden?'

It wasn't sudden, it had been gradual but inexorable. 'We don't love each other any more.'

He didn't try to deny it. There was another breathtaking spasm within her as she wondered if she should try to take back the words, if after all it might not be too late. 'Tom?'

'Yes. What do you want to do? You're not at home, I called there.' His voice was flat, weighty with resignation.

343

He wouldn't make himself the villain, she remembered. Nor would he put himself out to rescue the two of them, after their eleven years of marriage. The wringing in her stomach transmuted itself into a flutter of excitement, of liberation. 'No. I rented a place, I just want to stay here for a while to think things out. I called because I didn't want you to worry about where I am.'

'Thank you.' There was sarcasm now, a familiar weapon. He added, remembering, 'There is a worry here. The younger Duhane girl has gone missing. Her father called, she's been out all night.'

She said stupidly, 'What?' although she had heard too clearly. And she remembered the harbour wall and Doone's waterlogged body brought ashore. The bustling street had gone so still and she had watched in the middle of it with the condensed chill of the Ice Parlour bag squeezed to her chest.

Not again. Another adolescent, neither child nor woman. 'Leonie? Is this anything to do with you?'

Tom had made a connection. It was one of those sudden, blinding flashes of insight, which illuminate a landscape better left in merciful darkness. She knew it and she didn't care. 'No. I don't see how it could be.'

He didn't reply at once. There was some noise in the background, confused Beam voices.

Leonie drew herself inwards, even at this distance. 'I'll call John right now. There may be something I can do.'

'Yes. Let me know what you do decide, Leonie, won't you?'

'Yes,' she promised.

She lifted the receiver again as soon as the connection was broken and jabbed out the number of the Captain's House. The engaged tone sounded at her and with a twitch of impatience she hung up and walked the steps to the kerb. She gazed unseeingly at the litter of butts and candy wrappers washed up against the kerb stones, not letting her thoughts focus yet on what could have happened to May.

She dialled the number three more times, but it was always engaged. She fought against the impulse to race down to Pittsharbor at once. There was nothing to be done before she had spoken to John. Perhaps May was already safely back at home.

She left the shade of the store front and crossed the road to a wooden bench in a worn semicircle of grass. She sat down and bent her head, waiting. The yellow dog ambled up and lay panting at her feet.

Lucas pounded up the steps from the beach and ran across the hummocks of grass to the porch. He had wanted to do something to help find May, but had been unable to think of anything useful. He had been wandering along the tideline staring out across the water, then he had noticed something. The others looked up and watched him dashing towards them. 'The boat,' he shouted. 'The rowboat's gone.'

He pointed, and Marian and the others followed with their eyes. Once they saw, it seemed incredible that no one had noticed before. It was an hour past high water but the sailboat and the other dinghies rode comfortably on the swell of the waves. Nearer to

345

the shore, within wading distance, bobbed the little white plastic buoy where the Beams kept the tender moored. There was no line, no boat.

Marian stood up, her hand to her throat. 'I'll go and tell John Duhane.'

Elizabeth waited with Spencer and Alexander.

Spencer listened to the news as she relayed it and said, 'I saw her on Pittsharbor night.'

'We all did. She was at the barbecue party.'

'No, it was much later than that. There was a moon and I went out on the deck for some air. Someone was down on the beach, just sitting on the shingle looking out to sea.'

'She was by herself?' Elizabeth asked. The image of May out alone in the dark deepened her sense of foreboding.

'At first. I couldn't even see who it was. I wasn't particularly interested.' He leant across to a table and shook a cigarette from a pack. He tapped the filter but didn't light it. 'Then Marty Stiegel came rushing out of nowhere. Not running, but moving at a pace. The kid whipped round and I saw it was the young Duhane girl. They talked for a minute, then they went back across the beach together and up to the Stiegels' place.'

Alexander had been sketching in a notebook. Elizabeth tilted her head automatically and saw that he had been drawing her hands as they lay in her lap. They looked to her like ancient hooked claws. Now he snapped the book shut. He exchanged a glance with Spencer and Spencer gave the smallest shrug.

'She was at home until yesterday evening,' Elizabeth fretted. 'Her father said so. She didn't go missing on Pittsharbor Day.'

None of them recalled aloud the similarity to the circumstances around Doone's death. There was no need to.

'What can we do?' Elizabeth asked.

Alexander sighed, 'Nothing much at the moment. She's probably just run off to a friend, or to see some boy. The way thoughtless kids do.'

I know she hasn't, Elizabeth thought, but she made herself nod. She turned her head to look at the view of the bay.

Marty took the call from John Duhane. Justine had been fretful and Judith had taken her out in her stroller for a walk along the Pittsharbor road.

Afterwards he took off his glasses and held them clasped in one hand. His eyes were closed and there were furrows of concern over the bridge of his nose and pulling the corners of his mouth. He stayed motionless for a long moment then, as if having come to a decision, he jumped up and went to the locked filing drawer in the corner of his study.

He put on his loose jacket with its deep pockets and walked along the beach to the Captain's House. When he came to the porch door he peered into the shadows inside and saw John talking on the telephone, walking distractedly up and down as he did so. Marty tapped on the glass and John's head jerked up. Seeing it was only Marty he gestured briefly to him to come on in.

Ivy was sunk in the corner of one of the sofas. She gnawed at the corner of her thumb-nail, her face sharp-pointed and tight with anxiety.

'No, don't worry just yet,' John was saying. 'If Amy does hear anything from her, will you give me a call? Sure. Yes. Yes, thanks. Goodbye.'

Hunching his shoulders he looked across at Marty. 'None of the kids locally nor any of her friends in the city have heard from her. One of them got a postcard, that's all. She hasn't run to them anyway. She hasn't taken any of her clothes or belongings either. Nothing is missing.'

'Nothing at all?'

'Nope.'

'I came to see what I could do.'

'That's good of you, Marty. I don't know yet.' He shrugged, showing his helplessness, then glanced briefly at Ivy. 'There may be an explanation, something that isn't sinister. I can't think what it might be, that's all.'

'The police?'

'Not yet. But I'm going to . . .'

Marian Beam appeared in the porch doorway, cutting him short. There were red blotches disfiguring her neck and throat, and her hair was an uncombed mass of knots. She looked as if she might be losing control. 'Our rowboat is gone,' she said.

Ivy jumped up and they crowded to the window with Marty behind them.

'When?' John demanded. The white buoy bobbed naked on the ebb tide.

'I don't know. Lucas just saw it wasn't there. I came right over.'

The colour faded out of John's face. Beneath his tan he looked aged and grey. Marian went out again on to the porch and he and Ivy followed her to the beach steps. There was no dinghy drawn up on the shingle, nowhere else for it to be.

Marty was left alone. Quickly and silently he flitted up the stairs. Thirty seconds later he descended and followed the other three out on to the deck. He was pensively waiting, with his hands deep in the pockets of his jacket, as they turned back to the house.

'If she's taken the boat . . .' John began and let his words fade, because he couldn't voice the possibilities. 'I'm going to call the police,' he said.

Karyn and Elliot took the sailboat out to search the nearby bays for any sign of the missing rowboat, and Shelly and Richard paddled two canoes across to the island. They made a circuit of it, examining all the rock shelves and inlets, but they found nothing.

Under Marty's direction two groups, including Spencer and Alexander and Lucas Beam, walked the headlands to the north-east and in the opposite direction towards Pittsharbor. Tom and Marian stayed behind with Ashton and Sidonie. While the babies were taking their naps the two of them climbed to the widow's walk, which crowned the roof of the big house. They stood shoulder to shoulder in the small space, their hands on the warm metalwork spikes of the railing.

'I haven't been up here in so long,' Marian said.

349

The view was a tapestry of turquoise and silver-grey. Moon Island was a whale-back spiked with the silhouettes of spruce and the islands in the open water beyond seemed to sail through a fine veil of mist. The bay was busy with shuttling boats.

'Where has this child gone?' she breathed.

'I hope to God not the same way as the other one.'

Marian lifted her hands and clenched them again on the spear-tips. The metal left a fine deposit of salt and flaking paint in her palms. 'I don't know what's happening up here,' she repeated. To hear his mother express uncertainty gave Tom a jolt of surprise. She was different today; her looks and her bearing, and even her voice had changed. She seemed older and almost frail.

'I'm sorry about Leonie and me. It must have come as a shock to you.'

'I didn't know you were so unhappy.'

'Unhappy? Yes, I suppose so. In a long-term, low-level way that we didn't take notice of until it suddenly became acute. It was only this summer. Up here at the beach.'

The light-drenched sharpness of the view, striated rocks and wing-stretched gulls and shifting water ought to have made the notion of unhappiness seem murky and incongruous. But there was sadness here like a sea fog. It penetrated the bluff houses and lay in the corners as black as shadows at midday.

'She wanted a baby.'

'Of course,' Marian said. And after a moment, 'What will you do?'

350

'I don't know that there is much to do.'

'You don't seem to want to try very hard. Why don't you go and get her, wherever she is, and bring her back where she belongs?'

That was more like Marian. 'Because Leonie doesn't want to be got, or brought. We haven't been like you and Dickson, you see. You set an example for us all that was kind of hard to follow.'

'Did we?' Marian said. 'Is that so?' She was looking at Dickson's flag. It stirred and flapped in the light breeze.

The day ticked on and slid into a motionless afternoon. The searchers trickled back to the bluff, having found nothing except a fearful awareness that there was so much space and so little for them to go on. May had simply vanished. If she had taken the Beams' boat, then that had vanished with her.

John and Ivy sat on in the Captain's House, waiting, willing some news to come. The police had earlier taken the view that May Duhane was almost fifteen years old, there had been a family disagreement, it was too early yet to launch a full-scale search for her.

John shouted, 'Something has happened to my daughter. She has never done anything like this in her life.'

'Sir, we fully understand your concern,' the officer stonewalled him.

It was Ivy who showed her strength. After the first shock she became resolute, turning John from the comforter into the comforted. 'We'll find her,' she repeated.

351

Unable to sit still, she crossed and recrossed the room in a frenzy of contained energy, prowling from corner to corner and seizing the telephone every time it rang. It was only offers of help, never May herself. In one of her loops Ivy went up the stairs to search her room again.

She came down with the red-and-black book in her hand. 'We didn't see this before.'

John took it and flipped through the ruled pages. 'It's some kind of diary.'

'Yeah. Doone Bennison's.'

'Why didn't her parents take it?'

'Perhaps they didn't know it was here.'

The silvery artemisia bush shivered outside the windows of Elizabeth's evening room. 'Why aren't they looking on the island?' she demanded of Spencer.

'Karyn Beam and Elliot and Lucas walked right over it to the ocean. They didn't see anything.'

Spencer put down the magazine he had been pretending to read and walked through to the kitchen where Alexander was cooking. He mounded a neat heap of herbs on the wooden chopping block and rocked the mezzaluna over them. The scent of thyme rose cleanly. Spencer leaned against the dresser and stacked a pyramid of kitchen weights on the plate of the old set of scales.

'What are you going to say?' Alexander asked.

'To whom?'

'We should say something to somebody. In case there is a connection. We agreed last time that there

352

wasn't, that there was nothing to change and a lot of people who would be hurt. But *two* teenage kids?'

Spencer was making an inverse pyramid now. The brass discs rocked threateningly as he lowered the heaviest into place. 'Yes. I believe you're right.'

'The police?'

'No.' They went on separately with what they were doing, balancing and chopping, without the need to enlarge further on why the police and the usual channels and the straight world were antipathetic. The top-heavy pile of weights overbalanced and noisily crashed. 'Not first off, anyway. I'll talk to him and tell him what I saw.'

Alexander nodded. 'When?'

'You're concerned about this kid, aren't you?'

'Yes. I am.'

Elizabeth came in and began fussing around the margins of the kitchen. Spencer picked up the weights and replaced them, then smoothly changed the subject.

The tan station-wagon nosed down the bluff road. Hannah peered ahead of her, then hunched forward over the wheel to give herself a better view. Her first impression had been right, it was a squad car ahead. She could see the square heads of the two officers inside. They passed the path and steps that led down to the public end of the beach, but the car didn't stop. Its destination must be one of the five houses. 'Whatever is going on?' she muttered. Looking sideways, she saw that Aaron had briefly fallen asleep. Slumber came on him often, without warning. His jaw sagged open and his slow breath caught in his throat. He was ill, but he had insisted so vehemently on being brought home from the hospital that she had given way to his demands. As she turned towards the house she saw that the squad car had gone all the way to the end of the lane.

It took all her strength to manoeuvre Aaron out of the car and up the porch steps. He gasped painfully for breath and each small pace he took, with all his weight on Hannah's arm, cost him an effort. There was nothing left spare in him for talking, but she encouraged him forward with a little monologue of praise and reassurance. At last she had him in his chair beside the wood stove. She brought a plaid rug and tucked it around his legs.

'You know what I want?' he demanded.

'What's that?'

'A glass of five-fruit.'

It was the soda-fountain flavour of long ago. Neither of them had tasted it for twenty-five years. Hannah kept her voice light. 'We don't have any five-fruit. I'll get you a Coke.'

She was in the kitchen when she saw Marian Beam hurrying towards the porch. She sighed at the sight, but curiosity made her open the door and let her in. Marian didn't often come visiting the Fennymores.

Marian sat beside Aaron's chair. She had brought the news of May's disappearance, but once she had conveyed it she showed no sign of leaving. They talked a little about the police and the search that was under

354

way. Hannah took away Aaron's untouched glass of Coke. 'I have to go and buy some supplies,' she said, with her mouth tight.

'I'll stay with him,' Marian told her.

'Why thank you, Marian.'

When they were alone together they sat for a minute in silence. Aaron's eyes were closed, and the colour of his skin and the lines etched from each side of his beaky nose made him look like one of his whalebone carvings. Marian folded her two hands around Aaron's cold, knotted one. Then she lowered her head, very slowly, until it rested on his knee. He lifted his free hand and placed it on her hair.

A tear ran down the bridge of Marian's nose and lay like a bead on the hairy surface of the plaid rug. 'I wanted to come to the hospital.'

'There was no need.'

'*I* felt the need.'

His voice was bone-weary, hardly more than a whisper. 'It has been a long time, Marian.'

'Twenty years. Twenty-two since Dickson died.'

In his fifties Aaron had been still strong. There had been an unhappy violence about him, an original wildness just contained within the flesh of convention. He had seemed not to be afraid of anything, nor to place much value on anything either, and there was a powerful erotic attraction in that. Plenty of women in and around Pittsharbor had been drawn to Aaron Fennymore, Marian knew perfectly well. He had a reputation as a sexual aggressor. He had assaulted her widowhood and she had been pleased to give him

355

what he demanded; more than pleased, she had given herself up to him. It had not mattered, at first, that he returned so little.

'How are you?' she asked. His hand was so light she could hardly feel where it rested on the curve of her skull.

'I am tired.'

'Do you remember the woods?'

They used to climb up on to the headland and lie in the hollows between the spruce trees. Regardless of their age. Without thought of their grown children.

He spoke so slowly that his lips hardly moved. 'Full of sex.'

The woods *were* full of sex. It was true, but no longer theirs. She nodded her head, complicit and valedictory, with the weight of grief gathering within her. 'Where has this other girl gone?' she whispered.

'I don't know.'

They were thinking of the black tree trunks and the mossy hollows.

'How is Hannah?'

'She didn't need any supplies. I don't want her to be hurt Marian.'

After so long. 'I know that. I love you, Aaron.'

'Yes.'

Darkness fell early, bringing with it a shower of sharp rain. The change in the season seemed to have come within the space of a single day. Yesterday it had been full summer, but today there was the smoky, wet-leaf warning of autumn in the air. In a week it would be the end of August, then Labour Day and the summer visitors would empty out of their rental cottages and turn back to the cities.

All the lights were burning in the Captain's House and the open ground at the road's end was lined with parked cars. May Duhane had been officially declared missing, twenty-four hours after she had last been seen. With the dark the search for her had been called off, but it would resume at first light.

Marty put Justine to bed. He went through the routines of Pampers and baby-powder and sleep suit, and wound the musical box that stood at the side of her crib, but he was clumsy with her and she cried intermittently. She was teething, and her fat cheeks were flushed and prickled with a faint rash.

He held her on his lap and tried to soothe her, and at last she grew drowsy. Her fists relaxed and her eyes faltered shut, her wet eyelashes making crescents of tiny shadow spikes. He put her in her crib and settled the quilt around her. He was relieved to be briefly free of her unending needs and at once felt the needle of self-reproach. If there wasn't Justine, what worth was there in anything else?

Downstairs, Judith was waiting for him. She half-turned from the window and the invisible sea, and he saw her as a profile of abstract curves and mounds, flesh compressed and seamed by her clothes. 'Pour me a drink,' he begged. 'I thought she'd never sleep.'

'Wine okay?'

'Anything. Just alcohol.'

Their voices sounded flat, all the resonance leached out of them by the damp and the cloudy vapour of apprehension.

'Any news?'

'I haven't heard anything,' Judith said.

'I wish there were something . . .' Marty whispered. A knock at the door made them gaze at each other in hope and fear.

It was Spencer Newton, a cashmere sweater over his summer shirt. 'Do you have five minutes?' he asked.

'Sure. Come on in.'

Judith was behind them, nursing her glass of wine, listening.

'No, I wondered if we might take a walk along the beach.'

Marty looked back over his shoulder. He sketched a gesture of puzzlement at his wife and answered, all compliance, 'Right now, Spencer? Well, okay, if there's something I can help you with.'

Judith looked dubious, but she dismissed them with a reminder to Marty that they should eat before too long.

The rain had eased off, leaving the air cold and moist. The beach pebbles glistened like jet underfoot and long black waves with curling lips of grey foam seemed superfluous to so much wetness.

They had been silent as they made their way down to the water's edge. Marty was constrained, as if he knew and feared what was coming. When they reached the tideline they began to walk towards the Pittsharbor steps.

'Do you know anything about where May Duhane is?' Spencer asked now, without preamble.

'Nothing. If I did, I'd have told her father.'

'Or the police.'

'Yes, if it was relevant. What is this? What are you suggesting?'

Spencer's even tone didn't change. He told him he had seen May going up from the beach with him on Pittsharbor night.

His version of the scene sounded odd and Marty quickly defended himself. 'That was forty-eight hours ago, she's been missing for twenty-four. Plenty of people saw her in the meantime, including her father. I told John about the other night. May and I met on the beach, she said there'd been a family upset and asked if she could come up for a drink. She did, we chatted for maybe an hour, she went home. That was all and as it happened I didn't even catch a glimpse of her the next day. Judith and I went over to Bar Harbor for lunch with friends, if it's any of your business. I'll tell the police that too, when the questioning starts. If the kid doesn't come home before then.'

Spencer's head was turned away, towards the sea and Moon Island. 'Look, Marty, I'm sorry. I don't want to do this. I ask because of something else I saw.'

'Jesus.' Marty was angry now, with a quick defensive heat.

'Last year I was walking in the woods towards Berry Island. I lost the path and came down close to the shore, and I found myself overlooking an inlet I'd never come across before. Just some sloping rock

359

shelves and a finger of water. There was a cave or a funnel beneath me because the waves were booming in it.'

The darkness hid Marty's face. But he stopped walking and waited, his shoulders rigid.

'You were there with Doone. Her Mirror dinghy was made fast in the inlet.'

'I know what you saw.' Marty rapped out the words, cutting Spencer short. 'Do you make a habit of spying on people? Have you got a thing for it, you and Alexander?'

'No. But five days later the kid was dead.'

'Why didn't you report it at the time?'

'She was already dead. It was an accident, a drowning. Judith was about to have a baby.'

'But now another one's gone missing it's one too many, is that it, Spencer?'

'Yes.'

'Fuck you,' Marty spat at him. He swung round and Spencer automatically stepped back. He stumbled and a wave broke over his loafer, and he swore in his turn.

'Listen.' Marty advanced and pressed his face close to Spencer's. 'I took pictures of her. She liked posing for me. I took pictures of her with her clothes on, and that day she wanted the pictures with her clothes off. Spread out on the rocks, just like you saw. It was her idea. They were good pictures, too. I got rid of them, of course. Okay, she was naked. She was the model.

'But was I naked, Spencer? No, I wasn't, was I? I was just the photographer.

'Did I screw her? No, I didn't. She was a virgin, the

360

post-mortem showed that. Didn't you know? So you don't know quite everything, do you?'

'Why would a fourteen-year-old girl want to pose in the nude for you, Marty?'

The man hesitated. The wind of his anger dropped and left him deflated. For an ugly minute Spencer thought he would cry, beg for his silence. But in the end he only answered softly, 'She had a thing for me. She thought she was in love with me.'

'And you liked it, didn't you?'

'God help me. But this one's quite different. I don't know anything about her. Or where she's gone, or why. I swear I don't.' Marty's shoulders dropped, he spread his hands imploringly. 'Do you believe me?'

Spencer's mouth was twisted with distaste. But he answered truthfully, dismissively, 'Yes, I believe you.'

The sky was a perfect unbroken bowl of china blue. She lowered her head so it rested against the pillow of rock and let her eyes close. The sun burned coppery discs behind her eyelids and the heat of it radiated up from the rocks and entered her bones.

Here and now, she whispered to herself. He was here with her now, which was all that mattered.

After the happiness misery always came, but while it was with her the intoxication was worth anything, any of the jealousy or the loneliness.

When she opened her eyes again she saw him with his head bent over the viewfinder of his camera, the favourite old Leica. She heard the shutter click before her mouth curved into a smile. She felt powerful; what

361

she wanted she would have. 'Take some more pictures of me.'

He came and sat close beside her on the slab. She could smell his sweat and the muskiness of it excited her. She smiled at him, teasing, with the tip of her tongue nipped between her teeth.

'Haven't I taken enough pictures of you?' He laughed.

'We could do some different ones.'

'Different?'

The sea was blue-green, flecked with gold, big and easy in front of them.

In answer she undid the buttons at her front. She slipped her arms out of the sleeves and grasped her forearms, seeming to luxuriate in the sun's heat on her skin. Then with a quick movement she unhooked a strap and let the cups fall away to expose her breasts. His mouth opened a little and she smiled again, offering herself

'So perfect,' he breathed. 'A young girl's body.'

He moved to touch but she caught his wrist, playfully holding him apart from her. 'Wait.'

She undid and discarded the rest of her clothes. The nakedness, the warmth on every inch of her skin felt magnificent. For a moment she almost forgot he was there; she lay back and gave herself up to the sun. The shutter clicked, and again. She arched her back and put her hands up to her breasts, tilting her head so that her chin fined down and her hair fell in waves over the rock.

They were absorbed in the intricate, threat-woven

immediacy of the moment. Neither of them heard or saw Spencer Newton.

She spread her arms and legs now like a starfish, limpet- glued to the tideless rock, and laughed up at the sky. The shutter clicked.

Afterwards, while the power was still strong in her, she let him touch her and he responded because he couldn't help himself, that was just how it was.

It didn't last, it never lasted, whatever she offered him.

He was hers and not hers. Always giving not quite enough, holding back, then taking himself away altogether. The buttery gleam of her pleasure gave way to sudden hot anger. 'I won't let you go back,' she screamed at him.

'I have to go.'

They were sitting apart now. His eyes were shielded with one hand. 'Put your clothes on.'

She began to cry, without warning, oily tears, which ran down her face and dribbled from her jaw. 'Please,' she begged him. 'Stay here with me a bit longer. Another half an hour. I won't kick up after that, I promise.'

'Don't cry.' He hugged her, reluctance in every line of his body, and she turned her ravaged face against his shoulder and wept.

'I love you,' she insisted over and over. 'You don't know how much I love you.'

He stroked her hair, moving his mouth against her skull. 'No, you don't. You're too young to know anything about love. Next year you'll look back on this and you won't be able to understand what made you so crazy.'

'I'm not crazy,' she insisted, knowing she was. 'Last year I felt the same, didn't I?'

She remembered the first time he had taken her sailing, with the wind lathering the water and wrapping hair across her face, and how kind he had been to her. By gravely paying her attention he had lifted her out of being a kid and let her see that there was another world. Every detail of the day was clear in her head.

It hadn't been his doing, not at the beginning. She was the one who had stepped across into that other place, because she suddenly saw the way into it lit up as if the sun had come out. She thanked him for taking her out and kissed him. Not a peck on the cheek but a real kiss, which grew, like a flower opening. She had felt his surprise and another current: pleasure.

At once she had stepped back, sweet strength in her smile. 'See you tomorrow,' she'd promised.

He would have to, he couldn't resist it. She knew that from the first day. Her knowingness was her strength and her weakness.

She felt no regrets now. Anger and despair, but not regret. It would be like regretting having been born.

'It's time to stop,' he said.

She froze, even the river of tears seeming to dry on her face. 'No.' The word was a stone in her mouth.

He ignored her. 'It's time to stop seeing each other

alone like this. You will grow up and find a proper boyfriend, and you'll start doing all the things you should be doing at your age.'

'Going to bars and getting carded and smoking weed and making out, like the Beam kids?'

He stroked the hair back from her wet face. 'Yeah. All those things.'

'No.' She wrenched herself out of his grasp. 'Don't put me down with that. I don't want any of that shit, I want to be with you.'

He wouldn't even look at her. He was bent over with trouble and the wish to get away from her. 'Doone. Listen to me. This is wrong, everything we have been doing. I accept the blame, I feel more guilty than you can imagine. But I'm married to Judith and I love her. She's going to have a baby in just a few weeks.'

She put her head back then and screamed. It was like a thread of molten pain rising out of her throat and burning the air. The echoes shivered around them and seemed to catch and multiply. The voice of pain passed through the trees and all along the shoreline. The scream went on and on until he slapped her face. Then it stopped and the silence seemed absolute.

He whispered, and she felt the heat of his breath on her skin, 'I'm sorry, I don't want to hurt you, I never wanted you to be hurt.'

She tried to be cunning. 'Even though you did all that to me?'

He was quicker, cleverer by two decades. 'All what? You are a virgin, aren't you?'

365

The desolation of abandonment came down on her. He would leave her and he was already denying her. 'If I can't have you I don't want anything.'

'You won't feel like that for very long.' He was gentle, trying to soothe her, but she didn't want to be soothed. She needed to be alone now to taste the full flavour of her loss. To fondle it and explore its unseen dimensions.

'Come on. We'll go back to the beach now and we'll forget all this, and in the end you'll forgive me.'

He took her hand and drew her to her feet. He helped her on with her clothes, thumbed her eyes dry for her and led her over the rocks to the Mirror dinghy.

The sailboat her parents had bought for her, because she had asked for it. They were too busy to sail in it, of course, and were glad for Marty to teach her. And she would have to let him sail her back to them now, because she couldn't handle the boat alone.

As she stepped in, it rocked violently and she would have fallen in if he hadn't caught her hand and steadied it.

She sat in the stern while he busied himself with sheets and halyards.

The woman who was watching from the shelter of the trees lifted her hand to her.

Doone said, 'If I can't have you I don't want to go on living. I won't go on.'

Marty was busy with the sheet, he didn't even look round at her. 'Yes, you will. You have got your whole life ahead of you.'

366

The advancing footsteps grew louder. They were all around her and cold hands plucked at her clothes. May was stumbling backwards, trying to escape, then it seemed that the ground opened like a mouth and she was falling into it. A scream started out of her but it was abruptly silenced.

When she opened her eyes it was on the other side of some long, distressing interval. Time had passed, but she had no idea where it had gone. At first she could see nothing but blackness and her eyes searched the margins of it, not knowing if it was part of her or if she was enveloped by it. There was a cage of pain around her head, and her mouth was ragged and sticky with thirst. She tried to call out, struggling so hard that the cry should have been deafening, but no sound came.

The dark was diluted, then dispelled by the light she had followed into the trees. Someone was singing.

There was a woman with a lantern. May felt no surprise at the sight of her. It was the island woman, in her long clothes, her hair scraped back from her melancholy bone-white face.

There was a younger woman with her. Water streamed off her and her features were veiled with wet hair, but even so May knew it was Doone.

The singing stopped and the faces came closer.

Doone wound up her hair and fastened it, and knelt down beside May. 'Why don't you sit up?' she coaxed.

When she did so they put their arms around her. They leant back and made themselves comfortable, and Sarah linked her fingers in May's. Her hand was rough, but it was warm and reassuring.

'My head hurts,' May complained.

'Hurt, hurt, hurt,' Sarah repeated softly. 'Come with us and leave it behind you.'

'Come where?' The pain was diminishing even as she spoke.

'We'll show you.' Doone helped her to her feet and they took one arm each.

'How can you, if you're dead?' The cunning question pleased her; she would catch them out.

They only smiled.

'It's not so far.'

The membrane, May remembered. Forever threatening to dissolve and let one world flow into the next. It had gone completely now and there were no laws of physics or mortality.

They were in a room lit by smoky lamps like the one Sarah had held up in the dark. The walls were coarse stone and great yellow bones hung from wooden pegs driven between the stones; the jawbones of whales. The beams of the roof were so low that they were within easy reach of her hand, the earth floor was smoothed and flattened by the passage of heavy boots. They were not alone here; men in rough clothes sat at the tables. There was one more three-cornered table and the women took their places at it.

May thought of questions she must ask. If she could phrase them right she would learn everything she needed to know. She turned to Sarah, searching her oval face for clues, but her eyes had turned to colourless stones. 'Why did you die?'

'Because I believed I couldn't live. I thought I loved a man.'

'The Captain.'

Gravely Sarah inclined her head.

At the other point of the triangle Doone was just as she had been in Marty's photographs, her smile transfiguring her heavy face.

'Did you leave your diary for me to read?'

'No. I wrote it out of pain, for love.'

The rocks and sheltered hollows of the woods and the interminable sea. It wasn't love they wore and whispered about, rather the grimacing mask and the incoherent murmur of sex. May understood the absolute distinction. Confusion peeled from her. 'Were you so unhappy?' she asked tenderly.

Doone's photograph smile faded. 'Are you?'

May looked around her again. In a group of the silent men she saw a tall man in high leather boots, his clothes dark with blood and seawater. She understood that this place was all about pain and sadness and capitulation. All these people were lost. 'No,' she insisted. It was suddenly important to make them hear her. Their stone-eyed faces turned to look at her, row upon row, pressed flowers with the sap and scent all gone. The sadness was suffocating. 'No,' she shouted more loudly.

Sarah and Doone took her hands, drew her to her feet.

If these people were all dead, why wasn't her mother among them?

She gazed wildly around. 'Ali, Ali,' she screamed.

369

The sound was different. The words were coming properly out of her mouth, a hoarse, rasping croak.

I want my mother.

The cry came out of the depths of her. In answer all they did was pull on her arms. They dragged her to the window and made her look out. At sea beyond the island a ship was riding at anchor. The sails were furled and the rigging was intricate lacework against the silvery water.

'Come with us,' Sarah said. 'Sail away. Leave everything behind you.'

That was the song she had been singing. *Sail away, boys. Follow the whale, boys. Ah, far away. Ah, far far away.*

Doone put her mouth close to May's ear. There was a breath of cold, which fanned and chilled her cheek.

'Ali! Don't leave me here, I'm frightened. Mom? Mommy, are you there?' It was her own voice, small and plaintive, a child calling out in the night.

The ship rocked on the swell and the women tugged at her, tightening their grasp as the singing grew louder.

'I won't go,' May screamed. Terror surged up in her, compounded of the melancholy singing, the stone eyes and the fingers that dug into her flesh. She struggled and fought, and as she did so pain flooded through her body like sensation returning to a numbed limb. Needles of it darted into her brain and a crown clamped around her temples.

Her mother was dead, of course, she had died of a brain haemorrhage long ago, one of the random tragedies of life; why then was she calling out for her?

370

Strength fuelled by fear made her break free of the women. They were no guardians for her, they were horror itself.

She was lying in a pit like a grave. There were black crescents of earth from the steep walls in her fingernails, and her neck and legs were twisted. She felt droplets of rain prickling her face and in an agony of thirst she tried to drink them.

Thirteen

The night following May's disappearance passed and there was still no sign of her.

John and Ivy slept hardly at all, and at first light the search of the headlands and bays resumed. They begged to join the searchers, but were advised by the police to stay where they were. They waited in excruciating idleness, making detours around each other to fetch cups of coffee, which neither of them wanted or to look out of the windows that offered only the same changeless vista.

The red-and-black diary lay to one side. It was a jumble of girlish confessions and numbers, which neither of them could decipher or attach much importance to.

In the very early morning it had rained again, a heavy shower that thinned to a drizzle, then stopped altogether. The light brightened and by ten o'clock the sun shone in a clear-washed sky. Warmth drew out the scents of pine and wet earth; the blameless beauty of the bay was an added reproach. The houses on the bluff stood out in sharp detail. There was no-one to be seen on their decks or down on the beach because everyone was either out with the searchers or sitting inside, waiting. Up among the early arrivals from the town who were setting out their towels and folding chairs for the day near the Pittsharbor steps, two police officers were moving from group to group, asking questions.

Ivy sat in an upright chair at the kitchen table, turning a cup of cold coffee in scraping circles. 'I was such a bitch to her,' she owned flatly.

'No you weren't.'

'Maybe not all the time. If she comes back – God, if she's all right, I swear . . .'

'I know,' John said. He paused beside her chair and Ivy turned her face against his sleeve.

They remembered separately the distorting glass that had slid between them and the world after Alison's death. Looking through it at ordinary life had been to see the world foreshortened, stripped of luminescence and the resonance of promise. The glass shivered in the wings again now, grief waiting to assail them.

'I was thinking about Alison,' Ivy whispered.

'I know,' John repeated.

'What did you feel when she died?'

'Guilty.'

'You weren't the guilty one. Neither was she, after she was dead, was she? Only we couldn't talk about her because of what had been wrong and her dying so suddenly was a kind of door that closed her off. I liked it that May didn't know about her affair because it kept the goodness of her, the way May believed in it.

'Then I had to go and spill it out. Do you think it's why May went off?'

'No,' he said, hoping it was the truth. He was tidying the worktop restlessly, unseeingly, as he spoke. He slotted kitchen knives back into the wooden block where they belonged. 'When she comes back, when we're together again, we'll talk to each other about your mother. It isn't too late.'

Their fear was that too late was exactly what it was.

A woman police officer came to the door. She didn't try to soften the news: the Beams' rowing dinghy had been found empty, the oars thrown inside it, two miles down the coast on the rocks at Hays Landing. There was no way of telling if May had taken it there and abandoned it, or if it had been carried from elsewhere and washed up by the tide.

Leonie left the Saab parked outside the Flying Fish and walked the rest of the way to the bluff. Another call to the Beams – this time she had spoken only to Karyn – told her there was no more news of May. It was unbearable to think of staying up in the Haselboro cabin, although she didn't want to go back to Marian's house and she could hardly intrude herself at John's. She kept to the far, shady side of the road when she reached the Fennymores' driveway and with her head bent moved quickly towards Elizabeth's. Elizabeth opened her door immediately.

'Can I wait here with you?' Leonie blurted. 'I don't want to be so far away.'

Elizabeth held the door wider. 'I'd be glad of the

374

company. Alexander and Spencer have gone with Marty. They're out on the island. The boat's been found, did you hear?'

Leonie's eyes widened. 'And?'

'That's all. Nothing else.'

Looking around the table Lucas mumbled, 'She asked me if I thought she was *like* Doone.' He put down his hunk of sandwich only half eaten. The younger children gazed back solemn-faced and the adults frowned or picked at their food. 'I said she wasn't,' he insisted. 'Nothing like. We only went for a walk and fooled around for half an hour. She was kind of upset, yeah, but she made me leave her there. You know, I thought it was just girls' stuff.'

Richard put down his fork. 'You told the police all of this?'

'Sure. It was the night before, anyway. But all the questions, right? It makes me feel like it's my fault.' No one said anything. 'Jesus,' he muttered uneasily. 'I mean, they were totally different.'

'Perhaps May didn't think that. Perhaps she identified with Doone.' It was Marian who said it, voicing the possibility everyone else left unspoken.

'Not to the point of contriving to drown herself as well, surely?' Karyn snapped.

'That might depend on why she thought Doone did die,' Elliot said quietly.

'Jesus,' Lucas said again. He got up and left the table, and even Kevin and Joel were silent.

*

Aaron didn't fall asleep. He sat wrapped in a blanket in his chair beside the stove, watching the sunlight moving in rhomboids of dilute citrus yellow across the floor-boards.

'How long did Marian Beam stay?' Hannah ventured.

'Not long,' he denied her.

Hannah went on with her work, glancing at him as she moved around the room with a duster, but they didn't talk any more.

Judith telephoned her mother in Connecticut and held the baby up to the mouthpiece so her grand-mother could hear her gurgle.

'Where's Marty?' she asked when Justine was restored to her bouncing chair.

Judith explained that he had joined the search for a missing teenager.

'Another one?'

'It's not the same,' Judith said quickly. 'Last year there was a drowning accident. It happens, doesn't it? I think this kid has just run off somewhere. She had an argument with her sister or something.'

'Are you all right, Judith?' Her mother was a widow, prone to anxiety and over-protectiveness of her only daughter.

'Of course I am. Justine's teething, that's all.' She was regretting the call now and the anxiety of isolation that had driven her to make it was only intensified.

'And Marty?'

'Of course. He's just doing what he can to help.'

After she had managed to extricate herself from the conversation Judith squatted on the floor opposite the baby. Justine's face split into a smile at once, showing tiny white chips of teeth embedded in crescents of gum.

Uneasiness shifted and compressed itself inside Judith's rib-cage, at odds with the exuberance of her passion for the child. It was only when she became a mother that she had identified the similarity, but Marty who seemed so certain and formed when she married him also had a childlike aspect. He needed her protection, just as the baby did, although it was disturbing that she couldn't define properly how or why.

And now her own mother had scented today's unease, all the way from Connecticut, and it was seeding itself there too. The corners of Judith's mouth turned down in an approximation of a smile at the thought of this inexorable connection between mothers and daughters.

She held out her hand and Justine grabbed at it, double-fisted. Her co-ordination was improving every day. 'I'll be here,' Judith promised her. 'I always will.'

All day along the beach and the bluff, ripples of dread ran like a powerful tide coming in over the sand. The five houses were joined by its fingers, the same image of a waterlogged body haunting each of them.

Elizabeth and Leonie couldn't bear to stay inside where the air was weighty and stagnant, and the silence oppressed them. They went out into the garden, making a tour of it from the lane side round to the front of the house overlooking the beach. Elizabeth pointed out the dead heads and showed Leonie how to nip them off with a sharp snap of the secateurs. They worked together in the sweetness of the borders, stretching and kneeling, and teasing out weeds from between the kniphofias and hydrangea bushes. By concentrating fiercely on the job they were able to bear the terrible waiting. Leonie thought, *maybe some day I could have a garden, with roses and thyme and lavender bushes*. Tom had never wanted anything more than a small yard with an elaborate barbecue. To concentrate on such things helped her to think beyond today, with its rising swell of dread.

Marty dragged his aching legs through the next tangle of briars. The slope to the crest of the island was steep and bare of trees on this part of the seaward side. The rock was clearly visible in bald grey patches between the vegetation like a skull beneath tufts of hair.

Spencer and Alexander were further down the slope at distances of ten and twenty yards. They had agreed on this as the way to cover the most ground in their search. Marty was vaguely surprised by their stamina and tenacity. He thought he was strong himself, but he was breathless and flagging in comparison with them. The dragging progress over the inhospitable island was exhausting and the pointlessness of it chafed at him. He could only think of finding the girl and it seemed impossible that they were doing anything but wasting time up here. Clearly the police thought the same. 'She took the boat,' he panted during one of their rest stops. 'Surely we'd be more useful working down the shore instead of up here?'

'My mother is convinced she would have come across to the island and I trust her instincts. I always think there's a bit of the witch in her.'

Marty gritted his teeth. He hated Spencer's feyness and the suspicion that the two of them had asked him to join their search with the intention of watching him, of keeping him in view. To underline his innocence he could only agree, and keep walking and searching and calling her name through the mild afternoon heat. Spencer and Alexander thought he was guilty.

The summer afternoons of a year ago returned to his mind with perfect and unwelcome clarity. He knew how it had begun and how the entrancement had advanced by stages, so tiny as to seem unimportant, until the threshold of guilt had long been passed and nothing could be done to retrieve innocence for either of them.

But the diary had revealed nothing incriminating. Unless the code, the passionate scribbled numbers, gave him away. If it did happen that May was dead and if he had only destroyed the diary instead of panicking and putting it back, what other danger was there? He would have been safe from last summer. It would be his word against Spencer Newton's, no evidence but an account of a photographer taking photographs on a sunny afternoon.

Marty toiled on across the thorny slope.

May opened her eyes again. Huge segments of time seemed to pass, yet she couldn't populate them with thoughts or sensations beyond generalised pain and tormenting thirst.

The light over her head was hard and bright. How many hours or days had she been lying here? Would she have been missed? Were they searching for her?

Somewhere in a dream or delirium she had been calling out for her mother, the name was still shaped on her tongue. She was more properly conscious now; it was her father she wanted and Ivy.

The thought of Ivy filled her mind. Ivy was so admirable and strong. She only felt angry with her because she was so effortlessly what she herself wanted to be. There was no space left to fill because Ivy already occupied it, yet it was exactly the shape in the world that May wanted too. Of course jealousy would make her angry. It wasn't Ivy's fault, how could it be? Weak tears collected in May's eyes at the thought of how much she loved her. She pressed one finger into her eye socket and tried to lick the moisture off it. Her tongue was swollen and cracked.

Ivy would be worried. Ivy worried about her if she was an hour late coming home, although she pretended not to. 'Don't make me, you little bitch,' she had snarled once, only once.

'You don't have to worry about me.'

'Yes I do. Don't you understand anything? There's no one else to do it.'

It became suddenly of supreme, immense importance to relieve Ivy of anxiety. No one was going to

380

come and get her out of here, not Ali or John or anyone else. She would have to extricate herself or die in a hole. Leave Ivy. Screw things up for her for good. The whispers would follow her. *Her mom died, then her kid sister . . . did you hear? . . .* Ivy would have to be harder and brighter and tougher than ever to make up for it.

Climb.

Climb out of here and crawl home.

There was the singing again. Fucking singing. *Ah, far away. Ah, far far away.* Only it was Lucas's voice this time. Shit, it was a dream. What else could it be? Start climbing, okay?

The lip of the hole wasn't so far away. Perhaps twice the height of her head. Forget the cage of pain and the thirst, which had become the size of another complete individual shrieking inside her. She reached up with clawed hands to the stones that jutted overhead. A knuckle of rock made a place to wedge her foot. Her face scraped against the sour earth.

Not that way. The better way was to press her back to the side of the hole and jam her feet against the opposite face. It hurt her legs and there was a hot pain stabbing through her braced shoulders. A shower of small stones and chunks of earth rattled down, but she was able to lever herself up by a foot, then a few more inches. The light overhead seemed to come no closer and the pain radiated from her shoulders to possess the rest of her. She braced herself once again and shuffled another step upwards, then one more. But the effort of holding her legs straight was too much.

381

Her knees folded and she fell back down, the shock of the impact jarring a moan out of her.

She raised herself on all fours and looked upwards again. She saw that the only route was after all to climb, using the knobs and tiny protruding ledges of stone. This time she moved slowly, considering each hand- and foothold. Whenever she achieved an upward lift she hung motionless for a long moment, her face pressed to the wall, conserving her tiny store of energy. For a long, agonising series of movements the sky seemed to come no closer.

Suddenly the bottom of the pit was far below, a considerable drop. If she fell now she would be badly hurt; to climb up again would be impossible. The lip of the hole was within reach of her fingers as they strained upwards. She brought her feet level and hung on with her fingertips. She could see nowhere that might offer the next foothold.

Up. She focused on the thought with the last reserves of her willpower. There was a place about ten inches above her present toehold, no more than a shallow groove, but it might be enough. Cautiously she slid her right foot upwards, jammed it into the recess and tested her weight on it. Her fingers scrabbled higher and somehow the purchase held. Now her right hand found roots and stems growing beyond the edge of the hole. She grasped them and brought her left foot level with the right. Her body was balanced on her toes, her fists desperately clutching the grasses. There was a jutting stone higher to the left. She planted her foot and launched herself upwards, and there was an agonising moment when she had to give up her handhold and grope for another beyond it. She found a thorny stem, which tore her palm, but still she grabbed and hauled herself up by it. Both feet were level again, her face was mockingly tickled by the fronds of grass.

Her breath sobbed in her throat.

'Help me,' May whispered, but she had no expectation that help would come. There was no island woman, no Doone; neither Ivy nor her father would hear her entreaty. There was no membrane either, nothing but herself and the whistling emptiness of the brightening air.

'Again,' she commanded.

She tested her handholds by pulling on them. They seemed firm enough. Then she sprang up from the foothold. Her feet flailed and scraped as she tried for a purchase. It seemed that she was slipping downwards, but somehow she hoisted her hips over the edge of the hole.

Her feet swung in empty air and her face was smothered with soil and wet leaves. She dragged one knee over, then the other. She found herself crouched on all fours, panting like a dog.

Above her was the broken-down stone wall of what had once been the whalers' refuge. Behind and higher up the slope was the oak tree. The chinks of sky visible through the canopy of leaves were a mild, smoky blue.

May began to crawl up towards the humped back of the island. Her hands were torn but she couldn't find the strength to stand upright.

*

Marty had lost sight of Spencer and Alexander. He thought he must have crested the ridge and begun the descent before them. Either they were still on the landward side and were out of sight and earshot, or the agreed distance between them had widened and they were much further over to his right. He stopped walking and cocked his head to listen. There was the raucous screaming of the gulls and the rustle of the sea, and he made an effort to block them out. There was something or someone moving in the scrub below him; too far down the slope and in the wrong direction to be Spencer Newton.

Marty took a step forward, then another, and stopped to listen again. The crackle of leaves and twigs had stopped. 'May?' he called. 'May, Ma-aa-ay . . .'

There was an answer, a thin cry: 'Help me.'

He broke into a run, wildly crashing forward and slowing immediately because he made too much noise. She was still below him, not far away now, he could hear the repeated cry much more clearly. He ducked under the shade-spreading branches of an old tree and saw her. The tiny white oval of her face was turned imploringly upwards.

May knew that rescue and safety were approaching, then she saw who it was.

She understood everything that had happened in a sudden blinding instant and the knowledge made fear hit her all over again. It turned to a hammer-blow that made splinters of pain fire off in her chest so that she stopped crawling and crouched with her arms crossed to protect herself.

She was afraid of him. As soon as he was close enough he saw it and smelt it, a sharp, feral scent. Her fear ignited a flare of panic in him and at once his head was twisting, his eyes scanning the ranks of trees for witnesses. They were alone in the woods, no one else had heard her. She had been lost. She needn't be found. His fists tightened, white-knuckled, a terrible reflex.

'It was you, wasn't it?' The words wrung themselves out of her, burning in her parched throat. 'It was you who came and took her diary. You were the only one who knew about it.'

He took a step towards her. His hands hung heavy now, the fingers thick and clumsy.

'It was you she loved.'

'I didn't hurt her,' he protested. 'I didn't do anything she didn't want.'

May was very tired. Her eyes flickered and her head was heavy, much too heavy for her shoulders. The bars of her pain cage were closing in, tighter and tighter. *Everywhere, and there. Nothing she didn't want.* It was the truth, perhaps. 'Don't hurt me,' she begged. 'Please, Marty, don't hurt me.'

He knelt down in a hurry, his shadow blocking out the light. She flinched a little and the sign of her fear made his thoughts burrow on into the darkness. *If May was not found, if she was silenced, no one would know.* A tide of blood hammered in his ears.

Spencer was whistling, a sharp extended note that

shrilled through the trees. Relief surged through Marty. 'It's all right,' he whispered, locking his arms around her so that she whimpered with the pain of it. 'You're found. You're safe now. We're going to take you home.'

He held May's head against his chest, stroking her hair. He whistled in answer and shouted, 'She's here! I've found her!'

She closed her eyes. Later she remembered that he had picked the leaves and twigs tenderly out of her matted hair.

When Alexander had run for help and Spencer was giving her sips of water from a bottle he carried, Marty blindly turned away. He looked down into the deep hole, the old cellar of the whalers' retreat. He was white to the lips. Lifting his hand to rub a prickle of sweat from his face, he saw that it shook like an old man's.

Fourteen

The late sun shot an arrow of gilt across the sea. A four-wheel drive truck driven by a police officer in wraparound sun-glasses nosed on to the shingle and a knot of people immediately gathered round it. At the same time a fishing boat appeared in the channel between the headland and the rocks of Moon Island. The onlookers stood watching and in the quiet that fell the steady chug of the engine grew loud. A stretcher and blanket were unloaded from the truck and carried to the water's edge.

Up among the blooms of phlox and kniphofia in Elizabeth's garden Leonie and she stood together. Their elongated shadows pointed to the edge of the bluff like signposts. They could see Alexander down in the group on the beach, and the Beams, and Judith Stiegel with the baby in her arms. The black shingles of the Captain's House next door were warmed by the light to mellow grey-brown, but the house stood empty and silent. John and Ivy had run out and down to the boat, which took them out to the island.

Hannah stood watching too, from the corner of her

porch. Aaron was propped in his chair close to the open door. His head lolled and abruptly lifted again as the breath snagged in his chest. 'What?' he called out to Hannah.

'Nothing yet. The boat's just coming in.'

The boatman cut his engine and two or three men waded through the shallows to hold the prow of the craft. It rocked on the swell and the sound of voices giving orders came across the beach. Leonie felt Elizabeth's hand on her arm, and took it and held it in hers. The stretcher was laid out on the shingle.

May was lifted out of the boat by one of the men in the water. He hoisted her seemingly without effort and carried her the few steps to the beach. He made to lower her to the stretcher, and Leonie and Elizabeth both remembered the other motionless body, dark and heavy with water, and the tarpaulin that had wrapped it out of sight.

But May would not be made to lie down. Instead, the man set her gently on her feet and supported her with his arms. Ivy and John closed in on either side of her. May took one step forward and turned her face up to the sky.

'She's walking up the beach.'

Leonie smiled. The difference from the other one was so plain. Alexander had brought them the news before hurrying back to the beach, but to see her for themselves was the best reassurance. They put their arms around each other, and there were tears and relief at the same time.

Elizabeth took a folded handkerchief from her

388

sleeve. She dried her eyes and looked around her. 'Do you know,' she said, 'I don't think I've ever seen the garden look more beautiful than it does at this minute?'

And it was true that there was a luminosity in the early evening, which delineated every leaf and petal in an intricate arrangement of melting light and shadow.

Hannah said to Aaron, 'They're putting her in the truck now, with her father and sister. They'll be taking her to the hospital, I guess, but she looks well enough to me.'

'I'm glad of it,' he answered with composure.

Hannah lingered on the porch for a while longer, watching the groups of people on the beach break up and turn away in their separate directions. Spencer and Alexander peeled away from Marty and Judith, and the two couples traced a V-shape across the shingle to their steps. In the middle a clump of Beams jostled around Marian's bulk, like tugs bringing a liner in to dock.

The slanting light was distinctly end-of-summer. Within a month the last visitors would be gone, and Pittsharbor and the deserted bluff would be ready for winter. Another year's cold would be hard for Aaron to endure, but he wouldn't agree to leave the place. He was held here by his memories, which were more vivid to him now than the pallid and painful constrictions of reality.

'Fine evening,' Hannah observed calmly as she came across and settled the pillows behind his head.

*

389

May was transferred from the truck that had brought her up from the beach to a waiting ambulance. Ivy and John and a police officer went with her. One of the paramedics gave her tiny sips of water as they rolled along the lane towards Pittsharbor. She begged for more in a cracked whisper, but he wouldn't let her have it. Her lips were split by deep seams crusted with blood, and her tongue was dark and swollen. She wouldn't let go of John and Ivy. John supported her in his arms and Ivy held on to her hand. John kept lowering his head so his mouth brushed against May's hair.

Ivy wanted to smother her sister with love, to choke her and ram her throat full of it, so that if she ever vanished again she would at least take the certainty of it with her. And with another part of herself she wanted to vent her anger for the last hours, by hitting and hurting and clawing at her in a blaze of retaliation. She bit her own lip until it stung.

May opened her eyes. 'It hurts. My hand.'

Ivy loosened her fingers. They were cramped with the intensity of her grip. Anger felt like a blowtorch burning in her chest. 'I'm sorry. I'm so mad at you. I thought you were dead.'

The paramedic looked a warning at her. They were travelling faster now, gathering speed towards the hospital.

To her surprise May grinned, then winced at the pain from her split mouth. 'I thought I was, too.'

'Nowhere near,' the paramedic said, 'You're a tough one, aren't you?'

'I'm glad I didn't die.'

Beyond the tinted windows of the ambulance there were trees and rocks, and the striations of light and shadow, the real world. She had climbed up out of a dark place because she wanted to be back here again. The memory of the effort it had cost told her how much she had wanted it. She was not Doone, she was nothing like poor Doone or her melancholy predecessor. She felt a lightness, not just in her knocked head but all through herself, as if she had discarded a weight she had dragged about with her for much too long. She could see her sister's chipped nail polish and the worn denim of her father's Levis with intense clarity. The simplicity of it all was more precious than anything she had ever known.

They were all looking at her, the woman police officer and the paramedics, and John and Ivy. It dawned on her that she was more hurt than she realised. 'I am all right,' she said clearly. 'I am quite all right. I didn't want to be dead, like the others.'

The other world was there, but it was fading from her sight. The bigger and much darker mysteries were all about this one. She thought about Ali and Jack O'Donnell, and Marty, and Leonie, and Lucas, and the stories Elizabeth had told her. What people did and hid from one another and wished for in their hearts. Love and sex, longing and disappointment, those were the real secrets.

John stroked her hair. 'Of course not,' he soothed her. 'Of course you didn't.'

He thought, *Oh God, if only Ali were here*. He couldn't

be a mother to May, or to Ivy, and they needed her now. Ivy's face was puckered with warring emotions, made almost ugly for once by the force of them. And the loneliness of the days and nights he had just endured suddenly unleashed itself. He found himself belatedly crying for his wife. Ivy saw it and shifted herself closer to him, and the three of them hung on to each other's hands like an everlasting knot.

The ambulance turned on to the freeway and towards the hospital.

Marty and Judith reached the security of their house. For once Judith didn't get busy immediately with Justine's needs. Instead she challenged her husband. 'You look terrible. What's wrong?'

He shook his head, his mouth making a tremulous line.

'I want to know,' she insisted.

She planted her hands on his arms, shaking him. She was big and solid, and as seemingly imperturbable as one of her own sculptures, and the impulse grew within him to crack open and expose his failings to the solace of her massive calm. He could smell her familiar scent overlaid with the sour-sweet odour of baby. His mouth opened, choked with words.

'Yes?' Judith said. Her hair was slicked close to her skull, making her head and shoulders look like one rock balanced on another.

'I did it,' he said.

Her eyes widened a fraction, made blank with surprise.

'I killed her.'

'She isn't dead, Marty. We just saw her off to hospital.'

'Not her.'

'Who, then?'

He could see the surprise overwhelmed by a leap of fear and apprehension. But the longing to tell, to relieve himself of the guilt by sharing it, had grown too strong to contain. 'Doone. I killed her.'

Judith half turned to look at the baby in her chair, searching for reassurance in the sight. But then her gaze dragged back to Marty. The words couldn't be unsaid, although she did her best to deflect them. 'She drowned. It was an accident. I don't know what you're talking about.'

'Because of me. It happened because of me. She said she wanted to die and she did. She was in love with me, more than just a kid's crush. I let her, then I stopped her and she drowned.'

'Wait.'

She came closer, so their faces were almost touching. A monumental composure overlaid the depth of her shocked reaction. 'Are you sure you want me to hear this, whatever it is?'

Desperately he whispered, 'Yes. Oh yes, please let me tell you. I can't keep it in any longer.' He tried to rest his head against her but she wouldn't yield. He was like a child handing over his confession, waiting for the damage to be made better.

'Go ahead then,' Judith said.

Her expression never changed while he told the

story and the words poured violently out of him. Spittle gathered at the corners of his mouth; he made little gestures of entrapment with his hands to catch and hold her, although she made no move away from him. Just once she turned her gaze to make sure that Justine was still happy in her chair, with her fat fists waving at a mobile suspended in front of her.

At the end he buried his face in his hands.

'Is that it?' Judith delivered the words coldly, wanting to empty her mouth of them.

'Yes. I don't know how I can expect you to understand, let alone forgive me. But I did put a stop to it, you know. I told her that there would be no more sailing together. There were going to be no more times alone with her. I . . . wanted to put things right, Judith. They'd gone wrong, yes. But I did what I could, at the end.'

'Wait a minute.' Her voice grew colder still. 'Are you saying you interfered with her?'

'No, Jesus, it wasn't like that. I didn't make love to her or anywhere near it, what do you think I am? She came on to me. But yeah, I did things I shouldn't have done. It's the age, Jude, that just on the brink between girl and woman time, neither one nor the other. It's . . . *intense*.' He looked wildly around, at the pleasant room and the doors still standing open to the view of silvery sea. 'But I love you, for Chrissake. We were waiting for our baby to be born. I told her.'

At last Judith shook her head. 'And so you think she killed herself for unrequited love of *you*?'

He hesitated now. A trap opened at his feet. 'She

was unbalanced. I think maybe she didn't try to live. I think maybe that was it.'

'You didn't kill her.' It was a flat statement. There was a reprieve in sight.

Even more hurriedly he said, 'No, I think I see that now. Only the whole thing has been driven inside me. Yesterday and today there was the other girl, and we were out looking for her and all the horror of it came rushing back. I was out one day taking some photographs of Doone, quite innocently, and Spencer Newton saw me. He put a wrong construct on it, of course. But I think he and Alexander believed I might have had something to do with May's disappearance. Which I didn't, of course.'

'Poor Doone,' Judith said with sudden softness. 'Poor little girl.'

'Yes.'

'Who else knows about this, Marty? Apart from Spencer and Alexander? People at the gallery, maybe? Up here at the beach?'

'No one. I swear to God. Except for May herself. She found a diary, in Doone's bedroom. And I was the only person she told about that.'

'A diary. I see.'

Now Judith went to the window and looked out at the island. He followed her and rested his hands experimentally on her shoulders, feeling the reassuring pad of flesh on her back.

'Don't do that,' Judith said in a clear voice.

'Do what?'

'Touch me.'

'What do you mean? Judith, listen baby, I told you because I couldn't bear to keep it from you any longer, because you deserve better than . . .'

'Don't try to justify it to me. Don't ask me to share the responsibility for what you did.' She had already moved away. With shaking hands she was putting notebooks and work materials into her black holdall, moving quickly and distractedly, betraying her feelings at last.

'What are you doing?' he demanded in disbelief.

'What do you think? You don't expect me to stay, do you? I'm taking Justine in the car. We're going back to the apartment. I'll take advice, you must make your own arrangements. Don't stand there, blocking my way.'

He was amazed. 'You're just shocked, I'm not surprised, but you mustn't be so harsh. You can't walk out on me. I'm not Tom Beam.'

'You're right. You are much worse than Tom Beam.'

'Wait. What about Justine?'

'I have to think of *her*.' Judith's eyes were hard and burning as she nodded towards the baby. 'I'm going now,' she said. 'I'm going to pack my things and go back to New York.'

He tried to stop her, pulling her back and attempting to snatch the bag out of her hands. 'I'll come with you.'

'I don't want you with me.'

'Just wait, stay till the morning at least, we need to talk this thing out. You can't take Justine away from me.'

Judith squared up to him. Her bulk became threatening. 'Yes, I can. Whose case would anyone listen to? To yours? A child molester?'

Marty recoiled. 'You wouldn't. Don't call me that. This is *me*.' He beat his chest with his fists and Judith's mouth hardened at the theatricality of him. 'I'm her father. Your husband, did you forget that?'

'I can't change one of those. The other I can do something about.'

'*Judith*.' His voice rose in a howl. Justine started in fright and her face puckered. Before she could begin to cry Judith gathered her out of her chair and swept her out of his reach. She ran up the stairs with her hand cupped around the baby's head and the door of the bedroom snapped shut behind them.

An hour later, Judith and Justine were gone.

May had slight concussion, a bruised collar-bone and severe dehydration. After a day in the hospital she was fit enough to get up and sit in a chair, and to plead to be allowed home. John and Ivy sat with her, sometimes together and sometimes separately. For the first time since Alison's death the girls were content just to be together. Ivy lounged in a visitor's chair and flipped through magazines or jabbed at the television remote, but she showed none of the usual signs of wishing to be somewhere else. And sporadically at first, then compulsively as the old crust of antipathy began to break up, they talked.

'After Mom died I think I just went about being more myself than I'd been before. I wanted to be more popular, more hip, more in with everything. Kind of, *fuck you, world*. It gave me something to concentrate on, like non-stop performance art, maybe. It seemed the only way to deal with everything being so shitty, you know?'

May said wonderingly, 'Was that what you were doing? You seemed like you didn't care about anyone. But how can you *deal* with someone dying just like that? Walking out and never coming back, without a footprint or a message or anything left behind?'

'She didn't know she was going to die, did she? So how could she have left us a message?'

'I was the opposite to you.'

'. . . Naturally,' Ivy shrugged. 'Didn't Dr Metz take you through all that sibling rivalry shit?'

'I wasn't trying to be different. I'd have pulled out my teeth to be like you, but I was so scared of everything. That John would die, that you would die, that somebody would notice me or that I'd be ignored.'

'You were awful. Always ill, always clinging on, then going crazy and chopping her things up. Or going out to commune with some *tree*. I didn't know why you just couldn't say, this has happened, right. Nothing will bring her back, so the rest of us have got to get on with it.'

'Nobody talked about her. Nobody *talked*.'

Ivy gave a harsh hoot of laughter. 'We didn't want to set you off. Sniffing or cutting.'

'You really are a heartless bitch, aren't you?'

Ivy stopped laughing. 'That was a statement, not a taunt. You've changed. Must be the concussion.'

'What do you expect? And *why* didn't anyone talk about what was happening to us?'

'Partly because of history, because of Jack O'Donnell, I guess. I knew that Dad and Ali weren't that happy, that she might well have gone anyway. She left in a big way, though.'

May thought about the image she had crumpled up and stuffed away in her unconscious. When she unfolded it she saw it was only two people on a sofa. Having sex, Ivy said, having sex, that was what people did. As she considered the scene now, chips of disgust flaked away from it, diminishing its lurid brilliance and leaving a blurred image that seemed more striking for its banality than for anything else. Men and women, husbands and wives, were unfaithful to each other. It was sad. But it wasn't grotesque, loomingly fearful or threatening. It was just people.

'And partly Dad himself,' Ivy added. She spoke quietly, without emphasis.

'What did he do?'

'Nothing. That's just it. He's not like Ali.'

They contemplated the vividness of her, or the flashes and reflections and dressings-up of it that were left in their memories. They would not say it aloud but they acknowledged that John was passive by comparison, a done-to man rather than a doer.

'There's nothing wrong with that,' May defended him, out of love.

'Of course there isn't.'

They were quiet for a moment. Absently Ivy reached for May's Walkman but she set the earpieces swinging in little opposing arcs instead of putting them in her ears.

May felt grateful for this indication that the conversation wasn't over. 'Do you think he'll, you know, get someone else in the end?' she asked.

Ivy sighed. 'I suppose. I don't know why he should be lonely, living with us, but he seems to be.' Her face was so ironically expressive that May laughed out of pure affection.

'I'm sorry I punched you.'

'If we're in apology mode I'm sorry I said what I did about Mom and Jack O'Donnell. I'm sorry I wasn't on the island when you came looking, I'm sorry you fell into an old cellar and hit your head and hurt your shoulder, and we didn't find you until you climbed out on your own. I'm sorry I haven't been there for you all along, like I should have been, poor motherless girls that we are. Um, is there anything else?'

'That seems pretty much to cover it. Don't break my Walkman.'

'Sorry.'

'Mom won't come back, will she?' May said. The observation was important because it was final, at last. 'Nothing any of us does will mean anything different.'

She remembered climbing out of the pit and the determination that she would do it because she wanted to go on with her life. Not like Doone. Not like Sarah.

She wasn't going to tell Ivy about the ghosts because Ivy would classify all that with clothes-cutting and tree-hugging. Her sister was so sure of what she knew May

400

thought. Ivy had suffered enough, and yet she had managed to turn out so strong and smart. Better than smart; Ivy had a kind of wisdom, May realised. She admired her older sister as much as she had always done, but now it was admiration rooted in more valuable traits.

'You're right, I should be like you. Concentrate on myself as a work of art.'

'Mm. I wouldn't go as far as pulling your teeth,' Ivy said kindly. 'It would be a backward step. A waste of the braces.'

'Do you want Dad to find someone else?'

'Yes, I do. It's time he did. But all the ones he's had up to now have been such compromises. Like he wanted to please us by not going for anything too noticeable. Suzanne, for one.'

'"Good accessories are so important,"' May intoned. 'Jesus.'

'Do you think it could be Leonie?'

'I haven't a clue. What happens is what happens. But I think maybe we shouldn't stand in his way so much any more.'

May dropped her head to pick at the bedsheet and looked up again. Her cut hand was healed now. 'Yeah,' she said.

'Hey, there's another drama. Judith's left Marty.'

'Why?'

'D'you think they'd tell me? Next thing, the Fennymores will be splitting.'

It was something to do with the diary. Marty had seemed the incarnation of threat when he came on her

401

through the trees; even now she could taste the sour rush of fear in her mouth. Yet he had held her and stroked her hair, and told her she was safe. Judith's leaving him was something to do with Doone, of course. Last summer bleeding into this one, the past interfering with the present, for ever and ever. Faces watching from within the circle of trees.

'Are you okay?' Ivy asked.

'Um, I'm thirsty again. I'd like some Coke.'

'I'll get you some,' Ivy said tenderly.

The next afternoon Leonie came. May stared at her in surprise. She brought with her a bundle of magazines and two bottles of Hard Candy nail-polish, pale sky-blue and a gooseberry green with flakes of glitter suspended in it. She sat down on the bed. 'Hi, I didn't know what to buy you, so I got these.'

'That's neat. Really neat.' May struggled to unscrew the seal of the green one, but her hurt shoulder hampered her.

'Let me.' Leonie undid the bottle and feathered the brush invitingly with polish.

May unclenched her fists and reluctantly spread her fingers apart. She had cleaned the earth out from under the nail tips. 'I've got horrible nails,' she muttered. Their bent heads almost touched as Leonie deftly painted. She spread the little brush and worked it to the nail margins with smooth strokes, like a proper manicurist. When both hands were done May held them up in front of her to judge the sparkling effect. 'Thanks,' she said. 'I like that a lot.'

'How are you?'

May loved the nail polish. She would never have bought it for herself; it was Ivy's kind of stuff, so she would have pretended to despise it. But this gesture of Leonie's seemed to admit May at a stroke into a world inhabited by her sister and her sister's friends. Leonie hadn't brought her a little girl's present, or something boring like fruit or books. She had bought glitter-green Hard Candy and May understood that she had chosen it because she knew it was the right gift. Gratitude made her smile straight back at Leonie.

'I'm okay.'

Leonie nodded. 'I heard you were. But I thought I'd come by, just to see. I know you'll be going back to the city as soon as you're well enough.'

She had had the briefest of telephone conversations with John, all of it concerned with May. The vacation was over. Tacitly they avoided the question of whether the two of them might see each other again.

'Do you want to come out for a walk with me?' May asked abruptly. She hoisted herself out of the bedside chair. 'I'm allowed to go out in the grounds. It's so hot and stuffy in here, I feel I can't breathe half the time.'

'I'd like that. Is your polish dry?'

'I won't smudge it. I'll wave my hands around.'

The hospital was backed by a small park. They walked down a path bordered with hydrangea bushes, the mophead blooms turning dry and rusty as if they were already set out in basket-shop dried-flower displays.

'Are you going back to the city too?'

Leonie answered easily, 'I think I'll stay on here for a while. I can do some work and I like my cabin up in the woods.'

They made a slow circuit of the park. May blinked at the flowerbeds where summer daisies were giving way to pink and purple asters with cobwebs spun between them. The colours seemed emphatically bright and she realised that the warmth spreading through her was happiness.

Leonie was walking with her head down, her hands in her pockets. 'Tom and I have separated, you know.'

'I'm sorry. I don't know, is that the right thing to say?'

'Probably. For the time being. In the end I should think we'll both be happier, but that doesn't make it any the less sad now.'

They came to a bench under a plane tree. The circle of butts spread around indicated that it was where the hospital smokers came and the sight reminded Leonie of Pittsharbor churchyard. She had sat talking to Elizabeth, who had warned her not to let life's chances pass her by for fear of regretting the missed opportunities.

They sat down in the tree's shelter and May tapped her nails so the flecks of glitter caught the light. 'I didn't understand anything much, before,' she attempted. 'When I saw you with my father and smashed the window. It wasn't out of jealousy, not really. I just needed him to be my *dad*, you know? I didn't want to see him like he was with you. Do you mind me saying that?'

404

Leonie lifted her head and their eyes met. May thought it must be the first time they had looked at each other properly. They sensed the fluttery movements of estimation as liking measured up against mistrust. 'Not if it's what you feel.'

May said, 'The whole world seemed made up of sex. Everywhere I looked. It was seething, dripping from everyone. Even the *old* people, not just Ivy and Lucas.'

'It can seem that way.'

'I've got it in better perspective now.'

'That's good,' Leonie said gravely.

'What changed it was that I more or less did it with Lucas. On Pittsharbor night.'

Compassion and concern flooded Leonie's face. May was touched by the sight of it. 'May, you're very young. What happened?'

'I was wasted, so was he. Nobody's fault except mine. It wasn't anything amazing. You know?'

Leonie smiled. 'Yes. I do know. Did you want to because of competing with Ivy?'

'In a way. But it's just what people do, isn't it?'

She wouldn't tell even Leonie that it was also because of Doone, because she had thought Lucas was Doone's lover, that she was herself entwined with Doone. Anyway, had that really been the truth?

It was true that Doone had died because of sex. And so had Sarah Corder, betrayed by it. May bit her lip. It wasn't *just* anything, however much she wanted to diminish it.

Leonie took her thoughts and echoed them. 'It isn't just what people do, May. When it's good, sex is better than anything you know or could imagine; more exotic and more absorbing, and funnier and prouder and simpler. You can't forget it or rub it out, it's like a song running in your head, which carries itself down your spine and all through your bones. It's being so close to another person that they become you. Better than you could ever be separately.' Her words amazed her even as she spoke them, although she knew them to be true. She had thought that physical desire had deserted her and now she knew that it would come back.

'I can't imagine.'

'You'll discover for yourself. Not for a while, perhaps. Not with Lucas Beam, I shouldn't think.'

May laughed. The notion of Lucas was surprisingly diminished, it took up hardly any space in her mind now. 'Is it like you say for you and my father?'

Leonie hesitated, then said sadly, 'No. Not right now, anyway.'

May was embarrassed, feeling she had trespassed too far. 'I haven't helped things between you that much, have I?'

'Maybe not. But the truth is, if it's going to happen it doesn't need much help or hindrance.'

'I think I understand that, at least, after what you've told me.'

Leonie took her hand and squeezed it quickly, then let it go because she was afraid that May might object to such a demonstration. 'You're okay,' she told her, and it was an appreciation and a wider assurance as well as being to do with her injuries.

They left the bench and walked the circuit of the park once more.

When they came inside they found Ivy sitting by May's bed. She was rattling the bottles of nail-polish on the bed table and yawning, but she jumped up as soon as she saw the two of them. She was wearing a halter top and checked capri pants, and with the summer's end her arms and shoulders were brown and smooth as a bolt of mocha silk. 'Dad's just coming,' she said, eyeing Leonie in surprise. 'He stopped off to buy some shit for you, May.'

'I'll go,' Leonie said quickly. She didn't want him to think she was contriving a meeting, here of all places, or intruding into his family. 'Get well soon,' she said to May. 'And good luck, if I don't see you before you go back to the city.' She ducked her head at Ivy, an awkward greeting and goodbye in one.

'Thanks for the stuff,' May called after her.

It was too late. Leonie saw John advancing up the white-lit tunnel of the hall. There was no detour she could make and he had already seen her. They stopped, too close together under the inquisitorial lights, and stepped a pace apart again.

'I just looked in to see how she is.'

'Thank you.'

'I can imagine what you must have felt like, all that time she was missing . . .' Leonie broke off, reddening. 'At least, I can't imagine because I don't have a child of my own. But I thought about you.'

There was no explaining why she hadn't felt it right to go to him and help to share the vigil. It was to do

407

with presumption and also with offering what she feared being unable to sustain. But the withholding of her support made her feel small and mean in retrospect.

'Thank you,' he said again and added brutally, 'I missed Alison. I wanted her to be there so we could endure it side by side. It was the first time in a long time I have actually cried for her.'

Leonie acknowledged the admission with a brief dip of her head. There seemed to be no more to add; the tranquillity she had been feeling and the hypothetical flare of rekindled lust were not relevant here and now. She held out her hand and he took it briefly.

'Ivy and I have been packing up. I thought perhaps May wouldn't want to go back to that place and anyway we've only got a couple more days' vacation left. I don't know.' He was asking her for a pointer.

'I'm going to stay on at the cabin for a while.'

They were both thinking of the green bedspread, the hollowed mattress. Not now, but maybe some time; that was what they had agreed, could it be only three nights ago?

Just as she had done at the beginning, in the Pittsharbor car-park, Leonie moved close and kissed him on the mouth. 'If I do decide to move on, Elizabeth Newton will always know where to find me,' she said. She walked away from him, the rubber soles of her sneakers drawing a small squeak out of the plastic-tiled floor.

John found Ivy and May sitting head to head as May painted Ivy's fingernails. They were laughing together about something and with the same movement they turned their flushed faces towards him. They were suddenly alike, the same mouths, the same slant to their eyes. It was tough, he thought, that they should have to have been taken to the brink of a tragedy before discovering their connectedness. But plenty of discoveries were tough and the routes to them no less so. Hope for the future lifted suddenly inside him and the lightness revealed itself in his face. His daughters were looking steadily at him.

'Ivy said we could go straight home, but I don't want to yet. I want to go back to Pittsharbor and finish everything off,' May said.

He didn't ask her what her unfinished business might be. 'We can do that if you're sure it's what you want,' he told her.

'I'm sure.' May bent her head again to concentrate on the sky-blue finger-nails.

Fifteen

'You put it back, didn't you?' May locked her eyes on him.

He stared at her bare sandy feet, at the floor, anywhere but into her face. She had come in from the seaward side, materialising at the screen door and boldly walking into the room, before Marty had a chance to withdraw or to hide from her. He could not know how much of May's courage it had taken to propel herself here.

She repeated, 'You crept into my room and took it, and you read it, then you put it back again so it would look as if it hadn't been touched.'

The Stiegels' house was in disarray. There were boxes and half-packed bags spilling their contents on the floor, and already an atmosphere of neglect, as if dust motes were thickening in the stagnant air. The last grains of summer were running out, sand in an hourglass.

Marty straightened up and put down the concertina file he had held in his arms, reminding May that she had come across pictures of Doone by prying and snooping on her own part. 'Yes,' he agreed, 'I had to know what she had written about me.'

'And did you find out what you wanted to know?'

'It was in code, most of it.'

'I told you that.'

There was a silence, in which they appraised each other. May held up her head, keeping her resolve firm.

No one knew she was here, unless she had been seen as she slipped up the Stiegels' steps. She had told John she was going to call on Elizabeth, knowing that Elizabeth had driven to Pittsharbor with Spencer. It was a heavy, thundery afternoon with occasional fat drops of rain pockmarking the flat sea and the beach was almost deserted.

'What do you want?' Marty asked. He suddenly came a step closer and automatically, fearfully, May retreated by the same measure. It was as if they were dancing together.

But she did know exactly what she wanted: it was the first certainty she had ever had that was based on an adult's perception, not a child's.

She had dreamed about Marty Stiegel, in the hospital and twice more since she had come home to the Captain's House. They were superficially harmless dreams in which he served a family dinner of live lobsters in the New York apartment, or appeared smiling in her classroom at school dressed in a Hallowe'en costume but with the mask held out in his hand for her to take. Yet there was an undercurrent to

411

them, which stayed with her long after she had woken up, and she knew that it welled out of fear and washed in a cold flood right through her.

I want not to be afraid. The thought came to her as she sat on Doone's bed, looking at the diary on the shelf. If she dammed it up the fear would still burst out in the end and carry her away. She could confide in her father, perhaps, or Elizabeth, or even Leonie, and there would be more sessions with Dr Metz and she would be treated with concern and sympathy, but she would still be a flood victim. *I don't want that*, she thought. It would be to make herself passive again, to be at the mercy of fate or whatever random circumstances life threw at her, when she needed to be exactly the opposite.

The only proper way forward was to face down the fear and so to exorcise it. She could make herself unafraid by crossing the arcs of sand and shingle, and climbing the steps to Marty's door and looking straight into his eyes. 'I want to talk to you,' she answered.

He was, in truth, the only person she could talk to properly. To reveal her fear to anyone else would be to betray Doone's secrets too, who had chosen to take them with her beyond where they could be uncovered. Unless Doone had left the diary on purpose for her to read, and decode, and to inherit. . . . May blinked. She couldn't believe any longer that Doone possessed her, or influenced her. Doone had just hidden her diary where she believed it wouldn't be found, then she had sailed her boat out of the bay.

'Go ahead. There's no one here, as you can see.

Judith and Justine have left me.' With a shrug he indicated the dismantled room and his sad solitude within it. He screwed a piece of paper into a ball and threw it aside.

May felt a brief contraction of sympathy for him, twisted with dislike of his self-pity. It was very quiet; the ball of paper unfurled with a tiny scratching noise. 'I heard. I'm sorry.'

'I think they will come back.'

'What exactly did you do to Doone?'

He looked now, jerking his big head, pinning her with his narrow eyes. It was much too far to the door, May realised. Her heart was hammering. *I want not to be afraid.* But she was afraid of him, she couldn't escape it.

'You read what she wrote, didn't you?' he said softly. 'You know everything.'

'It was . . . oblique. She wrote what you made her feel.'

'You broke the code. That was clever of you. How did you do it?'

'I . . .' May's stomach loosened. She should have denied it instead of letting him see through her like a pane of glass. She eased away from him, another step towards the door, but he followed as if magnetised. Her hands came up in self-protection but he caught her wrists and held them down. The force of it made her wince with the pain in her bruised shoulder. Marty let go and smiled at her, as tender as a father. 'Listen. Your view is distorted. Of course you identify with her. But she wanted me, not the other way round. She was

413

hysterical. Do you understand what that means? I was *all* she wanted, May. In truth and in fantasy. I went along with it, further than I should have done, much further, but never as far as she wanted.'

Everywhere, and there.

May said slowly, 'I think she died because of you.'

Marty shook his head. 'She died because of herself, May. I told her that what was happening between us had to stop. She wouldn't – couldn't – accept it. She took out her boat and she drowned herself.'

'Was that how it was?' May asked.

At first he didn't answer. May thought he was preparing a lie and fear and dislike of him rose more strongly than ever. But then he lifted his head and looked straight into her face.

'I don't know,' he said. His voice was steady and May couldn't tell whether he was offering her the truth or concealing it. 'Maybe it was an accident or maybe she drowned herself. We . . . I . . . shall probably never know.'

She wanted to die, May thought. That was what you did to her. And you know it too.

'Was that how it was?' she repeated, pressing him.

He retreated now from the slip into honesty, if that was what it had been.

'Of course it was. What did she say different? What did she write that says specifically, incriminatingly, *Marty did this but I didn't want to. He forced me?*'

His breath warmed her face. She remembered the night of Pittsharbor Day, in this very room, when he

414

had comforted her, then come too close for comfort. It was the way he was, the flaw in the silky-smooth weave of him. Young girls. She thought of young girls now as she made a move beyond them, into the adult realm. 'Nothing.' Her mouth formed the word stiffly. Doone had been protective of her betrayer to the end.

He was close enough now for her to see tiny veins netting the whites of his eyes. His grip on her relaxed. 'There you are.' He was reasonable, even magnanimous.

Blood swished in May's ears. 'I'm not afraid of you,' she insisted. It came out too loud, almost a shout.

'Of course not.'

'On the island, when you found me. You thought you would kill me, didn't you? To protect yourself?'

He looked amazed, shocked, disbelieving; the expressions chased over his flexible features before he laughed. It was a gust of laughter that shook his chest, convincingly. 'My God. No, no. All I felt was huge relief and gratitude that you were safe.'

He had cradled her in his arms and picked the debris out of her hair. May's defiance softened and buckled, before threatening to collapse altogether. She couldn't discern what was the truth and what she had hatched from within herself, brooding alone in Doone's bedroom. 'The diary,' she insisted. 'Once you had it, why did you put it back? You could have destroyed it. That's what you should have done'.

'I didn't know who else knew about it by then.'

'Only you and me,' May said.

She studied his face again, watching hindsight and

rapid calculation adding up together, and pulled herself away from him. He didn't try to restrain her. She was still alone with him, the door was still behind her and at a distance, but the room shrank and became unthreatening. The place was just a holiday home in the process of being closed up for the winter. She had achieved what she had come for: she would walk away with distaste for Marty Stiegel and a queasy kind of sympathy, which weighted her heart, but she wasn't afraid of him any more.

'You could do it,' he urged. 'You could destroy it. Doone would want that. Not to have her secrets read and exposed and pawed over.'

'I don't know what to do with it, yet. I have to go now.'

He was going to stand in her way with further insistences, but in the next room the telephone began to ring. He spun round at once, with the eagerness of someone who had been waiting too long for the call. May walked quietly to the screen door and let herself out on to the deck once more. The sky had grown dark, with a purply tinge to it that faded over the sea to the flatness of lead.

'Judith?' When he heard her voice at the other end Marty closed his eyes and breathed a silent *O* of relief.

She was angry still and she wanted to hurt him. He let her talk, offering no resistance to her sharpness, but all the time he was thinking that it would work out in the end. Her fury would diminish, she would accept what had happened and allow it to be put in the past,

416

and he would have the relief of nothing to conceal. He would be at home and comfortable again, with his wife and his daughter. 'Listen,' he soothed at last, 'listen to me. I'm coming back home. No, wait. You don't have to do that. Just back to New York. We can talk, at least we can talk, can't we?

'We always did talk. Judith, We were always able to do that much.

'I've rented a car. I'll close this place up, bring back whatever needs to be brought. And when I get back to the city – Jesus, Judith, you left without taking any of your stuff. I'll bring it round for you. No more, nothing more than that.

'And – Judith? – How is she? My little girl?'

He listened again to his wife's bitter voice, his teeth viciously tearing at the margin of his thumb-nail.

'I love her so much,' he mumbled at the end. 'I will see you soon, both of you.'

But Judith had gone, cutting him off in mid-sentence.

Marian went to call on the Fennymores. She had telephoned, of course, as soon as she heard Aaron was home, but Hannah was adamant that he should have no visitors. Now Marian made the short walk down the bluff road, passing Marty Stiegel's rental car parked in his driveway. The sight of it made her thoughts travel from the Stiegels to Tom and Leonie. Their readiness to accept failure gnawed at her, opening unwelcome perspectives on her own life.

She knocked and rang for several minutes before

Hannah opened the door by a slit. Her bird eyes settled on Marian's face for an instant, before flicking defensively away again. 'It's you. Thank you for coming the other night. I'm grateful to you, Marian.'

'I was glad to do it,' Marian answered. Not for you, but for him.

They both heard the unspoken words. Hannah held on to the door as if it were a drawbridge. She had become the guardian of her husband's citadel at last and Marian saw that the new-found power filled her with grim triumph. She had waited long enough, poor Hannah, and had made do with so little of him. It wasn't much, especially in the face of the loss that must soon come. He was receding, slipping out of the grasp of both of them.

Marian wanted to push open the door and elbow past her to get to Aaron, while he was still there. 'I would like to see him, Hannah. Just for five minutes.'

The slit narrowed. Only one of the unblinking eyes remained visible. 'He's ill. He's asleep just at this minute.'

'Hannah . . .'

'I'm sorry.' She closed the door. It was a small, mean victory. But a victory, nevertheless.

Marian walked slowly away, wondering if Hannah was watching her from one of the curtained windows.

Instead of turning for home she crossed the headland on the Pittsharbor side, walking over Aaron's land where Spencer Newton wanted to put up rental cottages. There were only a few cars in the small car-park, which served the public end of the beach, but beside one of them a young couple were scolding two tiny children as they made ready for the drive home. The kids squirmed as their fat limbs were rubbed clean of sand and dry clothes were hastily zipped up to cover them. Marian would normally have stopped and exclaimed over their prettiness, but today her eyes slid past. She went on down the beach steps. The bluff houses reared solidly above the sea wall, each seeming tethered to the beach by its flight of steps.

Marian tucked up her skirt, revealing the puffy blue-and-white pillows of her knees. She walked into the water and stood with her back to the land, letting the waveless suck of the sea test her precarious balance.

Her love affair with Aaron had been conducted with Hannah always in the background. Hannah had known about it, of course, but none of them had ever admitted as much. Even before Dickson's death, Marian had been in love with Aaron Fennymore. The passion had fed her with energy and zest for life, and the summers at the beach had given the rest of the year meaning and shape. It had not seemed to matter that he had loved her so much less in return.

Marian turned to look at the houses and the water swirled around her calves. The Fennymores' presented a closed face to the bay, the Stiegels' upper windows were blanked with winter shutters. From the flagpole in front of her own house Dickson's Stars and Stripes hung motionless. There wasn't even a stirring of a breeze, and the air lay thick and heavy. The light in the west had turned greenish, almost luminous. There was going to be a storm.

Lucas came cantering down the beach with Sidonie on his shoulders, causing the little girl to scream with a mixture of delight and terror. After the quarrel with Ivy and May's disappearance Lucas had been sullen and uneasy, but the mood seemed to have lifted now. The other boys were close on his heels. They hollered at Marian and wheeled towards her.

'Grammer!' Sidonie yelled and the boys dashed into the water, sending up thick plumes of spray. Marian drew her skirts closer around her and the children halted in a semicircle, startled by her unresponsiveness.

'You okay?' Lucas asked.

I am not, Marian thought. Not any more. 'I'm old and very tired,' she said slowly. 'Just leave me alone now.'

They started up again, uncaring enough, and exuberantly ran away in another direction.

In the house, from his place beside the stove, Aaron asked, 'Who was that?'

'Marian.'

The deepening of the furrows beside his mouth might have indicated disapproval, or disappointment.

'It's time for your medicine,' Hannah told him. She brought a bottle and spoon, and poured the measure, and afterwards she wiped his chin with the cloth she kept at hand. Aaron's eyelids descended, shuttering his feelings. After a moment Hannah settled her spectacles in place and went back to her reading.

*

Ivy leant her elbows on May's bedroom window-sill. 'It's going to thunder. Our last night's going to be the same as the first one. Doesn't all that that seem like years ago?'

The Duhanes would drive back to New York the next morning. Ivy and May had done their packing; except for the last of her belongings the room was almost as it had been when May first saw it. The red-and-black diary and Hannah Fennymore's two books were centred on the top shelf.

'I'm ready to go,' May said calmly.

'What is all that stuff in there?' Ivy nodded at the diary.

'Oh, you know. I couldn't make half of it out.'

'Weird.' Ivy yawned in agreement. 'Listen. I'm going to go and hang out for an hour with Lucas and Gail. A goodbye thing, nothing heavy. Why don't you come with me? Maybe we could all go into town, get a drink or something?'

'You should go. But I think I'll stay here. I want to take Mrs Fennymore's books back.' It was easy to think about Lucas; May's face curved into a surprising smile.

'You sure?'

'Totally.'

The old Saab was parked outside the Beams' house. Ivy walked by without giving it a glance. The porch had been tidied somewhat, although the splintered boards were still dredged with sand.

Tom opened the door. He directed Ivy towards Lucas's room and she slithered past him and up the

421

stairs, raising her eyebrows at the silence in the house.

Leonie was in the kitchen, leaning against one of the counter-tops. She followed a crack in the floor tiles with the toe of her sneaker. Tom came back and sat down again at his place at the table. He knitted his fingers together and frowningly aligned his thumbs. They hadn't argued or even disagreed; they had simply made arrangements about what was to be done. It was a bloodless way to end a marriage, in restrained negotiations over property and bank accounts.

Yet what more did she expect, Leonie asked herself, from a marriage such as theirs had been? Of course it would not finish with operatic quarrels, or with cleansing rage, or even the bitterness of misplaced passion. The married Leonie made sad and reasonable provisions to put her married life aside and all the time the part of her that occupied the seedy cabin in the woods sang out with illogical hope.

The practical details were surprisingly few. They would put their apartment on the market and divide the proceeds equally. They had their own careers and had always kept their incomes separate. It seemed surprising, in retrospect, that they had never realised how detached they were.

'I don't want anything from the restaurants,' she said. She would have to live in a much more restricted way than she had been used to, but she did not think that would be too difficult.

Tom nodded with quick acceptance. He wasn't known for his generosity. 'Is there anything else?'

Leonie studied his face. The lines and hollows of it were familiar and at the same time he was a stranger, just a man she happened to know, no more and no less than he had been on the night of the beach bonfire. 'I don't think so,' she said. She took the keys of the Saab out of her purse and laid them on the table close to his hands. She had already bought herself a dented old Honda from a cousin of Roger Brownlow's up in Haselboro. It went well with the cabin.

'Can I . . . drive you anywhere?' Tom asked.

'Elizabeth offered and I accepted. Thank you.'

'Sure.' The screen door that led out on to the porch creaked and slammed shut in a swirl of gritty dust, making both of them jump. The wind was getting up in fitful gusts, which just as suddenly died into stillness again.

'Where's Marian?' Leonie asked. The house seemed punctured, with all the air leaked out of it.

'Resting.'

Leonie was surprised. Marian had never been known to rest, except in the handful of minor illnesses she had suffered over the years. 'Is she all right?'

'I think so.'

Leonie picked up her purse and slipped the strap over her shoulder.

'It is too late, isn't it?' Tom asked abruptly.

He wasn't looking at her. She couldn't tell if it was a question, or whether he wanted her to confirm what he already knew in order to make himself more comfortable with it. She waited for a sign, but there was nothing. The branches of the tree beyond the window

423

began an insistent tapping on the glass. In the end she answered, 'Yes.'

He came with her to the door, as if she had been a dinner guest, and she insisted that she didn't need escorting beyond there.

The first flash of dry lightning briefly veined the sky. It was almost seven o'clock and the light was fading fast as towers of grey and purple cloud mounted over the sea. May and Leonie sat on Elizabeth's porch seat with the three books on the buttoned cushion between them. In the garden beds the white faces of Japanese anemones stood out, while the brilliant reds and oranges of daytime colours dimmed into invisibility. The kitchen windows at the side of the house were open to catch the air, and the two women could hear snatches of radio music and the clinking of pans. Spencer and Alexander were cooking.

'Are you ready for home tomorrow?' Leonie asked. 'I'm going to miss you.'

'I'm glad to have been here but I'm not sorry it's over. I'd like to sleep in my own bed and have my own stuff around me. But I'll miss Elizabeth and you as well.'

This acknowledgement pleased Leonie deeply.

May was staring out at the sea. It was rising into a choppy swell, with threatening little wrinkles licked up by the gusty wind. 'Will you, you know, come and see us in New York?'

Gently Leonie said, 'If I may, I'd like to. But first I have to go some distance on my own. I don't know yet where I'll be taking myself.'

'I understand that.'

Elizabeth came out with a tray and glasses. There were vodka martinis for herself and Leonie, and cranberry juice in a frosted glass for May. Elizabeth raised hers to the two of them. 'Safe journey,' she said.

Over the rim of her tall glass May looked again across the water. There was a sailing ship in the bay. As she watched, it silently swept past Moon Island. The tall sails glimmered against the ridge of spruces and the long, steep bowsprit raked towards the southern headland where lines of breakers guarded the passage to the open sea.

The breath stopped in May's chest. She tore a single sidelong glance away from the ship and saw that the other women were watching it too. Another flash of lightning seemed to pin the vessel to a sheet of steel. In the darkness that fell after it Leonie whispered, 'It's one of the windjammers up from Rockland.'

Elizabeth shook her head just once.

May knew it was no elegant windjammer. This ship was heavy, with blunt bows and a sawn-off square transom. The fore and main masts were square-rigged, the mizzen fore-and-aft-rigged. And between the fore and main masts the deck was blocked by the looming brick try-works. She knew exactly, from the descriptions and the old engravings in *Voyages of the Dolphin*, what a whaling ship looked like. She reached out and with her fingertips stroked the book on the cushion beside her.

The ship sailed majestically away from them. It rode the breaking crests of the waves between the island and the mainland shore, and gained the open water beyond. They watched until it passed out of their sight beyond the southern headland. After it had gone they heard a sigh, distinct in the silence before the storm broke, like a breath exhaled from the beach and the rocks. It whispered in their ears and the three women sat still, not needing to speak or even to look at one another. They were connected now. The threads of understanding would grow stronger, and draw them deeper into friendship.

When May lifted her glass her teeth rattled against the rim. Elizabeth and Leonie drank too, and she noticed that under the porch lantern the lines of doubt and anxiety were smoothed out of their faces. The lightning flashed again, illuminating the deserted bay and printing its emptiness behind their eyes.

'I'm glad I saw that. I've never seen a ship so beautiful,' Leonie said. A vicious clap of thunder drowned her last word. Almost at once a scatter of raindrops ricocheted off the path. May stood up and took the books into her arms. She hunched her shoulders to protect them, then bent down and awkwardly kissed Leonie's cheek. 'Goodbye. Will you come and see my dad?' she asked.

'Yes,' Leonie promised. 'And you and Ivy.'

May was glad that Elizabeth got up and followed her across the garden to the side entry, past the glimmering moon-faces of the anemones and the extinguished blaze of brighter flowers. Benign raindrops spattered on their arms and shoulders. In the seclusion of the far side of the house they stopped and looked at each other.

'I saw it,' May said, as if Elizabeth might have doubted her.

All the windows in the Captain's House were lit up, making it look like a boat itself, riding at anchor against the clouds. Music floated from it, flattened by the humid air. Ivy and Lucas must be at home.

'He came for her at last,' Elizabeth said. 'He's taken her away.' She could feel that a weight had lifted from the beach. Sadness had broken up and drifted away, like fog in the sun.

'I hope so,' May said uncertainly. For herself she didn't want to sense the membrane again, or to risk breaking through it to whatever lay on the other side. She held the diary tight against her, the corner digging into the fold of her arm. Quickly, not trying to choose the words, she told Elizabeth where she had found it. Nothing more than that. 'What should I do with it?'

Elizabeth didn't hesitate. 'You should send it to her parents. It was hers, they would want to have it. They will know where it belongs, don't you think?'

She nodded, grateful, and leaned forward and kissed Elizabeth's cheek more gently and gracefully than she had managed with Leonie. It was an easier meeting and parting to negotiate. 'Thank you,' May said.

Her face in the house lights, young and soft-featured and full of life, made Elizabeth smile and catch her breath at the same time. 'Thank you,' Elizabeth echoed her.

May ran down the driveway and along the bluff road. She kept her eyes fixed ahead, but if she had

427

looked towards the Stiegels' she would have seen Marty lifting the last of his bags into the rental car before setting off.

Hannah opened the door after a long interval. May held up the books, keeping the red-and-black diary in the other hand, the weak one. 'I've come to return these. And to say goodbye. We're leaving in the morning.'

The big room with its clutter of books and curios was shadowy and smelt of long-enclosed air. Aaron was in his chair next to the stove, Hannah had been sitting at the table, writing by the light of the single lamp. She took the two books from May and slotted them back into their places on the shelves.

Aaron beckoned her closer with a yellow finger. 'You came to no harm, then?'

'Not really.'

'At your age you mend easily, if you're made right. You're nothing like the other one. Where are you going?'

'Back home. Back to the city. The vacation's over.'

But he had already lost interest, she saw, maybe even forgotten who she was. His mouth loosened and his eyes abandoned their focus, turning inwards instead to look at what she could not see. The terrible remoteness of old age struck her for the first time: Aaron was like a relic from another world. He seemed ten years older than the last time she had seen him, and much smaller and more palpably frail. Her legs felt like trees as she towered over him, her back like a pillar. She touched her free hand quickly to his shoulder and almost kissed the top of his head. Through the sparse hair she saw his scalp, blotched and discoloured with liver spots, and pity and distaste rose in her mouth He gave no sign in return.

Hannah was at her side. 'Did you find them interesting?' She nodded at the shelf where she had replaced the books.

'I did. In a way.'

'Yes. The *Pointed Firs* book is a Maine classic, of course. All you summer visitors like to read it. But the *Dolphin* story, that's different. My son Bobby found it in a second-hand bookstore and bought it for me, knowing my interest in such things.'

May nodded. This was a long speech for Hannah Fennymore.

'I often wonder if Sarah Corder was our island Sarah.'

May followed her gaze as it travelled beyond the blurred glass of the window to Moon Island. It lay low in the water, a spiny black hump against the graphite sky. 'Perhaps,' she said reluctantly. She wanted to shake off all these stories now. 'Did Doone think she might have been?'

Hannah shrugged. 'I don't know if Doone ever read it. She kept the books for long enough, but she never gave me the impression of being much of a reader.'

Probably, May thought, she had just used *Voyages of the Dolphin* to make her code. If she wasn't much of a reader, maybe there had been no other book conveniently to hand. Poor Doone. Whatever the truth had been, it didn't make much difference now.

Hannah was looking at Aaron. His head was lolling in sleep.

'I must go,' May said quickly. Hannah came with her to the door. When they shook hands, Hannah's felt tiny and light and brittle, like a claw. Then the door opened on to a gust of wind, which rattled the shadowy room. Rain slanted viciously beyond the porch.

'I'll run,' May yelled and darted away into it. Exhilaration swept through her as the downpour plastered her hair to her head. She thrust the diary inside her sweatshirt and ran through the torrent, working her good shoulder forwards as if the wall of water were solid. Lightning stripped the darkness once more, and the bang and roll of the thunder came instantly.

Lucas and Ivy were sitting on one of the sofas watching television, and John was at the kitchen end of the room, laying out food. 'You're soaked,' he exclaimed when May burst into the room. He came at once to lift the wet hair from her neck and help her to peel off her sweatshirt.

She was still laughing. 'It felt good, amazing. Not cold at all. You should see the lightning. Better than the Pittsharbor fireworks.'

When the diary was uncovered she put it aside. The black cover was smudged with damp, but it was otherwise undamaged. John rubbed her hair with a towel. She submitted to his attentions, luxuriously stretching her neck. Afterwards he hooked the feathery wings of hair behind her ears in a gesture implicit with tenderness. May closed her eyes briefly and bent her head until her forehead touched his shoulder. He cupped her skull with one hand, holding her against him. 'Go and change the rest of your clothes,' he ordered when he released her. As May slowly mounted the stairs the leaf and flower carvings of the banister felt voluptuously complicated under the palm of her hand.

When she came down again Ivy was in the kitchen stirring something in a pan on the cooker. Her earphones were firmly plugged in. 'Dad's gone out on the bluff for some fresh air,' she called to May in a too-loud voice over the beat drumming inside her head.

Lucas was sitting forward on the sofa with his hands awkwardly dangling between his knees. He looked clumsy and, for once, uncomfortable with himself.

May went quickly and sat beside him. 'I never thanked you for helping to look for me,' she said. She had seen him, in the confusion of searchers who surrounded her after Spencer and Alexander had come up behind Marty. There had been no distinction to him then; none of the spotlit glow that had followed him all the summer. He had just been Lucas. Nor, May saw, was there any distinction now. He was good-looking, sun-tanned, ordinary. There was none of Marty's silky threat in him . . . nothing to have enticed Doone beyond the point of reason. She didn't know, now, how she could have imagined there was. But she did remember her own infatuation with him. It was a pale thing compared with Doone's for Marty, but the memory of it made May certain in that instant that

431

Marty hadn't killed Doone. Doone had taken her own life, deliberately, in desperation.

'It was so bad,' Lucas confessed. 'When you were lost. I would have done anything. Not just what I did do, which was only walking over the island a few times, you know?'

'Thank you,' May said awkwardly.

'I didn't want it to be like Doone. Not with you.'

'I know. It wasn't. I'm pretty glad about that myself.'

He didn't give his high-voltage grin. Instead he glanced at Ivy and saw that her back was turned. 'Uh, May, listen. I wanted to say I was sorry. Again, okay? About that time on Pittsharbor Night?'

'It's fine.' May smiled at him. And at once she saw the infinitesimal change in his appraisal of her, as he reckoned with her smile, the way she tilted her head and the angle of her good arm on the cushions. Immediately she felt her own power as loud inside her as the beat of Ivy's music, and Lucas reddened and stared down at his fidgeting hands.

Poor Doone, May thought. Wound up in the skeins of sadness that netted this place, never to break free of them. She was glad of her own escape, tomorrow. New York had never seemed so alluring. 'Are you going to go on seeing Ivy?'

'That's kind of up to her.' He shrugged. 'Sure, I'd like to.'

You don't stand a chance, May thought. Ivy spun round and the sisters grinned at each other.

'We're ready to eat,' Ivy shouted. John came in from

the deck, with rain shiny on the shoulders of his slicker, bringing cold air with him.

Lucas shuffled to his feet. 'I better go.'

'I'll see you out,' Ivy said. 'Be at the Star Bar later?'

He waved at May, a mock-formal gesture that ended almost as a salute, and went on his way.

Once Lucas had gone, they sat down to eat. Ivy had laid three places close together at the top of the oversized oak table. They talked about the beach and Aaron, and about other holidays they had taken and might take in the future, and when she had eaten her tiny portion Ivy leant back and wound her sun-tanned arm through the slats of her chair back, continuing the conversation until May and John had finished too. Outside the rain slackened and turned to a soothing patter as the eye of the storm moved southwards.

Marty drove the unfamiliar car slowly down the coast road. It was a long thirty miles to the freeway in this direction. To his left were a dozen promontories, broken fingers of rock combing the spray from crashing waves, and on the other side dense swathes of conifers. The rain and the metronomic swish of the wipers, and the steady flicker of tree trunks in his headlamps, combined to make him overwhelmingly sleepy. He had slept hardly at all the night before, and very little the one before that. Thinking that music would help him to stay awake, he reached for the buttons of the radio, then remembered that it was a rental car and he would have to search the paperwork for the security code before he could make the thing work. He retracted his hand and stared ahead through the streaming rain.

The urge to let his eyes fall shut became irresistible. A yawn swelled in his throat and forced his jaws apart, and the tears it brought to his heavy eyes made him blink.

Some air, he must get some fresh air. He let down the window and a gust of salt-heavy wind drove rain into his face. He closed his eyes for a luxurious instant and clenched his hands on the wheel. The car strayed across the crown of the road.

The sea was very close. One of the inlets between the spines of rock must almost touch the road. He could hear the deep, insistent thunder of the waves driving into the confined space.

Marty opened his eyes and wrenched at the wheel to bring the car straight again. He pulled in to the side of the road, where dripping bushes swept the car wing, and switched off the engine. In the silence that followed a flash of lightning lit up the sky and sea. There was a ship under full sail, hardly a hundred yards off. He could see the pale canvas strain in the wind and the high bowsprit pitching against the seething water. His smarting eyes widened, stretching the orbits, and a snap of fear straightened his spine. He glanced into the driver's mirror, but the road behind him was black and empty. When he looked again there was only the darkness, the sea invisibly booming into the rocky inlets, and the rain hammering on the roof of the car and needling his face through the open window. His retinas burned with the lightning flash and the image of the vessel etched with it.

Marty sat for a long time without moving, until his arms stiffened on the wheel and cold numbed his torso. Lightning flashed again, but there was no ship. No cars came by and in his solitude he felt as if he were the last man in the world.

At last he shook his head, as though he were trying to clear it of some persistent dream. He reached out with cold fingers and turned the ignition key. The engine fired and he eased the car slowly forward. Like an automaton, he drove on towards New York.

Sixteen

He descended the steps very slowly, placing one foot in front of the other with extreme deliberation. Every facet of the beach was grey in the early light: wet grey shingle, sullen water and long lines of breakers setting up a dull, continuous roar. Aaron reached the bottom of the steps and began to shuffle, leaning heavily on his stick. Gulls rose in an arc ahead of him, wheeling away from the storm debris at the high-water mark. He watched them as they soared against the clouded sky. His own progress was painful but still he lifted his head, a flicker of exhilaration within him fuelled by the scoured air. It was his beach, in all of its moods, but he loved it best when it was wild and inhospitable like this.

He had planned this morning's expedition with great care, thinking of it as a break-out, and hoarding the energy and determination he knew he would need. Hannah couldn't keep watch over him for ever and sure enough she had gone out to Pittsharbor for an hour to buy supplies. He was irritable that the slow traverse of the bluff and the steps was taking so long, but it was also illogical to be concerned about the time.

He had made no arrangement, even though he might have picked up the telephone – that had never been his way – but he still nursed the hope that she would come, as she had done long ago.

The high-water mark was a tangle of wrack and line and shreds of garbage. He leaned on his stick to catch his breath, stirring the black fronds of weed with the toe of his boot. And when he looked up again she was walking to meet him. Her coat was wrapped about her and there was a scarf around her head. Sixty years had left her unmarked.

She reached his side. The surf was loud, but he heard her voice as clearly as if they had broken off their old conversation only an hour ago. 'I was watching the beach,' Elizabeth said. 'I woke up this morning and I knew you'd be here.'

She had told him exactly the same at the very beginning, when she evaded her mother and came down to meet him between the fishing boats. There was a difference about the beach today, an iridescence in the light and a full-throated cadence to the sound of the sea, which reminded her of those days. She felt as light as a girl. They turned together and began to walk slowly along the crescent of the beach, just out of reach of the foam-lipped waves as they ran out into the shingle.

'I am here,' Aaron confirmed.

The Captain's House and the Stiegels' were closed and shuttered. He pointed up to them. 'Gone back where they belong. You'll be next, won't you? You and Marian.'

437

She knew him so well. The distance of the years had telescoped, leaving only the mirage of time, which had ravaged their faces and seamed their skin. It was all a comedy, Elizabeth thought. She wanted to laugh, overtaken suddenly by the happiness of acceptance. There was nothing left for Aaron or for her to fight against. All their lives were embedded in the beach. They were no more than a comedy and an illusory ship, which seemed to carry the grains of tragedy away with it. Her eye was caught by the glimmer of a very small double shell lying among the pebbles. She stooped to retrieve it and examined the tiny gradations of rose-pink and pearl and silver. It was like a pair of baby's finger-nails. She held it in the palm of her hand, then tipped it gently back into the sea. All this she did while Aaron took a slow step and another.

'Back to Boston, for the winter?' She thought about it for a moment. Back to her bridge evenings and choral society, and good concerts, and the company of a few remaining friends she had known for most of her life. 'Yes. Marian and me, one, then the other. The way it always has been.' *Acceptance*, Elizabeth thought. *The final achievement, to accept what was not susceptible to change.*

'They all think I'm going to die.'

'It doesn't look that way to me.' She smiled at him, flirting, a girl again.

'I'll do it when I'm good and ready.'

'Just as you always did.'

They walked on, another handful of steps. Elizabeth sensed that he was tiring now. She touched

438

her hand to his arm, not quite connecting with his sleeve, just indicating that they should stop. They faced out, looking across to the island. The little beach was laced with driftwood. 'I saw the Captain's ship last night.'

He laughed, a sharp snort eloquent with a young man's derision.

'Little May Duhane saw it too, and Leonie Beam, although she didn't know it for what it was,' Elizabeth said.

Aaron's dismissive laugh was a contradiction. His face had darkened with exhaustion. It was an effort for him to make a half-turn and begin the chain of steps that would take him back to his chair beside the stove. He was glad of Elizabeth beside him, her arm close to his, separated by a chink of air. They passed between the Beams' sailing boat, swinging on its mooring line, and one of the rowboats pulled up high on the beach.

'Do you remember?' Elizabeth asked softly.

Once, one night before they learned to break into the Captain's House, they had crept together beneath the shelter of an upturned dory. The smell of fish gut and tar and salt was the same as the scent of today.

'I remember. Did you imagine otherwise?'

His sharpness pleased her. Of course he had not forgotten. They moved on, even more slowly, to the Fennymores' house. Ahead were the public steps. Aaron stopped again and took a long look, from the Captain's House up to the square façade of his own and on to the breadth of land that lay beyond it.

439

Without warning tears beaded at the corners of his eyes and ran down his face. He muttered an inaudible syllable and bent his head, and when Elizabeth moved to comfort him he bit at her, 'Just leave me be.'

'What is it?' Elizabeth asked.

'Weakness.'

'You aren't weak. You were never that. Impatient and inexorable and angry, but never weak.'

He lifted his chin. His neck was thin and yellow, roped with sinews. 'She'll be back soon.'

He would mount the steps again and shuffle back to his chair, and Hannah would resume her vigil over him.

'So I'll say goodbye, Aaron. I'm going back to the city in a day or two, after I've closed up the house.'

He inclined his head, his involuntary tears already drying. They had not even touched hands. The winter lay ahead of them, a passage of ascending stairs of ice and vortices of wind, and they both knew it was an obstacle too great for Aaron to want to negotiate yet another time. 'Until next summer,' he said.

'Next summer,' she answered, keeping her voice level.

He did not want an avowal of any kind and nor did she. They had adopted a different way, for all of their adult lives. She brushed his cheek with her mouth, so briefly that it was only the ghost of a kiss. She was already moving away, her hand lifted, when he murmured, 'Wait.'

She halted at once, watching his face and wondering.

'Don't let your boy put his houses up there,' he ordered. *After I am gone.*

'He doesn't own the land, Aaron. He can't build there.'

'If Hannah sells.'

After I am gone, she might not think it worth holding on. She may weaken and give way.

Long ago Elizabeth had disappointed him, and in retaliation Aaron had fought hard for his place on the bluff. He had kept it out of pride. She understood what it meant, but she didn't want to make a promise she couldn't keep. The sea made its admonition at her back and the sea-birds turned in circles over the land. But the acquiescent lightness of the morning didn't desert her. She knew the decision she should make. At last she said, 'Spencer can't buy anything without my money.' Aaron's eyes held hers. 'He won't have it, not until after my death.'

While she remained then, the bluff would be as they had known it together, in their separation.

He nodded and kissed her in his turn, the same dry, fleeting touch. Without another word he began the slow climb of the stairs and Elizabeth walked the beach. Neither of them looked back again. Nor did either of them notice they were being watched.

Marian was up on the widow's walk at the top of her house. She had seen the two of them come from their opposite directions and their slow walk together to the water's edge, and she had read the depth of their absorption in one another. Now she followed Aaron's painful ascent and the hesitant steps across the rough

441

ground to his porch. Elizabeth was lost in her own thoughts; she didn't look up to see Marian's bulk penned in by the fancy ironwork and silhouetted against the pearl-grey sky.

Seventeen

The letter from Chicago arrived almost by return of
post. May found it waiting for her one afternoon when
she came home from school. She left the white
envelope on the table while she switched on the TV,
fixed herself a sandwich, and sat down in front of it
with her plate and a glass of diet Coke. She ate half of
the cottage cheese on rye before replacing the bitten
chunk squarely on the plate. Then she took her knife
and deliberately licked it clean before slitting open the
envelope.

The letter was handwritten, on thick creamy paper
headed *Jennifer Bennison MD*. The script was small and
fairly legible. May read it slowly, taking in each word.

Dear May.

Thank you for sending Doone's book to me. I
knew she kept a diary, but we had thought she must
have destroyed it.

I am very glad to have this much of her, and to be
able to understand some of her thoughts and
feelings before she died. The rest of it, which I

cannot decipher, will have to remain a partial secret.
At least I know and understand a little more about
what preoccupied her in those last days. I also know
that nothing will change what actually happened,
nor will recrimination or bitterness bring our
daughter back to us again.

She was much loved by both of us, although it is
one of the characteristics of adolescence not to
recognise parental love, or to reject it, or to believe
that it is in some way not enough. In this sense
Doone was an ordinary girl, but she was also one
who was capable of rising to extraordinary passions.

We miss her in every moment of every day.

Thank you again for returning her diary.

With best wishes for the future,

Jennifer Bennison.

May folded the letter carefully and put it next to her
plate. She rested her hands on the table, palms down,
and waited for the rush of feelings to subside.

It was not her secret to reveal.

Voyages of the Dolphin was not her book, it belonged
to Hannah Fennymore, and all the connections to
Sarah Corder and the Captain's House belonged to
Moon Island and the beach and the summer, a long
way from where she was now.

None of them was her secret, she was only an
onlooker. She had stumbled on the diary and its key.
The only other interpretation was that there was a link
beyond the real world, which she couldn't and
wouldn't understand, not now, sitting at the table in

the apartment with her school bag and the faces soundlessly mouthing from the TV on the counter.

She wouldn't tell Mrs Bennison that she had broken Doone's code. Nor would she reveal what she knew about Marty Stiegel to anyone. Doone had hidden these things away and May did not believe that it was for her to disinter them. The ship had sailed out of the bay, carrying the rest of the secrets with it.

These things May was certain of, as far as certainty belonged with the cloaking fogs and stormy seascapes of Pittsharbor. It wasn't thinking of the beach and its blurred dimensions that disturbed her: it was the letter itself. She picked it up and read it again, although the words were already etched in her mind.

Jealousy, that was what it made her feel, jealousy that crawled up and pinched her with its iron-hard fingers. She was jealous of a dead girl because her mother loved her. . . .

She didn't even like the sound of Jennifer Bennison; the letter made her seem superior and cold, although she used the right words and what she said was no doubt true. But she had loved Doone, that much was plain. She hadn't died and gone away, she had stayed to miss her daughter in every minute of every day, not the other way round.

May got up from the table, pushing back her chair so that it scraped noisily. The phone rang at the same instant; she listened to Laurie from her class leave a message on the machine. Then, with silence for company again, she walked through the apartment to her father's bedroom, which had once also been her

445

mother's. She went to the closet where Ali's clothes used to hang and opened the door to empty space. A few naked hangers bracketed the rail.

May walked into the closet and closed the door behind her. She hunched her shoulders against the wall and the hangers rattled as she slid to squat on her haunches, then lowered herself to the floor. She could hear the trickling sand of silence in her inner ear and the darkness swarmed with colours behind her closed eyes. By breathing in hard she thought she could detect Ali's perfume.

There were no clothes. There was nothing left in which to wrap herself, nothing to tear or destroy. There was only silence and space, and herself.

The absurdity, the saving absurdity of it, squeezed a sudden laugh out of her throat, something between a cough and a gasp. 'Jesus,' May said aloud. 'What kind of a person am I?' She sounded like Ivy, she realised, and also like Ali herself.

The closet was dusty. Dust collected in the back of her throat and nose, and she sneezed, then let her head sink forward to rest on her knees. It was also warm and airless and comforting. *Closet womb*, May thought. *Womb closet. Safety, claustrophobia, safety.* The words ran round in her head until they lost their meaning and made a chain of soothing syllables, and she drifted into a doze.

She was startled awake again by John's voice. He was calling her name through the apartment. She scrambled upright and hit her head against the clothes rail, setting the hangers clashing together. She elbowed

446

the door open, stepped into the airy room and saw her father standing amazed in the bedroom doorway.

May looked back at where she had burst out from. 'I took a nap in the closet,' she explained.

It was funny enough to make them laugh until the dust turned May's laughter into a coughing fit, which made her eyes water.

'Come on. Come through here with me,' John said. He led her into the living-room and sat her down on the sofa. He turned on the lamps at either end of it because the room was dim. Then he sat beside her and drew her close, so that her head was beneath his chin. 'I was worried,' he said. 'I'm glad you were only napping in the closet, not lost.'

'Not lost,' she repeated comfortably.

'Where's Ivy?'

'With Steve, or somewhere.'

'Will you mind being on your own so much more, when she's gone to college?'

It was only a few days away now.

'No. As long as you're here.'

'We'll be good together. What were you really doing in your mom's closet?'

'I was looking for her.' She would show him Jennifer Bennison's letter, but not now.

'She's gone, May.' There was exasperation as well as sadness in his voice.

'I know that.'

The place where they were sitting, the settee and the fuzzy glow of lamplight, called to mind the other picture. May examined it in her head, trying not to

447

flinch. It wasn't merely banal, as she had earlier decided because she was trying to ape her sister. The pin-sharpness of the recovered memory was already fading, but she thought that the contrasts of it, light and shadow falling on interlocked bodies, brutal exposure and implicit shamefulness, would always stay with her. Her mother, caught in the act of love-making with a man who wasn't her father. 'Did she hurt you so much by what she did with Jack O'Donnell? Is that why we never talked about her after she died?'

John didn't pull away, as she had half expected he might. He held her loosely, went on breathing with his mouth against her hair. 'I loved your mother very much. I always loved her, from the first day I saw her sitting on a bench in the Frick with her tatty, brilliant clothes and that wild hair like a light was shining on her head. She was what I wanted, there was never another question for me after that day.

'Almost as soon as we were married I felt I wasn't enough for her and so she had to go looking for something more. The lack in me of whatever it was she needed, colour or strength or comedy, or maybe just sex, May, or most probably a mix of all those things and a few dozen others, made me feel guilty, and guilt makes you shrivel up, and you lose your courage and your sense of direction.

'I wasn't surprised when I found out about her affairs and if they had made her happy maybe it would all have been endurable. Not okay, but endurable. But she wasn't happy either, she always seemed disappointed, not just in me but in everything. Except when she was with you and Ivy. The two of you gave her an anchor, which I never could and no one else ever did.

'I didn't expect her to die. She was the last person anyone could imagine it happening to, because she was so strong. She was like a tree or a river.'

May stirred. Ali wasn't a tree or a river or anything of the kind. Dr Metz was wrong there too. She was *my mother*. But she let it pass, accepting that it was his right to interpret her in one way, just as it was hers to differ.

John clicked his fingers, a hard dry snap. 'It happened so suddenly. Immediately her absence was so entire and so absolute.'

It was, May thought. *Entirely absolute*.

'We had never really talked about what her affairs meant. About why she needed to do it. I always thought we would confront the truth next week, the next time she made it too obvious, the next time she had no explanation to offer. Then she died and it was as though she had just turned to me, with that sharp look of amusement on her face as if she was about to say something important, and I knew I would never hear what it was.

'I should have been able to talk instead to you and Ivy, but I couldn't. What I felt was . . . ashamed.' The word drifted and fell between them, as softly as a goose-feather settling.

May was thinking that she had expected it to be awkward to hear her father talk in this way, but it was not. It was natural. He chose his words too carefully and tried too hard to make simple what was shaded with nuance and complication, just because he had missed the fact that she wasn't a child any more, but he still said what she had needed to hear.

In her mind's eye she saw the island and the beach. She had travelled a long distance there, even though the horizons were limited, and the rock and sea boundaries of the place still shimmered when she tried to define them, and dissolved, to the point where time and space hummed out from her measurable orbit into fearsome infinity.

The outer door of the apartment slammed and dampening vibrations resonated through the inner walls. They heard Ivy calling out for them.

'There's one thing,' May said, sitting upright and raking her hair back from her forehead with a hooked forefinger, an unconscious echo of one of her mother's gestures. 'I think I won't go and see Dr Metz any more. If that's okay. No more trees and I have said every-thing I can to her about Ali being dead.'

'Are you sure?'

The light in the room was warm, and in its yellow reassurance she looked at the worn, rubbed details of the rug, and a vase with red and blue dragons, which Ali had brought back from Thailand, and the unre-garded family clutter that silted the tables and shelves. Suddenly she smiled. 'Yes. It means more to me to talk to you, like this.'

Her directness, and the conviction in her voice made him look at her in appraisal. May felt the pleasure of knowing what she wanted and the satisfaction of being heard.

'If that's what you want,' John said.

They looked up together when Ivy came in.

'Hi,' Ivy said, unconcerned.

The snow lay in thick blue-bevelled plates and layered cornices on the Pittsharbor roofs. On the ground, where it had been shovelled aside from roads and driveways, it stayed all winter in discoloured crags, visited by dogs and flagged with wind-blown litter, until the next fall came to round out the edges and purify the slopes. Then the onslaught of shovels began once more.

It had snowed yet again in the night. The trees lining the green were black outlines immaculately threaded with white and silver, and the white clapboarding of the church steeple looked tired against so much brilliance. A single bell tolled as the mourners left the churchyard. It was not cold enough to freeze the sea, although dirty grey crusts of ice rimmed the pebbles exposed by low tide in the harbour and it had not been too cold for the digging of Aaron's grave. Now the earth was heaped over it in a raw mound, which made a shocking contrast of darkness with the white landscape.

Hannah, in a black coat that was too big for her, was supported on her son's arm. Her daughters and their husbands came behind, followed by the groups of Hanscoms and Clarks and Deeveys and the other Pittsharbor families who had come to pay their respects.

Marian and Elizabeth walked near the back of the thin column. The sun had come out during the burial

451

and a line of diamond droplets glittered on the low branches of the trees next to the gate. But the threat of intensifying cold still stalked the gravestones, and made the people bow their heads and pull their clothes around them.

There were no funeral cars in Pittsharbor except the hearse that had brought the coffin from the house to the church. Now the mourners made a black clothes-line against the banks of sparkling snow as they trudged along the knife-edge of the wind towards the trucks and family station-wagons parked beside the green. Elizabeth's car was there and she nodded Marian to it, knowing that she had flown up from Boston and was staying at the Pittsharbor Inn instead of opening up her house on the bluff. The two women eased themselves into the car. Their dark clothes gave off the same close smell of storage.

Elizabeth reversed away from the snow bank and began the drive in convoy through deserted streets towards the bluff road. The tolling bell faded behind them.

'Did he always intend to go in the winter, when the place belongs to its rightful owners?' Marian asked, breaking the silence between them. 'Did you know how much he hated us summer complaints? He wouldn't have wanted a crowd of them gaping over the fence at his funeral, would he?' She kept her big face turned away, to examine this dignified version of Pittsharbor, which did not entice with tourist shops or jostle with visitors. Her eyes were puffy, and her cheeks and lips looked raw.

Elizabeth's gloved hands rested lightly on the wheel. Her face was powdered, expressionless. She had kept the same neutral demeanour all through the service. 'I don't know about intended. But Aaron always knew what he wanted,' she answered.

They left the ice-banded expanse of the harbour behind them and turned towards the bluff road.

'He didn't always get it, did he?' Marian still didn't turn her head. Her hair was drawn back and pinned in a new, flattened way that made her look older. 'He spent his life without you.'

The statement dropped between them, then faded like the church bell.

Elizabeth drew her colourless lower lip between her teeth, but she said nothing. Her eyes remained fixed on the road.

'Didn't you know I knew? Oh, he told me. Aaron and I were lovers too, of a kind. When we used to take our afternoons of middle age on the pine needles up in the woods he told me about his first and only love. Didn't he ever confide in you about me and him, Elizabeth? No? Let me tell you why. It was because I was a diversion – and not the only one, of course – a distraction along the route of a life that hadn't led where he wanted it to. We had sex, probably because sex wasn't Hannah's thing. I wasn't important enough to tell about.'

Elizabeth took Marian's declaration and considered it. The substance of it hardly disturbed her. She was thinking, *we're two old women dressed in black, driving away from a graveside. We've buried the man and we won't*

453

ever learn the differences in what he meant for each of us. And as for the similarities – the old rhythms are the same everywhere. She didn't think keeping or breaking silence, or even the totems of pride itself, mattered very much any more. But she did feel an affinity with her companion that she had never known before. 'You sound bitter, Marian.'

Their eyes met briefly now. Marian's were embedded in swollen flesh and Elizabeth recoiled from this evidence of the other woman's feelings. She returned her attention to the road and the rear of Chorlton Deevey's pick-up truck. They travelled in silence for a minute. Ahead Elizabeth could see the white-layered shack that in the summer became the Flying Fish.

'You think it's bitterness? You won't allow me the privilege of plain grief? If you lose someone you never truly had – and Aaron was never mine even though I loved him dearly – you suffer the loss twice over.' The five houses came into view. They rose out of a snow-sea that washed over the empty headland, seeming to ride on it to nowhere with the oyster-white sky as a sail. 'Twice over,' she repeated. Marian never could resist an effect.

Elizabeth lifted one hand in its black suede glove and placed it over Marian's. 'I'm sorry,' she said gently. 'I didn't understand.'

The end house was filled with people. Angela Fennymore had arranged a funeral buffet and there was a ham at the centre of a white-clothed table, shored up with baskets of rolls, and dishes of pickles

454

and relish. Hannah stood at one end of the room with her son, shaking hands with the people as they arrived and gravely accepting their condolences. Her grandchildren huddled in embarrassed discomfort in the furthest corner. One of the boys bore a strong resemblance to Aaron.

Marian and Elizabeth took Hannah's hand in turn.

'Marian, Elizabeth. I'm glad to see you both today. I know Aaron would have wanted it.' Her eyes were bright and her narrow back was straight. She looked as if she had been offered a glimpse of a different and better existence.

Glasses of sweet wine or whiskey were handed round on a tray by the second daughter and when everyone held a drink Doug Hanscom stepped into the middle of the room. He was wearing a dark coat and a rusty black necktie seemed knotted too tightly around his shirt collar. He had big, red, sea-scarred hands, which he held folded in front of him. Elizabeth thought of his lobster boat cutting the harbour water the summer before last and the waterlogged weight he had knotted to the end of his line.

He cleared his throat and the low rustle of talk died away. 'Neighbours and old friends,' Doug began, looking around the circle of attentive faces. He took his time, measuring the proper weight of his words. 'Aaron was a Pittsharbor man. He lived here all his life and he loved the place. He worked hard, never was afraid of a day's work. He married locally and he built this house with his own hands, to bring his wife and

455

family to. He lived a decent life. Hannah and he brought up their children to be respectable folk like themselves and they were proud of them.'

Hannah stood at his side, her eyes fixed on the window and the iron mouth of the bay beyond it.

'He was a part of this town. We all knew him and what he stood for. Today we put him to rest in the Pittsharbor graveyard. I can think of no better ending. And no better life to be remembered by.'

There was a murmur of assent and a respectful lifting of glasses.

The widow raised her head. She was as neat and proper and unrevealing as a starched handkerchief, just as she always had been. 'Thank you, Doug. I'm grateful for your kindness and for the help that all of you have given me in my loss. I am blessed with my children and grandchildren, and I am lucky in my life here in Pittsharbor.' The little speech was an ordeal for her. She stepped back to her daughter's protection, who signalled that they should all move on to help themselves to food.

Elizabeth sat down on an upright sofa. The tributes had been moving, perhaps just because they had omitted so much more than they stated. It was a version of a life, she thought, and of the person. A decent version, which gave no inkling of the pained and painful man she had loved.

Marian eased her bulk down beside her. 'I'm glad I don't have to live here all the time,' she muttered. 'The introversion of it. The narrowness of mind.'

'It wouldn't suit either of us.'

456

They had made their decisions long ago, for better or worse.

The ham was carved and plates passed round. The room grew stuffy with the heat of the stove and the pressure of people enclosed in a small space. The noise of talk swelled and there were one or two subdued coughs of laughter. Hannah moved among the groups, and at last came to Marian and Elizabeth. Caught between the two of them, Elizabeth was reminded of a photograph that Marty Stiegel had taken last year. The three old women of the beach, unwillingly connected, three faces of the same episode.

Sarah Corder had sailed out of the bay in her whaling ship and now Aaron was dead.

She felt calm descend and wrap itself around her. There were many different kinds of fulfilment, she thought. She had achieved her modest version of it.

Marian was asking busily, 'What will you do now, Hannah? Sell up and move somewhere comfortable?'

The other woman's sharp face grew needle points. 'I'll be staying put. It's where I belong.'

'And I always thought you toughed it out up here all winter because that was what Aaron wanted.'

The arrowtips of Hannah's features suddenly glinted. 'It will be what I want from now on.' It would, of course. Hannah too had won a version of freedom for herself

'How will you keep yourself busy? With none of your grandchildren close by?'

Elizabeth flinched. Marian was intolerable. But Hannah answered her straight. 'I'll set down to my books with no one to criticise me. I might write a bit of a history of the bay and the island. In my own time, with my own ideas.'

The rough shelves of books rose behind her, old brown volumes interspersed with modern editions of local history and fiction. Doone's two books were buried among them. On another shelf at the end were folders from Write it Down, the stationery shop on Sunday Street.

'I think that's a very good idea,' Elizabeth told her.

'Why, thank *you*,' Hannah returned.

The funeral gathering was breaking up. Edie Clark and her husband were already standing at the door with their outer coats on. Outside the sky was darkening from oyster to slate and the clouds were gravid with yet more snow.

Hannah hitched her chin towards the side window. Behind a loop of felt curtain an angle of the bay and the land that backed it were just visible. 'What about that, out there?' she demanded.

Spencer was in Boston. He had a private view scheduled at the gallery that evening. Two or three of Judith Stiegel's new, small and fierce pieces of work were included. Spencer was very taken with them. He was too busy to travel down east for Aaron's funeral. The Stiegels were back together again, he had told Elizabeth.

'The land?'

'I won't sell. Don't ask me. I know it's your money that wants to buy it.'

Elizabeth smoothed the black skin of her gloves over

her fingers. She felt a shaft of wicked cold at her back as someone opened the door on to the porch. 'I promised Aaron, the last time we spoke. But after I am gone, the money will be Spencer's.'

Hannah's mouth folded. 'None of us will be here for ever.' It was only an episode, all of it. Only a brief episode. 'Now, excuse me. I must see his friends out.'

Marian sniffed hard. 'Put up an apartment block and a couple of parking lots just to show her, I would.'

Elizabeth smiled at her.

She didn't stay much longer. She spoke to a handful of Pittsharbor neighbours, then kissed Hannah good-bye on each of her stiff cheeks. She followed Chorlton Deevey and his wife out of the porch door and began the walk towards her car. But on a sudden impulse she slipped aside and skirted the side of the house. The snow was deep and it ruffed the tops of her boots, but she pushed on through it, under the icicled eaves, to the seaward side of the house. She crossed the bluff to the beach steps, not caring in the least that Aaron's family and the last of the guests would see her, a jerky black figure moving like a marionette against the weighty sky.

The wooden steps were hummocked with unmarked snow. Elizabeth trod through it carefully, the snap of each unbroken crust loud in her ears. In her pocket was a note that had arrived at her house in Boston, from John Duhane. He had told her that both his girls were well, that Ivy was enjoying college and May now had a boyfriend. And he asked her to forward the enclosed envelope to Leonie Beam, whose

459

present address he believed she knew. Elizabeth had done as he asked.

As she walked, all the histories and the as yet untold stories of the beach and the island seemed to swell and sink around her, like the endless sea. She hoped with an old woman's dry clarity that Leonie and John would avoid the mistakes she had made. She remembered the meetings with Aaron, long ago, and the last time she had seen him, in almost this very spot. The years seemed briefly to dissolve and coalesce, so that Sarah Corder and her captain were part of the present, and Aaron and she and Marian, and John and Leonie and May, and all their loves and failures were no more than episodes played out against the shifting of the tides. Elizabeth found some comfort in this diminishment.

The tide was rising, the swell of the waves cracking beneath a tentative crust of ice. She moved slowly around the arc of shingle in the direction of her own steps, her face stinging and her body whipped by the wind. The stones were capped by pillows of snow and ice crystals bitterly ringed the craters between them. In the middle of the hostile beach she stopped and looked upwards. The roofs and chimneys loomed against the sky, and as she wept for Aaron the first black specks of snow whirled into her blinded eyes.

Across the bay, on the ice-bound wilderness of Moon Island, snow also fell on the low mound that had once been an unmarked grave.

Also by Rosie Thomas

EVERY WOMAN KNOWS A SECRET

What happens when you fall in love with the one person you shouldn't?

In the aftermath of a family tragedy, Jess Arrowsmith is powerless to resist her attraction to Rob, twenty years her junior, and the person she has reason to hate most in the world. As their love affair threatens to blow her family apart, Jess finds herself in a desperate struggle to defuse a crisis that puts at risk all she holds dear.

'Rosie Thomas has a special talent for dealing with everyday tragedies that can come along and blow apart ordinary lives … an intelligent and moving novel'
The Times

'Hard to put down'
Woman's Journal

'Rosie Thomas has excelled with a gritty, thoroughly modern drama'
Daily Mail

'Honest and absorbing, Rosie Thomas mixes the bitter and the hopeful with the knowledge that the human heart is far more complicated than any rule suggests'
Mail on Sunday

A SIMPLE LIFE

Hidden beneath the comfortable family life she shares with her successful husband Matthew and their two perfect sons lies a shameful secret that has haunted Dinah for fifteen years. She and Matt never speak of it or the impossible choice he forced her to make all those years ago; they think the cracks have been papered over.

But when a chance encounter brings the past into sharp focus once more, Dinah realises she can no longer deny the truth. She decides to risk everything – her husband, her sons, her perfect lifestyle – in order to claim what was always hers.

'She tells her story with seductive skill'
The Times

'Immensely sensitive, full of insight'
Woman's Journal

ALSO AVAILABLE